I0838288

Contents

TesseracT

Christopher T. Calogero

Chapter One
<u>The Mind With The Beaten Man</u>

The taunting weighed heavy on John's head. His mind was berating him again. *The perfect genius is all that is made. It is made by the working machine. I am its mortality.* The line repeated itself inside of John's brain for the forty-second time as its choke tightened. When he first arrived at the Davidson Hotel bar, John sat at a tall ninety degrees. But now, after an hour alone with his thoughts, his head collapsed flat on top of the teakwood bar. Nights like this were routine for John.

His research project began its decay back in March, and it was around then that the inner voice returned. For the first month or so, it would whisper the occasional remark of disappointment in John's ear. But after May had come and gone, the research project failed completely, and the insults arrived at the top of every hour.

It was not so much the ridicule that bothered him, however. After sixty-two years of mental self-slaughter, John learned how to take a beating. It was the delivery. He found the delivery beyond pretentious, and it did not even make sense to him. *The perfect genius is all that is made. It is made by the working machine. I am its mortality.* John winced as if he had just bitten into something sour. The words from his mind were such an obvious attempt to sound poetic, and John hated poetry. Wasted words were wasted time, as far as he was concerned. His conscience, on the other hand, settled for nothing short of Romanticism when it came time to hand John his lashes.

Each night, people would pass by the collapsed man, either thinking the worst or nothing at all. But little did they know, they were in the presence of a great debate.

John normally fired back. He argued how his life's shortcomings were typical of anyone within his department or with his inadequate budget. And if he got truly desperate, he would sink to the excuse that he was merely a human being.

After all, no one had figured out the Universe yet, so why let its weight rest on his shoulders? This all took place until about the time that he finished his second or third beer. Then, the remarks of the inner voice would sound less like charges of self-abuse and more like suggestions for self-improvement. But tonight was different. Tonight, John found that he had little fight left in him, so he decided to just sit back and enjoy the theatre of assault.

As he stared through his tall glass of red ale, he observed a rhythm. Every time his mind lobbed a slur his way, a tiny carbonation bubble rose to the top of his glass. John thought that if he were holding an instrument, he could write a song to its harmony, but then, the inner voice reminded him that he had no musical talent or ability. And with that pleasant remark, he drank.

John arrived in Amber Rock a few weeks back. He traveled to the mountain town each summer after his spring semesters at Colorado University where his colleagues and students knew him as 'Dr. John Robins'. The doctor, however, was never much for decorum, so he made it a point to just stick with 'John' outside of academic settings, the bar being no exception.

Just like in years past, John intended to use his summer escape as a mental reward, however, after his year-long research project went up in flames, John's mind made other plans. His punishment started off simple. He was forced to outline the entire incident and file it in the *Notable Humiliations* folder. Over the years, his mind had built an impressive mental library for cataloging his life's mistakes and failures. Letting things go was not in the policy. And even though he always argued with his mind as a means to save face, deep down, he often agreed with it. After all, John was, and will always be, John's biggest critic.

Perhaps if he allowed himself to take a step back and look at everything with some optimism, he may have been able to dust a lesson out of the filth, but he didn't believe in that. To him, there was no greater sin than wasted time. For that sin, he owed a penance, and therein lies the irony of John: A man who lived between the lines of very simple standards always managed to attract so much complication. And as it is written in the law of all-natural order, *Anything that finds its way into John's life, soon becomes very, very complicated.*

Chapter Two

Incident #7

October 5, 2014: Moctezuma, Mexico

The entire town gathered on top of the hill at the bank of the river. Maria and Victor made their way through the crowd. The look of devastation across hundreds of faces told the young couple that they found what they were looking for.

There were three large holes in the ground, all lined up in the middle of the river. Each one was twenty feet in diameter and so deep that no one could see the bottom. Maria and Victor did not know what they would find when they arrived in Moctezuma, but they feared that it would be extraordinary.

The first hole swallowed most of the water. It dropped deep into the Earth. Even when they shined a bright light into the ravine, the scattered, falling water made it impossible to see how far down it went. The small remainder of the river flowed into the second hole. The hole curved near the bottom and continued downward.

No water made it to the third hole, which was completely filled with vapor. The mist rose from underground and made its way to the surface. After the third hole, the hill declined. What used to be levels of small pools and waterfalls were now short cliffs of rocks and dirt. The dirt was still moist, but it would dry up by day's end.

At the bottom of the hill, there was an opening where the very end of the hill met the ground. Out of the opening flowed a small bit of water. It made up about one-fifth of the river's original volume, and nobody could understand why.

Panic grew amongst the crowd that surrounded the holes. The river served as their main water source, and overnight with no explanation, it was desolate. Maria and Victor were shocked by the size and sudden appearance of the holes, but unlike everyone else, they knew that something was coming.

Since the couple's first experience in Wisconsin, everything else followed in a pattern. They measured the time between each incident to be forty-two days, and they were now able to predict the locations down to the mile. They placed the seventh pin in their map, and the pattern was forming. However, even after a year of traveling and discovering new evidence, Maria and Victor still had no answers.

A friendly man named Ignacio told Maria everything that he knew. His grandson was the first to discover the holes in the early morning. Maria's father was raised in Mexico until he was a teenager, and he made it a point to speak Spanish around her as she grew up. Victor, who was monolingual, relied on his wife to translate.

As Ignacio spoke, Maria repeated it to Victor in English. "I think the government dug them somehow. Strange illnesses are going around the communities up river, and my neighbor saw government vehicles investigating the water a few miles north.

"We think they cut the water supply in order to stop the sickness from spreading down river…" The old man stopped and thought about what he was about to say. Maria and Victor watched Ignacio's face change as the fear of their new reality sank in. "We did not ask for the holes. Without the water, most of us will die anyway." As Maria repeated Ignacio's last words, the fear infected her as well.

Victor put an arm around his wife. He and Maria knew that the government had nothing to do with the holes, but they could not explain that to Ignacio. Maria's Spanish vocabulary was flimsy at best, and she and Victor failed to convince their colleagues of their paranormal experiences using English. The thought of crossing a language barrier was simply not possible. "Lo siento," repeated Maria, as she could only offer Ignacio sorrow and wish him good luck. The young couple was alone with their knowledge.

Ignacio's grandson ran up to him. He was a small six-year-old boy, dripping with energy. Maria and Victor smiled at his liveliness amongst all of the worry. The boy said something to his grandfather while holding up a picture that he had drawn. Ignacio continued to tell him "No" as the boy repeated something over and over.

"What is he saying?" asked Victor.

"I don't know exactly. 'It was the *something*. The *something* did it'... I can't understand the first part," said Maria.

Ignacio pointed at his grandson and gave him a final, stern "No." With that, the boy handed Maria his drawing and ran away. It was a picture of the hill and the river. There were three holes drawn on the top of the hill and a wall of water behind them. On the other side of the holes, there were three serpent-like creatures. They towered above the holes, and each of them had one big eye in the center of their bodies.

Maria stiffened. Louisiana, Idaho, and Wisconsin all had their share of strange, but the picture opened her mind to a place that she did not want to go. It suddenly occurred to Maria what the little boy had said to her.

"What's the matter?" asked Victor.

"He said, 'the *worms* did it'."

Chapter Three

Incident #13

June 14, 2015: Amber Rock, Colorado

Before he knew it, John finished another glass of ale. It was number four, and he usually called it quits after three. He could have penciled that into the list of grievances for the day, but the alcohol was doing its job; the chatter from his mind was temporarily muted.

"Another red ale, John?" John looked up to see Jack already holding a fresh glass under the tap, smiling as usual.

"No thank you, Jack. I think I'm a little ahead of myself."

"That's when all the fun happens, John," said Jack as he returned the unused glass to its rack. Over the past few weeks, John became friendly with the young bartender. The doctor was heavy-handed with his tips, and Jack had a knack for slipping him the occasional drink off the record. Jack cleared the bar space in front of John and found a drawing scribbled on a crumpled napkin. He flattened it out on the bar. "What's this?"

"Sodium chloride," said John. "Sometimes I draw molecules when I'm bored. I usually don't even realize I'm doing it." Jack admired John's rendition of the molecular structure. He smoothed out the napkin and slid it back to John, feeling guilty for ruining such a piece of art. John smiled and crumpled it up himself. "Don't worry. It's just a habit. I saw the salt shaker there and started drawing."

"What kind of science did you say you teach?" asked Jack.

"Particle physics."

Jack's face lit up. He leaned in close to John. "E equals M C squared." With a grin, Jack waited for his well-deserved praise from the doctor. John said nothing, assuming that Jack had more to it. "That's physics, right?"

"Yes... It is. Very good, Jack. That's Einstein's equation of energy-mass equivalence. That's a famous one."

Jack raised his chin in pride. "Do you teach that?"

"Yes, sort of, but my studies focus more on particles and what they call quantum mechanics," said John.

"Particles, huh? Particles like dust and rocks?"

"More like subatomic particles. Think way smaller. For instance, with sodium here, you see eleven electrons and protons, and twelve neutrons. Those are the dark ones here." John shifted into full teaching mode as he used his tiny napkin as a blackboard. Jack tried to keep up. "But even the protons and neutrons are made up of smaller things. We call them quarks. Basically, everything we see can be broken down into smaller units. Does that make sense?" asked John, hoping that something found its way through to his young friend. Jack's stoned face suggested nothing of the sort.

"Umm… Yeah, that's really cool. I think I've heard of this stuff before."

"Anyway, I'm slowly moving towards string theory. The more we break down these particles into even smaller particles, the more I realize that I need to just go right to the source."

"And what source is that, John?"

"Well, string theory in a sense is science's way of connecting quantum mechanics, which works with small things, and the theory of relativity, which works with large things. They call it '*the theory of everything.*' If it really is the answer for everything, then anything else is just a waste of time, right?"

Jack took a deep breath. After a moment of processing and computing, he stared back at John. "The theory of everything, huh?" asked Jack with a look of damning curiosity. "Maybe you're the guy I've been needing to talk to then… There are things going on here that are unexplainable. More than likely dangerous. Maybe you have an equation or something that can spell it all out."

John waited for clarification. "Okay. What is it?" he asked. Jack leaned in for the sake of privacy and looked John square in the eye.

"Ghosts. What do you know about ghosts, John?" John sat back in his stool and smirked. "There's been three sightings this year, the third happening just last week. This time one of the maids saw something on the fourth floor. I assume your string theory covers this to some degree," said Jack. John reached down for his wallet, still smiling.

"I'm yet to come across ghost theory, Jack." He took out a twenty-dollar bill and a five, and placed them on the bar. "As far as I know, they don't fall under the umbrella of my studies, but I'll make some phone calls and see what I can figure out." John stood up from his stool.

"It's all energy, right? If it's the theory of everything, you'll come across it eventually."

"That's a good point, Jack. Maybe I'll have to get a few minutes with that maid and hear her side of it. Thank you for the ale." John started his way to the exit.

"Be careful on your walk home, Johnny. They're out there."

★★★

The mountain town was so beautiful at night that John made it a point to always travel to and from the bar on foot, but tonight, he found himself walking into a thick fog. Heavy mist seeped out of the mountains and poured over the small buildings. The street lamps conjured up a glow of moisture and dark yellow light. As the visibility dulled, everything around John went quiet. He was remarkably alone. The sound of his footsteps bounced off of the mountains and echoed back.

An interesting feeling descended through his gut. It was not as harsh as fear, but certainly discomforting. John's usual fifteen-minute walk already seemed like thirty, and his feet were growing heavy.

John reached the top of the hill and started down its descent. After only two or three steps, he was greeted by the glow of his hotel's lights. John's relief was paired with a new lesson: Now that he was nearing his older years, beer number four should always be accompanied with either a full glass of water or a hot plate of food. Six-and-a-quarter decades did not have him feeling like an old man exactly, but drinking was much harder than it used to be.

After a third of the way down the hill, the hotel was in full view. John became aware of how fast he was walking and stopped to take a breath. He was nearly there. The flood of discomfort was on its way out, and the red ale began to numb his fears. But then he heard the bells behind him.

John jerked his head around. Nothing was there. The sidewalk was clear all the way up the hill. Stumped and a bit drunk, he ran the scenario through his mind. It sounded like chimes or small bells were dangled just behind his head and gently shaken.

John waited for his Follower to introduce Itself. The feeling of being completely alone was no longer a concern, and once again, the air was silent. After thirty beats of his heart, he turned around and continued on. Luckily for John, he did not believe in the supernatural. Otherwise, the rest of his one-hundred-yard walk would have been very uncomfortable.

★★★

The lights were off when John walked into his room. If it were up to him, they would stay off, and he would put the exciting evening to bed. Unfortunately, John's struggle to fall asleep was a fight as old as time. He grew up on a Wyoming farm with no siblings, so a wandering mind was inevitable. He handled the passing thoughts as well as he could for a five-year-old, but on the night of his sixth birthday, he was cordially introduced to insomnia, and his wandering mind soon had all the time in the world. Given no choice, John thought deeply about everything.

Science possessed him. By the age of ten, he memorized the roles of history's leading contributors from Aristotle to Newton to Einstein. By twelve, John debated his parents and teachers on the existence of God and the afterlife, demanding evidence for all claims. *All that exists can be measured in numbers,* he often thought. For that reason, John was never afraid of the dark. The idea of ghosts and the supernatural amused him in the pop-culture sense, but it all meant nothing until it could be supported with science.

After a full day of over-examining each and every thought, John would pass out for four or five hours, wake up in the middle of a new thought, and start all over again. And he did eventually fall asleep after that long evening, but unfortunately for him, the bizarre was not quite over with.

Somewhere in the ungodly hours, John awoke to a sensation up and down his body. He was covered in static electricity. He reached over for the desk lamp, and when his arm arrived twelve inches from the metal switch, an electric bolt jumped from his hand, to the lamp, and back. With a brash pop, the room lit up blue and John yelped.

He sat up and spewed out a blasphemy to the God he didn't believe in as his hand pulsated in and out of numbness. After he ran out of curse words, he flattened back out and stared at the dark ceiling. He no longer had to worry about shutting off his mind for the night; sleeping was now certainly out of the question.

Within a few minutes, his arm felt like it belonged to him again, but the fear of a repeat shock kept him from touching the light. The room was in absolute darkness – a negative black. He knew that the window was near, even if he could not see it. He considered opening the shades to catch some light from the street lamps, but when he sat up, a second rush of static drifted over him. He froze. The static inched up the back of his neck, over his ears, and to the tip of his nose. It likewise covered his forearms and chest. He watched his shirt lift off of his chest and stretch forward as if it was being pulled by a magnet. In one rush, all of the electric energy leaped from his body to the closet doors, fifteen feet straight ahead of him. The static hit the wood and crackled on its surface. It shot to the ground, and squeezed through the thin opening under the doors.

The closet itself was an aesthetic draw. Its double doors were made of a beautiful, dark wood with carved, symmetric patterns. Between the doors and the doorframe there was a slight gap, and through that gap came a dull glow. The light intensified until the inner closet was blinding bright. Then, as slowly as it lit up, the light faded back to darkness. And with a flicker, the bedside lamp turned on. John watched the incident in silence. His adrenaline, however, played at full volume.

It must have been his most primal survival instinct that kept him glued to the bed because John's curiosity wanted nothing more than to sprint to the closet and rip the doors open. After a quick and mild debate, he ended up with a compromise: He would head for the closet, but he would do so slowly and with extreme caution.

Sitting at the edge of the bed, John placed one foot down. With each pound per square inch that he applied from his body to the old hotel floor, there came a singing creak. He shifted his weight gradually and started his migration. He counted each footstep, considering the possibility that death waited behind the door. By the time he reached double digits, he was within a grasp of the doorknob. He took one last breath, turned both knobs, and pulled.

He stepped inside and tugged the pull-string light. The closet was silent. John looked across each top corner and then down to each bottom corner. A few shirts hung from hangers and his single pair of shoes sat neatly aligned on the floor. John saw nothing more, but he felt something. He felt a presence as if Someone was on the darker end of the closet looking back at him.

As John waited for a proper introduction, he caught himself panting. For politeness sake, he slowed down his breath to hide his fear from the Visitor. Once again, he ran his eyes along all eight corners of the closet. After a full minute passed, his heart beat dropped and his breath slowed down on its own. With some fraction of certainty that he was in fact alone, John shut the door. But when he turned and walked back towards his bed, a bell rang again.

John dug his foot in the floor and whipped himself around. Staring at the door, John waited on the edge of his toes. He knew what would happen next, and it happened. From behind the door came the sound of a ringing bell. John walked to the door and ripped it open.

In the center of the closet was a shining speck of gold. It started out as a glimmer and then expanded into a small bell. The glow reflected off of John's widened eyes. It grew to about the size of a fist. The bell, although simple in shape, was gorgeous. Light danced off of its armored plate and surrounded it in a halo. John felt the urge to fall to his knees. His legs were buckling due to fear, but also out of true admiration. Feeling inferior, John looked inward to his mind for any thoughts or suggestions. His mind was also at a loss. It was, however, able to submit that the bell looked to have been plucked from heaven's gate itself. But before John and his mind had the opportunity for further observation, the bell shook.

Audible vibration engulfed John. Despite its size, the small bell produced sounds greater than the ten church bells of Notre-Dame. John cried during his trip to the French Cathedral, but the small piece of metal in the closet now had him sobbing. He fell to his hands and knees as water poured out of his eyes. The precise emotion was too overwhelming to be clear, but it was as magnificent as it was excruciating. He was on two rockets in two opposite directions.

With all of John's strength, he strained his neck, lifted his head, and opened his eyes. As the bell sped up, angelic sound came screaming out. John endured. An ocean of sensation poured over him until he felt his heart reach its limit. Then the ringing peaked and the bell slowed. At a steady descent, the energy quieted and guided John down. The chorus of music simplified itself one note at a time, and eventually devolved into a single chime. The vibration in the air stilled and placed John gently back on the Earth.

The doctor found himself struggling to breathe through the tears and snot, so he inhaled through his mouth and expelled everything from his nose down onto the hotel carpet. John rubbed his eyes and sat flat on his behind. He looked at nothing but the bell. It hung still for another twenty seconds or so. John's mind began to hold court over the origin of the noise-making object, but before it could cough up a starting point, the bell shook one last time, and then it shrank and vanished.

John was panting again, but this time he could not hide it. His stomach bloated and his bowels had a near misfire. He was speechless, but what was even more astounding was that John's mind was speechless too. For the first time in his life, his brain was not flooded with thoughts. It was stumped.

With his system experiencing a processing error, John's auto-pilot took over. He found himself back on his hands and knees searching the floor for answers. He rubbed his hands all around the walls of the closet and creases in the wood, hoping to find a logical entry/exit point for the bell. When his brain was able to reboot itself, he realized that even if he found any openings, they would still not explain how it grew and shrank out of existence. So, he sat back down in disbelief and tried to gather his senses.

A few hypotheses bubbled to the surface, none of which had any real substance. The most obvious to him was to blame the alcohol and its possible effects. He certainly exceeded his regular quota for one evening, but then again, never had a few extra drinks caused extreme hallucinations. The next few thoughts had similar themes about not eating since noon and being sleep deprived, but they collapsed rather quickly as well, considering that he was nowhere near starvation, and he had a few hours of shut-eye just before the episode. So, in the absence of a plan or any idea of where to even start, John decided that the rational thing to do was to pull up a chair and wait to see if his Guest would return. And he did just that.

John remained focused and oddly patient for the first few hours, but once the first rays of morning light hit his shoulders, he decided that he should at least put something into his stomach if he was planning to stick it out. He did not want to miss another apparition, but he realized that he would need to eat and sleep eventually.

John took a quick trip down to the corner store to buy some breakfast and coffee before heading right back up to his headquarters for second watch. He now had something to do outside of drinking through a day of self-torment. The bell woke him up from a long sleep. His failures kept him unproductive, and he wasted so much time. So, as the amazing sounds of the bell rang over and over in his head, John gave himself one goal: Find the Ringer of the bell.

Chapter Four

The Collapse Of A Union

Alice rifled through Tom's clothes looking for more evidence. The woman's slip that she found mixed in with his work shirts did not belong to her, nor did the panties from his dresser. She ripped his suits from their hangers and his shirts from their drawers. Her rage drove her to find more clues of his infidelity, but underneath it all, Alice knew that it would soon not matter. It was over. Just one hour ago, Tom sat her down in the great room, asked her to put down her morning cocktail, and informed her that he had been seeing someone for over a year. Alice knew about Tom's flings for decades, but she never imagined that she would ever be replaced by one of them.

They met twenty-seven years ago when Alice waited on Tom. He was fresh out of law school, and she was on her third waitressing job of the year. He ordered a steak, medium rare, and a glass of cabernet with the request that she not bring it out until the steak was ready. She managed to get the order correct, which was some accomplishment, but upon transference from the tray to the table, she dropped the glass. Alice shrieked as the wine spilled all over the steak. Her two previous firings flashed before her eyes, and she felt the horror of knowing that her father was going to have to bail her out once again.

As the tears gathered along her eyeliner, she looked at Tom, but Tom was not upset. In fact, he found her clumsiness adorable. He laughed and placed his hand on hers. Alice calmed down immediately and joined him in the laugh. She took a deep breath, collected herself, and went back to the kitchen to get Tom another steak.

On her way back to the table, she tripped over her own feet and dropped the new tray onto the ground. Alice would never forget those shattering dishes as they smashed on the floor. They were the perfect analogy for how her young adult life was going. Having seen enough, her not-so-empathetic manager chewed her out right at the table. Alice never received many scoldings, being that she was raised under the care of overprotective, upper-class parents and a sweet, lower-class nanny, but before she could cry again, Tom interrupted her manager.

He insisted that Alice join him at another restaurant for dinner with the rationale that he was now very hungry because she had dropped all of his food, and she looked like she could use a meal herself. Tom was born with a true gift of persuasion, and Alice just happened to be in a persuasive mood. The two of them left right in the middle of her shift. She never went back, even to pick up her paycheck. They were married six months later.

Their relationship was healthy and exciting. In practicality terms, they were the perfect match. He started making money quickly, and by pure coincidence, she enjoyed not having a job. Tom took care of them financially, however, Alice did find ways to pull her weight creatively. She adopted little projects around the home and made herself responsible for tying together any of their day-to-day loose ends.

During their second year together, she convinced Tom to pursue a business venture with her father, William. William was a well-respected airline pilot in the southeast, and at that time, he was trying to broaden his horizons financially. His friend, Russell Thomas, devised an instrument that attached to a double-winged propeller plane in order to make it more aerodynamic during take-off, and inversely, allow it to have softer, more controlled landings. Individually, it was surprisingly cheap to make, but neither William nor Mr. Thomas had the kind of money needed for a full-scale production. William would never ask Tom for financing out of both politeness and the fear of losing his son-in-law's money. Alice, however, knew that her father had an eye for innovation and Tom had a mind for flipping investments, so she convinced them both to take the leap. Tom's persuasive skills had rubbed off on her somewhere along the way. He and William shook hands and started an investment that eventually grew tenfold.

Alice planned a surprise trip to Paris for Tom and herself to celebrate. She even learned a little bit of French to help them get around. For the first time in her life, Alice felt like she was building something real. She and Tom were perfect for one-another.

And then she found out about the cheating.

One night when he was in Atlanta on business, Alice was awoken by a phone call. She was greeted by a young woman screaming indiscernibly. After a few moments of trying to communicate over the woman's hysteria, she realized that the call was intended for Tom. The young lady was a former paralegal at Tom's firm, and she had been let go after the two of them were caught together in his office. Tom was a young asset, so they only got rid of her. She, of course, was not happy about being used and disposed of, so she went on to tell Alice every detail of their short-lived romance.

Alice heard everything the girl had to say, but processed very little of it. She could not believe that any of it was possible until the woman told her that it all took place over the same three weeks that Alice spent planning their trip. Throughout those weeks, she considered herself lucky that Tom was getting home so late because it allowed her extra time to make arrangements and study her French, but now, she felt betrayed. She felt like Tom had thrown her away.

For two days, she prepared for her confrontation with him. She prayed to God to give her strength through her sadness, which was quickly turning into anger. She spent hours feeling livid and thinking only the worst thoughts about Tom. Then, without warning, she would cry and break right back down into sadness. Every so often, she stopped to take a deep breath and find some clarity, but in no time, she would lose grip again.

When the morning sun finally shone through the window on that second day, a strange byproduct of feelings remained. The anger and sadness were still there, but they were no longer on the forefront. At some point during the restless night, she faced the reality of a more sobering emotion: fear. Not fear of what she or Tom might do to each other, but fear of where she would end up when it was all over. Going back to waiting tables was the path to a pathetic and humiliating existence, and crawling back to her father, defeated and desperate, was worse.

She used the rest of her time alone to write a letter to Tom, listing everything that she was feeling; the anger, the grief, and the betrayal. As she proofread the letter, she envisioned her plan coming to life.

When Tom got home, she would lead him into the bedroom where the letter would be waiting for him in a sealed envelope. After Tom finished reading and digesting it, Alice would explain out loud to him the torture that he caused her.

And only if she received an undeniably true apology from her husband, they would then find some way to start over and rebuild their marriage, God willing. But to Alice's total surprise, the letter would never even need to be opened.

Alice was still at the table when the front door flew open. Tom marched into the kitchen, dropped his bags, and looked Alice in the eyes. Tears poured down his face.

At first, he said nothing. He stared at her, but his heavy breathing told Alice that he was more nervous than she was. In a strange way, that gave her hope that he might actually care, but she did not dare to speak first.

Without breaking his glance, Tom kneeled down, took Alice by the hands, and sobbed. Out of all the mixed emotions still swimming around her chest, relief was the strongest. The sorrow and shame radiated off of him like warmth.

He explained the entire incident with the young paralegal and he swore to Alice that he regretted it from the moment it happened. He told her that he had already contacted a marriage counselor who agreed to see them immediately if she was willing. And then he explained how his father treated his mother the exact same way, and the thought of turning out to be anything like his father sickened him.

Alice was so overwhelmed by the conflict inside of her heart. Half of it could never trust him again. It provided her with a clear image of Tom on top of the girl at his office. With that visual, she felt like someone dumped ash into the open wound on her chest. It felt cold and dead. But then the other half of her heart reminded her about what Tom had said to her. She could not look past the fact that he may have inherited some of his issues, and who was she to walk out on him at his weakest point? He did come to her with the truth after all, and now he was crying for forgiveness. So, she decided at that moment, with her husband in her lap, that she would go as far as he was willing to go. She would fight as hard as he was willing to fight.

Unfortunately for her, Tom's gift of persuasion came second to his talent of melodramatic acting. What Alice did not know was that as soon as the young paralegal had hung up with her that night, she tracked down the phone number to Tom's hotel in Atlanta and fired off the exact same phone call to him. After she made it clear that she had just spoken to Alice, he decided that some preparation for his homecoming would be time well spent. He leafed through his catalog of characters and came across the *apologetic husband*. His approach to method acting really brought the role to life.

Of course, it was not long until Alice was accidentally introduced to the next young woman, and then the list grew from there. For the first few years, she threatened to leave him after each new girlfriend. That led to an apology which became more and more recycled with each use. Eventually, she stopped caring and started drinking, and he stopped talking to her all together. By their tenth anniversary, they knew nothing about each other, and only spoke either when she needed money or when he was going out of town. And like the spin of a dial, seventeen more years went by, and he finally informed her that she would no longer be living with him.

Chapter Five

Incident #4

June 1, 2014: Air Space Above Gillis, Louisiana

Alice ripped through the rest of Tom's closet, finding traces of his new girlfriend all over the place. She made a pile of the young woman's undergarments on the floor. Armed with a mound of justification, Alice prepared for her ambush on Tom. For good measure, she grabbed her glass of whiskey and slammed it back. The combination of alcohol and reality burned through Alice, and it put her into a rare moment of clarity: She was kneeling on a floor covered in the clothes of her ex-husband and his new girlfriend. She was no longer in her own home. She was no longer wanted. Alice stood up and made her way out of the ruins.

Her uniform was drenched in sweat and wrinkled, and she was not even at work yet. Work, of course, was a new trial for Alice, and it should have been the first clue to her upcoming eviction. Six months earlier, Tom told her that it was time to get a job so that she could start supporting her own drinking habit. Alice found it difficult to find work, being that her résumé had not been updated for three decades. Luckily for her, her father had been bailing her out for over five decades.

Although long retired, William's forty-year career allowed him to hold close relationships with the airlines and the union, and he landed Alice a job as a flight attendant. She struggled through the long hours and turn-arounds, but she had no other option. After being her lifetime safety net, William was out of tricks. So, she did what she had to, which mostly meant drinking heavily before each flight and then sneaking shots of airline liquor in the bathroom. But she was surviving.

Alice walked out from the bedroom, and turned the corner into the hallway. She heard Tom close a door upstairs and make his way out. The sound of his footsteps alone gave her flashing visions of his mistress' panties. Flooded with wrath, she stormed into the great room just as he passed above her on the upstairs balcony. She slammed her empty glass to the floor and shattered it. "I found her clothes!" she screamed with a southern drawl. Tom leaned over the balcony. His demeanor, in contrast, was calm.

"Well, they were not exactly hidden."

"How could you let another woman put her clothes in our closet? You couldn't wait to kick me out before she moved in?" Alice trembled with each word. Tom took his time before speaking, knowing that an argument with her in this condition was simply a war of attrition. She would implode at any moment.

"You haven't used that closet in years. I gave you half of this house. You could have picked any closet that you wanted."

"That was ours, but go ahead and give it to her. Eventually you'll just throw her away too."

Alice peered into Tom's eyes. Even after years of dejection, there was still a trace of her that wanted to share a closet with him. Upon looking at him, she realized that they had not made actual eye contact in ages. One thing that she discovered early on was that they could speak to each other using only their eyes. She knew how he was feeling and he could tell her almost anything with a look. Hope made its way back into her scarred heart. Her husband was looking at her. The longer she stared at him, the stronger she felt a connection reforming. At that moment, she wholeheartedly wanted him back. She melted into his gaze, and with her eyes, she begged him to melt into hers. She begged him not to let go.

He blinked.

"I think it's time for you to leave," he said. "Your new keys are hanging by the door. I know it's only eleven A.M., but you should probably go sleep this off." Alice cranked right back up.

"My new keys?! What new keys?"

"To the apartment. I already told you. Maybe if you weren't screaming in hysteria, you would have heard me. It's three miles from the airport, and I've already paid your first six months of rent. Feel free to keep the car."

Alice began to hyperventilate, but she stopped herself in order to not give Tom the satisfaction. "And what about my things? Should I just buy a new life?"

"Everything you need will be brought over in the next month. You can still come to the house, but I think it would be best if you go over to the apartment today and get a feel for it."

"I don't have time for this right now. I'm going to be late for work," she said.

"What do you mean late for work? How can you go to work like this?" he asked with sincere confusion.

"Like what?"

"You're drunk. You can't show up in this condition."

"I'm not drunk!" Alice's scream pierced through the house. "You're not getting rid of me like this! This is my house too!" Alice stormed up the stairs and into her room. A split second later, she walked out carrying her suitcase and headed down the stairs. She glared up at Tom as he stared right back at her. She opened her mouth to say something and then realized that no words could match her emotions, so she looked him over one last time, and marched out of the door.

***

The number of accidents that she almost caused on her drive to the airport was staggering. She hit two curbs and blew a red light. She also smoked a record four cigarettes on a fifteen-minute drive. To blame her behavior completely on the alcohol would not be fair. It was no doubt a contributor, but her nerves were playing the violin on her arteries the whole way. Somewhere along the freeway, she got tunnel vision and blacked out. She came-to while smoking another cigarette in front of the outdoor baggage check. She had no idea where she parked her car, and she knew that smoking that close to the doors was prohibited, but given her boiling, red skin, she assumed that anyone of authority would turn a blind eye.

By the time that Alice made it through security and to her gate, she was informed that her flight to Austin was delayed until four o'clock due to thunderstorms. Being stationed in Orlando, she was used to local storms holding her up, but apparently the sky was covered all the way from southern Alabama to western Louisiana. In order to have the civility to sit around with her thoughts for that long, she knew that she needed another drink.

Showing up at the bar wearing her flight attendant uniform seemed a tad inappropriate, so she threw on a fleece and bought a liter of whiskey from the duty-free shop. With a cup of ice, she walked into the smoker's lounge and set up camp.

Over the following several hours, Alice wrestled with the thoughts of her uncertain future: Where would she end up? How would she take care of herself? Would her job get the better of her? The only answer that she seemed to have for each question was another gulp of whiskey.

After half of the liter and a full pack of cigarettes, Alice saw that the clock read *seven P.M.* She shot out of her seat and hustled out of the lounge. After only five steps, her legs made it clear that she just drank half of a liter of whiskey. The airport was leaning left. So, she leaned right and trotted to the gate.

For the first time all day, she was relieved. The flight was further delayed, and Alice made it right on time to help with the pre-boarding process. She ate a handful of drinker's chocolates to cover up the whiskey smell and fell right in line with her fellow flight attendants. An hour later, the plane was full and they were in the air.

Alice looked around at all of the different faces of the passengers. For once in a long time, she felt a sense of luck with her situation. Here she was, completely intoxicated and unprepared for her duties, still humiliated from being dumped by her husband, and yet nobody noticed or cared. She considered that maybe working on a constantly moving vehicle would be a good fit for her. She would never be tied down to one place, and all of the people that she met each trip would be quickly replaced by the people on the next trip. Temporary randomness seemed far more appealing than permanent unhappiness.

Alice walked the aisle and served drinks to the tired passengers until the last reading light went out. When the plane turned completely dark, she felt okay with sitting down for a breather. She took a long, deep breath, and then said a prayer. Over the years, her relationship with God had been replaced by alcohol, perhaps explaining her growing depression. Alice decided that she would start mending that immediately. Knowing that she had taken a step towards a life of peace, she finished her prayer, sat back, and closed her eyes.

★★★

A deafening crack forced the airplane to jolt upward. Alice, who had fallen asleep, was shot to the limit of her seatbelt's guard and woken up. The emergency lights on the floor flickered on and off as the plane leveled itself. Nervous chatter filled the cabin. Alice froze in her seat while the other young flight attendant got up and ran into the cockpit.

The passengers all had an identical look of panic on their faces. As Alice's heart pounded, she imagined that this is what tragedy actually feels like. Her body stiffened. The young flight attendant came back out of the cockpit and ran over to her. Alice had no idea what her name was because she was drunk when they were introduced, but now that her adrenaline had taken over, she was fully sober.

"Okay, we have just been hit by lightning. The Captain said that we are going to be fine, but we need to land immediately," said the woman. Alice watched her speak, but failed to process her words. "A storm came out of nowhere, and we're right in the middle of it. We're over Gillis, Louisiana and there's a small airport where we can land." Alice blankly stared at the young woman. "Ma'am, are you okay? I need you to go into coach and make sure that all of the passengers are seated. I'm going to make the announcement, okay?" Alice snapped out of it.

"Okay… yes," Alice finally said. She stood up and gained her balance. The woman walked over to the intercom and held the speaker to her mouth. Just then, the plane got rocked by another crash of lightning. Alice fell to the ground as the passengers lit up with cries of fear. The plane went completely dark until the next lightning bolt flashed through the windows.

Alice lost her sense of awareness and crawled over to find her seat. The young flight attendant screamed through the pandemonium to sit down and buckle up. Alice felt her way to her chair and pulled herself into a half-seated position. With her hands shaking, she locked the seatbelt onto her lap.

As the lightning cracked again, she could see the fear-ridden travelers for a second at a time. Their heads were between their knees, and they held each other's hands as a last grip for life. The plane's rapid descent felt more like a nose dive to Alice as she mumbled through her prayers. Everyone except for her was crouched into a lump, including the other flight attendant. When the plane took a sudden turn, Alice got a clear look out of the window, and her fear of death was momentarily forgotten. The lightning that surrounded them was not striking between the clouds and the ground. It was all hitting one direct point that was level with their current altitude. That direct point was a glowing sphere that floated beneath the clouds, and every few seconds, it got struck by a thunderbolt.

Alice had never seen anything like it. She first thought that it may have been another plane getting battered, but it was not moving, nor was it the size of an airplane. It was spherical, and just before they descended enough for it to be out of sight, the entire sky sparked with streaks of lightning. They came from all directions and met on the round object. It looked like a spider web of electricity, and when the web disappeared, there remained the glowing white orb, mysterious and alone, floating in the void. It was imprinted into Alice's mind as bright as it burned in the sky.

Chapter Six

<u>Remembering A Year Better Forgotten</u>

John was beginning to feel like himself again. More than a week had passed since the manifestation, and since then, the only things to appear in his closet were freshly hung shirts. After wasting plenty of time obsessing over a drunken illusion, John washed his hands of it all and claimed ignorance. Of course, he knew that this was a total copout, but he could not justify a ninth day of sitting in front of his closet. So, for the time being, he got back to his previous obsession of over-examining his yearlong mistake.

There was a beautiful lake at the foot of the mountains that he escaped to when he needed to clear his head, and it was there that John chose to settle his mental struggle.

Upon arrival, he was happy to see that he was not alone. There were young families walking around and swimming in the lake. John sat at the edge of a small dock and dangled his feet over the water. On the most beautiful day, in the most pleasant setting, John waited for his mind to thrash him.

John settled in for a cross-examination of himself that would determine the severity of his punishment. His former penances ranged widely depending on what self-determined sin or violation he had committed, but something told him that this one would be the harshest of all. So, with no desire to delay it further, John rested his chin on his chest, closed his eyes, and sank deep into thought.

John's mind cared little about his efforts; it was always more interested in the end results. In this most recent indictment, the doctor was accused of wasting a year of his time on a research study that ended up being a total contradiction of itself. John tried to lessen his sentence by way of a plea bargain, but unfortunately, in the great court of John, deals were never given to lessen his punishments. So, a full trial was in order.

The first issue detailed by John's opposition was the fact that John acted alone. He failed greatly, and he had only himself to blame. Not only did he admit to that point himself, but he considered tattooing it across his chest as a form of self-punishment. He spent months playing back the entire study in his head, and never once did he consider casting blame to any outside person or stimulus. John had no problem recalling any part of what had happened because from day one of the experiment, he kept a written record in his notebook of each day's findings.

There were almost eight months of daily passages in that journal, but there were six days in particular that could sum up the entire experiment, from its start, to its highest point, to its lowest point, and finally to its closing entry. They were marked and ready for one final review. As his feet dangled over the lake, John opened the book and prepared himself to relive his downfall.

Excerpt 1:

August 19, 2014

I am writing this as an official record of my efforts in the chance that my research produces any results or otherwise advances our collective hypotheses. Because I am attempting something that I know is beyond my ability, I am entering this study with the most open mind that a man of science should allow. And because this composition will likely only act as a diary and never reach the eyes of another, I will write it informally in the interest of recording free thoughts as they come, as well as any experimental advances or shortcomings. However, I will share this journal in its entirety if I happen to find any degree of success.

As previously stated, my goal at hand is beyond my measure, as I do not have the proper technology, budget, or ideal counsel beyond my own knowledge and studies of the subject. However, if I could make the slightest footprint in the direction of progress, then I will know that my time was spent doing something of true worth. So, for the indefinite future, I am officially committing myself to aid in the discovery of the graviton. I have examined over the past decades that the forerunners of particle studies, of whom I most respect, have almost unanimously agreed on the existence of the gravity particle. Its place within string theory would have an impact possibly as great as the Higgs boson's impact on our understanding of fields and mass. And perhaps that in itself was my ultimate inspiration for starting down this long, undiscovered road.

Seeing the boson's progress from Higgs' hypothesis all the way to its physical discovery has opened my eyes to how powerful our collective minds can be. The 'God Particle,' as we have so nobly entitled it, is worth so much more to us than a function. It is hope and proof: hope that we will one day be able to answer the ultimate question, and proof that we are taking steps in the right direction. And so, in the dark corner of my office, I will work away, striving to do my part. As mentioned, I have a less than acceptable budget for research, and the technology available at the university is outdated at best. Therefore, instead of attempting the impossible of shaking hands with gravity's boson, I will work with mathematics to formulate the most up to date equation that could serve the current model. When I have reached my limit, I will seek the necessary assistance from a member of the mathematics department. If luck does exist, I will find the golden method of converting equations into material whether it be the way of the physicist, the chemist, or the alchemist.

Excerpt 2:

September 29, 2014

Today is day forty-two since the first step of my research. Keeping this daily journal has been helpful in unexpected ways, specifically for the recording of my thoughts that I would normally share with a colleague or research partner. I have chosen to stick with my decision of keeping this experiment in the dark from anyone else for now, simply because I still do not know where it will lead, and I do not want time to become any sort of factor on anyone's patience. My goal is to have something material by one year, however, that is fully subject to change should I find myself moving slower than expected or veering towards new discoveries.

As for any indication of whether this research will produce a desired result, I feel fortunate to say that the prognosis is leaning positive. My fascination with the subject has some degree of influence on that projection, but there is also no doubt that my understanding is also growing exponentially.

Although I have gone out of my way to familiarize myself with gravity and its properties, the consequence of focusing my career on quantum mechanics and the micro level of the Universe is that I have become much more accustomed to the electromagnetic and nuclear forces of nature. I find myself asking, if gravity dictates all of the massive objects of the Universe, why then does its force stop at the quantum level? It is the weakest of nature's four forces, yet it holds all galaxies in place. Perhaps the graviton is the ambassador particle that can lead the way to introducing general relativity to quantum mechanics.

I am finding myself visualizing the graviton particles interacting with every part of my world. I can sense their spin-two as they move in and around me. I understand that my mind is projecting it to be only what it can understand and relate to, but what are they truly? What if gravity is an endless field after all, and what if that field is made up of an ocean of these unseen particles? Are they finite? Is there shape or size to them as individuals? If they do share our space, what other great problems could their discovery solve? Maybe they will help explain the abundant mystery of Dark Matter.

For now, I am trying to make peace with the fact that these answers will never come in my lifespan. Whether we discover the graviton or not, there is simply not enough time to learn its absolute nature. But even in the face of such a bleak and honest certainty, I am uncovering the origin of my deepest curiosity. I now see that the root to all of my scientific wonder is the mystery of space-time. What is space-time? Is it truly a woven fabric, or is the fabric itself just emptiness filled with countless fields and waves? How much is there that lies beyond the perception of our ignorant five senses? Perhaps we are doomed to never know, but whatever the case, the craving is pouring out from my bones, and I may not sleep until I meet the answer.

Excerpt 3:

November 26, 2014

The campus is clearing out for the holiday tomorrow, but I will not be going anywhere. Around midnight last night, I added another piece to my puzzle, and I now have almost half of a major equation. There is still plenty to balance on this end, and of course an entire other half, but in just three months I am far ahead of what I could have foreseen back in August. I hesitate to celebrate a partial victory, but I will allow myself a nightcap at the halt of this entry. The project is still unknown to anyone else, and I have decided to request one less class for next semester. It was not my intention to cut back on my teaching, but in light of the current state, I believe that the extra time will come in handy down the road.

I will not let this slight turn for the better get into my head, however. I have been bitten too many times by the deceiving smile of optimism. But maybe it would benefit me to ignore reluctance and consider myself on par at least for one night.

Excerpt 4:

January 5, 2015

Today showed no more progress than yesterday. Things have slowed down considerably over the past twenty or thirty days, and I seem to be losing grip on my overall understanding. Perhaps the overabundance of focus that I have put on this subject is curdling into exhaustion. I cannot pinpoint exactly how or where I strayed from progress, but my lack of results seems to speak for itself. I will consider taking a weekend out of town to rest and try to resurface. If that does not help, then I will need to either rewind the project back or reach out for help. Neither one of these options are desirable, but if they will save the study, then what choice do I have? My tall drink tonight will serve as necessity, not celebration.

Excerpt 5:

March 19, 2015

I am writing this only because I need to step away from my work to clear my head, and because I have somehow not missed one day since I began this journal back in August. The past three weeks have been an inferno of humbling realizations, and today I was put in my deserving place of insignificance. Right around the three quarters completion mark of my equation, I noticed that something was not balancing correctly. As I wrote last Friday, there was hope that the mistake happened sometime within this most recent phase of research, and therefore would be malleable. I have battered through my notes over the past week, and upon close scrutiny, it is now evident that the error occurred in October when I was working through the 'Wave versus Field' study.

The consequential impact of my mistake has started a snowball effect leading all the way up to this very moment. Over the next ten days, I will work ceaselessly to figure out if there is any chance of reviving the project, short of starting over. If I determine that there is a salvageable portion, then I will devote two more months of time to come up with some sort of product. I owe the project at least that, considering how much I have already put in. If, however, it turns out to be as paper thin as I fear, then it will be terminated immediately. I do not know exactly where to pick up after watching such a solid devotion rot before my eyes. I will hang this project up on the wall as a lesson for what happens when I try to grab something beyond my reach, and I will sit directly under it where I belong. And that will be that.

Excerpt 6:

April 3, 2015

Today will be my last entry in this journal. I have written down my thoughts for two hundred and twenty-eight straight days. For just over seven and a half months, I have been building an equation that was meant to aid in the discovery of the graviton. And for seven and a half months, I have proved nothing more than my inadequacies in the fields of mathematics and my humanistic traits of believing that I was capable of something greater than those before me.

I have often thought of what I would do with this journal at the conclusion of my research. The optimistic goal was to use it as an informal reference to each day of my research after a success was reached. It was not exactly a traditional way to mark the steps of an experiment, but I have always believed in personalizing my data and information for context's sake. However, my most recent thoughts of this journal's fate are far simpler: Burn it. Erase it from existence as well as any evidence that this project ever happened. But that would be an injustice. I do not deserve to be let off with such little consequences. This journal needs to be preserved. I need a constant reminder of how and why I failed. Out of all my successes and achievements in life, not one comes to mind that holds any weight in comparison to this. And trying to bury it would be an even greater sin than the failure itself.

And now onto the final diagnosis of the incident: After the second half of my equation was halfway written, I realized that it hosted one screaming flaw: If I had continued writing it to its completion, then it would have completely contradicted the first half. As clear of a contradiction as 'one equals negative one.' And this all stemmed from a small miscalculation in the early months. Fittingly, if I had gotten that calculation correct in the first place, then I would have known immediately that this experiment never had a chance from the start. But why would something ever work itself out so easily? When does life ever provide the painless way? I am glad that I took the route that concluded in a full school year wasted, because now I realize that my place in the Universe is that of complete and total mediocrity. The gravest mistake of all would be one that allowed me to believe that I could make any difference in the grand scheme of existence. I accept my place in the corner of my meaningless world and vow to hold my solemn obligations as a man who will create zero change. Even long after I am gone, this paper and ink will remain to preserve my legacy.

Sincerely,

Dr. John Robins,

Professor of Particle Physics, Colorado University

John winced as he read the final entry, waiting for the hammer to drop. He took a deep breath and closed the book, but against all odds, his mind did not pounce. It allowed him to take the breath. After months of being held under a microscope, John looked up to find nothing there except for the clear, blue sky. It was only then that John was given the chance to consider the one major detail that was never written down in his journal. That was the fact that no one ever found out that his research study had even taken place. Not one person. All of the humiliation and shame that bore down on him was completely self-inflicted. An unfamiliar feeling made its way into his chest. It was not quite positive, but not negative either, which was good enough for him.

Perhaps as a side effect of his borderline-optimism, John was able to look at his mathematical performance throughout the project from a new light. He did allow a large miscalculation to lead him down the wrong path, but he also sifted through much of the multivariable calculus and differential equations with relative ease. For months leading up to the mistake, John conquered formulas in weeks that would have taken his colleagues months or even years to comprehend. And even after the mistake, he acquired a useful understanding of the current state of gravitational studies. So, all things considered, he asked himself: *Was it a waste of time?* As badly as he wanted to scream 'Yes' and convict himself of the cardinal sin, he decided that for once his ambition and efforts were good enough to carry his weight, even in the presence of failure.

So, there John sat, journal in hand, and feet dangling above the lake. It was time for him to face his long-awaited punishment, and it was handed down: time served. John took another deep breath and exhaled. He was given his final second chance. His mind offered him a rare bit of humility with his sentence, but as always, it came with a price. He owed something.

He opened up his journal, clicked open his pen, and took it to the page.

June 22, 2015

Sulking in my regrets about all the time that I have wasted is in itself a waste of time, and therefore an act of hypocrisy. I would like to drop this journal into the lake under my feet and move on with my life, but that would be unearned. I have a debt that can only be paid in my time and effort. If string theory is in fact the theory of everything, then devoting myself to finding it will give me true worth. If this theory turns out to be the manual for the Universe, then I will be there to see it through. If it turns out to be a fallacy, then I will do my part in dismantling it. Either way, this is my act of contrition, and I will see it through until death or completion.

The perfect genius is all that is made. It is made by the working machine. I am NOT its mortality.

John

Chapter Seven
<u>A Curious Introduction</u>

Just as the early twilight peaked through the clouds, John woke up. For once, he was able to fall asleep at a humane hour. Normally, a swear word would roll off the tip of his tongue if he woke up before sunrise, but on that morning, he was greeted with the kind of excitement that only a child feels. It was not his insomnia that pulled him out of his slumber; it was the static. The static electricity that introduced itself to him on that strange night weeks ago was back, and just like last time, it had covered him like a warm blanket. John was so happy that he could have smiled, but he feared that any movement might release the energy's grip from his body. So instead, he remained perfectly still, and he observed.

Even by not moving, John felt the static gently crackle and pop as it crawled from his head towards his feet. Out of the corner of his eye, he saw the small amount of sunlight in the room start to dim, and simultaneously, the closet glowed. It appeared as if the light that came in through the window was actually being absorbed by whatever was inside of the closet, like water to a sponge.

By the time that all of the natural light was gone from the room, he felt the static electricity speeding up its course towards the closet doors. Knowing that it would only hang on for a few more seconds anyway, John sat up to get a good look. The static immediately shot across the room. He heard it hit the wooden door with a crash, and then slip straight under into the glow.

The room was silent until a strange noise creeped out of the closet. It sounded like thousands of small feet tapping down on a hard surface. His excitement mutated into concern as the wet clicks grew louder. John remembered clearly the heavenly sounds that came from the bell. This was different; this was disturbing. With the mixed emotions of hesitation and curiosity, he stood up and took his first step towards the closet.

John walked slowly, giving his ears the chance to pick up any soundwave that came his way. As he got closer, the clicking sound increased. In fact, it doubled. His mind illustrated a number of interpretations of what might have been waiting for him behind the door, none of which were very welcoming, but he continued forward. Curiosity once again won the argument over caution.

He reached the doors and grabbed the knobs. They were cold, as were the doors themselves. His shadow in front of him deteriorated as the room darkened by the second. Even the glow from under the closet had disappeared. With no trace of an explanation for anything, he yanked the doors open and took a long step back, and his understanding of reality changed forever.

Two elongated creatures hovered out of the closet towards John. He did not know exactly what he was seeing, but they looked to him like enormous, black centipedes. They floated across air, and their legs moved in unison as if they were walking on solid ground. They danced forward in an elegant, corkscrew motion, and by every inch that they progressed, more legs appeared and disappeared along their bodies. It was beautiful and hideous. With each footstep came the clicking sound that he heard moments earlier. There were hundreds every second. John stood and watched as the distance between himself and the creatures shortened steadily. Although his eyes followed their every move, his body was paralyzed from astonishment. And throughout this unsettling introduction, one thought spun around inside of his head like a record on loop. It was simply: *Any moment now, fear will own me, but until then, this is the most important moment of my life.* Just as this thought repeated itself for the third time, the two entities reached John. They met him at eye level, but instead of making contact, they each took a separate direction around his head and moved behind him. He estimated that they had about a seven-inch diameter, and were close to nine feet long.

He had just enough strength to turn his head in their direction. His legs, however, remained unresponsive. The beings hovered over his bed, twisting and crawling the entire way. As they neared the top corner of the ceiling, each of them shrank down in size and disappeared. After a few seconds, they grew back into sight four or five feet away. Just as John realized that he should have been questioning how any of this was possible, the visitors turned and made their descent back towards him, and his mind went blank again. Sweat dripped down his face, and his heart pounded, but just as before, they did not make contact with John. They again took separate paths around him.

As they approached the closet, they slowed down. John could see all of the grotesque details of their bodies which were only inches from his eyes. Countless legs fluttered back and forth, propelling them forward. Other stringy flaps opened and closed on their backs and sides, revealing wet openings to their gruesome anatomy. John had trouble distinguishing any sort of facial features, but something did become clear to him; whatever these things were, they had intelligence, and they were studying him.

As the last bit of the serpent-like beings departed back into the closet, John noticed the most intriguing element of their visit. In the center of his closet was a sort of floating orb. It was not necessarily in the shape of a sphere or a cube, but those were the closest things that his mind could relate it to. When John looked closer, he saw that the object had absolute straight lines and corners that formed stark right angles. However, its outline was also curved like that of a circle or a ball. It was totally and perfectly straight, as well as rounded. But not both. John knew immediately that he could never explain it to anyone, nor could he understand it himself, even as he was looking at it.

The orb was about four feet from top to bottom, and it was illuminated with a hue of color somewhere between blue and purple, but not quite either one. John was mesmerized. He could not fathom how he was looking at a color that did not exist inside of an impossible shape.

As the orb swallowed the last bit of the creatures, John noticed that it did not emit any of its color or light back out into the room, which was pitch-black. He tried to wrap his head around the idea of a light vacuum, but before he could dissect its concept, the orb began to shrink. As it deflated in size, its color paled, and the room brightened. It condensed down into half of its shape, and then a quarter, and then an eighth. When it was no larger than the size of a dime, everything around John became visible again, and without a whisper of sound, the orb was gone.

John coughed up heavy breath. The massive weight of the situation crashed onto him. His body weakened, and he grabbed on to the nearest chair to keep from falling. It was not until then that he noticed the horrible stench that the creatures had left behind. He dry-heaved as he coughed and gasped for air. His mind spun in eight different directions until it had tied itself into a knot. Luckily, the last instinct that remained was his recognition of nausea. So, he dragged himself into the bathroom and got within vomiting range of the toilet. However, as soon as he was able to breathe the untarnished air of a new room, his stomach contents slid back down and settled.

John pulled himself up and sat against the wall. His heartbeat and breath came back down to Earth and, one by one, his thoughts began to resurface. *What just happened?* was the question that found its way to the forefront. He attempted to give it a shot, but just by repeating the question again in his head, John's pulse accelerated and his brain flooded. Images of the creatures flashed into his brain, and the nausea returned. John closed his eyes and took deep breaths. He and his mind agreed that he was not ready to tackle that just yet.

When his system cooled down, his mind handed him a question that was more appropriate and, perhaps, more important: *Did that just happen?* Whatever it was that John witnessed was certainly not possible, so consideration was warranted. On one hand, it was the second time that his closet produced something unworldly. *Consistency can support confirmation,* he thought, but then again, it could very well have been the confirmation of his insanity. He wondered if the hyperreal visions were actually hallucinations caused by the stress of his failed research. He had no history of psychosis, and everything that he experienced felt undeniable, including the smell that still lingered. However, even with the complete trust in his brain and his sharp five senses, there was one constant that John trusted more than anything: science. Not one second of that supernatural ordeal could be crammed into his scientific understanding. So, he debated. Was science wrong, or was he delusional? As much as he wanted to solve this thrilling mystery, he decided that now was not the time. Getting out of the room and breathing some fresh air seemed like a more desirable step one.

John got himself up to his feet. He took a few wobbly steps to regain his bearings and assess himself. After judging that he was fit to walk, he searched around his drawers to find something quick to put on. He did not dare to wear anything that was hanging in the closet until after a full examination, followed by a trip to the laundromat. He did, however, decide to take a peek inside just to see what kind of damage these things left behind.

The closet appeared untampered. His clothes were in order and the white walls remained white, but just before he shut the door, he happened to glance down to the closet floor. His journal was sitting next to a pair of his shoes even though he remembered sticking it on the top shelf when he returned from the lake.

When he bent down to pick it up, he recognized that something was off. The book felt lighter than normal, thinner too. He opened it to find that a good portion of the pages were removed. In fact, all of the pages that John had written in were neatly cut out. He leafed through the rest of the book and counted the pages. After subtracting the remaining number of pages from the total of three hundred and fifty original sheets, he came to the conclusion that there were exactly two hundred and twenty-eight pages missing. John was baffled. He could not understand why anyone or anything would be interested in his research, and failed research at that.

He knew that he had the book in his possession all day from the time that he sat over the lake until the time that he came back to his room for the night. He then put the book in the closet and went straight to bed. No person had entered the room which left the creatures as the only culprits.

John did assume that they had some version of intelligence as they passed him by, but he could not begin to figure out their motive. They had no business even knowing what a book was, so to think that they somehow located his journal among everything else in the closet, and then surgically removed only its important contents put John's head right back into a spin. He knew that the smart thing to do would be to search the room for more anomalies and try to further unravel the yarn, but that was a tall order for a man in his condition. So, he settled for the second smartest thing to do: head straight to the bar and self-medicate until something made sense.

Chapter Eight
<u>Out Of Money, Out Of Luck</u>

Mark coughed up a lung and woke up. The coughing replaced his need for an alarm clock. He followed his morning routine of lighting up a cigarette and rolling over to watch the six o'clock news. As usual, the television was on because he fell asleep without turning it off. His weekday routine was similar to his weekend routine, except on the weekends, he would light up a cigarette *and* open a beer before watching the news. During the week, he did all of his drinking at night.

Empty beer cans and food wrappers littered Mark's house. The walls were brown from cigarette smoke, which might cost him his security deposit if he could ever afford to move out. When the sports report came on, he dug around his night table to find the napkin that he wrote his picks onto. His losing career looked to be intact as he compared his drunken bets to the scores on-screen. He crumpled the napkin and threw it on the floor. The time had finally come where he had to choose between gambling and drinking. Knowing how important of a decision that would be, Mark told himself that he would figure it out over a beer after work, and he rolled over to get up.

As he lit-up another cigarette, Mark exercised the only good habit that he had left in his life. He took a ten-second gaze at the framed picture that sat next to his bed. It was of his father and his young son, Jake. His dad, who happened to be the only person in the midwest who smoked more than Mark, died seven years prior from lung cancer, and Jake, who was about to graduate from high school, did not come around much anymore.

In the mornings when his headaches were at their peak, Mark chose to blame his ex-wife for his non-relationship with Jake. She already took most of their money and their only working vehicle, but those he could live without. Jake was all that mattered. His morning headaches gave way to heartaches, and those turned into his reason to drink. However, when Mark found himself deep into a case of light beer, his guilt always caught up with him, and he could only blame himself. But that was for good reason. After all, he did blow the last of Jake's college fund at the nearby Indian casino.

Mark had an unfortunate night at the craps table, and then he had an even more unfortunate night at the baccarat table. That was particularly disappointing to him because, prior to that night, he lived his life by his father's most credible advice: "*If you like fun, play baccarat. If you like money, don't play baccarat*". He lost so much money that the casino comped him a free weekend stay along with a free breakfast buffet. However, as bad as Mark was at gambling, he happened to be an excellent negotiator. He knew that he could never stay a weekend away from his family, let alone one night, but he also knew that he could not show up sober and accept the tidal wave of rage that would be waiting for him at home. So instead, he parlayed the free room and breakfast into a two-hour open bar where he drank his weight in whiskey gingers.

After the bar cut him off, Mark made a run for his car. Somewhere along the way, he forgot that the casino was buying his drinks, so he ran away knowing that he did not have any money to pay for his tab. He never looked back, but of course, nobody was chasing him. He hopped into his car and peeled out of the parking lot, luckily avoiding the incoming cars. But unluckily, he smashed into two parked cars less than five minutes later. He was arrested and brought to jail. One phone call later, Mark's ex-wife learned not only about his DUI, but also about the fact that they no longer had enough money to bail him out, and by the time his brother came up with the money to bring him home, his family was gone.

Chapter Nine

How To Prove You're Not Crazy

Jack slid a tall red ale in front of John. Before Jack could let go, John grabbed it and drank it in three consecutive gulps. He put the glass down as he wiped the excess foam from his mouth. "Can I have another, please?" asked John. Jack was already in the middle of a new pour as if he had anticipated John's request. He placed the beer in front of John with a look of concern. John picked it up in stride and took another large guzzle, but only finished about half of it. He then sat quietly and stared into the mirror behind the bar. His face was void of expression.

"You alright there, Johnny?" John hesitated to answer, never removing his gaze from the mirror.

"Well… It's hard to say, Jack. The past few weeks were easily the strangest I've ever had. Waking up this morning was so horrendous that I might actually never be the same person again… which may or may not be a good thing. And on top of all that, this whole year, which has been a tremendous disaster, has more or less been a metaphor for my entire life, so..." John paused. "I may have to think about my answer and get back to you."

"I know what you mean, buddy. If you need to talk about anything, I'm something of a good listener," said Jack. John did not reply back, nor did he seem to acknowledge that Jack had even spoken. Deciding to give John his space, Jack turned to walk away.

"Do you know of any electronic stores around here where I can get a video camera?" asked John. Jack turned back around.

"Yeah, there's a place over on Magnolia. You filming something?"

"There's been some unusual activity in my room recently. I found a few things in places where I didn't leave them," said John. Jack stopped in his tracks and looked at John. His eyes widened to the edges of his face.

"Are you shooting me straight right now, Johnny?"

"What? What are you talking about?" asked John. Jack leaned in close to where nobody else in the room could hear him. John moved back, craving some personal space.

"Are you telling me that your room is haunted?" asked Jack. John shook his head and rubbed his eyes. "Did you research those ghosts yet like we talked about?"

"No, Jack. The room isn't haunted. I had a few valuables move around on me, and I just want to make sure that the maids or the hotel staff aren't going through my things. I want some very simple surveillance." Jack came back down from his excitement.

"Oh… I see. Well, until you prove anything, you should keep an open mind, especially if they're older valuables. A lot of the time, spirits are attracted to older things. There's some weird connection between antiques and ghosts. Not to mention, that place where you're staying is pretty old. No doubt that plenty of people have died there over the years. I would guess those hallways are swarming with phantoms." John tried to respond politely to Jack, but his effort meter was low. The alcohol was doing little to ease the shock from earlier.

His stomach moaned. He dropped a few pants sizes over the months, and he was having trouble remembering when he last ate. The kitchen door opened on the other side of the bar, and John received a strong whiff of a steaming fish.

John loved seafood, but something about the wet, salty aroma put him right back in his hotel room with the odor from the fluttering creatures. He would have lost his stomach if it was not empty. There were some bar cherries just within reach. He knew that the polite thing to do would be to ask Jack for a glassful, but he was all the way on the other side of the bar helping a customer, and time was a factor.

John picked up the cup and poured them out in front of him, causing a mess. He grabbed them by the handful and filled his mouth. He chewed them violently until the fresh, sweet taste doused his nausea. Feeling rather ashamed of his animal-like behavior, he cleaned up the juice with some napkins, and put the remainder of the cherry cup back where he found it. He rested his head down and shut his eyes, hoping that something would start to make some sense.

"I forgot to tell you." John jolted up to see Jack standing over him. "I speak your language now." Jack held out a book with the title, *A Man Named Albert.* "I saw this in the window of the bookstore the other day and I thought of you. I'm so glad I got it," said Jack.

"What's it about?" asked John.

"It's about Albert Einstein. Isn't it great? I've never learned this stuff before. I haven't gotten to the end yet, but I think it talks about how he discovered light or something," said Jack.

"Well not exactly, but he did…" John realized that any explanation would likely be lost, and he actually felt flattered that Jack took an interest in his subject. "You know what? I'll let you finish it. I don't want to ruin the ending for you," said John. Jack smiled and set the book down.

"Yeah, I'll let you know when I'm done, and we can talk about it." John got a closer look at the cover and noticed a bright green sticker that said *Great for Your Little Learning Scientist!* He smiled back at Jack, politely omitting any of his passing thoughts.

***

On the walk to the camera store, John's mind raced. Images of the creatures flashed across his vision. He wanted to label them as insects, but he knew that was too simplistic. Wherever they came from, their environment was likely much different and therefore required a radically different physical makeup, but it was not just their appearance that had John so tied up; it was their ability. They traveled through his room like nothing he had ever seen.

They moved in and out of reality, just like the bell that appeared and disappeared again. *Where did they go?* John asked himself. The idea of virtual particles popped into John's mind. He wondered if perhaps the entities were able to appear and disappear just like the quantum particles. *Were they gone, or did they go somewhere I could not see?* he wondered.

***

John returned to his room with the most expensive camera kit he could buy. The system included wires and cables that could translate all the videos to his computer, and two mountable cameras. He wanted to make sure that he had every angle of his room covered, including his closet.

He spent the better part of his day setting them up. He recorded, and he tested. He recorded again, and he tested again. John saved files, erased them, and repeated. He left nothing to chance. John trusted science more than his own eyes, but no one could argue with visual proof. If he could catch one of the apparitions on camera, he could prove to himself that he was in fact in his right mind, and then he could figure out what was actually going on.

Chapter Ten
The Artist And Its Solitude

It looked up from Its home at the great machine and at those who were building it. It lived alone for so long, and then without warning, the others came in and built their structure that spanned across the skies. The Artist and Its home were left buried in the shadow of the machine, and the constant labors from above produced a noise that never stopped. The Artist watched the creatures engineer their creation. They worked in unison, never halting or breaking formation. As It looked at the species that was so different from Itself, It grew repulsed and retreated back down into Its keep.

The Artist had feathers with colors that were never seen by man. As It made Its way down into Its home, the feathers brushed by bells that were built into the walls. Each bell hummed a low, soothing tone as the Artist passed by. The lonely Inventor hand crafted every bell out of the rarest metals from all over Its world. They were purely unique, and each one produced a different sound more beautiful than the last. All of Its creations were unique and beautiful.

The Designer prided Itself on the ability to develop things not for the purpose of function, but solely to express emotion through imagery and sound. Countless artworks covered the walls and ceilings of Its home. Individually, they all told brilliant stories through complex designs. Collectively, they formed an inter-connected masterpiece of colors and shapes. In the center of everything was a creation that was not yet complete, but already surpassed anything that the Artist had ever made. It spent most of Its waking hours perfecting it.

When the Artist stopped Its work to look up at the creatures in the sky, It winced from disgust. They built nothing for aesthetics and only for function. It watched them since they arrived and concluded that they must have no emotion and no means of inspiration. Function, only function. They never ceased, and they never stopped to appreciate their own work. They wanted only to build their machine, and that machine would alter the skyline forever.

Not only would this work be the Artist's greatest creation, but it could possibly stop the machine in the sky. The Artist vowed to complete it before the soulless militia completed theirs.

Chapter Eleven
<u>Bait It, Cast It, And Wait</u>

Weeks went by, and John had nothing to show for it. He spent most of the time in his room waiting, except for the seldom break to eat or catch a short walk around the block. When he returned, he routinely checked the footage on his computer to see if he had missed anything. His days were spent sitting in front of the monitor and watching the room from the view of the cameras, even though he was sitting right next to them. He knew that things were not going well when he realized that he was leaving the room just for the excitement of checking the video when he got back. It was becoming an obsession.

On his finest day, he decided to strip the bed of its sheets and bring them into the middle of the rug. He then put on a pair of shoes and slid his feet back and forth on the carpet while rubbing the sheets together. It was his master plan to create as much static electricity as possible in the hopes of triggering a reaction from his closet. Around the half hour mark, when he was pouring sweat, he realized that not only was it not working, but if a hotel maid had entered his room at that moment, then the idea of proving his sanity would be a lost cause. Right then, he gathered himself and promised that he would give it a three-day break in order to get back to reality. He would check the cameras each night after dinner, just in case of an incident, but other than that, he would get back out into the world.

It rained the first day, which was John's favorite weather for walking. The warm rain over the mountains put his mind in a rare state of calm. After a small breakfast, he took his coffee on a two-hour walk beside the foggy lake, and his mind wandered into a void of unimportant thoughts. John mentally planned his day of leisure, and the thought of the video cameras did not enter his head once.

He stopped by a used book store and bought an old science-fiction novel that he had never heard of, and then he walked towards the Davidson Hotel to grab a pint and sit with Jack. John felt guilty about his mood the last time that he was in the bar, and a red ale just seemed like a good middle step between buying his new book and reading it.

When he arrived, he was concerned to see a young woman behind the bar because that was the first time all summer that Jack was not there to greet him. However, the nice girl told John that Jack had gone to Aspen with his friends for an ultimate-frisbee tournament. John got a mental image of Jack smoking pot with his friends and running around on the frisbee field, and he laughed for the first time in a long time. He then ordered himself a tall red ale, and sat in a quiet corner to read his book.

One hundred pages and two beers later, John decided to go to his room and lay down before figuring out his dinner. On the trek home, John acknowledged that his day of relaxation was thoroughly enjoyable. He also considered that if he had not gotten out that morning, he may have never gotten out. The break was well needed.

As he came within a block of his hotel, his heart started to beat a little bit faster. It just hit John that this was the longest amount of time that he had been away from his room since his encounter with the centipedes. He bit his lip, trying to ignore it. On the elevator ride up, he made the decision to not check the cameras until after dinner in order to hold his obsession at bay. To his surprise, John's proactive mental efforts caused his heart rate to drop back to normal.

He arrived at his room and let himself in. As soon as he walked through the door, his heartbeat shot right back to manic. Something had been there again. The atrocious smell hit him in the face, and the air was hot and thick. He remained close to the door, unsure of whether or not he was alone. The bedroom light was on, but John could not remember if he had left it that way or not. He stood and listened for any unfamiliar sound, but there was only silence. John took a breath and forced his body forward into the bedroom. It looked exactly how he left it. Nothing was moved, nothing was missing, and the closet was still wide open. His laptop was also wide open, and John, of course, was out of patience.

He sped through the day's recorded video, waiting for his newest visitor to reveal itself. He played through it at thirty-times speed. He noticed nothing, so he slowed it down to twenty-times speed, and still nothing caught his eye.

Ten-times speed, seven-and-a-half-times speed, five-times speed, two-times speed. Nothing. No matter how slow John watched it or when in the video he skipped to, he saw no changes in his room, but the smell was there, as was the sticky, hot air.

John slammed his computer shut and paced the room. He missed whatever it was that came and went, and because the cameras did not record anything, he once again had no proof. His pacing turned into stomping as he blamed himself for ever leaving the room. By his twentieth lap from one end of the room to the other, John had found himself getting closer to the closet, and the closer that he got, the stronger the smell became. He finally acknowledged the correlation and stopped at its open doors. He took a step in, grabbed the pull-string light, and turned it on.

The smell was truly sickening, and the air was dead still. He glanced over everything and confirmed that it was all pristine and untouched. But then he noticed his journal. It was in the exact same place that he had left it, yet something was off. After the incident a few weeks back, it was left with two-hundred and twenty-eight missing pages. It was noticeably thin, but now, without even picking it up, John knew that he was staring at a full notebook. Of course, he could not resist swiping it up and leafing through the pages.

Upon sight and touch, John was baffled. The pages were perfectly reattached. There was no seam where they had been cut out, nor was there any adhesive to suggest that they were glued into place. They were simply back. John ran through the book and counted its original three-hundred and fifty pages.

His brain went blank again. His lack of explanations for anything that had happened over the last month was beginning to drive a hole through his brain. The only reasonable thought that crossed his mind during that moment was to forget about everything and go home. The agony was too great. He was getting nowhere, and he was losing his mind in the process.

For a brief second, John looked into his conscience to start the process of investigation, but in no time at all, it rejected his request. There was no more energy left for inquiry. He spent every mental cent that he had to that point, and there was only failure to show for it. So, he let go of the book and sat down against the wall. With no answers, no video evidence, and more questions than ever before, John dropped his head, closed his eyes, and shut down.

Chapter Twelve

Incident #9

December 28, 2014: Ninnekah, Oklahoma

Out of all the heartfelt, emotional pain that he suffered through every day, Mark still loved Thursday mornings. On Thursdays, his foreman brought bagels to work for the crewmen. Mark always had two. Normally, he would settle for whatever two flavors were left around. He had a principle that because he ate two, he would not pick and choose, but today, he laid rest to etiquette and dug out his two favorites: cinnamon sugar, and onion-salt. Savory and sweet. He decided right then and there that today was the first day of the rest of his life. Things have not gone well, and they may never go well, but he could at least change his attitude on it. *Happiness is a decision,* he thought.

He ate his breakfast and smoked a cigarette outside of the building that he had been working at for the last few weeks. It was an office building with a bit of a grandeur design for a place like central Oklahoma. Its opening had already been delayed for several months because of complications due to its over-ambitious interior makeup. When standing in the lobby, one could look straight up to the twenty-four-story ceiling that was complete with a glass skylight. The open-balcony hallways to the offices wrapped around the clearing, spiraling all the way up to the top floor. Despite being completely breathtaking to look at, it was a disaster to build. Mark was in charge of the scaffolding that led up to the higher floors, and today was going to be long and awful, just like every day that he had been there.

He did not care for the management or much of the other crewmen on the project. Most of his assignments were in Oklahoma City where he was surrounded with familiar faces. He did, however, make one new friend named Kenny who bought him lunch every day in exchange for cigarettes. Kenny promised his wife that he would quit smoking and considered it only a half of a lie if he never bought a pack. So, he bummed cigarettes off of Mark in exchange for food. Mark would have been happy to share without the free lunch, but Kenny insisted.

Right as Mark was about halfway finished his smoke, he heard the familiar, heavy footsteps behind him and knew who it was without even looking. He lit a cigarette and held it up. Kenny grabbed it in stride and took a puff. "Thanks, Moe," said Kenny. Mark noticed that Kenny called everyone 'Moe,' although he never asked why.

"Where ya been? I've been smoking alone all week," said Mark.

"I went to my wife's parents in Texas for Christmas. The kids haven't seen them in a while, so we stayed a few extra days."

"Yeah? How was that?"

"Awful. One bathroom for six people. I'd rather pay for a hotel, but my wife is too cheap, which she gets from her dad. I ended up arguing with them two the whole week about it," said Kenny. Mark laughed. "Thank God my parents are dead. They only had one bathroom too. We would be having the same trip to their house for Easter." Mark continued to laugh. "How was your Christmas? Do your parents have more than one bathroom?" asked Kenny.

"No, they're dead too," said Mark. They both laughed.

"Well, did you get to see your kid?"

"No, not this year," said Mark. "That doesn't happen too often anymore. But I did find out that my lovely ex-wife is suing me. So, that's great."

Kenny nodded. "Yeah that's good stuff. Somehow, I'm not divorced yet, but as soon as I am, my wife's gonna rip into me like a hyena and end up with everything… Although she's too cheap to pay for a lawyer, so we'll probably never get divorced." Mark nodded and smirked.

"Yeah… Divorce sucks. Try your best to avoid it. Especially if you like your kids."

"Yeah, I don't want to lose my kids. But on the other hand, I'd be able to smoke as many cigarettes as I wanted, Moe," said Kenny. Mark coughed up smoke laughing.

"Do yourself a favor and quit before you start looking like me," said Mark.

***

About seven hours into his twelve-hour day, Mark found himself building the scaffold from the eleventh to the twelfth floor. He was oddly focused all morning and avoiding distractions. However, he could not help but notice workers steadily migrating from the higher floors down to the lower floors. They were all walking down through the hallways as opposed to taking the elevator. Mark continued to work, but saw more and more wanderers out of the corner of his eye. He leaned his head out of the scaffold and looked up to find that every light in the building was out. It was still somewhat bright because of the skylight, but the indoor lights were out and the sounds of drills and other tools had gone silent. Two more crewmen walked by, heading towards the lobby. "Hey, what's going on?" asked Mark.

"All the power is out in the building. It was just the higher floors for a while, but we lost everything a few minutes ago," said the man. Mark looked up at the empty building. As the two men continued on, Mark shrugged his shoulders and continued to work with his battery powered drills. Within three minutes, the drill gun died. He popped the battery out, replaced it with a spare, and pushed down the trigger: nothing. He tried another, and it was just as dead.

Mark sat down at the edge of the scaffold and dangled his feet twelve-stories above the ground. From his perspective, he forgot about how difficult it had been to work on the building, and he admired how interesting and unique it was beginning to look. It almost leaned in one direction as the floors climbed to the ceiling. From the floor to the glass ceiling, Mark was in its dead center, and at the moment, it was completely silent. He thought that the building may never be that quiet again for as long as it stood. So, instead of walking out into the cold to join the mass of other workers, he decided to smoke a cigarette by himself and enjoy the view.

He thought about the deal that he made with himself earlier in the day, to make the choice of happiness. Although he had not made any real changes yet, his attitude towards the world did seem to be a little brighter. The work day was moving fairly quickly, and looking back, he had actually enjoyed it. He was only on his fifth cigarette of the day, so it still felt crisp as opposed to the twentieth or thirtieth which would feel heavy and full of tar. His favorite smoke was usually the second of the day when he first walked out into the cold air. The chilled air mixed with the bite of the tobacco was so refreshing to him. Thinking about all of the smoking gave him the sudden craving for a soda, and luckily enough, there was a cooler directly below him on the lobby floor full of them.

He leaned his head over the scaffold's edge to locate it, but before he could even see the floor, he was punched in the face by a horrific odor. It came without warning and surrounded him. The stench was salty and bitter, and physically thicker than the smoke from his cigarette. Mark began dry-heaving. After coughing uncontrollably, he vomited all over himself and then over the edge of the scaffold and onto the lobby floor. He would have heard it hit the ground if his senses were not compromised by the smell.

After a minute or two, his body habituated to the fragrance just enough for him to catch his breath and regain control of his nervous system. He leaned onto his hands and knees and steadied himself. While looking down at his hands on the surface of the scaffold, a large, dark shadow blocked out all of the light from the skylight window above him. As it passed, he looked up. Mark was not sure what he saw at that moment because it disappeared so quickly, but he was sure that it was large and it moved across thin air. Assuming that his eyes were deceiving him, a scraping sound rose from the floor below him. He looked down and saw the tail end of a large, cylinder shaped creature making its way up the wall and into the hallway. He saw enough to judge that its size was at least twenty or thirty feet long, and wider than the building's elevator. It was covered in dry, grayish-pale skin.

Mark heard it traveling around the long balcony hallway. He looked across the way and waited for it to reach the other side of the building where he would be able to see it in full. He considered that his heart might stop if it turned out to look like what he thought it might look like, but he decided that he was better off seeing *it* before it saw him. And as his eyes followed around to the spot that it should have been moving, another creature appeared out of the air four floors above him. Within the matter of one second, an elongated entity grew out of nothing into a humongous snake-like being. It gravitated upwards towards the ceiling until it stopped around the twentieth floor. It then slithered over the balcony wall and began exploring the hallway.

Mark watched it until it was out of sight, and then he hyperventilated. His chest became tighter as his basic *fight-or-flight* instincts were reduced to *sit still and wait to die*. After a loud crash from the floor below him, he snapped out of his trance and somehow got back his ability of *flight*. After determining that all of the hallways and staircases could be compromised, he concluded that the safest route to the exit was to climb down the scaffold straight to the lobby floor. And with colossal creatures spontaneously appearing all over the place, Mark felt a real sense of urgency.

He hopped to his feet and ran to the ladder. Despite Mark's obese stature, he could climb up and down a scaffold like a five-pound spider monkey. He dropped and slid down the bars by the dozen. He made it down to the eighth story in less than twenty seconds. When he loosened his grip to slide down to the seventh, a strong crash caused the scaffold to shake. He dropped down and landed hard on the next surface, nearly falling over the edge. His ankle was badly twisted on the impact.

Mark limped over and grabbed the next ladder. Just as he was about to climb down, he found himself no longer alone. Another entity sprouted up out of the air about ten feet in front of him. It quickly grew into a full-formed vertical body that hovered still. From bottom to top, it was thirty feet high and at least eight feet wide. Mark reluctantly looked the creature up and down. He needed to find something of familiarity on the beast to help his mind label it. The best that he could come up with was that he was looking at a giant earthworm, bigger than a city bus. This label gave him no comfort. In fact, it left him feeling completely helpless. He thought that this must be how those people on the news felt when they fell into the lion's den at the zoo. Except they at least had the benefit of being mauled by a landlocked animal. Mark's opposer did not seem to be bothered by gravity or nature.

The worm remained vertical, but slowly descended to Mark's level. Its body shape was unchanged from top to bottom: No real limbs or features except for one area in its center that looked to Mark like a mashed, closed fold. Before he could figure out its purpose, the fold opened, and Mark was met with the gaze of the creature's single eye. It stared at him, and Mark stared back. The eye itself was dry and rotten. It was gray and full of cracks, as if the worm had died and dried out.

It hovered closer to Mark and slowly circled around him on the ladder. He dared not to move as it passed him, over and over. Keeping with the theme of predatory animals, he now imagined a shark circling its prey before ripping it into pieces. As his brain marinated in that comforting thought, he saw out of the corner of his eye that the other two worms were hovering over from across the way to join their friend. They stopped about fifteen feet away and began to float around in a figure-eight motion, completely in sync with each other. Their bizarre dance gave Mark a chill up his spine, and fear took over his body. He wrapped his arms and legs around the ladder, closed his eyes, and prepared to die. He heard nothing but silence and his own heart beat for the next five seconds. Then, after a loud crash, he felt the scaffold disperse into countless pieces. Mark was sent flying through the air along with the piece of ladder that he held so tight.

Chapter Thirteen
<u>Self-Diagnosis</u>

John found himself in his all-in-one physician office and pharmacy: the Davidson Hotel bar. His head rested on his forearm as his mind mocked him. *The perfect genius is unbreakable. It is everything intertwined, and I will break it. The working machine will have worked for nothing.* Sometimes these idioms that made no sense were the only things that made sense to John. As he wondered if his own doom would become the doom of all others, his primary physician/pharmacist came to greet him.

"You alright there, John? You're looking a little deflated." Jack stood over John with a look of concern. John was unshaven and drained, down about fifteen pounds since the start of summer. He sat up with the intention of telling Jack that he was fine as usual, but something inside of him needed to be honest.

"I'm struggling a little bit, Jack. It's been a tough summer."

"Yeah? How so? Lay it on me," said Jack.

"Well for one, I haven't exactly been truthful with you. Do you remember the other day when I asked you about where I could buy a camera because my belongings were moving around on me?"

"Yes, of course. I suggested that there was a paranormal explanation," said Jack.

"Right. Well, I'm not saying that it has anything to do with ghosts, but it turns out that you might be right... more or less," said John. Jack's eyes lit up.

"What are you saying, John? Are you telling me that something happened from the beyond?" Jack leaned into John's personal space, impatiently awaiting an answer.

"It was more... I don't actually know. About a month ago, there was something going on in my closet. My room became very dark, and my closet lit up, so I walked over to see what was going on. When I opened the doors, there was a bell."

"What kind of bell? Your bell?"

"No, not my bell. It was floating, you know, like nothing was holding it. Then it shook and it made these sounds like I was in the middle of a gothic church. The ringing was deafening."

"Where did it come from?"

"I have no idea! Something was ringing it and it lasted for a few minutes. The sound put me into some kind of trance. I couldn't stop crying and I almost vomited and shit myself, then it stopped and just disappeared."

"What do you mean it just disappeared?" asked Jack.

"It vanished. It was gone," said John. Jack was engrossed, hanging on to every word. "A few weeks later, the closet lit up again, so again I opened the doors to see if the bell was back. This time, two giant creatures came out into my room. Giant… bugs or something. I mean they were close to ten feet."

"What did they look like?"

John's speech accelerated as he became more worked up. "I don't know exactly. Centipedes. Except they had no faces, and the more they moved around, the more legs would appear and disappear."

Jack covered his mouth in shock. "What are you telling me here, Johnny?"

"And as they hovered around my room, they would shrink down and disappear and then come back to full size… I know this sounds ridiculous, but I'm not making it up."

"Of course you're not making it up! You're the most honest guy I know."

John looked at Jack, confused. "Well, thank you, Jack, but you've only known me a month. I can't imagine I'm the most honest guy you know."

"I'm a great judge of character, John."

"Okay well… thank you. Anyway, these things hovered around my room for a few minutes before going back into the closet. That's when I saw inside my closet, there was a floating orb that they went into. I guess it was some sort of portal, but it was no shape or color that I have ever seen in my life. If you gave me a hundred years I could never redraw or even describe exactly what it looked like. It was round and flat and sharp and smooth all at the same time."

"Wow," gasped Jack.

"As soon as they left, the orb faded away, and the only sign of them left was this horrible stench. I almost vomited again." Jack's eyes widened as he took everything in. John sat up and leaned in. "But here's the strangest part, Jack. Whatever these things were, they went through my journal and stole pages out of it. They went through my notebook and removed pages. Only certain pages. Why? Why would they do that, Jack?"

Jack stood up tall. He expressed befuddlement, surprise, and excitement. "John, this is incredible. Do you understand what's going on here? You need to get this story out there. You're a man of science, and you have proof of the supernatural. Why are you not excited?"

John sighed. "I'm not excited, Jack. I am not fabricating one word of this story. I mean, I personally saw everything that I just described."

"Yes. I believe you. Why are you not excited?"

"Because, Jack. It's not real. I'm crazy. None of these things actually happened. I'm just losing my mind."

"No, you're not! You're opening your mind. I've been trying to tell you about this stuff since you got here."

"It doesn't exist. None of it. And I have proof."

"How do you have proof? You saw everything yourself."

"Seeing it is not proof, Jack. I have proof. I recorded it. I walked into my room the other day, and it was covered in the smell. So, I checked the closet and found that the pages in my journal had all been returned. The book was completely back to normal. I checked the cameras, and nothing. Nothing came in or left my room, and somehow the smell was still there and my book was back. Do you know what that means? None of it happened. I'm just a man who is losing it. I'm a bit young to lose my mind, but it happens. Plenty of people go crazy, and that's just how it goes sometimes."

Jack stood his ground and thought. He was determined but at a loss of ideas. "John… Don't make any decisions just yet. Think about it." John shook his head in disagreement. Jack spoke over him. "You're a logical guy. You can figure this out."

"I've figured it out. I'm nuts, Jack."

"You're a man of science. You can handle this. Let's figure it out together."

"Listen. You're a good kid. Let this one go, okay?" John stared Jack down. He waited for an agreement, but Jack did not oblige. John stood up. "Let it go. Let my mind whither in peace. But don't worry, I'm going to be in here much more often. I plan on drinking a lot heavier." John placed his money on the bar. "You got a long life of clear thinking ahead of you. Don't waste any more of it on me." John turned around and walked away.

Chapter Fourteen

If It Isn't Real, It Sure Looks Real

John sat on his bed and dug his teeth into the large leg of a roasted chicken. It was accompanied by tomato bisque soup, a plate of hot bread rolls, a large ice-cream sundae, and a six-pack of red ale. He decided to spend his money on the things that he wanted before his mind shriveled into complete disarray.

The radio blasted a classic rock song as John used the chicken bones as literal drumsticks. The pressure that squeezed him for his entire life had let go, and he experienced the sweet taste of liberation for the first time. Right then, John determined that losing his mind might have been the best thing that ever happened to him.

With six full beers and a long night ahead of him, he looked around the room to find something to do. Ordering a movie came to mind. It had been years since he watched one from start to finish, and the television was only collecting dust all summer. However, when he stood up, the open laptop caught his eye. It had been running for weeks, but he had not checked it since the night that his journal was returned. He shook off the temptation and walked over to grab the remote. When he picked it up, he found himself eye-level with one of his surveillance cameras. Again, he was drawn to the idea of the video, but he turned away and went back to his seat.

He switched on the television and flipped through his movie choices. He had never heard of any of the titles, and had no idea how to search for one that would interest him, but it didn't matter. Even while skimming channels, his mind was stuck on the open laptop. He tried his best to pretend that he would rather watch T.V. than check the video, but at some point, he realized the absurdity of lying to himself. So, he let out a reluctant sigh and shut the television off.

John pulled up the video of the day that he believed his room was breached. He rewound it all the way back to the morning when he first walked out the door. He then left it on real-time-speed and watched. John had an incredible talent of being immune to boredom as long as his time was spent on something of true worth. He could live in a laboratory for weeks if the experiment had the slightest hope for success. So, he sat there and watched for an hour. He finished two beers. He sat there for another hour, and finished two more. After another half-hour, he sat up straight and stretched his back. His eyes were stinging from dryness and the alcohol was making him tired. Just as it hit him that he might actually be wasting his time, it happened.

The screen flickered. It lasted no more than half-a-second, but considering that this was the first change to happen over the past two-and-a-half-hours of video, he decided to rewind it and see if it happened again. It did. He went back and slowed it down to the very frame of change. He found it, but even when he paused it, there was no detail to be seen. It was just a blank screen.

John then switched to the video from camera-two and synced up the times. Sure enough, camera-two's video flickered at the exact second as camera-one. He knew that this was too interesting to be a coincidence, so he began to explore possible causes. Just like the static electricity that found its way to the closet or the light that faded whenever the orb appeared, perhaps the cameras lost either the light to visibly see anything or the energy to keep recording. This possibility felt more probable the more that John thought about it, but being the good man of science that he was, he decided to try and rule out his theory before just blindly jumping down the rabbit hole.

He racked his brain to figure out how he could prove that the power in the room had gone out over a week ago. It may as well have been a year ago, because he had no idea where to start. Nothing electronic was acting funny or blinking. In fact, other than the lights, he hardly used much power in the room. This was the first time in a while that the television was turned on. The smoke alarm light was glowing green, the air conditioner appeared untampered with, and the clock on his nightstand had never stopped running, nor did he ever need to reset it. And then it hit him... *The clock.* The clock beside his bed was not electric; it was an old-fashioned wind-up. He noticed that the maids would wind it whenever they cleaned the room. Most importantly, it would not stop running if there was ever a loss of power.

John looked at camera-two, which was placed at a high angle in the room. And by pure luck or pure coincidence, both of which meant the same thing to John, it happened to be pointed in full view of the clock. He loaded the video to about one second before the flicker. Because he went a little expensive on the camera's quality, he was able to freeze the frame and zoom in clearly. The time on the clock read *one-forty-two*. He then skipped ahead one second on the video past the flicker. As soon as the clock returned to frame, it read *one-forty-eight*. Within one second of video time, the clock jumped six minutes. He backed it up just to make sure that he was seeing it correctly, and without a doubt, the minute hand teleported a good inch across the face of the clock. John's heart pounded. For the first time all summer, he may have found proof that he was not crazy. Even though the video did not provide any visual evidence of the creatures, to him, it was proof by omission.

On a whim, he had the urge to read back through his journal and see if he had overlooked anything on the day that it was returned. He took it out of the closet and quickly flipped through it. Everything looked normal. The pages were well-attached and it seemed to be in perfect condition. However, there was a page about a quarter of the way in that caught his eye. He always dated his entries, but this particular day only read *October*. All of the previous days had the month, day, and year. The page just before it had a date that read *October 15, 2014*, but this page's numbers were absent. He flipped to the next page and found the exact same thing. It simply read *October*. The next page read the same, and the page after that, and it continued all the way until he hit the day of *December 17, 2014*. After that entry, all of the numbered dates remained. John did not understand why, nor did he believe that he had left all of those dates out. He went back to the first day in October where the numbers were missing and he began to scan through the excerpts to see if anything else was off.

Within a few pages, he noticed more and more blanks. It did not take him long to figure out that anything that was missing was either one of his math equations or a date. "Numbers," he said to himself. All of the numbers from those pages were completely removed from the book. He felt a rush of nerves, fear, and excitement. All of his hair stood straight up and his vision darkened. *This is real,* he thought. *All of it is real.* He closed his eyes and absorbed it. John understood that his new discovery would likely lead to countless more months of no answers and many questions, but he accepted his fate. He vowed to solve the incredible growing mystery. After another rush of adrenaline from his new reality setting in, he took a breath and calmed down. His heart rate dropped, his vision returned to normal, and his hair… remained standing. He looked down at his arm and examined the hair that was standing straight up. It all slowly but steadily leaned in the direction of the closet. And as the tingling set in, John knew that it was not his nerves that were causing his hair to stand. It was the static.

He looked at the closet, and awaited the inevitable. The room darkened as he felt surges of static electricity flow passed him and into the open closet. A small point of light appeared below his hanging shirts. It was no larger than the head of a pin, but its glow lit up the entire closet. John stood about ten feet away. This time, he was not scared or even nervous. He was entranced by the small orb. It grew into the size of a marble and turned into the beautiful, unexplainable color that he had remembered from before. It stayed that size for a few seconds until it slowly grew. It looked like it was being inflated from the inside and expanding perfectly in all directions. As it grew larger, it became brighter and more vibrant in color, but emitted less light. Like last time, it absorbed light from the space around it until the room was completely dark.

The orb reached full size, around four feet, and silently hung in front of John's eyes. He approached it slowly. In the back of his mind, he knew that any contact with the object could result in death, but he accepted the risk, knowing that he may be the only person in existence to meet something so mysterious and wonderful.

John got about arm's length from the apparition and bent down. At first, it looked like it was twinkling, the way light dances through a diamond, but now that he was so close, he could not tell if the orb was moving or the light inside of it was moving. Furthermore, he could not make out its exact shape. From certain angles, it was the roundest sphere he had ever seen. He thought that if he held a cue ball next to it, the cue ball would be insignificant in comparison to such a perfect circle. But when he leaned to the other side, the orb appeared to be an absolute cube. The sides were so completely flat, and the corners were perfect, mathematical right angles. And as he examined the foreign geometry of the orb, John developed a strange thought: *negative mass*. It took up space, but it also appeared to be a void. It was a solid hole.

The air closest to the horizon of the hole felt very cool, almost refreshing. A breeze crossed John's face as it glided into the orb, and he was met with a rush of nostalgia, as if his body had been waiting a long time to experience that breeze again. Curiosity overcame him. When the creatures entered his room last time, they came directly out of the orb, and they exited back through it when they left. John started weighing the risks of finding out what was on the other side, leading with the assumption that the portal must go two ways. Knowing that the greatest consequence of all would be to miss his opportunity, he decided to make contact.

John held up his hand. Because he was right-handed, he used his left hand just in case it was incinerated upon touch. The closer he got, the more he could feel the air being pulled into the object, like water flowing down a hole. He stalled for a moment in order to enjoy his left upper limb one last time before its possible mutilation, but while he was so close, he peeked into the orb and got a vague glimpse of what was on the other side. It was hard to see because the shape of the exterior created a fish-eyed view, but among the eccentric colors and hues, he saw a number of odd shapes floating around. His best guess was that he was looking into the open sky of an extraordinary place. Flying figures moved across that sky, leaving behind streaks of color and light. He did his best to comprehend it all, but from his vantage point, it was as if he had opened his eyes underwater and then tried to see what was happening above the surface. It was not working and the clock was ticking, so he decided to dip his fingers in. If he would be able to pull them back out, then he would go in head-first.

John touched his hand to his face and nestled it. He nodded his head and moved his fingers to the ready position, just inches away from the orb. He took a long, deep breath. "Au revoir," he said, and then he moved his hand to the surface and just as it was a hair's length away, something popped up in the entire lens of the object. John fell back and shouted. He stared at the entity and it stared back. It was a giant eyeball that filled the orb. It was wide open and lurked over John with a soulless gaze. John was flattened to his back. He was as white as a ghost, and so was the eye. The orb began to grow. It inflated larger and larger, and the eye remained dead center. It looked like death itself. As the orb widened, John could see that the eye was surrounded by dry, grayish-pale skin that was covered in cracks and scars. He felt no compassion from the creature, nor did he feel any confidence in the notion of self-defense.

The orb floated out of the closet and now was nearly the size of the room. "Get away!" John shouted. He began to look around and saw that in every direction that he turned his head, the eye was there looking right at him. It was above him, and at all sides at once. Even when he looked down at the floor below him, the creature was there, examining John like a rat in a cage. Suddenly, everything glowed with a blinding-bright light. Its intensity forced John to cover his face. He yelled at the top of his lungs. The light became brighter, and brighter, and brighter as John clenched his fists over his eyes. He screamed "Enough!" as loud as he could. And then like the flip of a switch, the light was gone.

John remained on his back, covering his face for a long minute. When he finally uncovered and looked around, the room was back to normal. It took him a moment to be able to think again, but when he could, the first thought that popped into his head was: *Nothing that happened was possible, but it happened.* The man of science was on the cusp of throwing in the towel. He did not yet call it paranormal, but it certainly was not explained in any physics book that he had ever read.

That particular episode had put him inches away from a heart attack, or a hemorrhage, or something. Whatever it was had his head spinning. He took deep breaths and let them out. After five minutes of panting, he got the feeling back in his legs. He turned over onto his hands and knees and slowly stood up.

Although the room looked exactly the same as before his visitor, it felt much different. John now considered it the pinpoint location in all of the Universe where the unexplainable comes to happen. And the energy was swelling. He felt watched and important. No drug in the world could have given him that feeling. He found himself walking laps around the room. He continued in circles for ten minutes or an hour; there was no telling. He couldn't make much out of his thoughts, but he did have an overall mood that was forming itself. It was that of scared, excited, and alive. He hated the idea that he was completely alone with his knowledge, but John considered that he had nothing but time to figure out how to make his story explainable. He would sell his house and move in to the hotel full-time if he had to.

As these wild thoughts were churning around in his head, there was one that gradually worked its way to the surface. That was the hope that his new friend would have left another clue in the closet. The fact that these things were not killing him upon their arrival made John think that they either wanted him alive, or they did not care either way and were just using his room as their canal. Regardless, he decided to embrace it, and he hoped that it would continue.

The last two visitors had borrowed some pages from his notebook and then returned them with some major editing. This latest traveler had made the grandest of all entrances, and in turn, had the promise of leaving behind the grandest clue. So, with no more patience for surprises, John made his way to the closet. The door was left wide open, and without even needing to search around, right in the middle of his floor sat the next gift from John's new friends. And indeed, it was the grandest one yet.

Chapter Fifteen

<u>When It All Gets Put Together, The Picture Becomes Clearer</u>

John had not left the room in three days. He drank water out of the sink, and he ate whatever scraps he had in his fridge, but his attention was glued to his new toy. It was a small, metal ball about the size of a golf ball. It was non-reflective and rough, but a perfect sphere. It was currently attached to the tub, but that had only happened when John entered the bathroom. When he walked into the bedroom and placed it on the floor, the ball would roll itself over to the bed and stick to it like a magnet. In the vending room, it found its way to the ice-machine, indicating to John that it liked to acquaint itself with large objects.

It started after the eyeball and the orb had come and gone. John walked to the closet and saw the metallic ball on top of his shoebox that sat right in the middle of the closet floor. As soon as he crossed the threshold of the open closet door, the ball leapt from the shoebox to John's leg and stuck. He shook his leg and then swatted it off, but as soon as it hit the ground, it rolled right back over to him. Deciding that fear was becoming a waste of time, he pulled it off of his leg and took it into the bedroom to further examine the mysterious sphere. As soon as he crossed back into the bedroom, he felt it being pulled toward the bed. So, he set it on the ground and watched it roll straight to the base of the bed frame. And ever since, he has taken it room to room, trying to understand its nature. There were no conclusions yet, but he could not deny its desire to connect with big things.

John held magnets to the ball to see if it possessed a charge in order to determine the type of metal that it was made of. The magnets neither stuck to nor repelled the ball. This ruled out iron and nickel, but the rough texture of the surface could have told him that anyway. It was like nothing he had ever felt. When he touched it, it seemed to have a powdery-rub, like it was covered in soot, but his fingers always came out clean. It also stayed warmer than room temperature at all times. He decided that he would wrap it up in a cloth and take it out of the hotel to experiment with the ball's motion outdoors. Just then, the phone rang.

John picked up the ball and walked into the bedroom. He dropped it on the floor and as it rolled over to the mattress, he picked up the phone. "Hello?"

"Dr. Robins, this is Anna from the front desk. How are you?"

"I'm okay, ma'am. How are you?"

"Very good, thank you. Doctor, we have an important voicemail for you. Over the past few days, you have received a number of phone calls from a man named Jack. We tried to call up to you many times, but there was never an answer. If you would like to hear his voicemail, I can transfer it up to you." John knew that the phone rang at least ten times over the past few days, but he paid it no mind. But now that he heard Jack's name, he realized that his disappearance from society may have been slightly alarming, even if he only knew one person in town.

"Um, yes I'm sorry. I've been very busy with my work. I guess I haven't checked in over the past few days. Please, transfer the message," said John.

"Absolutely, Dr. Robins. As soon as I hang up, the voicemail will begin."

"Thank you, ma'am," said the doctor. Anna hung up and John heard a click and a beep.

"John dude, it's Jack. Listen, I know you told me to let it go and I'm really not trying to bother you. But the other day this married couple came into the bar and started asking me all these weird questions. They wanted to know if anything strange has been happening in town lately. Apparently, they're investigating different paranormal stuff around the country and this was their next stop. Maybe they know about this town's reputation with ghosts or something.

"Anyway, I told them that they came to the right place because the Davidson always has haunting stories. But after we got to talking, they told me about some guy from Oklahoma that saw these weird creatures that tried to kill him. Long story short, don't get mad at me, but I told them about what happened to you. I'm sorry man, but it seemed way too weird to not say anything. Since then, they've been begging to meet you, John. They've come in everyday and asked if I have gotten a hold of you. They said that they can really help you, and they may even need you to help them. I know you said to drop it, but it may be worth it just to hear them out.

"Give me a call or come down to the bar if you want to meet them. I'll give you free beer. Don't be mad at me, dude. Call me back, Johnny. I'm sorry." There was a long beep. John put the phone down. He exhaled and thought about whether or not to be mad at Jack. He was not happy that Jack had already revealed their conversation, but he also could not help but be curious as to what the married couple had to say. A few questions bubbled through his head: *Why are they here? What have they seen? What do they know?* Some part of his ego wanted him to stay in his room and figure everything out himself, but in the end, John knew that his curious mind would be ultimately in charge of his decisions. He sighed, picked up the phone, and dialed a number.

"Davidson Hotel. How may I help you?" asked a man on the other line.

"Yes, sir… Can you transfer me to the bar, please?"

Chapter Sixteen

<u>A Meeting Of The Minds</u>

John walked into the Davidson Hotel wearing his long rain coat. It was not raining, but the coat offered deep pockets in which he could stash the metal ball. Even after three straight days in his room, he was not ready to let it out of his sight. And as he crossed the doorway of any given room, he felt it shift around in his pocket. When he finally walked into the bar, it leaned hard towards the bar itself. John was taking mental notes and formulating theories about why.

The room was crowded and full of conversation. John kept a low profile as he looked around for his summoners. There were many groups and couples, none of which stood out by any appearance. He looked to the bar and saw that Jack had already spotted him. There was a tall red ale waiting for him at the bar. Jack slid it to him. "Hey, buddy. I know I went a little far with this one, but hear these people out." John took the beer and said nothing. "I don't know if it's a coincidence, but I've never heard anything like what you said and what they said. That's them over there." Jack pointed to a couple on the other side of the room. "They've been waiting a long time to talk to you. If at any point you get uncomfortable, just give me a wave. I'll make sure they don't come here to bother you anymore, but I think you might find them interesting." John took a long gulp of beer.

"Thank you, Jack," said John. He walked over to the table and stood over the couple. They quickly noticed him and smiled. John remained reserved, almost reluctant. "Hello. I'm John." The couple stood up and shook John's hand.

"Hi, I'm Dr. Maria Delphi and this is my husband, Victor Delphi."

"Hello, John," said Victor. John nodded. "Please, take a seat." They all sat down. John placed his beer across from their glasses of wine. Maria leaned forward.

"Thank you so much for coming, we know this must be a little strange. Jack said that he was having trouble getting a hold of you, so we're glad that you were kind enough to speak with us," said Maria. John continued to look but not speak.

"So, you must be wondering who we are and what we're doing here," said Victor. "Might as well get right to the point. We know you're probably skeptical of any story from a couple of strangers, but basically Maria and I believe that we were the first to experience something similar to what you have experienced yourself. Jack told us a little bit, but, of course, we would like to hear your story from you." John kept his poker face.

"So, maybe in the interest of opening it up, I'll tell you a little about how we found you." John nodded. "Well, we met each other at the Wisconsin College of Science. She was in a doctorate program and I was getting my masters, and after graduation, we both separately got hired. About two years ago, Maria became wrapped up in an experiment. Maybe it's a bit much to explain in one conversation—" Maria cut Victor off.

"Well he does work in science, hun." Maria looked to John. "Jack mentioned that you are a scientist. May I ask what field?"

"I teach Particle Physics at Colorado University."

"Well, that certainly makes this a lot easier. I'm an Astrophysicist, and over the past few years, I've devoted my studies to the make-up of space-time. It's something that I've always been interested in, and we've been lucky enough to gain some extra funding and equipment due to donations. So, in this particular experiment, I was attempting to examine the texture of space-time to determine whether the quality was smooth or grainy. To help make that possible, Victor was able to create a machine that aimed at measuring the form of space at one exact surface-layer."

"Are you an engineer?" John asked Victor.

"I am. I work mostly in solar energy, but Maria has gotten me more involved with her projects."

"Just as a guess, did you use light as your measurement tool?" Victor's eyes widened.

"Yes, Doctor. That's exactly right."

"Don't give me too much credit. I've read articles in the past that hypothesized how space-time fabric may have a rough texture. They talked about how it could affect the travel of light at different wavelengths. Frankly, I think it's impressive that you were able to put it into practice. Did you obtain anything significant?" asked John.

"Well, yes and no," said Maria. "As far as the machine creating a precise layer of readable light energy, it worked perfectly. But we could never quite get it to output the right figures or information in the way that we intended."

"Essentially, it turned on and did exactly what I wanted it to do, but it did not have the ability to tell me what it was seeing," said Victor. "In that sense, it turned out to be a dud. However, there was a very interesting side-effect from pressing the *on* button." John awaited an explanation curiously, but he hid his emotions. "This is the part where we generally lose people, Doctor."

"Okay…" said John.

Victor sighed and took a deep breath. "Have you done any work with spatial dimensions?"

"Sure, I've actually just begun to concentrate on string theory," said John. "We're up to ten dimensions of space."

"Exactly. Well, we believe that we have discovered the second dimension." said Victor. John's face squinted as he grew confused.

"You're telling me that you've found flatland? As in a place without depth?"

"Yes, and we know how it sounds," said Victor.

John paused. "I apologize, but you may need to clarify that one a little bit."

Maria leaned forward. "We know this is strange, but you need to see our machine to understand what we are talking about. In essence, we believe that we have isolated an absolutely flat dimension. It functions as a complete domain on its own, but it exists within our shared space. It's as if it was there all along, and we just had to find it."

"When we turned on our machine, it lit up something that we could not explain," said Victor. "Strange figures moving around, outlines of objects, an unexplainable color palate, and all of it had absolutely no depth. Maria's told me about spatial dimensions in the past, but we never intended to look for one when we started this project. We have extremely detailed notes of each day that we were able to study our discovery. And again, all of this would make a lot more sense if you were to see everything in person. We'd actually love it if you would be our guest next weekend. We would like to put you up in Wisconsin and give you a first-hand look at all of our data." John looked down at the table while he tried to figure out what to say.

"Listen, that all sounds very interesting, but I'm failing to understand where I fit into any of this. Trust me, if someone were to show me some proof that they have breached the second dimension, then I would be delighted to dive in on some research, but honestly, you've managed to just confuse me, and the truth is that I'm actually quite busy with my own problems," said John.

"You know what? I think we're getting ahead of ourselves. It's just that we have been dealing with our issues for so long now, and we've had no one to talk to that would begin to understand. Suddenly, we've heard about your story and I think we are just pouring everything out at once. Let me just try again to clarify what we are saying," said Maria. John was shifting in his seat, becoming noticeably less patient.

"The part where you tie in to all of this is that after a few weeks of first turning on our machine, some strange things started to happen in our lab. Equipment ended up in places that we did not leave it, or it would disappear altogether. And then the machine would turn on when we were not around. And I don't mean that it would just pop on; I mean that something would turn it on. It has a very specific, physical start-up process, and something was putting it through the motions.

"We have plenty of cameras around the room and the hallways outside. At first, when nothing was showing up, we thought that we were just losing our minds, but then we began to realize that whenever one of these incidents would occur, the cameras would stop working completely. Whatever was coming in was somehow draining all of the power from the building." John did not want to say it, but Maria was making him think about his own encounters.

Victor did not want to lose him, so he continued Maria's story. "A little over a month after the machine first turned itself on, we experienced the heaviest thunderstorm that we have ever seen. We heard thrash after thrash of lighting from inside our lab, which is almost soundproof to the outside world, but that night, it was deafening. We ran outside to see dozens of lightning bolts all slamming into one little point in the sky. It looked like a glowing ball of energy.

Even after the sky cleared up hours later, the ball never left. It just floated there and burned all night," said Victor.

"How big was it?" asked John.

"I'm not sure exactly because it was so high up, but it couldn't have been too big. The only reason we could see it was because it was so bright. Does that sound like something that you might have seen around here? asked Victor.

John looked back at him, not wanting to show his cards just yet. "How did that lead you here?"

"Well, through the news, we heard about an airplane that got struck by lightning twice in one night over Louisiana. Turns out that one of the flight attendants they interviewed saw a glowing light in the sky that got hit by multiple bolts of lightning. Maria and I thought that sounded very similar to what we had seen, so we headed down to Louisiana to see if we could talk to this woman ourselves.

"Not only was she very helpful, but while down there, Maria came up with the idea to investigate the town below where the light had appeared. We thought that maybe there was an off chance that someone might have experienced something like what we did in our lab. No one had any missing equipment or machines that turned themselves on, but we found a fig tree farm that began growing figs the size of basketballs overnight. The owners had no explanation, and the fact that it occurred directly below the area where the light showed up certainly raised the possibility of a correlation.

"Then another storm happened in Idaho. We were never able to find any sort of activity on the ground, but the storm lasted two straight weeks. That allowed us plenty of time to get there and see the light appear for ourselves. After that, we noticed a pattern. I have to give Maria credit for this, but as we pinpointed each location on the map, we saw that they were popping up in three corners of a square. Not only that, but every incident was happening on a schedule. Forty-two days apart from one another. So, we figured instead of waiting for the next one to occur, why not find it before it comes? And that's what led us to the all-confirming location. Moctezuma, Mexico. We actually got there the morning of the incident, just about five hours late.

"Three mysterious holes developed in the ground overnight that drained a river nearly dry, leaving an entire village without water. The holes were so deep that we couldn't even determine how far down they went." John shook his head as he tried to fathom everything that he was hearing.

"Is any of this documented? Why is no one else helping you if all of this is so public?" asked John.

"Because no one believes us. No one will come to read our data. The people in Louisiana just thought that the giant figs were some sort of farming miracle. They were more excited about calling the record books than figuring out how their crops could grow tenfold in one day. And the villagers in Mexico were convinced that the government created the holes in order to stop poison or illness from traveling down the river. But who could blame them? That makes a lot more sense than what we think."

"Tell him about the creatures, hun," said Maria. John's ears perked up.

"Well, if we have not lost you yet, then this part is sure to scare you away. Or maybe from what Jack told us, you'll know exactly what we're talking about. When we were in Mexico, we met a little boy who supposedly saw some… things creating the holes. He called them worms. He actually gave us a picture that he drew of them. All of that said, he is a little kid. Kids have imaginations, kids lie, and honestly, we would never run around the continent chasing down giant worms off of the word of a six-year-old. But then the storms led us to Oklahoma. "We met a carpenter there who told us a story about these *'giant, floating beasts'* that tried to kill him when he was working on a scaffold. He described them exactly how they were drawn by the child in Mexico. We showed him the picture and he recognized them. Oklahoma led us to New Mexico, and New Mexico led us here. Amber Rock, Colorado. This is the seventh location that we've been to in the past year-and-a-half.

"We've gotten better about figuring out where an incident has happened. When you walk into a town and start asking people if they've seen any floating insects or orbs in the sky, they generally start walking in the other direction. But lucky for us, this is a famous ghost town. This one was easy. We came to a popular landmark, The Davidson Hotel, and we asked the bartender if he knew about any new paranormal stories. It just so happened that he knew a guy who had just recently experienced some *'other-worldly'* visitations. And that's you, Doctor. You are the most recent victim of a very frightening and very real traveling occult. You're one of the few people who can truly understand what it is we are talking about. And we sure could use your help," said Victor.

"The carpenter and the flight attendant will be joining us next weekend," said Maria. "But we could use another scientific mind. We apologize for laying all of this on you, Doctor, but we need you." John sat quietly and looked at Maria and Victor, but his brain was working in sixth-gear. The couple's stories of insanity were right on par with his own. He wanted to pretend that none of it had anything to do with him, but his conscience would not let him. It made too much sense. He fired one last question to completely conquer his doubts.

"What do they look like, the creatures?"

"The best way to describe them is earthworms. But they're very big, about thirty-feet tall. Dry, white skin. They supposedly have one large eye in the center of their bodies. The carpenter said that it looks like the eye of death... Is any of this close to what you saw?" John sat still, looking at the table. The rational side of his brain still did not want to believe that any of the stories were true, even his own. But he was tired of hiding from it. He reluctantly nodded his head *yes*.

"Where were they?" asked Victor.

"In my room. I saw the orb too. It's happened at least four times. I saw it twice, and there's been three different kinds of entities to visit me that I know of. One of them had the eye."

"How about the static?" asked Maria. "Did you feel the static? We also lose power in the building when they show up."

"Yes. Whatever the orb is, it seems to absorb light and energy from the room. I tried to record it, but my cameras shut off too. I've been trying to figure it out, but nothing makes any sense..." John paused and let out a sigh. He suddenly looked defeated. "This has not been easy. I've seen things in the past month that were straight out of a nightmare. I apologize for keeping my guard up, but you must understand what I'm feeling. My sanity and reality have been flipped sideways, and I don't know how to handle it."

Maria reached across the table and placed her hand on John's. "Dr. Robins, this may be hard to believe, but we know exactly how you feel. We've been feeling this way for two years. And trust me, it still does not make any sense. But something is happening, and it can only be best if we figure out what it is. Come with us to Wisconsin. Let's figure it out together." John looked Maria in the eye. For about one second, he had an incredible feeling of relief. He knew that even if they never did get to the truth, at least he was no longer alone. He nodded to her in trust.

"Thank you," said John. He looked at Victor and gave him the same reassuring nod. "So, what's the next step?"

"Well, we're in town for another day. Does your building have roof access?" asked Victor.

"I'm not sure."

"Let's find out. We're predicting a thunderstorm tonight."

Chapter Seventeen

—

A thick ray of light blasted into another, creating a ninety-degree angle. With an absolute force, another ray came striking down, forming another ninety-degree angle. And then another. The complex corner where the rays met was bolted together like rods of steel, and with total control, they had turned a hoard of awesome energy into another link of the structure. It was nearing completion.

The Artist chose to remain hidden. It knew exactly how the creatures were intending on using their machine and the impact that the great device would have on the humans. It decided right then that Its previous methods to interfere were proving to be ineffective. The only option left was to introduce Itself to the humans and warn them, but Its beauty and presence would not be enough. It needed to speak, and Its exact choice of words meant everything.

Chapter Eighteen

Incident #14

July 26, 2015: Amber Rock, Colorado

John, Maria, and Victor stood on top of the roof of John's hotel. The misting rain was getting heavier by the minute. John stared up into the night sky as the number forty-two circled around in his head. Just as Maria and Victor had predicted, it was exactly forty-two days since the first episode of the static and the bell that rang in John's closet. And now they waited to see if another orb would appear above them. If they were correct again, they would have forty-two days to locate the next place of incident. They had an idea of where it would be, but they would worry about that later. For now, they awaited the fire in the sky.

Maria and Victor stood a few feet behind John and watched him. They were nervous. Not exactly about the storm, but whether or not that it would show John what he needed to see. They were confident that lightning would strike as intensely as it always had, but there was a small concern that the orb may not be as easily seen. They worried that if John was not totally convinced, then he would not come with them to Wisconsin.

John, on the other hand, stood tall under the mustering clouds. Fear was miles away. He wanted nothing more than to see the orb and take the next step towards an answer. Everything was happening so fast, and he had hardly a moment to process it, but unfortunately for him, there was no time. The young couple was there and they seemed to know something more than he did. So, he grabbed on to the situation and kept his eyes open. One concerning thought to John was that if he had not decided to join the young couple for a drink that afternoon, then he most likely would have missed the storm and, in turn, conceded any chance of ever moving forward. A lesson was learned to keep his mind open; a lesson he's needed to learn his entire life.

Crack. The first bolt of lightning lit up the sky, and the rain came down in sheets. "It's starting," said Victor. He and Maria walked closer to John and looked up at the clouds. Another strike exploded across the high air. It was the loudest that John had ever heard. Another happened, and another.

"Oh my God," said John. "You were not kidding." The wind and rain picked up twice as hard.

"Just wait," shouted Maria, trying to be heard over the weather. "It gets heavier." As they looked on, four consecutive bolts slashed through the clouds. They began coming in sets like waves in the ocean. John watched them in awe. A modest smile grew across his face. Each strike of lightning felt like a defibrillator shocking a piece of his life back into him. There was so much light from the electric bolts that they could see across the town as if it were daytime.

"This is amazing," said John.

Victor gave him a pat on the shoulder. He did not yet know if John was sold, so he clenched his fist waiting for the signal. He reached out and grabbed Maria's hand, which was even tighter than his own. They squeezed each other and stiffened to the point of holding their breath. They knew that this storm was the most important of all. And then, they let everything out and hugged. Relief washed over them with the pouring rain.

They walked up to John and stood by his side. The three of them looked up at a brilliantly lit, perfectly defined orb in the sky. They watched in serenity as spark after spark crashed violently into the small ball of light. John nodded his head. "I think it goes without saying that you might be onto something here, Dr. and Mr. Delphi."

"Just wait until you get to the lab," said Maria.

Chapter Nineteen
"It Is True, We Shall Be Monsters"

The Wisconsin College of Science was a small school in size, but quietly became one of the nation's most important foundations for astrophysics and aerospace engineering due to the contributions of Juan Carlos Vasquez. As a young student of chemical engineering in the late 1970's, Juan Carlos found himself obsessed with the concept of *efficiency*. While growing up in Mexico, he was one of six children, and he was raised in a poor home in an exceptionally poor town. His father and mother owned a car, but it was used seldom because gasoline was both expensive and difficult to come by. At a young age, Juan Carlos became fascinated with the fact that the things that were most important were the things that were the hardest to maintain: money, food, and energy. He learned to take the little that he had and stretch it beyond its worth.

Juan Carlos was the third oldest of his siblings, but the first to learn a second language. His school had a small library that existed because of the philanthropy of a local landowner, and it was there that Juan Carlos spent all of his free time. When he was twelve years old, he came across *Frankenstein* by Mary Shelley. He enjoyed the unique mix of science and horror, but the aspect of the story that captivated him the most was the way in which the monster learned to speak:

The tragic creature was abandoned by his creator because of his brutish appearance. While on his own, he discovered a small family who lived in a house out in the wilderness. He knew that if he presented himself to the family, he would only scare them away like he did the man who conceived him. So instead, he hid away and watched them. For months and months, the monster studied them from a distance and learned from them how to communicate. The concept was innovative and extremely cunning, and it gave Juan Carlos an inspired idea.

When he finished reading the book, he wrote a letter to the wealthy landown-er who donated the library and asked him if it would be possible to find the

English version of *Frankenstein.* Juan Carlos explained that he would read the English and Spanish texts side-by-side in order to learn the language of the original text. The landowner told him that not only would he find him an original version, but if he could write him a summary of the book in English when he was finished, then he would pay for Juan Carlos to receive a private education. After four months of intense study, Juan Carlos hand delivered the landowner a twelve-page paper written in beautiful, Romantic-era English, and the landowner kept his word of paying for Juan Carlos' private education. The setting of that education was in the landowner's hometown of Medora, Wisconsin.

St. Peter's Academy was a boys-only boarding school that offered one of the best educations of the northern states. Because of Juan Carlos' cultural background and quick absorption of language, they tried to guide him towards a concentration on linguistic studies. But as much as he had appreciated its importance, he knew that learning English was only a tool for his advancement in the world; it was not his purpose. So, he began his pursuit in the field of science with an interest in chemical energy. He could never forget about that car on his property and how much easier his parents would have lived if they only had access to fuel.

He eventually graduated with an outstanding transcript and a full scholarship offer to the Wisconsin College of Science, which he graciously accepted. He was randomly placed in the John Paul Jones freshman dormitory, and was given one of two keys to room two-twenty-eight. The second of those two keys was given to a young man named Harper Thomas. Harper came from a family of southern crop dusters, and had flown small airplanes his entire life. Even though he was a gifted pilot, his true desire existed even higher than the skies that he frequented: outer space. He did not want to become an astronaut per se, but he did want to help create a machine capable of navigating the cosmos, or at the very least, something that could safely explore the Geospace closely adjacent to Earth. And just like the lone raindrop that lands on the single, dry seed in the garden, Juan Carlos and Harper learned that they had been introduced to each other for a very specific reason.

Juan Carlos excelled in his studies of chemical engineering, and in a parallel effort, Harper quickly handled the vast concepts of mechanical engineering.

After hundreds of sleepless nights, and many arguments and disagreements, the unlikely pair came up with a small prototype of an engine that would hypothetically burn Juan Carlos' clever mix of liquid oxygen and liquid hydrogen at a calculated, rationed manner as soon as it hit zero gravity. If it worked according to plan, it would burn to the effect of six-times slower than a normal rocket fuel engine, while still producing the same amount of energy. The fuel itself was effective enough on its own, but Harper's intricate engine chambers allowed the fuel to expand within its unique containment design that maximized the propellant's effect the second that it reached weightlessness.

The two roommates could not finish their graduation walk before the school's science board informed them that they had been in a long-term discussion with NASA about the pair's prototype and fuel formula. They were both offered jobs in Washington D.C. within a week of receiving their diplomas. Harper was born with a travel bug and headed East as soon as he packed up his car. Juan Carlos, on the other hand, decided that Wisconsin had been nothing but good to him, and came up with a counter-offer. He asked if he could stay at the Wisconsin College of Science and set up a remote laboratory. He thought that it would benefit both him and the school to carry out his work in the satellite location. The school board came to an agreement that they would split the cost of renovations of an older building if NASA was willing to pay half. In NASA's eyes, Juan Carlos was young, brilliant, and seemed to be driven by loyalty, and because the renovations were not greatly expensive anyway, they shook hands and considered it a charitable donation.

The laboratory was going to be renamed after NASA, but after a last request, Juan Carlos convinced them to allow Harper to receive some credit. He pleaded that none of it would have been possible without his roommate. Juan Carlos worked in that laboratory every day for over twenty-five years, earning his pay by developing many more innovations in the line of efficient energy sources. Throughout that time, his friend, Harper, orchestrated more donations from NASA by having older equipment sent to the lab when it was no longer of use to the government. It became a small stockpile of technology that allowed the college's research to advance tenfold. Somewhere along the way, Juan Carlos had a daughter named Maria who would eventually grow up and take the reins from her father.

Chapter Twenty
<u>The God Machine</u>

John stood next to his car, in the parking lot of the two-story building. It looked like any building on a college campus, which sort of made him feel at home. Since the storm several days back, his enthusiasm about the entire situation had retreated ever so slightly, but he could not help it. It was in his nature to always keep his guard at arm's length.

The weather was beautiful: sunny with a breeze. John had never been to Wisconsin before, but he was already impressed. The building sat on a hill that overlooked the campus. It was small, but pleasant. The building itself had a heavy, rocklike structure as if it were carved out of one piece of natural stone. Next to the front door, on a well-kept lawn, stood a sign that read, *The NASA/Thomas Laboratory of Aerospace Studies.* John found himself getting a little too comfortable being on the outside looking in, so he walked to the front door and entered.

The lobby was empty of people, but it was lit up and welcoming. When John stuck his head out of his office back in Colorado, half of the lights would be turned out and the floor was filled with a heavy silence. The NASA/Thomas lab, in contrast, was bright with sunlight from the open windows, and had a natural echo from the campus below. And by the time John reached the first hallway, he could hear the faint voices of his new colleagues having a discussion.

The east wing laboratory was set up similar to a classroom or small theatre. It was big and open, and descended from back to front. From the back doors, a slightly declining ramp ran down the center of the room.

About halfway down the long walk, the benches stopped and opened up into a work area. There was an island desk that sat in the middle of the floor that was used as the main work and demonstration table, similar to a teacher's desk, but much bigger. Beyond that, at the very front of the room, there was a dry-erase board that doubled as a projection screen. The center and right side of the board were messily covered in math equations and various written-out ideas. On the left side, there was a big, detailed map of North America that had been stretched out and attached. A series of short pins and long pins were stuck into specific places across the map accompanied by yarn that ran through and connected each pin. However, the eye-catcher in the room was the display on top of the island desk: a glass cube of about four feet in measurement. There were small machines connected to each of the eight corners of the cube as well as one larger machine in the center. When John walked in, he made a quick assumption as to what it was.

He entered quietly and stood by the doorway with his hands in his pockets. Maria was seated in the front of the lab on a stool as Victor stood near the dry-erase board. He was answering a question asked by Alice, who was sitting in the front row bench just to the right of the walking ramp. To the left of the ramp, in the same row, was Mark. They were both dressed much more casually than John, Maria, or Victor, and were both smoking cigarettes. It was illegal to smoke inside of a building on campus, but Maria and Victor gave them permission in the hopes of keeping their stress levels manageable under the given situation. Alice and Mark were taking full advantage of said permission by using the last puff of one cigarette to light the next.

Maria spotted John standing at the top of the room and gave him a smile and a nod. John nodded back. Victor finished up answering Alice's question, which had something to do with aliens or bacteria, or maybe even alien bacteria. He was beginning to understand that she was not grasping the concept of what he was suggesting, but his patience and politeness kept him from saying that outright. He looked up mid-sentence and saw John. His natural smile told John that his presence was appreciated. Victor waved him down.

"Forgive me for a minute, Alice, but our final guest is here," said Victor. "Alice and Mark, this is Dr. John Robins." John began his descent down the ramp. "Doctor, this is Alice Day and Mark Schmidt. We briefly mentioned them in our meeting last week." John found his way to where Alice and Mark were sitting and shook their hands. They offered each other a brief hello. "We are finally all here now, and we can get started."

Maria stood up. "So, before we get into anything involving our own indi-vidual stories or plans or theories, Victor and I just want to say thank you for coming. It was really brave for each of you to take it on faith and travel all the way here to try and figure this out with us.

"Victor and I have been through so much over the past couple of years, but the hardest part by far was knowing how alone we were with everything. Just getting anyone to sit down and listen to us has been impossible, so thank you all for trusting us. We thought that it might be a good idea to start off by getting on the same page and filling you all in on where everyone is from and what happened to each of you. Alice and Mark, I think you two have had a little time to get acquainted, but maybe for John's sake we'll catch him up on your situations," said Maria. "Mark, do you want to start?"

Mark sat up and put out his cigarette. "Yeah, that's fine. Well, I'm Mark. I'm a carpenter out in Oklahoma City, although I'm actually now fired, so I guess I should say I'm unemployed… I kind of feel like I'm in A.A. right now. I've only been once, although I'm told I should go more often… But anyway, right around Christmas I was building an interior scaffold for a new office building. Things seemed pretty normal for most of the day, but then about halfway through, maybe around lunch time, I noticed that all of the other workers were walking out. Someone said that the electricity had shut off, which can happen from time to time in a new building, but the strange thing is that my batteries stopped working too.

"Then um…" Mark paused to try and figure out what he wanted to say. "Listen, frankly, I'm not the best story teller as far as explanation and build up and all that, but long story short, I found myself alone sitting on the scaffold, and all of a sudden, I smelled this horrible smell, like an odor right in my face. Before I knew it, I threw up all over myself. That's how bad it was."

Mark turned further around in his seat to face John. "I was sort of leaning over the side of the scaffold and I saw something moving around on the floor below me. This particular building had a big opening that went all the way up from the lobby to the top floor, and the hallways were open and wrapped around above the lobby. Whatever this thing was, it looked like a huge snake, but bigger than any animal I've ever seen. A minute later, I saw another one appear out of nowhere about fifty feet above me. And I mean appear as in grow from nothing into something.

"Right around this point, it occurred to me that if I valued my life, then I should probably get moving before they saw me. So, I started climbing down the scaffold. After a few floors, I fell on my leg, about a ten-foot drop. I got up and started limping back to the ladder… Then I was stopped. One of the things, the fuckin' creatures, whatever you want to call it, was floating right in front of me. It looked like a giant worm, but real fat. Somewhere between twenty-five or thirty-five-feet tall and ten-feet wide, suspended in thin air, like there was no gravity. It didn't really have a face, but there was one huge eye. It was looking right at me.

"After about a minute, it threw itself into the scaffold. Lucky for me, I got sent backwards and landed on the nearest floor's hallway, but the scaffold completely collapsed. If anyone was in the lobby, they would've been crushed. Anyway, I stayed still on the ground for a few minutes figuring that if this thing wanted me dead, then I should act like I was dead.

"After five more minutes of lying there, I heard footsteps coming down the hallway. Apparently, every worker on the site came looking for me. I hate to fake an injury, but I made the decision to pretend that I was unconscious. Who was going to believe that a giant worm destroyed the scaffold? I was hoping that they would take pity on me if I had gotten seriously injured. Unfortunately, I was fine and I was fired pretty much immediately. In fact, the owners of the building are trying to sue me for damages because I was in charge of the scaffold. I can't imagine how I'm ever going to get another job in the state of Oklahoma… But anyway, that's it. Sorry, sometimes I ramble. I'm really not much of a story teller."

Mark's account hit John in the face. As unbelievable as it all was, he could visualize just how Mark felt.

"That's so scary," said Alice.

"After the storm led us to Oklahoma, it took us a while to find Mark," said Victor. "We looked around for a few weeks before we heard about the accident in the building, but as soon as we met him, we knew that he had seen something. He had that look of fear that I think we've all had."

"Alice, do you want to tell him your story?" asked Maria. Alice looked at Maria and nodded.

"Sure, although mine is nowhere near as exotic," said Alice as she chuckled. "After hearing what y'all have been through, I almost feel guilty sitting here, but basically, I'm a flight attendant, and I guess this was just over a year ago. I was working a flight from Orlando to Austin. It had been delayed for a few hours due to weather, and by the time we got into the air, I think they probably regretted not just canceling the flight.

"About an hour in, we were over Louisiana, and the plane got struck by lightning. I had always heard that planes get hit more often than you think, but it doesn't really have much of an effect because the electricity just bounces off, but this jolted the entire plane. Everyone that was sleeping got thrown around and woken up. We tried to get everyone in their seats and buckled up, but before we even had a chance to know what was really going on, we got hit again.

"That one really scared me. It hit a lot harder than the first. We went straight into an emergency landing, so I got in my seat and buckled up. And as I was looking around the plane, everyone else had their heads between their knees or were just closing their eyes. I think I might have been the only person who looked out the window, but I'm glad I did. Maria had mentioned that y'all saw something similar just a few days ago, so maybe you will know what I'm talking about, but right in the middle of the sky was this bright ball of light, as bright as the lightning, but it wouldn't blink out. And every few seconds, it got struck again.

"Thank God we made it down safely. There were news reporters at the airport because the plane nearly crashed, and apparently, I'm the only one who saw the ball of light because when I told the cameraman, everyone looked at me like I was crazy. But at least it helped Maria and Victor find me. And I guess it turns out that we weren't the only ones."

There was a long silence as John fell into thought. He no longer had any doubt, but he was still a bit uncomfortable sharing his experiences with strangers. It was beginning to feel like an unorthodox support group, but he knew that the only way to progress was through communication, so he swallowed his feelings. "You are certainly not the only ones," he said.

The Doctor proceeded to do more than just tell them his own story. He told them his life story. He went into great detail about how science pulled him in from a young age, and how it shaped his beliefs and world views. Each decade of his life revolved around whatever different field or theory he was studying at the time. He talked about his struggles over the past year when he failed to make ground on the graviton, and he broke down all of the ways that his wasted studies affected both his professional life and his personal psyche. And finally, he explained to them his encounters with the orbs, and the bell, and the creatures, and the utter disarray that they caused him. He wrapped it all up by illustrating the complete contradiction that these experiences were to the past sixty-odd years of his life.

In fact, the only detail that he left out was his daily journal that had been borrowed and altered by the visitors, and the metal ball that was left behind, which was now securely strapped to his ankle like the gun of an undercover cop. He was not yet ready to reveal it to anyone, at least not until he had more time to try and understand it himself.

After he finished speaking, John received a look of support from each of the other four volunteers. "Okay, now that we're caught up on each other, maybe it's time to try and piece together the bigger picture," said Victor. "That map is a project that Maria and I have been working on since our second discovery in Louisiana." He was referring to the large North American map that was attached to the board. Maria illuminated it with overhead lights. "This is a map of every incident to date, and as you can see, we've marked each occurrence with a pin. The short pins represent the ground incidents and the long pins represent the storms. The storms always take place directly over their ground counterpart."

"How did you figure out the last couple of them before they happened?" asked Mark.

Maria walked to the map. "The first ever experience happened right here in this lab, which we have marked in white. Forty-two days later, the storm came along and we saw the orb in the sky. So that gave us our first two points. Then, after we heard about Alice in Louisiana, we headed down there and discovered the fig farm in Gillis. From that point, we had two more pins, and a pattern was forming, each having a duration of forty-two days in between. The next location came from the northwest in Idaho."

"Did you meet anyone from there?" asked Alice.

"Not exactly," said Maria. "We never did find any evidence of activity on the ground, but exactly eighty-four days after your sighting, a two-week storm developed just outside of Dubois. Even after showing up a week later than it started, Victor and I were still able to see the orb for another six days. We obviously can't confirm it, but we think that something happened on the ground that was either too far from a town for anyone to witness or purposely hidden, so we pinned it to continue the pattern.

"With all of the locations mapped, we realized that we were looking at three corners of a square. It was a perfect ninety-degree angle. Of course, the next incident, if there was even going to be another one, could have happened anywhere, but we decided to go out on a limb and try to beat the clock. So, we headed to location number four."

"Mexico," said John.

"That's exactly right, Doctor," said Maria.

"Maria's being humble, but she was way ahead of me on predicting any of the future sites," said Victor. "And Mexico was absolutely the most important place of all. Not only did it complete the first portion of the map, but it also allowed us to find the next few stops with much better accuracy.

"Look at the four places that we just mentioned. They create a square, and if you notice, it's actually a cube," said Victor. Wisconsin, Louisiana, Idaho, and the spot in Mexico each had a low pin and a high pin sticking out of them. The low pins had a square of yarn that ran through them, as did the high pins. Together, with the pins acting as corners and the yarn acting as edges, they created the outline of a cube.

"And here's the most interesting piece of evidence that we have," said Maria. She turned on the projector and slipped a piece of paper in front of the focus. The drawing that the little boy had given them appeared across the dry-erase board. It showed the three tall creatures on top of the hill and the holes that swallowed the river.

"This was given to us by a boy named Lucas in Moctezuma. These holes that he drew were actually three large holes that showed up in a river overnight. Nobody could explain how they got there, but they completely drained the river, which the locals used as their main water source.

"Oddly, at the bottom of the hill, they dug out another hole that let out a small remainder of the river flow. Lucas kept saying something over and over. 'Los gusanos lo hicieron. Los gusanos lo hicieron.' It means, 'the worms did it.'"

"Those are exactly what I saw in Oklahoma. Those are the worms," said Mark in a state of shock. "Can we get a hold of this kid? I mean, obviously he knows as much as we do."

"Unfortunately, he's only a small child, so bringing him here is not possible. His grandfather didn't even really allow him to speak to us, but clearly, Mark, it matches your physical description of the creatures pretty well," said Victor.

"Have you been back to the river since?" asked John.

"Yes, about six months ago," said Maria.

"Did you speak to the locals? Have there been any changes?"

"Yes, actually. The holes are still there, but the river has gotten a little more flow back. It's at about half of what it was before the holes first appeared, but no one's mentioned anything in the way of giant worms," said Maria.

Alice smiled and almost laughed. "What are we talking about here? I can't believe y'all are actually saying that you saw these things. Where did they come from?"

"That's what we're all doing here," said Victor. He let out a chuckle. "Really, this isn't funny at all, considering that it's happening, but sometimes the absurdity gets to me too. The five of us and that little boy are the only ones who even know that any of this is going on."

"So, after Mexico you found me?" asked Mark.

"That's correct," said Maria. "And that was the start of the second pattern. After Oklahoma, we found a storm in New Mexico. Vaughn is a smaller town that had reports of an intense thunderstorm, but the real incident happened a few miles outside of town. There's a lake called Lake Sumner. It's fairly large and out in the middle of nowhere. This one actually got the most public attention. Do you remember how they described it, hun?"

"Yes. The township officials said that there was some sort of chemical dump in the lake that caused the fish to breed at an unexplainable level. Of course, that does not make any sense. Essentially, there are three main types of fish in the lake: smallmouth bass, largemouth bass, and flathead catfish. Along the shoreline, there were three piles, one for each type of fish. The bodies were completely dissected and laid down neatly. And maybe pile is actually not the right word because they weren't stacked on top of one-another, they were organized in rows and columns. All of their intestines, bones, and organs were placed on their bodies."

Victor pressed a button on the projector which displayed a picture on the board. It showed rows of fish laying across the sand, turned completely inside-out. He pressed the button again and a new picture popped up. It showed the surface of the lake which had thousands of fish floating on top of the water.

"This is from a few weeks after the storm, so maybe two-months after the initial incident at the lake. Those are all dead fish. Countless. They multiplied so fast that there was not enough room for them to survive. One of the men told us that in the period of a month and a half, the fish population went from four or five thousand to well over fifty thousand. A lot of people used the lake for fishing, but they closed it down because they thought that someone was dumping chemicals into it. Obviously, they had no other explanation. After we pinned the lake onto our map, we had enough information to figure out the next location which, of course, was Amber Rock, Colorado. We met Dr. Robins the day of the storm, and he confirmed the incidents that took place inside of his hotel room.

"And now, we have three more corners in the second cube of our map," said Victor. On the map, the first cube of strings surrounded the second. It was a small cube inside of a bigger cube. "All of the storms for the first pattern seemed to happen a lot higher in altitude than they did in the second, therefore, we placed the pins higher. But it's definitely happening in the exact same order, and in about one month, we will have the start of the fourth corner. It's going to show up in the town of Sutton, Nebraska. Maria and I plan to try and figure out what we can before it's time to head down there."

Mark laughed. "Well, how the hell are we going to figure it out? You've been going on this for two years, and you got no idea. I mean, what do these sex-fish have to do with the worms that tried to kill me?" Alice joined Mark in his laugh.

John stood up from his seat and began pacing the aisle. Mark looked back at him. "Doctor, you teach any classes about this in Colorado? Help us out. You seem pretty calm about it." John continued to walk the floor and look down at his feet.

"Well, Mr. Schmidt, like all of us, I've been trying to understand this since my first encounter, but unfortunately I've been hindered by a lack of information. Today has been enlightening, but if I'm being honest, I have to admit that my attention has been more focused on the one thing that we have yet to discuss."

"What would that be, Doctor?"

"Are you telling me that you're not curious about the large, glass case that's been sitting on the middle of the desk?" asked John. Mark and Alice turned to see it. They both had certainly noticed it when they walked in, but only John had predicted what it was, based on his conversation with Maria and Victor at the Davidson.

Maria grinned. She was proud that the only other physicist in the room happened to be the man that had the sharpest eye. "As it so happens, we were just getting to that, Dr. Robins," she said.

John looked at her, already knowing the answer to his next question. "That's it, isn't it?... The God machine."

Chapter Twenty-One
<u>The Inception Of The Light Pidima</u>

Maria stood in the laboratory and looked at all of the unused equipment that had accumulated over the decades. Regardless of its age, she saw every last scrap of metal for its potential, and she had her father to thank for that. Because of his long tenure with NASA and the help of his good friend, the government made annual donations of old instruments, machines, and devices that it considered obsolete. She considered them unutilized. Now that she was given the keys to the kingdom at the Laboratory of Aerospace Studies, Maria decided that she would not waste time trying to appease the department's budget or requisites just to make herself look efficient on paper. Instead, she would build towards something worthwhile.

There was one memory that had been roaming around her mind since her early childhood. The details were never crystal clear, but she could see the image of her father speaking to a younger colleague. The young man was very passionate about some new hypothesis that centered around the idea that the fabric of space was not smooth or continuous, but rather grainy and rough if examined at the most minute level. The last bit of Maria's recollection was of the man telling Juan Carlos about a recent gamma ray burst that had made its way over millions of light years to Earth, which ignited his wild presumption. This kind of language meant nothing to Maria as a child, but she retained just enough of it to look further into the subject over the years.

She would later learn that the discovery of the gamma rays that the man spoke of happened in the early eighties. Scientists in Sweden observed an inordinate amount of low-energy gamma rays collide with Earth that likely traveled across a few million light-years. The interesting detail was that one minute later, another group of high-energy gamma rays reached the same spot, seemingly originating from the same burst.

While researching the story, Maria was just as confused as the Swedish scientists because she knew that according to the theory of relativity, all light photons travel at the exact same speed, regardless of energy level or wavelength: a speed referred to as *'the speed of light.'* Maria learned that the scientists concluded that over the course of a few million years, the low-energy, longer wavelength photons somehow gained about a sixty-second lead in the race against the high-energy, shorter wavelength photons. Everyone involved was baffled because they all knew how long sixty seconds was in terms of a lightspeed reaction. Juan Carlos' young colleague, however, put forth an outsider's suggestion.

He forwarded the option that perhaps their pathway of space was not as smooth and open as everyone had believed, but instead grainy and interrupted. Maria had no way of contacting this man who's name she did not even know, nor had she heard of any experimental results from the world of science that could be linked to his ideas. But that did not convince her that his hypothesis was wrong. So, she took the snippet of memory from the day that she had met that man and combined it with the Swedish data in order to advance the thought even further.

She landed on the point that if space itself was at all wrinkled, spotty, or rough at even the most micro of levels, then maybe it could have an impact on the travel of something that was also micro. She visualized two balls rolling down a road that had imperfections and bumps in it. Each ball would be affected differently depending on its size. Therefore, if a longer wavelength caused a photon to avoid the bumps easier than a photon traveling at a shorter wavelength, then it was possible that the first photon could arrive at its destination that much sooner, even if it was just one minute over the span of millions of years.

Maria was well aware that the idea was radical, but she was also aware that if she could find some way to prove it true, then it could affect the study of not only aerospace travel, but of all physics. And that bound her to the obligation of her time and effort.

★★★

Victor was overworked and bored with his mundane tasks. When the school hired him to use his degree in solar engineering, he had much higher hopes than designing solar panels for the campus buildings in order to save money on power. Victor appreciated his employment, but his gut was burning for a greater challenge.

He was certainly no expert of astrophysics, but being married to a doctor in the field subconsciously fed him a meal's worth of knowledge. Over a few weeks' period, Victor noticed that Maria was going through a drawn-out investigation in her head. Most of it stayed in her head, but bits and pieces found their way out, and whatever it was that held her attention so securely began to intrigue Victor as well. By the time that she was ready to share it with him, he was fully ready to jump into anything that didn't involve building another simple energy panel.

On a Friday night after work, they went to their favorite Italian restaurant to discuss a plan for their first ever joint project. Over some pasta and wine, Maria laid everything on him. She started with her long-etched memory of her father and his colleague, and then proceeded into her research and hypothesis. She was never great at explaining complex issues in layman's terms, but Victor had learned the art of reading her signs and over-explanations somewhere along the way. The more passionate that she was about something, the harder she was to follow, but he loved that about her.

After they had talked it over for a few hours, Maria arrived at the most important point of the night. "I want to create a machine that measures several types of radiation at different wavelengths and frequencies simultaneously. Radio waves, microwaves, infrared, visible, ultraviolet, x-ray, and gamma all in one machine. Maybe that's not all possible, but the more we can line up, the better."

Victor smirked at Maria's ambition. "Maybe it's not possible? Let me save you the trouble, honey. It's not possible. Where are we going to find a machine like that?"

"You're going to build it!"

Victor laughed. "I'm going to build it? How many glasses of wine have you had?"

"Three too many, but let me finish. We have an unlimited amount of government space technology, which, by the way, no one from Wisconsin has ever said, and you have a brilliant mind that can create any number of solar panels in your sleep. Maybe you can even use one of your panels for parts and disassemble some of the NASA equipment and put it all together. If you ask me, I've already done the heavy lifting by coming up with this idea. You just need to build it." Maria pinched Victor's cheek, which was her favorite act of affection when she drank too much. Victor pretended that he hated it, but he actually loved it.

"Well, let me be the first to say, thank you Dr. Delphi. I'm honored that you're allowing me such a simple task in your experiment of measuring space-time, but I think we might need to pump the brakes. Whether or not this machine is even possible is one thing. The bigger question is why you would think that I am capable of creating it. Not to spoil the twist ending, but I am certainly not, even considering all of the technology that we have at our disposal. I think that you have come up with a wonderful, bold idea, but don't let me stop you from achieving it."

Maria locked eyes with Victor. She leaned in close, never allowing him to look away. "Are you a talented engineer?" she asked. Victor raised his eyebrow, not appreciating the request to give a self-righteous answer.

"I've met many who were much better," he replied.

"Victor, that's not what I asked you. Are you a talented engineer?"

"I'm okay," said Victor, reaching for a loophole.

"Are you happy in your current assignment?"

"I am not."

"Do you think you are capable of something greater?"

"It would not take much to be greater than this… but yes."

"If I pull some strings and get some funding, which I could easily do because I am an extremely influential and important asset to this college…" Victor rolled his eyes at Maria's ridiculousness. "… would you drop everything and give me your best efforts at helping me study the intricate weavings of the fabric of space?"

Victor looked Maria dead in the eye. Before he even had a chance to get serious with her, a facetious smile grew across her face which spoke a clear message to Victor: She was his wife, and he, of course, could never allow her to take such a leap by herself. Victor returned a phony smile of his own. "Well, if we both get fired, then you will be the one finding us a new line of work."

Maria came around to Victor's side of the table, sat down next to him, and pounded his cheek with kisses. He had many reservations about the idea, but he too had been staring at the pile of NASA equipment trying to figure out the best way to take advantage of such an incredible fortune. *Why not try to change history?* he thought.

***

Over the next week, they organized all of the equipment into categories. They found telescopes, microscopes, lights, lasers, small generators, electric hand tools, spectrometers, high-efficiency cameras, space shuttle silica window panes, safety tethers, and medical supplies including defibrillators. Victor immediately started separating what would be useful from what would not. The medical supplies and tethers were not so much relevant, but the silica panes could provide a heat and light resistant barrier for his machine, and the lights and lasers could be an obvious source of the photons needed for their trials. But the real gems among everything were the microscopes and spectrometers.

The microscopes not only offered magnifying lenses for an intensified beam of light, but they were also equipped with small mirrors for redirection. And the spectrometers would be used to receive the light and compute the energy into readable data. Victor had to tip his hat to his brilliant, lovely wife. To his surprise, after an inventory of their stockpile, the machine's manual was already writing itself.

For the following two months, the couple gave each other some space. Victor stayed in the lab and figured out the subtleties of his prototype. Meanwhile, Maria surrounded herself with books and computers, and learned everything that she could on the subject. They would spend about an hour together every night before bed and discuss the day's progress, then they would sleep, wake up, and start over. After starting a few small fires and breaking some priceless equipment, Victor had finished what he considered his first meaningful creation.

Late one night, he woke Maria up and asked her to come with him to the lab. He could not wait until the morning, and she was as excited as him, so they drove over to campus. In the middle of the desk in the laboratory was an object covered by a sheet. Maria walked over and examined it. They met eyes and, without words, exchanged the kind of involuntary smile that only comes along once or twice in a lifetime. She nodded to him and he nodded back. He pulled away the sheet and revealed his machine. It was about eighteen inches long, eight inches wide, and six inches in height. It looked like a large, metal shoebox. It sat on a firm metal rack that kept it suspended from the tabletop. He removed a lid off of the top of the box, which was there to protect the silica glass pane. Maria leaned up and looked through the pane to see the sleek makeup of the machine's internals. "Oh my God… Victor," said Maria.

"Yeah, tell me about it."

"This is incredible. I can't believe how compact you made it."

"Well, thank yourself for that. That night at the restaurant, you said that I could use an old solar panel for its parts. Turns out, one of my old panels was perfect for an exoskeleton. I was able to gut it pretty cleanly and fit everything inside," said Victor.

"How does it work?"

"I thought you'd never ask." They both laughed. Victor removed the window pane using a series of secure attachment clips. "This is silica glass. They use triple panes of this on space shuttles for both pressure and temperature protection. No matter how hot this light gets, we'll never feel it. It will also protect us against radiation. Now look at this." Victor shined a small flashlight into one side of the box. "You see these lenses?" Maria nodded. She had the grin of a small girl looking at the boy of her dreams. "There's six, each having a light source behind them." He pointed down the line at the lenses. "Radio, microwave, infrared, visible light, ultraviolet, and x-ray. I love you very much, dear, but gamma was not possible. I know that it's essentially the reason that we're here, but there's no way I could fit it safely into our machine.

"When I turn it on, the lights and lasers behind the lenses all shoot off at the same time. They're all aimed at the first set of mirrors over here." Victor pointed to the opposite side of the box. "The light and radiation bounces from this side and back to the other, and then back again over and over. If I lined everything up right, each beam should bounce back and forth thousands of times before it slips past the mirrors into the spectrometer. Then, the spectrometer will tell us if there is any delay from one ray to the next."

Maria shined a flashlight into the mirror side of the panel. The light twinkled off of countless, little mirrors. "Wow. How many are in here?" she asked.

"A few hundred," said Victor. "Honestly, the majority of the time that it took to make this was lining up the mirrors so that the light would bounce at exactly the same rate. It was not easy."

"Have you tried it yet?" asked Maria.

"I've turned on each one individually just to see if they would be read by the spectrometer, and it worked perfectly. It can measure each radiation type down to a ten-trillionth of a second. I've hooked it up to receive one quick jolt of electricity at a time, just enough to send a small bit of light and not overload the meter."

Maria searched her mind for more questions, but then just smiled again. She was satisfied. "This is amazing, honey. When can we turn it on?"

"I think we should be ready to record everything the second that it's on. There are going to be a million kinks to work out, so let's wait until tomorrow when we're both rested." Maria smiled. Victor smiled back. "If you win the Nobel Prize, I want at least an honorable mention."

"You'll get a nod in my speech," said Maria.

Victor looked down at his creation. His face grew serious. He hoped that whatever this machine did, it would change things, and something in his gut told him that it would. "Let's get some sleep, Maria. Tomorrow, we see what our light pidima will bring us."

Chapter Twenty-Two

The Light That Shined Across Dimensions: Incident #1

December 15, 2013: Medora, Wisconsin

They were back right at sunrise after three hours of sleep, but they were more alert than ever. The pidima sat on top of the metal rack, two-feet above the desktop. Victor hooked up a power cable to its outer socket, and gathered all of the necessary safety gear in case of another fire or small explosion. Maria took the time to set up a video camera to record the first trial, and stood by as Victor's aide.

Victor had a specific surge protector that was not only designed to shut down a rogue spark, but also manually set up for an important task. In order to work precisely, the pidima required very short bursts of electricity as opposed to a constant circuit. If a constant beam of light was shone onto the spectrometer, it would not be able to decide when to start and stop reading the light rays. So, Victor set up the surge box to pump small bits of energy into the machine in scattered spurts like a machine gun. Then the meter would output a few dozen readings over the thirty-second runtime. Maria started the camera.

"I am turning on the power box to charge now. It should take about sixty seconds," said Victor. He and Maria watched as the light on the box slowly lit up green. "The power is ready. Test number one will begin in ten seconds. Stand back, Maria." After ten seconds, Victor pressed the power button. The surge box began a metallic hum that quickly rose in volume. After a short silence, the box started to fire quick jolts of electricity into the pidima. It was as loud as a gun, and the pidima illuminated with each pop. The electricity blasted for half-a-minute straight, before coming to a stop.

"Wow. Is that it?" asked Maria.

"Yeah, it should be. Let's see if we have any results." He walked over to his computer which was connected to the pidima, and began searching for data. "Hmm…" murmured Victor.

"What's the matter?"

"Well, it shows a start time for every jolt, but no end time. That's strange. Each one that I tested individually produced both."

"Is it because you ran all of them at once?"

"Perhaps, but I don't understand why that's a problem. It seems fine recording all of the start times… I guess let's run it again." Victor walked over and charged the surge box again, and then went through the motions of another trial. After the full process, he found that the spectrometer had again only recorded half of the results, except this time, it was half of the start times and half of the stop times. Growing frustrated he ran it again, and again. After the fourth time, the machine had finally produced the full results of the infrared light rays, but nothing else.

"Why?!" shouted Victor.

"Okay, maybe it's an issue with the computer reading the meter, hun. Maybe the information is getting tangled up."

"Then how do I fix that? Why is the problem different every time?" asked Victor. Maria saw that he was losing patience and she knew that he needed to step away for a few minutes, but his ego would not allow him to do that.

"Could we try keeping a constant beam on to see how the meter reacts? Maybe it needs more time to adjust to the multiple lights," said Maria. Victor was rubbing his forehead, trying to not rip his own hair out. He sighed.

"It's just not making any sense. Everything was working fine. I don't… Yeah, let's try it. Why not?"

Maria unplugged the surge box and plugged the pidima directly into the wall socket. On her way back to the desk, she picked up a second fire extinguisher and walked it over with her. Victor was looking down at the pidima, but Maria could tell that his attention was stuck behind his eyes, thinking about where he went wrong. "Will this overheat it?" she asked. Victor was zoned out. "Hun, will this overheat it if we leave the lights running?" Victor continued to stare blankly.

"Should be fine," he said. Maria felt that his clock was ticking down, so she leaned over and turned the machine on. The pidima lit up with a stunning light for the first few seconds, but then settled into a grayish-blue glow. Seeing what was happening beneath the window of the pidima, Victor's eyes came back to life as the color in his face replenished. Maria leaned in beside him, also unable to look away from the phenomenon.

Just below the surface of the glass was a brightly lit area of moving, flowing shapes that shifted back and forth across a thin field. With the backlight in place, it almost appeared to be a hologram of squirming organisms, existing on a totally weightless, flat plane. Each individual shape drifted around like splotches of oil floating on water, however, they seemed to move with a purpose or intention. Maria and Victor knew immediately that whatever they were looking at were true living creatures.

Chapter Twenty-Three
Needing More Information

"What do you mean they were alive? How would you know that?" asked John with the most enthusiasm that he had shown all day.

"Yeah, and what do you mean they were flat?" asked Mark.

"I was just going to ask that," said Alice.

"They were flat. We truly believe that this was the second dimension," said Maria.

"But how could you possibly measure that? You can't measure something that exists without depth," said John.

"Obviously we did not realize all of this at once, but we had over a month to study these creatures and we're sure that they existed as independent life. Beyond that, we don't know much because we could not figure out how to communicate with them."

John began pacing as he attempted to visualize everything. Mark was also having trouble figuring it out, but Alice held back a grin, more or less enjoying all of it. "Do you have any pictures or videos of them?" she asked.

"Unfortunately, we had the same amount of luck as Dr. Robins when it came to any video evidence," said Victor. "Something about trying to record the light-plane distorted the camera to the point where the picture was just whitewashed."

"What did they look like?" asked Mark.

"In the very narrow field that we could see them, they appeared just as splotches that flowed in and around each other. I would best describe them as some sort of aquatic, liquid being as opposed to any solid shaped animal that we are familiar with," said Victor. "Have you ever seen a red blood cell magnified in the bloodstream? They almost seemed to fluctuate and flow with their surroundings."

"What were your methods at attempting communication?" asked John.

"We tried a number of things," said Maria. "The first issue came when we tried to move the pidima from its platform. Victor lifted it off of the rack and the second that it moved an inch, the creatures disappeared completely. The lights were still on, but there were no longer any figures. We later realized that the dimension was so flat and precise that the light had to shine only at its exact location, or it would be invisible.

"It took us three days of adjusting the pidima millimeter by millimeter until we finally got it right and the organisms popped back into frame. That told us just how precious its location was. So, with that understood, we carefully bolted the rack into place and sealed the panel to the bars. Our next question was finding out if we could make physical contact with them. With the pidima secured, we removed the glass pane. The plan was to touch a small needle somewhere in their field of vision to see if we could get a reaction, however that strategy evaporated right away too.

"As soon as the window was removed, we felt an intense heat pour out of the machine, and along with it, the image of the creatures faded away. We reattached the glass, and about five minutes later, they became visible again," said Maria.

"Maria and I talked about it for a few days while trying to remove it a few more times, and we came to the conclusion that their dimension is on a completely different energy level than our own. That's why light does not escape from their world into ours and vice versa. We were right in front of each other the entire time, and we could not see them. But the mixture of the pidima's heat and light was a perfect blend to connect our world with theirs. So, we thought about a few different ways of how we could encapsulate their existence while still being able to connect with physical touch, so we created this." Victor put his hand over the glass cube that enclosed the original pidima. "It was not easy figuring out the measurements or even building it, but we discovered that this four-by-four glass terrarium gave us enough room to work while still protecting us from the radiation. It also allowed for perfect light and temperature control.

"In fact, even after we had it completely sealed with our prodding instruments inserted, the open space was still letting too much heat escape from the sweet spot of their dimension. And that's why you're seeing the extra gear strung around the corners," said Victor.

The original pidima was still sitting on top of the rack in the dead center of the terrarium cube, but the top window was stripped and the bottom panel was removed, leaving the lighting field in the middle open and bare. And in each of the eight corners of the cube were smaller machines that looked like modified pidimas, all pointed directly at the original, center machine.

"In order to keep the whole environment at the right energy level, I created eight more small pidimas and planted them in the corners. But the difference is that these all only work one way. Instead of bouncing light back and forth, the light shoots straight to the center light field and keeps it healthy with heat and light. Now, we could open it up as much as we wanted and not lose any visibility."

Alice walked up to the container and examined it from all sides. She peered inside with the smile of an entertained child. She grabbed the handle of the long poking device and toggled it back and forth. "Please tell me you could touch them with this thing," she said.

Victor could not help but smile himself. "Yes, we did finally make contact."

"How did they react? Were they solid to touch?" asked John.

"Not exactly," said Maria. "We did not poke the creatures directly as a precaution of not harming them, but we placed the prodding needle essentially right in front of them where they could sense its presence. And to the best of our determination, it scared them. They scattered in all directions, bumping into each other and squirming away. A few times, we trapped them in the middle of two needles, but they squeezed their way around them without a problem."

"Over the following days of making contact," said Victor, "the creatures started behaving different, almost intelligently. They formed synchronized patterns, following each other in circles, forming up and breaking apart, basically communicating as far as we were concerned. All of a sudden, the dimension started to slowly fade away. Hour by hour, it was getting harder to see. So, I adjusted the corner pidimas and intensified the light until we could see it clear again. The next day, they started up with new and different patterns, and visibility started fading again. This happened for a few days until I found myself adjusting the pidimas every hour. And then one day, the dimension was gone. It disappeared and we've never been able to get it back since."

"It sounds like they may have somehow blocked you out," said Mark.

"It did seem that way, but we don't understand how considering their simplicity," said Victor. "Then, the real twist came about three days after it was gone. We came in to find that all of the pidmas were turned on and in use. On top of that, whatever turned it back on had plugged in the original surge box and was shooting jolts through the machines. Naturally, we checked the cameras and found a complete time lapse. Twenty minutes of video were missing, and we found no evidence of anyone entering the building from the lobby cameras. We now refer to that day as *Incident Number One*. It happened exactly forty-two days after we first turned on the pidima. And everything else that followed patterned forty-two days after that."

"Let's contact the government. We need to tell someone about this," said Alice. "Do you still have connections with NASA?"

"Absolutely. In fact, we wasted no time informing them about everything," said Maria.

"What did they say?"

"Well, considering that we had no videos, pictures, or proof, they threatened to confiscate all of their old equipment back. They didn't want their name tied up in any of our 'ghost stories,' and insisted very harshly that we keep all of this to ourselves. They now look at us as the quacks who have been wasting their equipment when other schools would die to have it. Obviously, we were appalled by their response, but it's also reasonable to see their point of view. After that, we cooled down on reaching out to anyone of authority. We decided that if no one was going to help us, then we at least needed to keep our lab and figure it out ourselves."

"Did you ever think of other ways that you could have communicated with the flat creatures?"

"We tried," said Maria, "but besides their synchronized movements, we couldn't even figure out how they communicated with each other. Frankly, we're not even sure how a flat object could have functioning organs. How do you communicate with something that doesn't have eyes, ears, or mouths? I thought about the possibility of trying to use math as a communication tool, but we did not have nearly enough time with them to decide what kind of math they could comprehend, if any. They obviously had a form of collective intelligence, but math or organized measurement is certainly a stretch."

John thought it over. His hungry mind felt again impatient. "Can we draw some sort of outline of their movements to the best of your memory? I'm curious about their patterns. "

"Honestly, Doctor, why don't we call it for today? We've given you all a lot to think about, and we could use a rest ourselves. Maria and I have taken the liberty of getting you three dinner reservations at a nice place down the road. It's all on us, drinks included of course."

"Thank God," said Mark.

"Take your time and relax. When you get back, we have some dorm rooms furnished for you to stay over. We can get into everything tomorrow."

"Thank you, that sounds great," said Alice. John shook his head, understanding their fatigue.

"That's very generous. Thank you," said the doctor.

"Let's all meet here around ten," said Victor. Mark and Alice gathered their things and made their way up the aisle. John puttered slowly behind them. When Mark and Alice filed out of the door, one last question hit John.

"Just out of curiosity, if you had done this experiment with the pidima in another lab in the building, do you think we would even know that this dimension was here right in front of us?"

"Doctor, if we had positioned that rack one inch to the right and turned the machine on, you would never have met us. This chain reaction wouldn't exist," said Maria.

John nodded, turned, and walked away.

Chapter Twenty-Four
<u>An Explanation To The Layman</u>

"I've grown up always drinking what people consider disgusting beer, but I love it," said Mark. "I've never gotten into any of that craft or foreign shit."

"There are so many of them though. I'm sure you can find something that you like," said John.

"Not a chance, Doctor. I like what I like. You can't help what the heart wants."

John smiled at Mark's stubbornness. "How about you, Alice? You don't drink beer?"

"Only as a last resort. I like whiskey, but I know what you mean, Mark. I'll never change my cigarettes. I've been smoking *Fayette Lights* my entire life. Had my first one in eighth grade, and I've never gone a day without one since."

"Well maybe you should write them a letter," said John. "I think they owe you a couple free packs for all of your loyalty."

"That's another thing," said Mark. "I can't smoke regulars. My best friend in high school, a guy named Shoe, gave me my first menthol. I never looked back. To this day I can only smoke these." Mark took a long puff from his cigarette. The three of them were comfortably set up on a patio table at Choo's Bar and Grill. As Alice smoked her own cigarette, she crossed her left leg over her right to rest it, and revealed a gorgeous pair of high heels.

"Whoa. Nice boats you got there," said Mark.

"Thank you. I stole them from my husband."

"Why does your husband own a pair of women's shoes?" asked Mark.

"I found them in my closet just before he kicked me out of the house. I'm guessing he was planning on giving them to his girlfriend, but I figured that I would take them as a first payment of alimony."

"Oh man... Sorry to hear that. My ex kicked me out of the house too. I probably deserved it more than you, but at least you got shoes out of it. All I stole was toothpaste on my way out," said Mark.

"Trust me, I'd rather have stayed in the house given the choice. I can imagine you would trade the toothpaste back too."

"I would trade it back for a lot of things that I used to have."

"Well, you enjoy your healthy teeth and I'll enjoy my expensive shoes. Maybe we can convince ourselves that we're better off, huh?" Alice looked down at her feet as Mark sat back in his chair. Neither of them said a word or even took a drag of their cigarettes for close to a minute. John sat behind his sunglasses and really observed them.

He saw two people who were truly unhappy and unsure of what to do with themselves. They scraped by day after day trying to find some way to just get back to even, but they continued to only sink deeper. John wondered what it was all for. To him, human nature was an even bigger mystery than the Universe itself. Sometimes, he believed that most people experienced much more bad in their lives than good. He often said that the question that received more lies than any other on Earth was: 'How are you?' And sitting there with Mark and Alice, he felt the incredible weightlessness of three people who were totally alone, sharing a table.

"John."

"Yes, Alice?"

"What the fuck is the second dimension?"

"Oh my God, thank you!" shouted Mark, as if he had been desperately wondering all along. John smiled.

"Have you ever heard of it before?"

"Yeah, a million times, but I never actually knew what it meant. I know we're in the third dimension, but honestly I've never really thought much about that either."

"Well, then it's good that you asked," said John.

"I understand the simple math of it, like a square versus a cube," said Mark, "but I don't understand how they claim to have 'found the second dimension'."

"Yes, I'm curious about the finer details of that myself, but I can at least explain my own understanding of it. As you said, Alice, we live in the third dimension, specifically the third spatial dimension. We also live in one dimension of time, but that's a separate term. The third spatial dimension means that we exist in a space that has length, width, and height, or depth if you prefer.

"Every direction that we travel is either forward, backward, side to side, up and down, or anywhere in between. As far as we're concerned, that means every possible direction, but it's not exactly that simple. Things in the second dimension only perceive and experience length and width. Height or depth does not exist to them."

John took out a pen and drew a line on a napkin with two dots on either end of the line. "The first dimension is only length. So, if I have point A and point B like you see here, the first dimension only exists on the line between these two points. In other words, it has no depth, no width, no real area. If anything lived in this line, it could only travel forward and backward. Not side to side, and not up and down. As far as it is concerned, none of these other directions are even real. It would have to be impossibly flat and impossibly thin. Even by drawing a line, it now has a little bit of width, but imagine no width at all. Does that make sense?"

"Yeah, but how could something exist if it had no shape? Where would it be?" asked Alice.

"Well, that's a good question. Try to think of the first dimension as the absolute basic unit of space. It's very hard for us to imagine something existing in a place that has no volume or form, which is what makes quantum physics such a frustrating field, but in a way, the first dimension may be where everything comes from," said John. "Have you ever heard of string theory?"

"I think I have actually," said Alice.

"Yeah, I know it's a theory in physics, but I have no idea what it's about," said Mark.

"It's commonly referred to as 'the theory of everything,' and without getting too lost in the weeds, essentially string theory breaks down all of the fundamental particles of force and matter into terminally basic entities called strings. If these strings exist, then they are smaller than anything in the Universe, and depending on their individual vibrations and behaviors, they develop into what we know as the basic particles."

"Doctor… I build scaffolds and drink beer for a living. You're losing me here," said Mark.

"Understood. I apologize, and frankly I couldn't explain this in under a year. The point I'm making is that these *'strings'* are called strings because they are nothing more than the immeasurably thin lines between point A and point B. Our minds fill in the blanks and create lines or strings, but in reality, they would not be visible in any way. Therefore, they exist in the first dimension."

"Wow," said Alice as she glared wide-eyed into nowhere. "That's confusing."

"Try taking it on for a career," said John.

"I don't think I'll do that."

"So, to take it further and move up the dimensional ladder…" John drew a second line on the napkin perpendicular to the first line, forming a cross. "By adding this line going side to side, we now have width. So, the second dimension is length times width. Anything within this dimension can move backward, forward, side to side, and anywhere in between. So, it has infinite space to move in all of the directions on a flat surface, but it can never go up or down. Furthermore, if there were a creature within this dimension, it could be as long or as wide as it wanted to be, but it would be completely, unimaginably flat.

"Think about a piece of paper. A piece of paper is a flat rectangle that has a few inches of width and a few inches of length, but it has no depth or height. It's flat. Except here's the real difference: If you picked up the paper and looked at its edge, you would see a tiny bit of thickness to it, probably somewhere near a tenth of a millimeter. It's extremely thin, but it does have some height. And that's because it's a solid object in the third dimension. But if you turned up an object from the second dimension to measure its edge, you would see nothing. It's absolutely without depth. And according to our young, new friends, that's what we're dealing with. A society of flat, weightless creatures."

"Like a hologram basically?" asked Mark.

"Yes. That's actually a great analogy. Imagine if you projected a picture onto a flat whiteboard. You can see it from an overhead view, but you could never look at it from the side."

Alice picked up the napkin and looked at it. "So, our dimension is just these two directions plus height?"

"Correct, but imagine just what adding height means. Take the cross in the picture and then add a line going straight through the middle up and down. Obviously, we can't draw a line into the air, but you get the idea. As far as we are concerned, adding depth means that we can travel in any direction possible, and It also adds mass into our existence. Without depth, there can be no weight, right?"

"But if these creatures can't see up or down, then how could they even know that we are here? What would we look like to them?" asked Alice.

John cleared a space off of the table. He took the flat coaster from under his beer and put it down in front of him. "Imagine that this coaster is a living being in the second dimension, and the dimension itself is this flat tabletop." John put his hand on the coaster and slid it back and forth around the table. "It can travel in any direction back and forth and side to side." He then slid it into another coaster and stopped. "As far as we would think, if it ever met another two-D object, they would collide much like we do if we walk into a wall, but there is an issue with that. If they have no depth, then there really isn't anything to bump into, so who knows if there would be any disruption? But just for our explanation, let's just assume that they could not pass through each other.

"Now imagine what an object would look like to them. Here is a circular coaster and here is a square coaster. If the circular coaster could somehow see in front of it, and it ran into this square coaster, it would only see the very front of it. I have issues believing that a flat object has the ability to see anything, but just for the sake of understanding, pretend that it sees only the front line of the coaster in front of it. It has no vantage point above or below it to see anything more.

"And here is where we tie in to all of this. If this coaster is existing on this flat table, and I hold my hand one inch above it, the coaster will never know that I am here. It has no ability to see up. I could wave my hand above and below it all I want, and it will never see me. However, If I lead the coaster to the edge of the table, and then I rub my hand flush with the edge of the table, then all of a sudden, I am entering the second dimension.

"So, the coaster can now see my hand, but remember that only the thinnest, flattest, tiny section of my hand is even within its dimension. So to them, my hand is only a flat, thin line like everything else, except that line will shrink and grow as I move my hand further down the edge of the table, and that is because my arm gets wider and thinner at different sections as it passes my fingers, into my palm, into my wrist and forearm, until I fully dip below the table and disappear altogether."

"Then I can see why they are so frightened by us," said Mark. "If Maria and Victor were sticking needles into their homes that came out of nowhere, I guess I would be scared too. You'd think that you were seeing ghosts or demons."

"Exactly," said John. "And just think about the control that we could have over them. We actually have a bird's eye view of everything in their world. Whereas we can only see the front side of objects in the third dimension, we can see every side of objects in the second dimension at once. You can see all four sides of this square if you look down at it. Imagine if something appeared in front of you, but along with your face, it could see your back and your sides all at once."

"I guess I understand why Maria and Victor had such a tough time trying to communicate with them," said Alice. "Even if you were trying to help them, how would you ever get them to see that? It would be like trying to talk with insects."

"I think it would be even harder. It would be like trying to talk with bacteria," said Mark.

"Well, now that I'm beginning to understand it better, Maria made a really good point. Maybe trying to use math would be a good way to get through to them. Don't you scientists call math the language of the Universe?" asked Alice.

"Yes we do, but try thinking about it on such a simple level as theirs. Even if they have some extremely basic form of math, so much of its functions would be lost on them. Think about cubing a number and what that actually means," said John.

"You mean because the numbers would get too big?"

"Well yes, but it's even more than that. If you take the number four and square it, you get sixteen. But what that actually means is that you can take a four-inch line in length and square it by multiplying it by a four-inch line in width. That gives you a literal square of four inches on all sides and sixteen square inches in the middle. But if you cube the number four, you're not just multiplying four by four by four, which is sixty-four. You're actually taking a four-inch line in length, multiplying that by four-inches in width, and then multiplying that by four-inches in height. That gives you a cube that measures four-inches in all directions, and sixty-four cubic inches inside, like a Rubik's Cube that has four tiles in every direction of its six sides.

"But here's where we run into trouble: A second dimensional creature has no idea what a cube is. It could fathom a square, but a cube is impossible. So, right there, you run into an immediate problem. How can you talk math with something that does not share the same mathematical laws with you?"

"Are there higher dimensions than ours? How many do you think there are?" asked Alice.

"According to string theory, ten, but who knows? It's still all very hypothetical."

"Maybe God lives in the higher dimensions. That would explain a lot," said Alice. John nodded his head. Even though he was far away from Alice on the spectrum of beliefs, he did not find it his place to argue or dispute someone's faith. He knew that he would never change anyone's mind, and he didn't exactly want to. Furthermore, he always left room open for the possibility that maybe he was wrong and the theists were right.

"Yeah, maybe He does," said John.

Alice, Mark, and John sat at the patio for another couple of hours, having more drinks and countless more cigarettes. They eventually got off of the topic of dimensions and math, and into more menial terms such as life, the Universe, and existence itself. For once in a very long time, John felt like he was a part of something meaningful.

***

When they arrived at the dorm rooms where they would be staying the night, John was exhausted. His brain had run a full marathon of questions, ideas, and thoughts. He had not felt like that since the first few weeks of his graviton studies, long before it fell off the tracks. With a deep sense of mental satisfaction, he laid down flat and fell asleep.

Chapter Twenty-Five
<u>The Night Visitor</u>

Alice was tired, but unable to calm her passing thoughts. The conversations from the day continued to spin around in her head. Although she understood John's explanation of the second dimension much better than she thought she would, Alice still had a feeling that they were all missing something. She could not connect the flat creatures discovered in the lab to the massive creatures that came out of the orbs.

She sat up in bed and turned on her bedside lamp. The room illuminated. It was an empty dorm room that she assumed housed freshmen because of its simplicity and lack of a private bathroom. The only thing that really stood out in the bland living space was her stolen pair of shoes that sat next to the door. The reflection of the light happened to shine directly off of their glossy black finish and straight back into her eyes. The combination of the glare and the eight glasses of whiskey from dinner conjured up an evil headache. All of a sudden, Alice did not like the shoes. In fact, she could not stand the sight of them. They reminded her of her husband. And just like Tom, they had a fake, glossy exterior, but they only caused pain the longer she wore them.

Alice hopped out of bed, walked over, and grabbed the shoes. She opened the lid of the small trash can, slammed them in, and then closed the lid on top. She figured that no one would be emptying the trash until the start of the next school year, but maybe the young lady that moved in next could get some use out of them. She stomped her way back to bed, turned the light off, and flopped down. She took a few deep, meditative breaths to calm down and then she shut her eyes to go to sleep.

After about five-minutes, she felt a slow Breeze move through the room, followed by the sound of a soft touch on the metal trash can. It took her thirty seconds before she convinced herself to turn the light back on, but she finally did. She looked across the room and saw her shoes sitting on top of the closed trash can lid, shining right back at her just like they had moments earlier.

***

Mark was experiencing a similar headache in his own room, but he hardly noticed it because he was fighting back tears. When he drank too much, he usually found himself lying in bed and looking at the few pictures that he had of his son, Jake. This normally would not make him cry, but over the past couple of weeks, Jake was not returning his calls. Mark figured that Jake's mother was to blame, but it was hurting him all the same. He grabbed his sock from the floor and blew his nose, then lit a cigarette. When he first arrived in the room, he stretched a shower cap around the smoke detector. He never traveled anywhere without his smoke-assistant shower cap. After he tired out from crying, he put the pictures back into his wallet and stared at the ceiling.

As he smoked his cigarette, Mark found himself calming down. His headache relaxed, his back loosened, and his mind started to drift. He began to imagine the sounds of windchimes until he sank into a point of near sedation. He was of absolute peace. If he had thought about it for a second, the sudden spell of serenity would have spooked him because he had no reason to feel at ease. He never felt at ease. But he had no chance to think about it. He had reached nirvana.

His body grew warm, and the inside of his eyelids produced the vision of a swirling pool of colors, colors he had never seen before. He became numb. The loneliness and pain that he had felt about Jake just a minute ago was gone. He heard a gentle Breeze pass by his ears as the sound of chimes and bells gently echoed in his mind. And just before he completely gave in, his cigarette burned down to the filter and smoldered between his fingers.

Shouting in pain, he sat up and threw it across the room. Mark stuck his scolded finger in the glass of water next to his bed, and then nursed the burn with his other hand. As he winced in grief, he glanced up and saw that there was a soft glow of Colors passing by his room. Shining through from beneath his door appeared to be the same celestial colors that he had envisioned in his mind. And as they passed by, he heard the faint sound of bells and chimes. He stood up and slowly made his way to the door.

***

John was sleeping soundly. He forgot to turn off the bedside lamp, but the light had not affected him. Half of his clothes were still on, and his travel bag sat open on the floor. The room was silent except for his breathing. The only thing that was out of the ordinary was the metal ball. John had taken it out of his pocket when he came into the room and placed it on the desk. It immediately hopped off and rolled to the heavy frame of the bed where it now remained.

John rolled over onto his side and readjusted. Although he was not fully awake, he heard the ball make its way from the bed frame over to the desk. He kept his eyes closed, but took auditory notice of the movement. As mysterious as the ball was, it was predictable. It never moved once it positioned itself onto its target. John was comfortable and not in the mood to get up and check it out, but in the midst of thinking about it, he decided that the light was becoming an annoyance. He opened his eyes and looked at the lamp. The brightness caused him to squint. He sat up. From his position, he could now see the ball on the floor, which caused him some concern. The ball was not touching anything. It just sat still on the floor about one foot from the desk.

John leaned over and looked down, confused. He reached his foot down to the floor and gave the ball a shove toward the door. It rolled for a short distance before slowing down and stopping, then it switched directions and paced back over to the same spot one foot away from the desk. John was befuddled. Just as he thought he was starting to understand its nature, it did something so out of character. He began a mental debate over whether or not to abandon his best night of sleep in months and really delve into this mystery, or just give himself a break for once in his life and lie back down. But before he could reach a verdict, the ball rolled itself into the base of the desk.

John picked his foot up off of the ground and gathered himself on the bed. Silence filled the room. He stared at the object with a sense of insecurity, almost as if the ball's behavior had been some sort of betrayal of John's trust. Then, right in front of John's eyes, the desk lamp's pull chain jerked itself down and the light shut off.

John yelled out a profanity as he shuffled to the opposite side of his bed and put his back against the wall. The room was black. He breathed heavily in and out, unable to move or make any decisions. A small Breeze grazed the window shades, giving them a shudder, and then moved across the room. John then heard the ball rolling in the direction of the Breeze, although he knew that it was not wind that was guiding it. Realizing that his ears were his only sense of judgment, John reached over and pulled the lamp chain, turning the lights back on. The ball followed the Breeze all the way to the door and bumped into it. As soon as it made impact, the ball rolled its way back to the bed frame and froze itself to the wood.

John leaned over and picked it up. Out of all the crazy thoughts that rushed through his head, the one that held rank was an idea that the ball was not just rolling around aimlessly, nor did it turn off the light. Something else turned off the light, and the ball followed it.

Still breathing heavily, John did his best to listen for any more signs of activity as his eyes searched the room. From the crack beneath the door, a glow of striking, bright Colors shone through. They stayed for only seconds, and then made their way down the hall. John snapped to his feet and ran to the door.

He powered his way into the hallway and ran in the direction that the Lights were headed. He made it only in time to see a glow of Colors turning the corner. He pursued them at the best pace that a sixty-two-year-old man could.

★★★

The only idea that Alice had to calm herself down was to pull out her Bible and read it, hoping that it would distract her from her self-moving shoes. Unfortunately, she could not make it through more than one sentence at a time without digressing back into panic. On top of moving themselves, she never heard the trash can lid open or close. This told her that not only did the shoes go from being inside of the trash can to outside of the trash can, but they accomplished it by moving through solid metal. If they simply walked out like a pair of phantom feet, then she may have been able to fall back asleep, but this act of pure voodoo was a little hard for her to shake off.

She finally worked up the muscle power to get up and walk over to get a closer look. Sure enough upon inspection, there were no holes in the can, and the way that the shoes had been carefully posed on the lid told her that whatever did this had a sense of style. Alice grabbed hold of a pencil that had been left on the desk beside her, and poked one of the shoes. After a few prods, she concluded that the footwear did not bear life, nor was it animate.

With the pencil as a tool, she swept the high heels off of the bin, and then used it to pop open the lid. The can was empty, just as it was when she arrived. With no explanation, she attempted to trick herself into believing that she never actually threw the shoes away, but just placed them perfectly on top of the lid and went to bed. But before she could even finish that nonsensical, self-deception, she grabbed the shoes and slammed them into the bin again, and then smashed the lid on top. She knew much too well that she did not want to believe what was happening, but she had no choice in the matter. *What happened, happened,* she told herself.

Uncomfortable beyond discomfort, Alice walked back to bed, slid under the sheets, and turned to face the trash can. She stared at it as if she was looking at a rabid animal in her path, hoping it would leave her be and just go on its way. Her breath trembled as she prayed that the night would quickly end so that maybe John or Mark would knock on her door to wake her up, but she knew that sunrise was hours away. It was not until a tear dripped down her cheek that Alice understood how helpless and alone she actually was. A small, warm Breeze passed by her, caressing her ear and neck. She tightened up as she felt a conscious presence make its way to the other side of the room.

The trash can began to move, inch by inch. It slid across the floor from the wall into the middle of the room, as if being pulled by an invisible force. Alice's eyes widened as she watched the shoes get removed out of the still-closed, solid bin and raised into thin air above it. They hung weightless for three long seconds, and then dropped onto the metal can, causing a loud crash. The shoes fell to the ground along with the toppled lid. Alice shot out of bed and ran out of the room. She sprinted down the dark hallway. When she made it to the far side, she turned the corner and slammed into a large body, knocking both of them to the floor. "Jesus Christ!" shouted Mark, taken by surprise. Alice climbed up to her knees.

"We have to get out of here, now," cried Alice.

Mark painfully rolled onto his side. "Did you see it too?"

★★★

John made his way up the stairs to the fourth floor of the dormitory. The last that he saw the Lights, they had entered the staircase door and headed upward. He was behind, but he had stayed close enough to not lose them. He reached the door that would lead into the highest hallway in the building. The door had a frosted-glass window that read *Fourth Floor: Resident Assistant Suites.* Even though the glass was too opaque to see beyond it clearly, the glow of the Colors still shined through. John had figured out that whatever this Thing was, It was not trying to evade him. It had shown enough intelligence and swiftness in his room to avoid being caught by an aged man in a barefoot chase. This Being was leading him, and maybe even drawing him in. But John had made too many thoughtless decisions in his hotel room in Amber Rock to decide to fear away from this one now. He had committed weeks ago.

He grabbed the doorknob with his right hand. His left tightly clenched the metal ball. As soon as he began to turn the knob and pull, the Colors vanished and the hallway went dark. He stepped forward. A few old exit-lights by each end of the hall created a dull, red illumination throughout the space, and John looked into its void. There were three doors on each side of the hallway, wide open, and one closed door that faced him from all the way on the opposite end. Which room that the Entity had chosen was a question to which John could only guess, so he thought about checking them one by one.

He began down the stretch of the hallway taking slow, silent steps. Without warning, all of the six open doors slammed shut with violent strength. John recoiled. He quickly regretted taking on the pursuit alone, but it was far too late to turn away. He was going to meet the Visitor, and they both knew it. John looked ahead to the closed door at the other end of the hall and took a deep breath. Just like a reoccurring nightmare, he was well aware of what was about to happen before it actually happened.

The doorknob twisted itself, and the door slowly opened. A sinister creak echoed towards John, offering a most unwelcoming greeting. From inside the black abyss of the room, a colorful Light began to glow and pour delicately into the hallway.

In an effort to not insult his Host, John fixed his posture upright and walked straight forward. Every nerve in his back and shoulders trembled, afraid of being snatched from behind at any moment, but he kept onward. Something told him that this Thing would not present such a theatrical introduction, just to saturate it with a cheap scare. So, putting all of his trust into the hopes of polite formality, he stepped to the threshold of the door. He recognized the room to be a bathroom, and he was immediately awestruck. The glossy tiles glistened and shined from the reflection of the angelic colors. It was visual ecstasy. From that point on, John made no more voluntary decisions. He was driven by an instinctive lust to see more.

The deeper he was pulled into the room, the more he was overwhelmed by its grandeur. From floor to ceiling, he was surrounded by an existence that no earthly man had ever experienced. As the unfamiliar hues filled his sight, a perfect breeze embraced his skin and filled his lungs with a scent that he could only describe as pure. He was relieved of the burden of walking, and now glided across the floor. When he came to a stop, he stood in front of the large bathroom mirror, and there It was. John was face to face with his Summoner.

Instead of seeing his reflection in the mirror, he saw a great figure. It was a large Eye, but nothing like the eye that he had seen in his hotel room weeks ago. This Eye was one of majesty, and reverence. It was filled with a brilliant, gold spiral that went on endlessly. Christened along the spiral were diamonds. They were countless in number, but each one was placed so perfectly that John could only imagine that its design was the work of an ingenious creator. The Eye itself was surrounded by an infinity of lush feathers, each one bearing a different color that John had never seen and could never understand. When the Eye blinked, the feathers came together, creating an abundance that John could only describe as *Magnificence Itself.*

He was drunk with admiration. All of his extreme emotions boiled to the surface: amazement, wonder, fear, intimidation, and most profoundly, the urge to worship. John had little control over his mind, but there was just enough left to question who or what this Apparition was. He exerted all of the energy left in his body in an attempt to speak, but nothing came out. And just as his thoughts and feelings began to turn petrified, his ears were enriched with a harmony of bells. The sound was divine. It put John at ease, and somewhere through the bells, he heard a message. The Visitor said to John, "Do not be afraid."

John felt all of his muscles loosening. His body was giving in. And the Being spoke again. "I am who has known you, and I have found you." John's heartbeat thundered as his body weakened, and the metal ball pulled away from his grip. "I am here, John. I am with you."

As John lost his last bit of strength, the metal ball shot out of his hand and drove itself into the mirror. John fell to his knees, and the mirror shattered and sprayed glass in all directions. The colors and lights disappeared, and the room went completely dark.

"No!" shouted John. He put his hands to the floor in order to stand himself up, covering his palms in broken glass. He rose to his feet and scrambled for the mirror, which was now just an exposed board. John slammed his blood covered hands onto its surface and pounded it. "Come back! Who are you?!" He slammed the board over and over, screaming into the wall. "Show yourself! Why are you here?!" John beat the surface over and over until his hands went numb. He fell to the floor and screamed in rage. Blood leaked down his slender forearms as he continued to slam his fists into the ground. The metal ball clung still to the heavy countertop just above his head.

Chapter Twenty-Six
The Farmer From Nebraska

Enoch sat down at the dinner table with his wife, Delilah. There was enough food for both of them to have their fill, but comfort was brief. Their stock was dramatically less than it was the year before, which was only about half of the year before that. The farm was drying up and the crops were dying.

Enoch had been an excellent farmer and agriculturist for all of his life, as was his father and grandfather, but something was happening that was beyond his control. Three quarters of his corn yield had diminished over the past five years because of nutrient depletion in the soil and environmental pollution caused by larger commercial farms in the surrounding areas. Enoch had learned a traditional style of cultivation, and his personal and professional ethics prevented him from ever considering any type of synthetic fertilizer as a means of enriching his soil. His father often spoke of learning the proper method, and then applying that method to God's natural Earth the way that all of man had done before them. And although Enoch would always put his faith into God's hands, his mind would often wander into the crudeness of human nature and recognize the very real problem that was in his own hands.

His harvest had gotten so low that he could no longer keep up with the demands of shipping his product nationally, and now he only survived by selling to the local markets around Sutton and its neighboring towns. And after being forced to lay off the last of his laborers as a result of the previous winter, he now worked the fields alone, desperately searching for a solution to the looming demise.

He and Delilah sat quietly and ate their corn and beef, as neither one of them had spoken a word since they concluded their prayer of grace. Silent dinners were common. They had been through countless trials over their forty-year marriage, this one being the last that they could handle. Living as an interracial couple in twentieth-century Nebraska brought more unwanted problems to their doorstep than they could ever ask for, but in the long run, it only pulled them closer together. The real test came about twenty years after wedlock when they believed that their prayers had finally been answered.

For two decades, they tried to conceive a child. It became apparent after five years of failure that one or both of them was infertile, although they never found out for sure because they did not believe in seeking medical help for something that was not up to them. Instead, they took to their knees every night and asked God to reveal to them His plan. As time came and went, they made peace with the fact that raising a child was just not going to be a part of their journey, to which Enoch never complained. He accepted their situation and carried on in the way that he knew how: If he would not contribute fruitfully to the world by way of children, he would produce as much vegetation and livestock that his land would allow. Delilah, however, had harder feelings about it.

For many years, she found time to cry when Enoch was working out on the farm. Most days, she could spend at least one or two hours crying alone before having to resume her share of the work around the property. Enoch and his employees were in charge of tending to the fields and cultivating the crops as they grew. He also handled all of the business deals with the companies that he sold his corn to. Delilah spent most of the day feeding and taking care of the animals as well as keeping up with the housework. She also had a love for quilting, knitting, and reading.

On an average week, she read two or three books and knitted a dozen blankets, hats, and scarfs. Once a month, she made a trip around to the local schools where she gave all of her homemade quilts and clothing to the children and spent a few hours teaching them how to make clothes for themselves. But as the years went by, she found herself creating less garments, and crying much more often. She hid her emotions from Enoch because he did not understand them.

One night, he awoke from sleep and found her crying. When she shared with him how sad she was that she could not get pregnant, Enoch reacted sternly with her. He demanded that she accept God's plan for them and that by getting emotional, she was questioning the Lord's intentions. He insisted that she was reading too much nonsense and threw all of her books away so that she would only read the Bible. He firmly believed that all of her questions could be answered directly from the experiences in the texts. From then on, if he ever did find her weeping, she would lie and say that one of the school children was sick, and she was sad for the family. She slowly became a shell of a woman, deeply saddened by years of repressed emotion. On the outside, she programmed herself to drift through her daily tasks, but on the inside, she was a desolate soul. But that changed on her fortieth birthday.

After weeks of nausea and irregular menstrual pains, she finally succumbed to professional medical help. She was pregnant. At the moment of discovery, she was flooded with an unequivocal rush of euphoria, relief, and regained faith. Her body underwent a transformation from a lifeless discontent to a blissful spirit of purpose, all in the matter of one second. Even Enoch felt an awesome breath of liberation that he never thought he could feel. He was happy to be a father, and he was truly happy that Delilah would be a mother.

They gave birth to their son, David. David was born with beautiful, blue eyes that were different from any ancestor he had before him. His eyes lit up every room that he was ever in, starting with the hospital room where he was born. But his body was not perfect. He was born small with weak bones and inadequate muscle tissue. The doctor warned them that he would be susceptible to physical injury throughout childhood and most likely well into his life. His weakened state also left him vulnerable to immune issues down the line. Enoch feared for David, as he only knew life through the eyes of hard labor. Delilah, on the other hand, did not care. She took one look into David's perfect face and knew that he would find his own way. She knew that he would go far away from the farm and influence the people that he met along the way. Even on the day of his birth, he had enough hair to tell that it was bright and curly, and his looks alone would get him as far as he wanted to go.

He grew up smiling. As Delilah tended to her work, she would bring young David everywhere with her around the farm. His calming presence even seemed to have an effect on the animals. They took to him like their own, never making a sound or a quick movement once David was around. By the age of two, he became fascinated with the pigs. Delilah let David help her feed them every day, and while they ate, they allowed David to pet them. Because of his small stature, Delilah was very careful as to not let him get trampled or hurt, but the day came where she stopped worrying. As if they knew that he was so fragile, the pigs would move gently around him, doing little more than rubbing their snouts to his head, and David loved them and enjoyed their friendship.

At night, when Enoch was finished with his work, he would walk David through the endless cornfields. He would teach him about how the plants grew the way that Enoch's father taught him. As Enoch held David in his arms and felt his child's love, Enoch too grew to understand that David would never take over the farm. He had a special heart, and Enoch decided that David needed to use his heart somewhere else in the world. From that time forward, Enoch understood that he was not just working to feed his family. He was working to give his son a different life.

By the time David was four, he was growing just as the doctor had predicted. His head was of normal size, but his body was weak and trembling. This led him to be top heavy and clumsy, but where he lacked in physical ability he made up for in creativity. Over the years of watching his mother create blankets and quilts, and watching his father build structures around the farm, David spent time creating his own toys. With Enoch's help, David had handmade a series of small model airplanes out of the extra wood from his father's workshop. He was recently obsessed with the variety of airplanes that were flying over the farm.

David played with his toy planes for hours at a time. Eventually, he discovered that he could open his bedroom window and throw the planes outside to see them fly. After a number of them broke, Enoch helped him put some more thought into the wing design that allowed the bodies to catch more air. He also found some lighter wood that he could thinly carve by hand. Soon enough, they had a convoy of trinket aircrafts for David to sling around at his leisure.

For weeks, he threw them out of the window and watched them sail down into the front yard, then he would run down the stairs, collect them all, and do it again, always trying to sail them further.

During that same summer, the farm had a booming production of crops due to a full year of mild weather. Enoch used the extra profits to expand the farm's livestock and house more animals, so he began the construction of a forty-foot barn adjacent to the house. David watched the men build the structure more each day.

One Sunday when there were no workers on the property, Enoch worked alone in the fields and Delilah sat on the porch sewing. She bought a white silk handkerchief from the suit store in town and made something special for David. Using colored silk thread, Delilah hand sewed a golden *D* on the handkerchief's face, and she outlined it with different bright colors. Even before it was finished, she knew that it was perfect. *A fit for King David,* she thought.

David had been throwing the airplanes out of his window all morning. She watched him run in and out of the house to collect them over a dozen times, amazed at his constant entertainment. On his fifteenth run, she got up to make a phone call to their church. David found himself alone in the yard, gazing up at the massive barn. It was only about halfway through construction, but the framework was complete as was the bottom level. With his airplane in hand, he was struck with an idea.

David entered the barn and had a look around. There were stalls built to hold the different animals, and there were a lot of windows and doorways to encourage airflow. All of it excited David, as he knew that he would soon be able to spend time with his father and help care for the animals.

He explored around until he reached the tall staircase. Looking up at the giant, he realized that his father never carried him up to the next floor. He made his way up the tall incline one stair at a time. The second story had a full floor installed but no proper ceiling or walls connected to its frame. However, there was a twenty-foot ladder that stood from the base of the second floor to the top of the barn's highest arch. David had no fear of heights and recognized a perfect launching point for his airplane. He stuck the plane in his pocket and made his way up the ladder.

His legs wobbled from the tough upward climb, but he took his time with each step. When he reached the peak, he could see the entire farm. There was nothing but corn as far as his beautiful eyes could see. With the sun high in the sky and shining on the green grass below him, he felt a small breeze blowing towards the house. Using his wit, David wound up and threw the toy in the direction of the breeze and watched it glide over the yard like a real airplane. He cheered and laughed as he saw that it had gone further than any previous flight from his bedroom window. He immediately thought about how to throw it even further on the next toss.

David started down the ladder. When he took his second step, his foot slipped. He reached for the barn's frame and grabbed on. The ladder shifted and toppled over to the floor a full story below. David wanted to scream for help, but he needed all of his strength to hold on. He hung on for four or five deep breaths until his small fingers gave out. David fell forty feet straight to the ground and slammed down feet-first. After his legs hit the ground, his ribs shattered, and then his head whipped to the dirt. His broken ribs punctured his lungs and David remained still on the ground for three minutes until he suffocated and died.

Delilah came out one minute later and sat on the porch, unaware that her son's body was lying only forty yards away from her. Enoch dashed out of the cornfields. He ran towards the barn and screamed for his son. From some distance away, he saw the ladder fall and then David fall after it. Delilah jumped out of her chair and ran over to meet her husband. Enoch arrived at his son's body and shouted David's name as loud as he could. David's lifeless eyes stared up at Enoch, but they no longer had their perfect blue glimmer. They were grey, and his mouth was full of blood. Delilah fell to the ground and shrieked the sound of absolute dread until she could no longer breathe. Her gift from God was dead.

★★★

Twenty years later, neither one of them had come close to fully recovering, but Enoch was much better about hiding it. He continued his daily work and just focused on each problem that came next, which in this case was the failing crops, but something still held them together. Enoch would say that it was continuing in God's plan that got him through everything, and Delilah would say that she agreed, but that was a lie.

Delilah was never the same after David's death. She would forever blame herself, and Enoch's apparent recovery did not help. She never understood how he could just carry on and never cry about the past, but she could not bring herself to ask him about it either. She learned to swallow it and accept her misery in the hopes that she would meet her son soon enough after her time was up.

When she absolutely needed to cry, she locked herself in David's room and cried on his bed. She always used the special handkerchief that she made her son to wipe up her tears. David never got the chance to cry into it himself, and something about the silk's touch on her cheek made her feel close to him. She decided to keep it a secret from Enoch. He would only see it as a sign of sadness for his wife and most likely ask her to get rid of it, so just like her emotions that she kept hidden away in her chest, the handkerchief would stay between only her and her lost son.

And there they sat, alone in the same room, eating in silence, waiting for the next day to come.

Chapter Twenty-Seven
Running Sleepless

"Something turned it on again!", exclaimed Victor. "Whatever you all saw in the dorms turned on the pidima. After the first time the machine turned itself on, I've always left it unplugged. Something plugged it in last night and turned it on." Once Victor and Maria awoke to the phone calls from Mark, Alice, and John, they rushed over to meet them at the lab. The sun was not set to rise for another hour.

"This must have happened before It visited the dormitory," said Maria. She turned to Mark and Alice. "Did either of you see what It looked like besides the colors?"

"I didn't even see the colors. I didn't see anything, but I was definitely not alone in that room," said Alice.

"I think John was the only one who got a look at It," said Mark.

"But did you feel anything?" asked John. "Besides the Apparition, I experienced a feeling that I've never felt in my life. Despite losing all control over my motor functions and decision making, my body was in a complete euphoria. I've never taken any drugs before, but I can't imagine that they could match how incredible that felt... I can't put it into words."

"As a man who has taken many drugs, I have to agree with you. I felt that when I was laying in my bed before my cigarette burned me," said Mark.

"The only thing I felt was fear," said Alice.

"How are you feeling now, Doctor?" asked Maria.

John's hands were wrapped up in bandages. The bleeding had stopped, but the cloth was covered in dry blood. John, however, paid them no mind. "I feel enlightened." John sat and said nothing for a moment, but his eyes indicated that he was of total cognizance. "Something happened when I looked into that Eye. I was given knowledge. I can't quite explain it, but my mind was opened."

"Please expand on that, John. My brain is running on no sleep," said Alice.

John stood up and began pacing. "There are numbers sitting in my head right now. A simple equation. *X equals four to the fourth power.*"

"X equals four to the fourth?" repeated Maria.

"Do you remember, Alice, when I explained what it meant to square a number and cube a number, and how that relates to a lower dimension?"

"Yes."

"Well, I think that you were right to ask if there are higher dimensions than ours. If you recall, taking the number four and squaring it meant that you could actually create a physical, four-by-four square. And if you multiply that by four again, then you could create a cube, but that is where our visual understanding stops.

"We don't imagine anything more complex than a cube because we've never seen anything more complex than a cube. But I think that's exactly what has been coming to us." John walked to the white board in the front of the room.

"If you take that cube of four and multiply again by four, you're not just coming up with the flat number of two hundred and fifty-six. You are creating the fourth dimensional version of a cube."

"A tesseract," said Maria.

John looked at her and nodded. "Precisely, Dr. Delphi. A tesseract. Are you familiar with a tesseract, Victor? Some also refer to it as a hypercube."

"Actually, a few years ago, Maria showed me some Carl Sagan videos where he was explaining shapes in higher dimensions. I wouldn't say I understand it all that much, but I am slightly familiar."

"I thought that the fourth dimension referred to time," added Mark as he lit a cigarette.

"Yes and no, Mark. In layman's terms, you're not wrong," said John. "We exist in three dimensions of space and one dimension of time, and that is why they refer to time as the fourth dimension. But what we're dealing with here are spatial dimensions.

"We need to start thinking in terms of progression, and the best way to understand how to progress from one dimension up to the next is by adding right angles." John walked to the white board and drew a line. "Look here. In the first dimension, you have a line that represents length, and if you add one more line perpendicularly to create a right angle, you now have length and width. That gives you an entire flat field in which anything can exist. You can illustrate this field with a square. If you take the square and add another right angle that travels north and south, you have the third dimension in which depth or height is now available within your field of space. Obviously, we represent this with a cube.

"Now, to get to the fourth dimension, we want to take our cube and add another right angle, but how do we do that? Every possible direction that a new angle could exist in is already covered in three dimensions. This is where we look to our friends in the flat world. As far as they are concerned, their dimension has every direction fathomable, length times width. There is no up or down to them, but little do they know that we are here right above them existing in a world of length times width times depth. We are right here and they can't see us. And just like them, there is another direction above us that we cannot fathom, and it is in that direction that the next right angle is laid to create the fourth dimension: a complex reality that stretches in ways that our minds cannot understand, but they are there, and they exist in the space of the tesseract." John pointed to the square that he drew on the board.

"Let's look at a pattern. The flat square has four right corners. If you fold six squares over a hollow space, you create a cube. The cube now has eight corners. To make a tesseract, you must take eight separate cubes and intertwine them in such a way that you form one even shape." John drew a tesseract on the board to the best of his unartistic abilities. "As I've said, it is not possible for us to fathom a fourth dimensional object because it spreads out into areas that we could never see, but this is a rough translation of what one would look like to us. We see one smaller cube inside of a larger cube with all of their corners connected. If we were in a higher dimension, however, all eight of these cubes would be of the exact same size, simultaneously existing as one object in the same way that six squares on the sides of dice make up a cube.

"If you count all of the corners, you get sixteen. A square has four, a cube has eight, and a tesseract has sixteen." Mark walked up to the board and examined John's drawing as the others took it in from where they were standing. Maria made her way over to the incident location map and saw it in a way that she had failed to in the past.

"Oh my God," said Maria. "Look at the map. He's right." As everyone looked over at the pins and strings of yarn, they began to understand exactly what John was getting at. "Each location is a corner of the tesseract."

"Where do you see that?" asked Victor. Maria began pointing out positions on the map.

"The lab was location one. That makes up the bottom corner of the outside cube, then the storm in the sky would be the top corner. Louisiana is the second set of corners, Idaho is the third, and Mexico is the fourth. Then, Mark's incident in Oklahoma makes up the bottom corner of cube number two, and the storm makes the top. New Mexico was the next set, Doctor Robins' hotel room and storm made the third set, and finally…" Maria took two more pins from the edge of the board and stuck them into the map. She then connected the two final threads of the yarn into the new locations and completed the second cube of the location map. "Sutton, Nebraska. And that's it. That makes the tesseract." Maria backed up and saw the map in its entirety.

"Wow, Doctors. Not too bad," said Mark.

"But why are we seeing these things pop up in the corners? What's so special about those locations?" asked Alice.

"I think they saw Victor's light pidima model and then created their own. His machine is basically a glass cube with access points attached to each corner. They're entering our world in the same way that Maria and Victor entered the world of the two-dimensional creatures," said John.

"But how did they find us? How did they know to start building their hypercube around our lab?" asked Victor.

"Maybe they didn't find us. Maybe the pidima found them," said Maria. "What if when we turned on the machine and illuminated the second dimension, our dimension was simultaneously illuminated to them? Maybe the energy and light that was needed to connect us with the flat world was the same amount of light and energy needed to connect us with their higher world."

"They looked at your pidima terrarium and used it to make their own, only it's billions of times larger," said John.

Victor stood under the map and drank it in, almost dumbfounded. "I can't believe they stole my idea."

"I think it's very important that we take a moment to realize what has happened here," said John. "We have discovered a cross street in the Universe that spans at least three functioning dimensions, and who knows how many more? This is more than a significant discovery. This could help explain every unanswered question that we have ever come across. I mean, this could be a solution to the mystery of dark matter. Dr. Delphi, what if the unexplained effect on gravity in galaxies is not actually dark matter, but rather the effects of that galaxy's mass existing in a higher dimension where we cannot see it? If gravity was able to travel across dimensions, then maybe it could carry the unseen weight that influences the odd speed of revolution. This is incredible."

Maria sat down and placed her face in her palms. "You're right. Everything we know, or don't know, is going to be different."

"Whoa, whoa, whoa," said Mark. "Before you guys get all goddamn scientific, can we discuss what this means for us, please? I mean, are we going to die or what?"

"I agree a hundred percent," said Alice. "How long do we have to live?"

"Well, that's one thing I may be able to answer," said Victor. "I can't tell you whether or not we're going to survive, but I can at least give you a timeline on when they will complete the whole thing. The next incident in Nebraska will happen in a few weeks, and then if Dr. Robins and Maria are right, the tesseract will close forty-two days after that. So, we have just over two months to get a handle on the situation."

"That shouldn't be too hard considering these things can move in and out of our lives without us even knowing," said Mark.

"Unfortunately, Mark, you're not wrong," said John. "If they are building this tesseract as a means of a portal or doorway, then we will be faced with some uncomfortable truths. The first being that it's big. It spans thousands of miles, and if they build it to completion, they will not only have total access to walk around our world, but they could possibly have the ability to pull us into theirs. It will be an open door greater than the size of middle America. So, the obvious question is, what do they want? Do they want to help us or hurt us? Are we so insignificant that they will just treat us as the study of a simple experiment, or do they have personalities that could sympathize and coexist with us?"

"What kind of culture do they have?" added Maria. "Are they a science-based society? I have to imagine so considering the structure they're building. And how about their math? Our most intricate theories may look like first-grader homework to them. If the flat creatures in the second dimension practiced mathematics, it would be so simple to us, like counting your fingers on one hand. The higher dimension is probably that much more complex than we are."

"Forget about their numbers. What if they want to get rid of us?" asked Victor. "At any point that Maria and I chose, we could have driven that needle right through one of those flat creatures, or just ripped them out of their world. There is nothing that they could do about it.

"We don't believe in violence of any kind, especially to something so small and fragile. Our goal was to make communication with the flats and learn about them, but think about if someone else would have been in our position. Countless examiners would have no problem extracting and dissecting those things. Imagine if the government had made this discovery. Why assume anything different about the four-dimensionals? They could exterminate us."

"But they could also help us," said Alice. "What if the flats trusted you? You could change their lives tremendously. If you really had the ability to pick them up, then you could relocate them to a better place or create a new way for them to travel. You could build them structures like they've never seen. The fours could do the same for us, and probably a lot more."

"That's great, but it's always easier to destroy than to build. Which one is more likely?" asked Victor.

"In the times of facing an impasse, it's always best to consult the evidence. We need to strongly consider the examples that we have experienced ourselves," said John.

"That's fine. Let's start with the river in Mexico, or the fish crisis at Lake Sumner? They took away the drinking water of an entire village, and they caused a fish population to multiply to the point that they died from a lack of space to move," said Victor. "How did any of that help? The only argument against their antagonism is that maybe they don't care about us for good or bad. Maybe clearing that river helped them build their structure."

"But the river recovered to half-volume," said Maria. "The village is still surviving. I can't figure out why they would dissect fish and then overproduce them, but I think we should still keep an open mind about everything before we absolutely decide that they are hostile."

"How about we ask Mark about their hostility? He almost got killed by one of these things," said Victor.

"But they didn't kill him," said Alice.

"No, they didn't, but it certainly didn't feel too good. I think I have to side with Victor on this one." replied Mark.

"If you're arguing that they're *good* because they did not kill him, Alice, then what was the positive side? I don't think throwing him onto concrete helped him very much," said Victor.

"Well, I can't say that I know why they did what they did, but I have to assume that if they wanted him dead, then he would be dead. And on that note, if that Thing last night wanted me dead, then I would be dead. I don't doubt that it wanted to scare me, but I don't think death was Its motive."

"What was Its motive then? You said it yourself that you felt nothing but fear," said Victor.

"I did, but everything made a lot more sense to me when I went back into my room to call you guys," said Alice.

"What happened?" asked Maria.

"Do you believe in God?" asked Alice.

"I do."

"Victor?"

"Yes… Sort of."

"Well, I certainly do," said Alice. "And I've been trying to figure out His involvement in this since the night that I saw that light in the sky. After hearing all of your stories, I don't think I've found it yet, but I do know that whatever came into my room last night was not sent by God and, in fact, I sensed evil. I've had one experience in my life where I believe I crossed the presence of something demonic, and last night felt very similar to that."

Mark began to laugh. "I'm sorry, Alice, but I'm not really seeing the connection of how this makes you feel any better. If I believed in God or demons, I think your story would send me running back to Oklahoma." Mark continued to laugh.

"Do you remember last night when you came into my room and we called Maria?"

"Yeah," answered Mark, still giggling.

"Well, I didn't say anything about it, but you may have noticed me looking for something around my bed. I flipped the mattress trying to find it."

"Yeah, I guess I remember that. I just thought that you went a little crazy."

"That Entity stole my Bible."

"What do you mean?"

"It stole my Bible. I was reading it to try to calm down after the first time my shoes moved. I remember exactly where I left it on the bed, but it was gone when we went back into the room."

"Ok… So then why are you arguing with Victor? I think you're only convincing me more that we want nothing to do with these things," said Mark.

"I'm just giving my opinion that we're dealing with many separate beings. I can't make up my mind about the worms because I have not seen them myself, but as far as last night goes, that Thing was evil. But when evil is present, God is present. I don't believe that God would allow us to face such an incredible danger without a plan of His own, and if that's the case, it's not our place to get in the way," said Alice.

"But with all due respect to your faith, I don't believe in God, so what should I do? It's very strange that it took your Bible, but in my opinion, it's still up to us to figure this out, and there's a lot at stake here," said Mark.

"That's fine if you don't believe in God, but just think about the difference of our experiences last night. John felt euphoria, and you felt euphoria. I felt fear. I think we may have all been deceived. Something wants to confuse us. When it comes to evil, nothing is what it seems."

"As someone who works in a peripheral of science, I'm supposed to keep an open mind to all possibilities. I hear what you're saying, Alice, but I don't feel a whole lot better about it, and I strongly disagree with leaving the decision up to God," said Victor.

"Why would it take your Bible?" asked Maria. The group shared a long silence. No one knew exactly what to think.

"I've been hiding something from you guys," said John from a seated position. "I apologize for the dishonesty, but I had to figure it out for myself before opening it up for debate." Everyone looked to John. "After the large centipede creatures came to my room, the first time that I saw the orb, they took a book from me too. I had a notebook that I kept as a journal for my studies on the graviton. I went through a lot of mental debate about what they could possibly want with my hand-written book. It drove me crazy.

"Eventually, it showed back up, and I began to question if it had ever even been gone. I started a new mental debate on whether or not any of this was actually happening or if I was just losing my mind. But then I looked at the book closer. As I turned the pages, I began to notice that all of the numbers that I had written had been removed. All of my words were still there, but anything involving numbers was gone. Dates, equations, everything. It was as if they were never written at all.

"I tried piecing it together using the cameras that I set up in the room, but as we now know, they were no help at all. And then finally, after my meeting with the worm in my room, I found this." John pulled out the metal ball from his pocket and revealed it to the group. "This was waiting for me in my closet."

"What is that?" asked Maria.

"I've been trying to figure that out for a long time, Doctor Delphi. I can't decide its exact purpose, but I can show you what it does. What would you say is the heaviest object in this room?" asked John. Everyone looked around the lab. There was a lot to choose from.

"I'm not sure. Do you mean just one solid object?" asked Maria.

"The top of the work desk is made of solid granite, and the base is some type of steel. NASA built it for heat resistance when Maria's father was working here. I have to imagine it's heavier than anything else in here," said Victor.

John placed the ball on the ground. As soon as he lifted his fingers, the ball rolled directly to the island desk. Everyone was amazed. "Very good observation, Mr. Delphi," said John.

"How did you do that?" asked Mark.

"I didn't. The ball moves by itself. Whenever I enter a room, the ball favors the heaviest object in that room, and it rolls itself towards it. It took me a little while to figure that out, but it only failed me once."

"What happens when you leave the room?" asked Maria.

"As soon as I cross the threshold of a doorway, it will find the heaviest object in the next room and gravitate towards that. I've been testing it for weeks."

"But why do you have it?"

"I'm not sure yet. It clearly has functionality, but I haven't been able to grasp its purpose. I'm beginning to think that it's some sort of tool." John walked over and picked the ball up. "If you're looking for any signs of a positive outreach from these worms, I would submit this as evidence."

"You got anything else from the beyond?" asked Mark.

"Just the ball. And again, I apologize for not being open about it. From here on out, anything that I know, you will know," said John.

"What did you mean when you said that it only failed you once? You mean the ball miscalculated the weight of an object?" asked Maria.

"Last night, I had it clinging to my bed frame, but once the Entity entered my room, the ball began to follow it around. I could not see It at this point, but I could hear It and feel It, and the ball followed It until It left the room," said John.

"Well, Dr. Robins, to me that stays consistent with what we have been saying all along," said Maria. "If these creatures are from the fourth dimension, then they would have a mass that's infinitely greater than ours, just like we are infinitely greater than the flats. Even if a billionth of a fraction of them entered your room, it would outweigh you or any other piece of furniture."

"When you saw that thing in the mirror, John, was it stretched out in all these imaginary directions that you were talking about?" asked Mark.

"No, but I would not expect it to be either. We live in a three-dimensional space. Even when a fourth-dimensional creature enters our space, we will still only see a third-dimensional cross-section of them. If Maria or Victor were to stick their hand through the world of the flats, the creatures would only see a flat, two-dimensional version of them. Basically, we only see a summarized form of these things, but there's much more complexity just above the surface."

Victor stood up and walked over to a drawer in one of the desks. He pulled out a menu. "It looks like we have a lot to talk about here. Let's order some food and a lot of coffee. If you're all only here through tonight, then we don't have much time to spare."

"That sounds terrific. And if you'll excuse me for just a minute, I need some fresh air and a cigarette. Alice? Care to join?" asked Mark.

"Absolutely."

★★★

After a break and a replenishing breakfast, Victor, Maria, Mark, Alice, and John debated back and forth for hours. They broke down all of the known incidents into extreme detail and examined every possible angle with the intention of finding a motive. With the majority of them running on no sleep, they pushed themselves to delirium until dinner time when they broke for one last meal. Just after eating, John checked his cellphone for the first time all weekend. He listened to an alarming phone message before returning to the group. Maria read his look. "Doctor, are you okay?"

"I have a situation back in Colorado," said John.

"What's the matter?"

"I have messages from the hotel where I am staying and from the police. Apparently, my room has been broken into. Everything has been ripped apart and destroyed."

"Jesus," said Mark.

"What do you think happened?" asked Maria.

"Well, given the situation, I'm leaning towards thinking that it was not a simple break-in."

"You think it could have been one of the fours?" asked Victor.

"I don't think that it's out of the question. I have to head back tomorrow and deal with everything. It may take a few days to clear it all up. I don't really know the extent of the damage or the legal process since the police are involved."

"I'm worried, John. Maybe it's not the best idea to stay in the room alone," said Maria.

"Yeah, I think you're right. There's another hotel across town that I can stay at."

"Let us know how we can help," said Victor. "As far as we're concerned, you can stay out here with us as long as you need to after you take care of everything."

"Thank you, Victor. I'll get back here as soon as I can," said John.

"I have a flight tomorrow night, and I'll be working all week, but I can be back for a longer stay by next weekend," said Alice.

"Maybe it's best if we just plan to meet again next Saturday. That will give everyone enough time to clear their heads and come back fresh. Are you staying or going home, Mark?" asked Victor.

"Well, I still have a few months of unemployment left, so if you think you need a hand around here, I'm happy to stay."

"Absolutely. We live in a duplex, so you can stay in the apartment below ours. That way you're not alone if this Thing decides to come back."

John sat down at the table with everyone. He pushed back his uncut hair and took a deep breath. "Before we leave here, it's very important that we understand one very real possibility. If in fact we are dealing with a malevolent species, we could be looking at the death of our kind. And I do mean all of humanity. Whatever route we decide, whether we sit back and watch this happen, or if we try to stop it, we cannot lie to ourselves. The decision that we make in this room will astronomically affect the future of everything.

"First, we need to establish their intent. If they are trying to help, then it may just come down to a waiting game. Perhaps we can even help them if we figure out how. But if we decide that we need to try and prevent them, we damn well better figure out how to do that. And I will give you every brain cell and effort that I have, if that's what we agree. But then again, it may not be up to us at all. From what I've seen, personally, I don't think we have a chance against these things if they choose to get rid of us. They have complexities and intelligence so far beyond our comprehension. They think outside of us, and they move outside us.

"And let me be clear. We should try with every option afforded to us to decide our own fate, but I fear that the ultimate decision will be left out of our hands and in the hands of our guests. Basically, in this equation of circumstance, we are no longer men and women; we are goldfish in a bowl. The only question is: Will they give us fresh water, or will they dump the bowl?"

Chapter Twenty-Eight

-

The two creatures looked one another in the eye. They knew what had happened, and they knew how it would be perceived. Their plan was being obstructed by the Speaker, but they had no ability to communicate it through words. There was too much time between the present and the completion of their machine. Speeding the pace was no option, nor was physical interference with their Enemy, but without action, failure would be certain and permanent. Through a shared understanding, they decided that reaching out was the only means to success. But in a competition for communication, words outweighed numbers by the ton, therefore, a demonstration of practice would be their only chance at winning over their simplistic counterparts.

Chapter Twenty-Nine
<u>A Signature From The Poet</u>

The room was torn to shreds. Everything that John owned was mutilated and doused in the stench that he had come to know all too well. The walls were splattered with a foreign goo, and the furniture was flipped and uninhabitable.

John spent hours speaking with the police. It was obvious enough that he had nothing to do with the ransacking, but just for good measure, he was equipped with a signed alibi from all four of his new friends along with an agreement of their cooperation if need be. So now, accompanied by two officers and the hotel manager, John searched around the room in the hopes of salvaging anything that was not ruined by the intruders. He stashed away his cameras and computer before he left for Wisconsin, although there would be no video evidence regardless.

All of his clothes were ravaged, as well as the few small possessions that sat on his bedside night table. The picture frames and paintings, all of which belonged to the hotel, were shattered and broken. The refrigerator was gutted and smashed, and the lightbulbs were suspiciously unscrewed from the lamps. But there was one piece of value that was left completely untouched. Right in the middle of the floor, nowhere near where he left it, sat John's journal. It was spared of all wrongdoing.

After leafing through the pages, John determined that it was indeed unharmed, which surprised him considering that whatever had entered his room this time clearly took special care of the notebook.

After another lengthy conversation with the police, John decided that he would find a different hotel to stay at for the next week, which was a relief for the hotel manager. And lucky for John, he was friends with the bartender at a very nice hotel just across town.

★★★

John had become quite used to anything unusual or bizarre, so when he entered the lobby of the Davidson, the only real emotion that he was feeling was an excitement to have a drink with his friend, Jack. He got settled into his new room, which in person was very old and gorgeous. He still did not believe in ghosts, but he could see why a spirit would want to spend an eternity there. The wood framing and walls that surrounded him possessed a character that could only be earned after a century of existence. He placed down his travel bag and journal, and headed down to the bar, hoping to see a friendly face.

When he sat down, he saw no one of familiarity. It took the barkeep nearly ten minutes to tend to his order, and she did so in an unfriendly and straight-to-the-point manner. He watched her pour his red ale, along with three other drinks for the customers around him and then move on. Even when he tried to hold her attention to ask if Jack would be working, she moved right along to the next order.

John took a few gulps and walked his drink over to the more polite woman who was working the front desk. "Excuse me, ma'am. I was wondering if you knew whether Jack would be working the bar tonight."

"I'm sorry, Dr. Robins, this completely slipped my mind when you checked in, but he actually took a leave just a few days ago. He left a note for you. He mentioned that you would be around sometime in the next week or two."

"He took a leave? Is he okay?"

"Yes, Doctor, he's fine, but he had some family business that came up unexpectedly. He was hoping that you would have the chance to read the note." She handed it to John.

"Thank you, ma'am," said John. He walked over to a couch away from the front desk and opened it up. He immediately chuckled at the presentation. It was short with sloppy handwriting, but otherwise decently written. The mystery of Jack continued.

Dear Johnny,

I hope you get this letter, buddy. I wanted to hear about your trip and find out what's going on with those people from Wisconsin. Anyway, my brother Eric had a hiking accident out in California. He's okay, but he banged up his legs pretty good. I have to fly out there and help him out with his recovery and take care of his small business in the meantime. At the moment, I ran out of money to pay for my cell phone, but I'll figure out a way to contact you at some point. And hopefully I'll be back out there before the summer ends anyway. Keep yourself safe with whatever you guys find. Also, talk to a maid named Cindy. Another ghost sighting happened the night that you left. Phantoms lurk those hallways, man. Start writing down some math problems to help us prove it. See you soon, buddy.

Jack

P.S. - I stole some money out of the register and bought you a six-pack with it. The new bartender sucks, but it's already paid for, so make sure she gives it to you. It's in the bar fridge under your name. Good luck, Bro!

John smiled and folded up the letter. He already missed Jack, but he figured that there would be no sense in wasting his gift. So, he walked over to the bar and waited fifteen-minutes to receive his beer, and then he retreated to his room to get some thinking done.

He had some thoughts of heading back to Wisconsin in the morning, but then he remembered how hectic the last weekend had been. Furthermore, his current room looked to be the perfect, quiet sanctuary for working out new ideas. His first order: Drink four out of the six beers and watch some television. Step one went just according to plan. He caught a few episodes of a British mystery show that he had never heard of, and he impressed himself by solving most of the mysteries before the lead character detectives could, who both happened to be sober unlike himself.

With a newly earned confidence from solving crime, John turned off the television in the hopes of applying his skills to his own life. He stared at the ceiling for quite some time, thinking about the awesome difference between himself and the creatures from the higher world. The alcohol dulled anxiety out of the equation and left him feeling only awe.

For the first time, he could see Alice's point of view. *Maybe they are here to help,* he thought. So far, there was little evidence to support this position, but given the infinite nature of the world above, he knew that anything was possible. He also gave weight to the idea of there being a contradiction between the visitors. Perhaps one fraction of them were friendly and the other were contemptuous. Or maybe it was even more complicated than that. And as he explored deeper into the abyss of possibilities, his grip on consciousness weakened, and he wandered off to sleep.

***

Twelve-hours later, John awoke. The world outside was noisy and awake. He sat up in bed and felt a stiffness in his back from the long slumber. His lack of exercise and flexibility was taking its toll. Not yet ready to get up, he scanned the unfamiliar room, wondering what he would start his day off with. His travel bag was across the room, the television remote had somehow ended up on the floor, and the few books that belonged to the hotel all seemed too thick to commit to on such a groggy morning. But his journal happened to be sitting on the night table just beside him.

It had been some time since John had really read through his work, and for good reason, but he thought that maybe it had been long enough since its conclusion that he could get something out of a good skim. He opened it up to page one and read his manifesto. It sent him right back in time to the ambition that allowed him to embark on such a task. He intended to just flip through, but as he read each day's entry, he could not help but get caught up in every discovery and emotion that he had experienced the year prior. An hour later, he found himself in the heart of his slipups, and all of the frustration and anger that he lived through came back as if he was feeling it for the first time.

He suffered through every single log in that last month and felt all of his hard-earned confidence rinsing away in the tides of self-pity. But some small part of the new John held on because as he concluded the final day's notes, he reminded himself that if he had not agonized through every last mistake, then he would have never been delivered the gravity tool from the visitors. And maybe he would have never been visited at all. And like a small triumph from the last man who finishes the marathon, John finished reading the last sentence and breathed a sigh of relief knowing that, if nothing else, he at least finished. Feeling an uncharacteristic sense of entitlement, he turned the page to start a new series of entries, beginning with that very day. He wanted to tell the second half of the story, which would hopefully be the more important half. But as he turned the page to a fresh sheet, he noticed something strange in the texture of the paper. It was slightly thicker than all of the sheets before it.

He held it at eye level and saw that there were actually two leaves stuck together. John carefully peeled them apart. As they lifted, a sweet-smelling aroma graced his nose. A pinkish-red glaze lined the edges of the page, acting like a fine, soft glue. The glaze was laid in a formulated, yet effortless pattern. The more that John peeled, the more that he was leveled by the beautiful and complex design. When he finally had the paper separated, he was greeted by a text that took up the top portion of the page followed by a drawing that filled the bottom two-thirds.

When his eyes settled enough to read the text, he understood that it was a poem. He read it out loud.

"They came to find your numbers.
For then, they will need you no more.
They will complete their working machine,
and then open the unclosable door.
They will devour your brain, discard your body,
and then, they will seize control.
But I know your real worth, John.
It is not your numbers. It is not your mind.
Your true value is your soul."

John read the poem over and over again. His heart flooded, specifically when the Author had addressed him by name. Images of the great Entity from the bathroom mirror flashed into his mind accompanied by screeches of alertness. No longer could he feel alone or unwatched. And as his eyes drifted to the drawing below the poem, he realized that it was not just a picture. It was a signature.

At first glance, it was an extremely detailed illustration of a beautiful meadow, covered in flourishing plants and creatures of marvel, like an intricate rendition of the Garden of Eden. With only what appeared to be the workings of a charcoal utensil, the Artist managed to tell a story for every countless organism that was represented in the image. Even the water and air seemed to come alive as John's eyes wandered the extraordinary landscape. He could feel the breeze and smell the sweet moisture. And as he pulled back to take in the picture as a whole, John recognized the outline as the shape of the letter *D*. If he moved his eyes quick enough, all he could see was the capital initial, but if he allowed his gaze to settle, he would again be lost within the endless terrain.

Eventually, he was able to pick himself up out of the trance and return to his hotel room. He set the book down, knowing that he could spend the rest of his days exploring the boundless world if he was not careful. He looked across the room into the vanity mirror and stared back at himself. Right then, he knew how little he actually was, and the only weapon that he and his friends had at their side was the unreliable, worthless blanket of hope.

Chapter Thirty
<u>Vocations And Roles</u>

"I've more or less kept my mouth shut about everything," said Mark. "Frankly, I don't know what the hell I'm talking about when it comes to science and physics or whatever, and you guys seem to be on top of it, but I have had a few thoughts that I wouldn't mind sharing," Mark had a tall American light beer in front of him on the bar. Next to him sat Maria and Victor, each with their own cocktail.

"Sure. Go for it," said Maria. "We can't explain any of it, so we'll listen to anything."

"Okay, then I have a theory, as you guys might say. Have you ever looked at building plans or blueprints?"

"I don't think so. Not in person at least," said Victor. Maria shook her head *no* as she sipped her drink.

"But I'm sure you're aware of the basic idea. They're plans for a three–D structure drawn onto a two–D piece of paper. As a carpenter, I've seen thousands of them. I've never drawn them myself, but in order to do my job I need to understand them as well as anyone. Some guys I know will never bother to learn how to understand architecture, and those guys will never be great carpenters. The point I'm making is that when you guys looked down into the flat world, you had no idea what you were looking at, but if I'm getting a clear idea of what you saw when you looked through your machine, it sounds a lot like looking at building plans. I'm not saying that you were looking at actual blueprints to a building, but you were seeing an extremely basic world from an angle that allowed you to see its full makeup.

"So, my theory is that whatever came looking at us from the other world is something that understands the craft of building. They're the architects and carpenters of their society. If you were able to take a picture of what you saw and show it to myself or someone in the business of building, then we may have been able to better understand their landscape and constructions.

"Just think about it, if these worms are smart enough to knowingly build a pathway into our space, why would they send the ones that didn't know what they were looking at? You guys didn't know what you were seeing because you're not architects. You're a bunch of science nerds... I mean, no offense." Maria and Victor looked at each other and agreeingly shrugged. They were in fact science nerds.

"I don't know a thing about science, but I do know how to look at a two-dimensional piece of paper and build something three-dimensional out of it. And if everything in their world is just one step higher than ours, then it would make sense that they would use three-dimensional paper to draw out their ideas as opposed to our flat paper. So, if they looked at our three-D world, they probably understand what they're looking at."

"Wow... That's actually logical," said Victor. "It also might explain why they move around here so easily."

"Do you know any of the architects from the buildings that you've worked on?" asked Maria.

"Not personally. I may have met one or two down the road, but I'm not close with any of them."

"Sounds like we should all learn a little architecture," said Maria. "I was up last night thinking about what Victor said. I don't know whether or not I think they want to help us or hurt us, but if they do wish to hurt us, then we need a doomsday plan. Maybe from a builder's perspective, you could help us figure out if the tesseract has a weak spot."

"There's a million books and videos on building demolitions. I only know how to build them, but how hard could it be to knock them back down?" asked Mark.

"But let's not forget, this isn't exactly a solid structure that we can touch. It's more like metaphysical coordinates that may or may not be connected in some way," said Victor.

"Well then maybe you two and John should figure out the technical details, and I'll start working on the plan to raze this thing if that's what we decide," said Mark.

"Speaking of them, what are your thoughts on Alice?" asked Victor.

"What do you mean?"

"I mean her and the whole good versus evil thing. Don't get me wrong, I believe in God, and maybe if he does exist, he can see all of this, but I don't think waiting around for Him to save us should be our go-to plan," said Victor.

"Well, it goes without saying that I couldn't agree more. I mean, with all due respect, I don't think there's a chance that God exists, but even if He did, who's to say that we're any more important to Him than the worms? Let's do everything we can to control our own destiny here," said Mark.

"Any thoughts on this dear? You're the only one who seems to be on her side," said Victor.

"I understand where she is coming from, and if my mother were still around, she would have said the exact same thing as Alice. But I'm not ready to decide either way. Right now, I'll keep an open mind, but side with caution."

Chapter Thirty-One
Where Did The Time Go?

John woke up distraught. The clock read *nine A.M,* but he had no recollection of falling asleep the night before. He had no recollection of anything the night before, or the night before that, or the night before that. The last thing that he could remember was the morning that he had woken up and discovered the mysterious poem and signature.

He sat up and realized that he was fully dressed, including his jacket and shoes. As he got up, his journal tumbled off of his lap, still open to the poem. He picked it up and looked again at the intricate sketch. As soon as his eyes hit the paper, it occurred to him where his last few days and nights had been spent: staring down into the Artist's endless world. Even now, after countless hours of admiration, John was still seeing details that he had not yet noticed. The bizarre and beautiful creatures that he found so interesting to observe seemed to multiply since his last visit, and the closer that he moved the book to his eyes, the bigger and more spacious the world became. At every angle that he shifted the page, he opened up a new valley to explore, more shades of texture, and a grander feeling of excitement. Then the book slammed shut.

John threw his journal across the room. The last crumb of self-control that he possessed saved him from another day-long viewing. He looked at the clock again, expecting to read *five-after-nine,* but instead was smacked in the face. The clock read *twelve-thirty P.M.* John could not believe it. Hours had flown by in moments. Seconds even. If not for some thread of instinct in the back of his mind, he could have been lost in the page for days.

His room was a small disaster. Food trays were thrown everywhere, hand towels were scattered, and every light in the room was left on. But he could not remember when he found the time to eat or who even brought the food to his room. Looking at all of the dysfunction, he spun himself into a web of absolute confusion, and he asked himself the most obvious question: *How long was I in here?*

★★★

John ran down to the lobby to grab a newspaper. He dry-heaved at his first sight of the date: *August fifteenth, two thousand and fifteen.* After rereading it, he vomited slightly in his mouth. But his reaction was just. Two weeks had gone by since the night that he first checked-in to the Davidson Hotel. He knew that he had lost some time due to the work of the Poet, but fourteen days was impossible.

John walked over to the nice receptionist at the front desk to find her smiling as usual. "Excuse me, miss. Would you be able to tell me the date?"

"Yes, Dr. Robins, it's Monday the fifteenth."

The information sunk through John's gut. "Thank you, miss." John turned to walk away, having no idea of where he was going.

"Dr. Robins, will you be extending your stay again?"

John stopped and turned around. "I'm sorry. Come again?"

"Will you be extending your stay again? Today is your final day with us. In fact, your check-out time is in about a half-an-hour."

"Yes, I see... And when you say 'extending my stay *again*,' what do you mean exactly?"

"Were you looking to add another extension to your stay? We haven't heard from you since last week."

Rather than trying to hide the confusion on his face, John ran the numbers in his head. Nothing was adding up, and his system started to shut down. Out of empathy, the young woman refreshed John's memory. "If you recall, Doctor, the maids entered your room last week for the final cleaning, and you asked them to extend your stay another week. I called up to you and we spoke about it."

"Oh, yes thank you… I apologize." John stood motionless as his heart dropped into his guts. Everything that the young woman had told John came rushing back into his memory. As if his mind was wiped clean and then re-imprinted, his entire experience over the last two-weeks slowly appeared back into his head. He could visualize all fourteen days while he did nothing but stare diligently into the drawing in his journal, only stopping for the occasional room-service meal. It all happened, and he was there.

"So, would you like to extend it again? We're happy to accommodate, but we only ask that you allow us into the room to clean. We respect your privacy, but we would also like to freshen the room since it has been over a week." John stayed in his head for a few more seconds before shaking out of his daze.

"Oh, no… Please, check me out. I'm sorry. I guess the time had gotten away from me. Would you allow me an extra hour though? I would like to straighten up a bit and gather my things."

"Absolutely, Dr. Robins. Take all the time that you need."

★★★

John fumbled around the room for some time before he was able to get out into the parking lot. He sat in his car and charged his cell phone after realizing that it had lost its battery well over a week ago. He listened to several messages from Victor and Maria voicing their concerns about his safety and asking him to please give them a call back. He was already a week later than he said he would be, and tardiness or truancy were not in his nature.

He then listened to a separate message from Alice asking for a call back. She mentioned that she had also not returned to Wisconsin since their meeting two weeks back, but her absence was by choice. John called all three of them separately and assured them that he was on his way. Maria and Victor answered and spoke to him at length expressing their relief that he was okay. Alice, however, did not pick up the phone, but John left her a voicemail insisting that he was heading straight back.

Chapter Thirty-Two
Suspension Of Awareness

Alice sat with her hands gripped tight to the steering wheel, although the ignition was turned off and the car was parked. She was not ready to go into the building, and she was still hopeful that she would not have to walk in alone. She was clouded with shame. She did not feel good about abandoning her peers without notice, but her intuition simply did not allow her to continue without some reflection. She had not yet come to any final conclusions, but she did decide that John was the only other person that she felt comfortable opening up to. And after an hour of waiting alone in her car, she saw him pull into the parking lot behind her.

She did not return John's call, but after he assured her of his likely arrival time in his voicemail, she showed up and waited for him. Alice felt that their conversation would be much better understood in person. She rolled down her window. "Hey," she said. John stopped as he was walking by her car. "You made it."

"Hey. I did," said John.

"You okay?"

"Sort of. I had one hell of an interesting week. How are you? Have you gone in there yet?"

"No, I've actually been waiting for you. Do you think we could talk for a minute?"

"Sure," said John. He walked around to the passenger side door and sat down next to Alice. "What's going on? Are you okay?"

Alice hesitated to speak as she gathered her thoughts. She had not said too much out loud over the past two weeks. "John… I'm scared. I'm scared about what's happening and how we're handling it."

"I think that's very understandable, Alice."

"Are you scared?"

"Yeah, I think I am… But I'm trying not to let it weigh me down. As much as we are doing our best to figure everything out, we may have absolutely no control over it. I've been working on only worrying about what I can control. You know… Whatever is going to happen will happen."

"That's why I waited for you before I came back. I don't think any of us have a clue about what's going on, but if anyone has a chance to figure it out, it's you. I'm well aware that I have more faith in religion and God than y'all do, but I don't think that it's ridiculous to consider it as a possibility. Whatever we are dealing with is clearly much bigger and greater than we are, and I don't think that it's up to us to interfere. I know you're not on the same side as me when it comes to God, but I'm just asking you to consider it."

"You know what, Alice? You're absolutely right. There is not one shred of me that believes in God, or a god, or anything supernatural. Even with all of that's going on, I fully believe that there is a physical explanation. But that doesn't mean that I'm right. For all I know, I'm completely wrong and God does exist. The truth is that nobody knows; neither me, nor you, nor anyone in that building. But you should stick to your gut. Do you know what Mark Twain said about thinking like everyone else?"

"No, I don't," said Alice.

"Mark Twain said, 'Whenever you find yourself on the side of the majority, it is time to pause and reflect.' If we all start thinking exactly the same, we will either be completely right or completely wrong. Having multiple voices is always the better option. So, as much as I completely disagree with your basis of thinking, I need you to keep myself and those three in check. We need you." John patted Alice on the hand.

"Thank you, John. That's nice to hear."

"It's true. And we also have no reason to conclude that the tesseract is a threat. We're here to figure that out."

Alice nodded her head. "Okay."

"So, what were you doing all last week?"

"I stayed at my father's house. I didn't feel comfortable coming back."

"I see. Did you let them know that you weren't coming?"

"…No."

"Why not?" asked John.

"I can't trust them. I don't understand half of what you say, but you are blatantly honest and far smarter than the rest of us. When they called me last week, they left a message saying that they hadn't heard from you yet. I didn't see any way where I could bring myself to help them try to do something that I don't believe in. I don't think they would listen to me anyway. That's when I called you and left you the message. I'm just glad you're okay. What happened to you anyway?"

John smirked. "Well, I received an interesting gift from something on the other side." John pulled his journal out of his inside jacket pocket. "It's quite powerful."

"They gave you that book?" asked Alice.

"This book belongs to me, but they added something to it."

"Can I see it?"

"Honestly, Alice, I really do think it's best if I reveal it to everybody at once. Believe it or not, it may not be safe for the two of us to look at it alone."

"Okay… Now I'm worried."

"Don't worry. You'll understand when you see it. And listen. Anytime you need to talk to me privately about anything, you let me know. I'll keep all of this between us. I do prefer to be open with them about things that they need to know, but if you need to talk privately, I'm always here for that."

"Thank you, John. I'm sorry for sounding so neurotic."

"Don't mention it. I run on neuroticism."

★★★

Mark, Victor, and Maria sat in front of the large projector in the lab and watched a video of a building's implosion. "Do you see how it falls into itself?" asked Mark. "They rig it like that in order to encapsulate the wreckage. I'm not quite sure yet if that's the best option for our safety, but it does make it easier to take something down with a modest amount of ammunition."

"But what kind of ammunition can we use?" asked Victor. "We're not exactly dealing with brick and mortar here." John and Alice walked into the lab at the top of the aisle.

"I hope that's not your plan for the lab," said John. All three of them shot their heads around to see John and Alice walking their way.

"Whoa, look who's here," said Victor.

Maria ran up and gave John a hug. "Oh my God. Thank God you're both okay." She then gave Alice a big hug. Alice smiled with a little bit of relief. Mark and Victor walked up and offered both of them handshakes.

"Jesus. Good to see you two," said Mark. "I didn't think you were coming back."

"Yes, I have a pretty good story for you," said John.

"You okay, Alice?" asked Mark.

"Yes… I am. I'm really sorry for my absence. I think I somehow lost it a little bit after that night in the dorms. I should have let y'all know that I wasn't coming last weekend, but… I don't know. It's hard to explain, but I am very sorry." There was silence among them. Maria reached out and rubbed Alice's arm.

"We're really glad that you're okay, Alice. Thank you for coming back."

★★★

After settling in and catching up, John found himself in front of the group explaining his long-lost week. Maria stood at a podium holding the journal, but she had not yet opened it under John's strict warning. "So, just by looking at the drawing, two-weeks flew by? You don't remember anything?" asked Victor.

"I do now, but my memory did not return until the hotel clerk reminded me of a conversation that she and I had. You might say that I was on autopilot. I ate, I slept, I went to the bathroom, but it all went by in the snap of a finger," said John.

"Well… Do you think you time traveled or something? How could it just go by so quickly?" asked Mark.

"I didn't time travel. In fact, I don't think it was an issue of time at all, but rather a practice of advanced psychology. I think that I got so lost in the artwork that I ceased to recognize the flow of time in a standard duration. Let's call it a mental time compression."

"Well, I'm hooked," said Mark. "Let's read the poem."

"Okay, but remember, it's the drawing itself that entranced me, not the poem. So, after Dr. Delphi reads it aloud, we should only look at the picture one or two at a time. It is truly a Siren of sight." John walked over and sat next to Mark. "Doctor, whenever you're ready," said John.

Maria opened the journal and flipped to the end of John's entries. She held the final page for a moment and braced herself. She turned it. As soon as she spotted the poem, she quickly forced her hand over the drawing just as John had instructed. She scanned over it before reading aloud. And then she spoke.

"They came to find your numbers. For then, they will need you no more. They will complete their working machine, and they will open the unclosable door. They will devour your brain, discard your body, and then, they will seize control. But I know your real worth, John. It is not your numbers. It is not your mind. Your true value is your soul." She kept her hand over the drawing as she processed the words.

"Holy Shit!" yelled Mark. "What does that mean?" Alice held her hand over her mouth, shocked by the message.

"Read it again, hun," said Victor. Maria read the poem aloud a second time with a strain of unease.

"Who wrote that, John?" asked Victor.

"I don't know for sure, but I have a strong idea."

"They know your name," said Alice. John nodded. "Didn't that Thing in the mirror call you by your name?"

"Yes, it did. And yes, that's what I'm thinking too," said John.

"Okay, I'm not much of a poetry expert or anything, but I can't seem to get past the part about eating brains and seizing control. Can we devote a little bit of time towards that please?" asked Mark.

"Yeah, I have to agree with Mark," said Victor. "What I'm gathering here is that not only can these things create massive holes in the ground and build portals that span thousands of miles, but also their plan is to '*seize control*'. Remind me again why we're still considering the possibility of a good outcome."

"Because we have no idea of the Author's intentions. It sounds a lot like It's trying to warn us, but who's to say that It's trustworthy?" asked Alice. "We don't know what It wants."

"It sounds a lot like It wants us to live. Let's take some good advice while we can get it," said Mark.

"Both of you are not wrong," said John. "If we take it at face value, then we need to destroy the tesseract immediately. As the recipient of the poem, I assure you that I do not want to be devoured, but Alice brings up a good point. We know almost nothing about the Poet, assuming It is even the same entity that visited us in the dormitory two weeks ago. There could be countless players at hand. We need to waste no more time assessing every possibility and figure out why these things are here and whether or not they're acting in our interest."

"Well, then here's our options and outcomes," said Victor. "We can do nothing, and either we will be destroyed or not. Or we can try to stop them, in which case our lives are in our own hands. I've never been much of a gambler, but continuing to exist sounds pretty attractive to me."

"I'm a person who is very addicted to gambling and I still agree with Victor. My life sucks, but I somehow still really want to keep living," said Mark. "At the very least, we should try to find a way to shut this thing down just as a backup plan."

"You're absolutely right, Mark. We need a plan to close the structure should we choose, but we still have time to decide. Jumping to conclusions now, knowing as little as we do, would be foolish," said John.

"I hope you're right because on the clock of the tesseract, it's a-quarter-past-eleven. It will be midnight before you know it," said Victor. "Sweetie, feel free to jump in at any time. We're brainstorming here. Apparently, there are no bad ideas." Everyone looked up at Maria. She was motionless and emotionless. She stood at the podium and stared dead into the journal. "Maria? You okay?" asked Victor. Maria had no response.

"She's okay. She looked at the drawing," said John. Victor popped out of his seat and walked up to his wife. He approached her slowly, studying her fixation. He put a hand on her shoulder.

"Maria. Can you hear me?"

John walked up and stood next to the couple. "You're about to understand why I didn't call you back for two-weeks," said John. Victor looked at him with confusion, then back at his wife. He grabbed the book's cover and slammed it closed. Maria slowly looked up at him. Her eyes were full of tears.

"That's the most beautiful thing I've ever seen," she said.

"Are you okay?" asked Victor.

"Will you look at it with me?" asked his wife. Victor looked at John. John gave Victor a nod of approval. Victor carefully opened the book and turned the pages. He glanced over the poem until his eyes met the drawing. He sank in.

John walked down near Alice and Mark who were baffled. "Is it really that powerful?" asked Mark. John nodded. Alice looked up at him with a mix of fear and wonder. She did not want to look, but she knew that her humane curiosity would leave her with no choice.

After five minutes of allowing the couple their time, Mark stood up from his seat and made his way to the aisle. John took Alice's hand and guided her up. She took his hand and stood up, and then followed Mark up to the podium. Mark gently shut the journal and held onto it. Victor and Maria looked at him the way that a baby looks at its mother when she puts it down and walks away. For a moment, they were lost. John walked up to them and guided them down to their seats. They sat silently and reflected.

Mark placed the book on the podium and prepared to open it. He looked at Alice to see if she was ready. She looked him in the eye and nodded. Mark opened the journal and they both surrendered to the work.

Maria and Victor sat and allowed their colleagues a turn for what seemed to be an eternity. They were jealous of the two, but also knew what they were going through. And the more that they watched Mark and Alice, the more they realized how right John was. This picture was dangerous. When enough time had gone by, John took to the podium and removed the book. And just like the good couple, Mark and Alice retired to their seats in silence.

"Now you understand. It's humbling," said John as he remained behind the podium. "This Creature possesses a talent light-years beyond history's greatest artists. Just imagine how magnificent it would be to see it in its full fourth-dimensional state, full of color and depth. It would probably crush our sanity.

"So, here is what I want you to think about. While trying to find the master plan for destroying the great gateway that is being built just above us, what are we losing? We could be saving our own lives, but we could also be shutting out a paradise that's more beautiful than any heaven we could imagine. This flat, colorless drawing that you all just fell into could represent an actual euphoric kingdom that we get a personal invitation to. Is it worth the risk? Is the possibility of torture and death worse than the possibility of spending the rest of our days in the true Garden of Eden?

"Just remember once more what these beings are, in comparison to us. They may look three-dimensional to our eyes, but that's because our eyes cannot see past the limits of our own space. And just as Maria and Victor could see all sides of the flat creatures at once, these greater beings can see all sides of us at once. They can see our faces, our backs, and every side of our limbs at all times. We are almost massless compared to them. We are simple weighted, simple minded bodies. And to us, they are gods." Victor, Maria, Alice, and Mark all sat staring at the seats in front of them, but they felt every word that John spoke.

"So now, we proceed, but we proceed with caution as well as intellect. There is an infinity of importance that rests in our hands. We each have a unique intelligence, and we each bring our own point of view. We must debate, but not argue. Every suggestion must be explored in full. If we disagree, we explain why. When the final day comes, there will be room for only one decision. We must choose precisely."

★★★

The group eventually came back into their senses and gathered up some organization. It was decided that over the remaining few weeks, until the next corner of the tesseract was expected to open, two things should be accomplished. The first was for exact coordinates to be calculated based off of the previous locations. Maria and Victor had never been able to witness the opening of one of the orbs because of trouble predicting the precise place in which it would happen. John and Maria volunteered to tackle the geometry, and Alice offered to assist them in any way that she could. The second step was planning an effective way to destroy the tesseract, should they decide that its existence would be their demise. Mark and Victor decided to put their brains together and figure out a strategy of termination.

Throughout the week, Mark continued to study the destruction of many types of buildings and structures. With the tesseract in mind, he learned how to attack the weakest points that carried the most amount of load.

While Mark focused on where to strike the tesseract, Victor focused on how to strike it. It was not a solid, visible object, nor was it detectable outside of the rare appearances of the orbs. However, he thought about his pidima terrarium and how he discovered that the proper housing and enclosing of energy was needed in order to keep the second and third dimensions at an equilibrium. Only then were they visible and tangible with one-another. He began to imagine the structure that needed to be built. It would require an amount of energy that would be difficult to obtain, and it would need a new set of pidimas that were designed to pour all of their light into one point. Its purpose would be to cause a collapse at the location that Mark would deem the weakest.

***

Mark cracked open a beer and handed it to Victor. He then opened another beer and lit a cigarette. He took a long inhale and let it out. They tapped cans and both took a sip. "Don't tell my wife, but do you think I could have one of your cigarettes?" asked Victor.

"Absolutely," answered Mark. Mark lit a new cigarette and handed it to Victor. "You deserve it, kid. We may have just started the plans that will save all of mankind." Victor chuckled. "So, what do you think about all of this? Everything that John and Alice have been saying."

"I don't know," said Victor. "Maybe John's right to say to wait, but I'm still not convinced that letting anything happen is a good idea."

"Do you find it strange that they showed up here the other week at the exact same time?" asked Mark.

Victor took a long sip of his beer. "Yeah, I've been thinking about it."

"I'm not saying they're hiding some plan or anything like that, but I do think that Alice is getting in his ear," said Mark.

Victor took a sip then nodded his head. "Yeah."

"We can't let that happen. John's obviously on top of his shit, but I think if we're being honest, we need him on our side. In my opinion, she's not helping the situation."

"I've spoken to Maria about that. Between you and me, I was hoping that she wouldn't show back up."

"What did Maria say?"

"She likes her. She's a little more religious than I am though. I guess she thinks it's possible that Alice is right about God."

"Yeah, I mean, I don't actually care what she believes in, but I can't let someone's faith get us all killed. Unless something dramatic happens in Nebraska that convinces us we're going to be okay, I don't see any situation where we don't try and shut this thing down."

"I don't disagree. What are we going to do about Nebraska?" asked Victor.

"My kid called me last night. I was going to tell you guys today that I have to skip the trip. He's going to be in Oklahoma for a week, and he said that he wants me to come see him. I haven't spent more than a few hours with him in years," said Mark.

"Really? That's great, Mark. I'm really glad he called you."

"Yeah, I want to come and see what happens down there, but I can't blow him off. I want to be able to see him more regularly, and I don't know if I'll get another chance."

"You absolutely should go see your boy. We'll let you know everything that happens when we're over there."

"I appreciate that…" A thought popped into Mark's mind. "Listen. Call it selfish or whatever, but if I'm able to see my kid regularly again, there's no way I'm going to be in favor of opening this thing up. We can't risk everyone else's life over something that we're not sure about. It's our responsibility to do something. Sorry to Alice and John, but God and this fourth-dimensional paradise aren't worth the death of every kid on Earth. I know you don't have kids yourself, but I think you can understand how I feel."

"Well… That's not exactly true anymore."

"What do you mean?" asked Mark.

"Maria's pregnant."

Chapter Thirty-Three

Incident #15

September 6, 2015: Sutton Nebraska

"We have about one-and-a-half square miles of possible area. Maria and I ran into a strange measurement when we were studying the past locations. We found an extremely detailed virtual globe on the internet that allowed us to measure down the inch," said John. They all gathered in John's motel room in order to plan their night precisely. They booked three rooms in a motel just about a mile outside of Sutton.

They had a paper map of the town laid out on the bed. "Maria, what's the program we were using called? It was a very good find."

"Google maps, John," answered Maria.

"Oh yes, right. Google. I'm glad you're good with the internet."

Maria patted John on the shoulder. "Essentially, all of the points of the tesseract were measuring up perfectly, until we reached the bottom of the second cube. For instance, in Wisconsin, the orb in the lab was exactly the same length from the storm in Louisiana as it was from the storm in Idaho, and the distance from the lab's orb to the orb that appeared in the sky above it was the same distance as Louisiana's and Mexico's locations. And the eight total locations made a perfect cube." said Maria. "That was all also true for the inner cube, just in smaller ratios, until we began measuring the ground locations to each other. For reasons that we don't understand, the ground locations create an imperfect square. Judging by the three that we have, we could not nail down this last location perfectly."

"Why not? Why did it line up perfectly everywhere else?" asked Victor.

"We can only assume that the tesseract shapes up exactly in four-dimensions, but it gets slightly warped when they apply it to a sphere, similar to how a paper map gets distorted when stretched onto a globe," said John.

Victor chuckled. "So, we're just going to drive around all night, hoping that we find the exact spot at the exact right time?"

"This is all we have, hun. We got it down to nine-hundred and fifty-five acres. There was no way to get it perfect."

"I guess we can't split up since we only have one car," said Alice.

"We don't even know what time it's going to happen," added Victor.

"Well, we do know that most of them occurred in the dark, either very late or very early," said Maria.

"Except for Mark's. His happened in the middle of his work day," said Alice.

"I say that we map out a street route right now that will cover as much of the area as possible and hop in the car and loop it all night. At the very least, we can learn the area and determine if there are any places of interest," said John.

Victor scratched his head and reluctantly shrugged. "Yeah... Well... I guess there's no sense in wasting any time."

★★★

Delilah washed a sink full of dinner dishes as the AM radio quietly played music from a gospel station. She cleaned the dishes delicately and slowly. Delilah did everything delicately and slowly. She had a relatively steady day emotionally, as she spent most of it keeping up with the house, but that was a sharp contradiction to the previous night where she cried herself to sleep again. The pain came and went.

Enoch worked the fields for about twelve hours before calling it for supper. He sat at the table well after eating, working in his notebook, trying to figure out the farm's weekly finances. As usual, he kept his feelings to himself. He was slowly accepting doom, and he recently decided to make an effort to not burden Delilah with his temper. He would rather die working in the cornfields than sell his family's farm to a larger commercial company, but he knew that an egotistical decision like that would only leave Delilah hungry and alone. He was also well aware that the land was losing value every day that he watched it wither.

Delilah finished the last plate and hung up the dish towel for the night. Weariness was getting the best of her. She walked out of the room and left her husband to his work. They had spoken in the morning before Sunday service, once before Enoch left for the fields, and they shared a few words over dinner about a fund-raiser for the local elementary school that Delilah had volunteered for. In between, there was only silence.

Their nightly routine involved taking turns bathing and shutting down their portion of the house before bed. It was mundane and unchanging. Every day was exactly the same. The only element that changed was the growing level of stress that each of them buried down into their chests. They drifted side-by-side physically, but existed in complete solitude emotionally.

As Delilah shut her eyes for the night, Enoch sat up and read a few pages of the Bible. He was looking for answers, and even though he was yet to come across those answers this late in his life, his faith was left unfaltered.

***

"Alright, who's ready to loop around it for the fourth time?" asked Victor with a good bit of sarcasm. They had just finished their third consecutive trip around the planned route with nothing gained but wasted time.

"Victor, you're more than welcome to give your input if you have any great ideas," said Maria. "What do you want us to do?"

"I don't know, but this is not working. Even if anything were to happen, we would never know about it. We should think about parking somewhere and getting out. Maybe we can even break off into twos."

"That's not a bad idea," said John. There was a long silence.

"Let's play *I Spy* to pass the time," said Alice. Maria chuckled and John smiled. They looked to Victor to see if he was still tense.

"I spy another cornfield," said Victor. Everyone laughed and the mood lightened. "Listen, I'm sorry for my edge. I just think that we've been waiting for tonight for so long, and we don't have a plan. I'm not blaming anyone because I can't think of anything either, but this is not productive."

"You're right," said John. "Maybe we should find a good spot to park and walk around a little bit. There's nothing but corn in every direction, but maybe it wouldn't hurt to get out and open our ears a little bit."

"Can we stay together though?" asked Maria. "I know we can cover more ground in twos, but on the off chance that we run into something, I think that we would be safer in numbers."

"I can agree to that," said Victor. "How about we turn down this road and find an easy place to leave the car? If we don't see anything in an hour, we'll move on."

***

"Enoch. Wake up," whispered Delilah as she sat up in bed.

"What is it?" Enoch gathered himself and sat up. Delilah tip-toed to the bedroom window and inched open the blinds. "Delilah, what is it?"

"I heard something outside. It sounded like something fell over near the barn."

"Is it one of the animals?" asked Enoch.

"Did you leave a light on in there? I can see light through the window."

Enoch jumped out of bed and walked over to the window. "That doesn't look like the barn light. Is it a flashlight?"

"But it's not moving," said Delilah. Just after she spoke, the light from the barn faded and went dark. "It went off. Is somebody in there?" As they continued to watch, the barn's visibility dimmed. Within seconds, everything outside was swallowed into a cloud of darkness. The moonlight shone down onto the cornfields brightly, but anything within one hundred yards of the barn was completely black.

"I have to go check. Call the police and lock the bedroom door."

"You can't go out there, Enoch. What if there are people?"

"I'm taking my gun. All of my equipment is unlocked. We cannot afford to lose any of it. Call the police." Delilah ran over to the phone and picked it up. She pushed down on the base switch over and over.

"The phone is dead." She tried to switch the light on but got no response. "The electricity is out. Please don't go out there, Enoch."

"All of my equipment is in there, Delilah. Lock the door behind me and take the pistol out of the closet. I will be back in five minutes. I will not let anything happen to you." Enoch turned to leave the room. Delilah grabbed his arm. Enoch stopped. They actually looked at each other for the first time in years. Delilah's eyes filled with tears. She grabbed her husband and kissed him, and he kissed her back.

"I Love you, Enoch."

"I love you too, Delilah." A loud crash sounded from the barn, followed by a door flying open. "Take the gun, and lock the door," said Enoch as he moved out of the room.

"Please, be careful!" shouted Delilah. "God, help us."

Enoch trampled down the stairs and walked out of the front door, locking the doorknob behind him before closing it. He slowly stepped across the lawn. Although the darkness was beginning to clear, he could still see very little, and he could hear nothing. He approached the barn with his shotgun facing forward. He thought about yelling at the intruders, or even firing a warning shot, but he was not in an ideal spot for cover if the intruders decided to fire back.

When he was close enough to see the front door of the barn, he stopped. He counted his breaths and surveyed the building in order to determine the safest place of entry. The pounding of his heartbeat made it hard for him to think, so he approached the window and crouched below it. He lifted his head just high enough to see inside without being seen himself. Across the large, open room, there was nothing but darkness, until he looked into the back corner. With complete befuddlement, Enoch gazed upon a floating sphere that was full of swirling colors and lights. Its beauty took his mind off of the intruders for a moment, but before he had the chance to really take it in, the orb shrank down into the size of a marble, and then disappeared.

The moonlight poured back in through the windows and revived the large room with some of its definition. Consequently, Enoch saw the vague outline of three massive bodies lined up across the room, filling up nearly the entire first floor of the barn. He froze at the first sight of them and tried to convince himself that his eyes were playing tricks, but then they began to migrate. Slowly, they inched their way to the open door, and as soon as the first creature reached fresh air, they shot out of the barn and rushed towards the cornfield.

With an unexplained dash of courage, Enoch hopped to his feet and pursued the silhouettes. They moved so fast that by the time that he rounded the corner of the barn, he was only able to watch the last of the three shoot through the corn stalks into the field. He grabbed a flashlight from just inside the open barn, and then he ran as fast as his waned joints allowed. When he reached the perimeter of the field, he stopped at the gaping path that the entities had filed through on their departure. It was wider than any two of his tractors put together. With a moment's hesitation, Enoch pumped his legs again and continued his chase.

After about one hundred yards, he was able to spot them again, but they were so far in the distance that he knew he would never catch up. He stopped to regain his breath. He found himself at a fork in the road both mentally and literally. He could either continue after the monsters that were ravaging through his farm, or he could run back to his house and protect his wife. His only real worry about going back to the house was tied to the possibility that the creatures would follow him when they were already so far away, which would only put Delilah in danger. But he knew that his shotgun would be proven useless in a contest with three beasts so mighty. So, after a thirty-second break to fill his lungs with air, Enoch made the safer decision of retreating home.

He stood in the middle of the folded path of corn and looked in the direction that the creatures had last been seen. For the moment, he saw and heard nothing, so he picked up his feet and trotted towards the house. He thought about the plan for when he reached Delilah. If they were to stay inside, they had some chance of remaining hidden. But then again, they lived in a house that was not much bigger than one of the creatures. The deadbolt locks were a little light for the task. On the other hand, if he decided to hop in the truck and try to escape, they would at least be moving freely, though his twenty-year-old truck stood no chance in a race against anything. But as it happened, the worms made Enoch's decision for him.

***

When he turned around to check on his safety, he saw that his uninvited guests had doubled back for him and were already within a few hundred yards. Enoch turned around and faced them. He saw no sense in letting his gun stay cold, seeing as how it would probably never be shot again, so he stood up straight and took aim.

The large moving targets grew larger and closer. Enoch did not lie to himself with any optimism. As his mouth whispered prayers to his Lord, he exhaled a sigh of relief. Enoch had a hard life, and a strenuous life, and every day that greeted Enoch brought with it a test for his soul. He was tired. The giants had swallowed up all but forty-yards of space between themselves and the farmer. He cocked the shotgun and watched as they bore down on him. And his last free thought brought him joy.

He knew that his death would crush Delilah and leave her completely alone, but some part of him also knew that being alone would finally free her. She had been locked in a cage of her own grief for most of her life, and Enoch accepted his share of the blame. As much as he only wanted the best for her, he was well aware that his need to control their lives had smoldered her. He could finally give himself up and allow her to enjoy the end of her time in any way that she pleased. There was no doubt that they would meet again. He stood up straight and smiled as he felt the wind of death upon his face, and then his smile turned to shock as he watched three humongous, worm-shaped bodies burrow into the ground just before his feet.

As if they had been met with no resistance, they tunneled through the dirt underground at the same incredible speed that they had traveled on top of the dirt. Like a synchronized team, they headed out into the cornfield in three parallel paths. Enoch watched as the cornstalks collapsed into the dirt as the worms tunneled underneath. Each stalk then slowly rose back up above the surface in a new, organized pattern. He ran over to one of his unhitched trailers that sat on a nearby dirt trail and climbed on top. With his higher perspective, he now saw that the worms had already covered over ten acres in their lightning-fast dig. The entire field fell and rose again as the corn spiraled into a mutilated garden.

After what seemed to be only thirty seconds, the creatures made their way back in his direction and shot out of the ground again. They sped towards where they originally came from. Enoch hopped off of the trailer and ran after them. Knowing how much faster they were, and guessing where they were headed, he cut down a small opening in the field and took off. By the time his yard was in sight, he saw the three intruders blaze into the barn and slam the door behind them.

***

"I hope this isn't illegal. I don't want to get arrested for trespassing or something," said Victor.

"Yes, and now they'll have our DNA," said John as the two of them finished urinating in a cornfield.

"How much longer do you think we should go before we call it a night?" asked Victor.

"I guess we should ask the girls. At a certain point, it makes more sense to get some sleep and come back out in the daylight."

"Do you think there's any chance that nothing is going to happen?"

"I suppose it's possible, but honestly I hope that something does, and I hope we see it. I really need to know what's going on. I imagine you feel the same way. You've been chasing this longer than any of us."

Victor let out a long breath. "John, I don't know. I'm certainly curious. I've been curious for two years, but I'm also getting scared. If it was totally up to me, we would all go to bed and wake up tomorrow to absolutely nothing. I'd rather get back to my life and take care of my wife and kid." John gave Victor a peculiar look with that last sentence. Victor caught on to John's feeling and grinned. "We have one on the way. We found out last week."

John looked at Victor and smiled. He gave him a hug. "Congratulations," said John as he patted Victor on the back. John truly felt happy for Victor, but he also knew that any chance of convincing Victor to consider his or Alice's opinion was gone. Victor was no longer just thinking for himself or his wife. He was thinking for his child.

★★★

"I feel like it's a boy, but Victor wants a girl," said Maria.

"I think every mother wants a boy," said Alice through a genuine smile. "How are you feeling?"

"I feel fine so far. I didn't know what to expect with the morning sickness and everything, but nothing has happened yet."

"How is Victor handling it?"

"He's very happy about the baby, but I can tell he's more stressed too. I'm sure you can see how irritable he's been lately."

"Well, that's understandable. It's not the best timing. How are you feeling about all of this? You seem to keep it to yourself for the most part."

"Yes… I guess I don't like to make decisions out loud until I make them in my head. Victor's pretty adamant about being cautious for the baby's sake. I think you make a lot of good points, Alice, but I'm still not sure about anything yet."

"None of us are."

"What about you? Are you still liking your new apartment?" asked Maria.

"It's umm… Yeah, I'm learning to like it okay. It's different having people living around you that you don't know. I always have to make sure I'm not being too loud."

"Tell me about it. We had renters under us for the longest time, and we're finally just enjoying the space." Maria chuckled, but Alice was quiet. Maria stopped smiling and looked at Alice, truly understanding her pain. It was obvious that Alice's life did not turn out like her own because Maria was happy with her career and felt fulfilled with her marriage. Alice had accomplished almost nothing, and she was struggling to keep herself above the surface.

"You know what, Maria? I lived with my husband for almost thirty-years, and we could not stand the sight of each other. We spoke to each other about once a week, and never in a nice way. But I never knew how lonely I could feel by myself. I try to avoid bothering my dad so much, but honestly, he's the only person I have to talk to. I despise my husband, but I keep hoping that one day he'll call and ask me back just so I have someone to be around."

Maria placed her hand on Alice's back as Alice began to tear up. "Alice… I'm so sorry you're feeling that way. I think it takes a lot to say that out loud. You're very strong for going through everything that you did and still taking care of yourself."

"Well, I'm clearly running on no sleep," said Alice as she grinned and wiped her tears away. "I didn't mean to lay that on you."

"Don't apologize. There's nothing wrong with feeling lonely." Alice nodded. She chose to not say out loud the next thought that came to her mind. Like John, she concluded that Maria and Victor would most likely head in their own direction regarding the tesseract, but for that moment, she did not judge them. They were happy, and they had a bright future. Her future was uncertain with the exception of a high probability of loneliness. She had nothing to lose, and they had everything to lose.

***

Enoch had absolutely no clue how three giants could just up-and-disappear. When he reached the large barn doors to lock the beasts inside, he saw that they were gone without a trace. Completely baffled, he headed back into the cornfield to assess what sort of damage had been caused to his already-depleted stock.

He wandered through the path that was laid down by the worms. Although flattened, the majority of the corn stalks began to stand up again around Enoch. He walked far out into the northern quadrant. It amazed him how quickly he ran back earlier without even noticing the distance. It took him several more minutes to reach the trailer on which he stood when he watched the worms tunnel through the field. He climbed back on top of it and looked out. The field was mangled in the strangest way. The rows of corn were intact, however the individual stalks were rolled in a pattern through the ground over hundreds of thousands of square-feet.

Enoch climbed off of the trailer and walked towards the warped field. For a moment, he forgot how close to death he came from the worms, and instead dreaded the loss of his corn and the financial plummet that awaited him. As Enoch walked into the disaster that finally sank his farm, he lost his weight and fell down to his waist in soft dirt.

Like quicksand, the ground swallowed Enoch down to his belly. In a panic, he squirmed his way to an overhanging cornstalk, and pulled himself out. He got himself up to his feet and looked down to see his freshly imprinted hole. Using his foot, he felt the dirt. It was soft and airy from the worms tilling it. Unable to comprehend it all, he cautioned his way more into the field. After a short distance of feeling his way forward, Enoch came upon a sight, and he immediately reached a point of understanding.

He gazed upon the offering that had been placed at his feet, and he dropped to his knees in worship. Then Enoch broke down and wept, for he was kneeling upon sacred ground.

***

Mark sat next to his son Jake who was all grown up. He looked like Mark in his face, but he took better care of his health than Mark, and he was already much taller than him. They sat together on a park bench. Mark faced his son, but Jake could not bring himself to make eye contact. "Maybe we can head down to that pub off of the highway that we used to go to and get you some ribs," said Mark. "Remember those? We used to love that place."

Mark knew that he was not getting through to Jake. It was obvious that their time together would be short-lived, so instead of continuing his small talk, he swallowed his pride and ego: "Jake, I'm sorry. I'm very aware of what I've done. You're my buddy and my son, and I screwed it up. I know it's my fault."

Jake looked at Mark for the first time. His young face showed no signs of either acceptance or denial of his father's apology. It showed the effects of abandonment and confusion for how he was treated. "It's hard to forgive what you did, Dad. I appreciate that you've admitted to your problems, but you've missed a good part of my life, and we can never get that back. And you can't keep blaming Mom. You need to stop that. She didn't do anything wrong. I would have done the same thing."

Mark looked at the ground as he fought back tears.

"I don't know if I can see you right now. I'm not saying no permanently, but I don't want to get your hopes up if I'm not ready to do this again soon. I'm sorry, Dad." Mark nodded and accepted his son's decision.

"You make me very proud of you, Jake. You're being honest with me and yourself. It's not easy to do. You know how I feel. I'm not going to press you on it, but if at some point you decide that you want to talk again, then you call me and I'll be there."

"Thank you," said Jake. They shared a silence.

Mark sniffed and wiped away his tears. "So, what do you have planned for the rest of the day?"

"I'm meeting some friends to see a movie. How about you? Have you seen uncle Scott since you've been back?"

"No, I don't think uncle Scott wants to see me, buddy. I was actually thinking about riding down to Ninnekah and checking out the building that I was working on. I haven't been back since they let me go. I want to see how it looks."

"You were working at the Ninnekah building? I didn't put that together. I haven't seen it yet either. I hear it's a huge mess," said Jake.

"What do you mean it's a mess?"

"Most of it isn't cleaned up yet."

"Wait, what do you mean? What isn't cleaned up?"

"The building. Did you not hear? About two weeks ago, the roof collapsed and a lot of the building caved in."

Mark sat up and turned more towards Jake. "The roof collapsed? How did that happen?"

"I'm not sure how, but it killed almost twenty people. Workers … Oh my God, I guess maybe you worked with some of them."

"The Office building in Ninnekah? The high-tech one?"

"Yeah. Dad, I'm sorry. I thought you would have known about it. I hope you didn't know anyone." Mark sat speechless. "You should be careful if you go over there," said Jake. "I'm not sure if you're able to get too close." Mark continued to stare aimlessly. He was flushed with thoughts and fears about not only who may have been included in the twenty souls, but also what was responsible for the collapse.

Chapter Thirty-Four
<u>What Hath --- Wrought</u>

The sun beat through the car windows on the unseasonably hot day. They had gotten only about four hours of sleep before heading back out on their search, which they were now another five hours into. "I think I have to stop and eat," said Victor. "I'm sorry, but I'm dying here."

"No, that's a good idea, hun. I'm really hungry too," said his wife. John remained quiet as he struggled to keep his eyes open, and Alice sat across from him with her head against her window.

"I'll go towards that diner that we passed earlier. Might as well try something local while we're here," said Victor.

"Yeah, I want some grits," said Maria. "I bet you grew up on grits, huh Alice?"

Alice saw something outside that caught her attention. She lifted her head up and stared out the window. "Wait a minute. I think I saw something back there."

"What was it?" asked John.

Alice continued to look. "I don't know. Something in that cornfield."

"Haven't we been by here already today?" asked Victor as he pulled the car over.

"I don't know, but go back," said Alice. Victor turned around and headed down the road slowly. They all kept their heads perched. "Right there. Do you see it?" They all moved their heads around to get a better look.

"What are you seeing?"

"Look at the corn way out there. Look at the pattern."

"Do you see it, hun?" asked Victor.

"No. There's too much glare."

They drove another twenty yards onto a slight incline. "Oh my God, she's right," said John. "There is a pattern. About two hundred yards that way." Victor stopped the car, turned it off and got out. The rest followed him. Victor stood on his tip-toes and looked out into the field.

"Well, Ms. Day, I believe I owe you an apology. Good eye," said Victor.

"That's about as obvious as any sign we've seen yet, isn't it?" asked Maria. "So, should we walk out there and check it out?"

"That's why we're here," said John. "Let's cut through the field."

"You know what? I know we trespassed on about ten different properties last night, but maybe we should head to the owner of this place and ask permission," said Victor. "It's daylight and they might see us. I just don't want to get shot or something."

"But what if they say no?" asked Maria. "I don't think we're going to get shot, and if they say no, then they'll be watching the field for us."

"He may be right, Maria," said Alice. "If my father ever saw four strangers walking across his property without permission, he would at least have a gun in hand and possibly take a warning shot. We don't want the future little Maria or Victor growing up with one parent." Alice gestured towards Maria's belly. Maria smirked.

"Okay, for the baby's sake we'll ask permission."

★★★

They made their way up the long dirt driveway to Enoch and Delilah's house. As they got closer, they saw Enoch and Delilah sitting on their front porch in rocking chairs. As they got even closer, they noticed that Enoch had a shotgun in his lap. "Good call, Alice," said John. "You may have prevented Victor from becoming a piñata."

"If I know anything at all, it's the behavior of country folk." They pulled up to the end of the driveway, which met the start of a beautiful, green lawn.

Victor sat and looked at the farmer and his wife, but left the engine running. "I feel really weird about this. Am I the only one?"

"How so?" asked Maria.

"Well, if these people's field was overhauled last night, then why are they just sitting there? You know that they can see it from up there. And why is he just looking at us? Wouldn't you get up if you were him and someone just pulled up to your house?"

"Well, we're just sitting here too," said Maria. "Maybe they're thinking that we're the ones acting weird."

"I don't like this, hun."

"You know what, Victor? I agree. But the guy has a gun. Let's not turn it into some *who's being weirder* competition. Let's get out and say hello," said John.

They exited the car. Side-by-side, they walked up to the porch where the farmer and his wife were sitting. "Good afternoon..." said Victor with some hesitation. "My name is Victor Delphi. This is my wife Maria, and this is Dr. John Robins and Alice Day." John, Maria, and Alice each said hello and offered a smile. "How are you?" The question sat in the air as Enoch and Delilah only stared down at them. "We apologize for the unannounced visit, but we happened to be driving down the road there, and we noticed some interesting farm patterns in your cornfield. I know that this may sound strange, but we were wondering if we could take a bit of a closer look."

"Who told you to come look at our cornfield?" asked Enoch. Victor was off put.

"Well, nobody, sir. We were just driving by and we happened to notice that the way you were growing corn in a certain section was very interesting. If it's not too much trouble, we were just wondering if you would allow us to take a quick look. We will not bother you for long."

"Why are you so interested in my corn? There's over one thousand acres of corn in this town. Why would you need to look at my property?"

"Sir, if I may," said Maria. "We do apologize for the intrusion, but we work at the Wisconsin College of Science and we have been studying some strange agricultural cases that have been happening lately. I don't want to scare you at all, but it looks like your farm may have been affected."

"Thank you for your concern, ma'am, but you're not scaring me. And whatever is growing on my property is only the business of myself and my wife. I think we would appreciate it if you left us to our afternoon." Maria nodded her head and thought about her next response. She knew that it would be her last before they were asked to leave in a less polite way. Instead, Alice jumped in.

"Did you happen to see any strange creatures either last night or this morning? Or any unusual sources of light?"

Enoch looked at Alice. He was clearly caught off-guard. His attempt at intimidation had left. Now, he was reading her to see what she actually knew. "Come again, ma'am?"

"Did you see anything out of the ordinary last night? The reason I ask is because all four of us have seen something unexplainable on our own, and we think that something may have happened here recently."

"Where did you come from?" asked Enoch.

"I live in Florida, he's from Colorado, and they're from Wisconsin. And we've all seen something different."

"What have you seen exactly?"

"More than anything, we've seen the appearance of some sort of orb of light," said Maria. "Most of them have been in the sky, but Dr. Robins has seen one at ground level as well."

"What did it look like?" asked Enoch.

"Well, sir, it seemed to be a floating sphere, but the more that I looked at it, the more that I realized it had an indescribable shape," said John. "And it glowed, but it also seemed to absorb all of the light around it." Enoch stared at John. He made no sound except for his breath.

"And there's also the creatures," said Alice. "We have not seen them ourselves, but another member of our party who is not with us right now said that he encountered some very large creatures. He described them as giant worms." Enoch looked to his wife. She looked back at him and softened a bit. "You two may be very confused. But we are too. We've been working on this for quite a while. We might be able to help you," said Alice.

Delilah leaned over and whispered something to Enoch. He subtly shook his head as if to say *no*. Delilah whispered something else into his ear. "How did you find our farm?" asked Enoch.

"Well, these different occurrences have made sort of a pattern. We were able to follow it here," said Victor. "We didn't know that it would lead us to your farm exactly, but we kind of had a general idea of where to look."

"We're not interested in anyone else knowing about what happened to our property. We have not decided what our plans are yet. If we show you a few things, we need to know that you will honor our privacy."

"Absolutely," said Alice. "Besides the four of us, there is only one other person who knows any of this. We promise that it will stay only among us."

"My name is Enoch Pricherwood. This is my wife Delilah."

"How do you do? Please excuse our demeanor. We have had quite a night," said Delilah. They all returned an excusing smile and another hello.

"Go around to the backyard and we will meet you back there," said Enoch.

They stood over the bodies of three cows. The cows were placed flat on the ground in an even row. All of their bones and their brains had been cleanly removed from their bodies. All that remained were organs inside of flesh.

"Oh my God," said Maria. "What happened to them?"

"We do not know. I found them like this when the sun came up. I had spent a few hours around the barn after the beasts had left. I knew that they were missing, but I just thought that they had gotten out during all of the commotion," said Enoch. "When the sun came up, Delilah spotted them in the yard."

John walked around the cows and got as close of a look as he could without disrespecting Enoch's request to not touch anything. "It almost looks like they were dissected. All of the slits and holes are so neat and elegant. Have you found the missing bones or brains?"

"We have not. And I don't expect to," said Enoch. John found that response strange. He found it even more strange that Delilah had a pleasant smile on her face the entire time.

"So, what do you think happened? Why would they kill them like this?" asked John.

"Let's go into the field. Perhaps you will understand if you see everything together." John gave Victor a nervous look. Victor returned it right back.

"I will go in and make some tea and cookies for you," said Delilah.

"Oh, please don't do that. That's very nice, but unnecessary," said Maria.

"No, don't worry, dear. It's no problem. It will be ready by the time that you are back."

"Well, thank you," said Maria with the internal hope that she would not be forced to consume anything made by the strange strangers.

***

They made their way deep into the cornfield, sifting through the tall stalks. Enoch led them with a steady haste. When they arrived in front of a wall of corn, Enoch stopped. They all stopped in sync.

"It begins just beyond here. It's very important to step lightly. The dirt is very soft," said Enoch. They all nodded and agreed. "And please, do not go near the holes. I've been down them this morning, but I would appreciate it if you just observed from a distance." Enoch looked each one of them in the eye and then nodded his head. He peeled back the thick stalks and walked through.

Maria was the first to see the other side. On the surface of the ground, cornstalks pointed out of the dirt at all different angles, but they did so in a flowing pattern. It seemed as though the rows had been twisted into spirals. When Maria walked further out, she saw large openings into the ground that led down to tunnels. The openings were close to twenty feet in diameter, and the tunnels stretched out into the field for several hundreds of yards. John, Victor, and Alice walked up beside her and gazed in awe at the magnificent sight. There were tunnels running parallel to each other under uniform rows of twisted corn. It was the calculated work of masters.

"They must be mathematicians," said John.

Just then, Enoch came out of the closest tunnel with his arms full of ears of corn that measured three and four feet each. He added them to a pile that he had collected earlier. The pile had one hundred other ears lying atop one another.

"Where did those come from?" asked Victor.

"Come have a look," said Enoch. They walked over towards the opening of one of the tunnels. "Don't get too close. It's very soft dirt." They looked down into the dark tunnels and saw thousands of corn stalks growing out of the ceiling of the tunnel. Enoch walked down inside and began plucking them from the dirt. Within seconds, he already had another dozen masts of corn in his hands. He walked up to the surface and handed them each one to hold.

Victor studied his in amazement. "Did this really just happen overnight? I've never seen corn this big."

"Yes, sir, it did," replied Enoch.

John looked back into the field. "How long were they out here for?"

"Oh, it couldn't have been more than two or three minutes. Maybe less."

They sat on the porch and ate cookies and drank iced tea. Maria had opened up a little bit. In fact, she found the cookies to be quite good despite her earlier fears. John and Victor had not spoken about it out loud, but somehow, they were both on the same page about not revealing everything to their new friends quite yet. Enoch and Delilah were hard to read, and trying to squeeze two more opinions into their already way-too-complicated debate seemed counterproductive.

John decided to go with a more deductive route and allow Enoch and Delilah to take the lead. "Can I ask you two why you think they dug into your cornfield or killed your cattle?"

"You may ask. We understand exactly why," said Delilah with a look of joy.

"Please, share. I think that we're even more confused than when we started."

"Twenty years ago, we lost a son. His name was David. He was four years old," said Enoch.

"I'm very sorry to hear that."

"As you can imagine, we were devastated. We were not able to conceive for the first twenty years of our marriage, then God blessed us with a boy. But He made the decision to take David away from us. And although we did not understand why, we continued to respect His plan. This property has belonged to my family for three generations, and about five years ago, the farm started to show signs of depletion. We have been losing a large percentage of our corn every year until the point where, recently, we almost had to sell the land. But Delilah and I never gave up. And last night, God answered our prayers. He let us know that He has not forgotten about us."

"When you say, 'God answered your prayers', what do you mean exactly, Mr. Pricherwood?"

"I mean that those creatures were celestial. He sent us three of his angels in the form of beasts, and they blessed our farm. They created a miracle. In that area, I now have what looks like fifty-times the amount of yield that was there yesterday. And it has increased greater than that even since this morning. Delilah's first thought went to the story of Jesus sharing the fish and bread that fed the multitude," said Enoch.

"God has taken our small share of corn, and he has spread it out in ways in which nobody sees. Now we will share it with everyone in our town, and we will still have enough to keep the farm flourishing," added Delilah.

John looked over at Maria and Victor. They were growing more discomforted by the moment. Even Alice did not look like she could keep up with their theory. "Yes, I see…" said John. "I can understand the corn and how much of a relief that is, but why did they kill your cows like that? Why would they remove their brains?"

"It is certainly mysterious and even brutal, but we believe that the angels had to take them as a sacrifice to God. God knows that the animals are ours to use, and we believe that he wanted to take them as a sign of trust for our covenant. I understand why their appearance may make you uncomfortable. Delilah was quite upset when we first found them, but after we put it all together, we knew that God was here."

"This is why we acted so unfriendly to you when you arrived. We did not know who you were, and we were afraid that you would tamper with our gifts," said Delilah.

The four of them sat in reflection, not knowing exactly what to say. Maria finally realized that no one had answered Delilah. "Well, this is…. certainly incredible."

★★★

They shared a silence for the first leg of their car ride back. They eventually stopped to wash their hands and buy some refreshments at a gas station. When they loaded back into the car, the heavy air had dissipated.

"Listen…" said Alice. "In case you're thinking it, I'm not nearly on the same page as those two. I still believe what I believe, but in no way do I think that God sent the worms to their farm and killed their cows as a sacrifice. Whether God is behind this or not, those two are wrong."

"We can all agree with that," said Victor.

"That whole thing was disturbing," added Maria. "The fields and tunnels were absolutely incredible, but the way that those cows were severed and probed will be with me for a long time. The fish in New Mexico were pulled apart in the exact same way."

"I was just going to ask you about the fish," said John from the back seat. "Is that what they looked like? Why are they dissecting animals like that?"

"Can we get a quick consensus here, please?" asked Victor. "We all think that they're crazy, and we should probably not tell them too much for the time being, right?"

A unanimous and confident "*Yes*" came out of the other three passengers in the car.

"Terrific," said Victor. "Let's just go ahead and make that an unwritten rule. Then, as far as the worms and everything else, maybe we can list a few of the common occurrences and get on the same page about it. For instance, the removal of the skeletal system from the animals."

"The holes, just like the holes in Mexico," said Maria.

"Absolutely. Those were extremely similar to Mexico. What else?"

"How about the multiplication of fruits and vegetables? You said that the fig farm in Louisiana produced those giant figs overnight," said John.

"That's right, Doctor."

"And now that we're talking about the fish, we can say that they were also multiplied overnight. It seems that these things have an interest in studying or killing living organisms, and then reproducing them in mass numbers," said Maria.

"On that same point: So far, not one person has been killed or hurt, and the only thing that has been tampered with was either plant food or animals that we eat," said Alice. "I understand the hesitation to jump to any conclusions, but can we at least agree that there's some sort of pattern going on? There's no real evidence yet that these things want to hurt humans. They've had many opportunities."

"I'm not agreeing or disagreeing, but you certainly have a point," said John.

"You're right until you're wrong though. As far as we know, they haven't killed any humans, but I don't ever want to see the day where we're being dissected and then recreated. I don't want to even know what that would look like," said Victor.

"I don't either. But she's not wrong, Victor. It hasn't happened yet," said Maria.

Victor held a stubborn silence as long as he could, and then he broke it. "It has not happened yet…" Maria looked at her husband. As much trouble as she had keeping an open mind, she knew that Victor was digging through rock to stay open. She was proud of him for giving up some ground. There was a long, healthy silence throughout the car. "I think I need some goddamn grits. Now, I'm hungry," said Victor. Maria smiled.

"Not a bad idea, Mr. Delphi," said John.

Chapter Thirty-Five
<u>On The Other Hand</u>

"So, they pulled their skeletons out of their bodies? How does that make you feel better?" asked Mark with a look of disdain.

"It's not what happened to the cows that makes us feel better; it's the fact that their behavior is starting to add up and make sense," said John.

"The only thing that they're adding up to is the line from your poem. '*They will devour your brain, and discard your body.*' They're doing exactly what the poem said they would do."

All five of them sat at a table at *Choo's Bar and Grill*. Mark took a large swallow from his beer. The hope that was briefly collected in the car ride home a few days ago was steadily being deflated by Mark's blunt tone.

"It's not happening to human beings, Mark. As long as they're only dissecting animals and vegetables then we--"

Mark cut John off. "It is happening to human beings, John. Seventeen people died in Oklahoma."

"What do you mean seventeen people died?" asked Maria in shock.

"I figured I would wait to tell you in person, but yeah, seventeen. The building where I saw the worms, the same worms that are ripping brains out of animals, the roof fell in and killed seventeen workers two weeks ago."

"Jesus Christ. Did you see the building?" asked Victor.

"Yeah, my son told me about it so I went over there. They're just starting to clean it up. We would probably have heard about it if we were paying attention to anything outside of the lab." Alice could only look down at the table, Maria was tearing up rapidly, and John's mind launched into one of its old, familiar spinouts.

"Did you know anyone who died?" asked Victor.

"Yeah, a guy named Kenny who I became friendly with before I got fired. A few others who I met too." Mark took another long sip of beer. Everyone remained speechless. "I don't know about cows or fruits or vegetables or any of that bullshit, but I do know that we're no longer safe. I watched those things fly around that building, and now it's a pile of rocks. They tore up John's room, and everyone in that hotel is lucky that it didn't come down."

"Well, what about everywhere else?" asked Victor. "Are we even safe in the lab? Maybe we should move everything out."

"That's not possible. We have all of our work in there. Without the lab, we can't get anything done," said Maria.

"Would you rather be dead?"

"No, Victor, but there's nowhere else to go. They could kill us anywhere if they wanted to, and we have no chance if we don't have the lab."

"Maria, we're not going to be the only people using that building in about two weeks. We can't be responsible for everybody else dying." As important as the subject was, Mark, Alice, and John allowed the couple their chance to argue.

"Then we will find a way to keep everyone out, but if we leave there, we're giving up. And it will look even more suspicious to them if we suddenly leave."

"Maria, I'm sorry, but you're speaking nonsense right now. Most likely, they're sitting there watching us as we try and destroy the very thing that they're building. All they have to do is drop the ceiling on our heads and it's over."

"Exactly. That's all they have to do, and they can do that to anyone that they want to. We have zero ability to conduct anything useful outside of the lab. Not right now at least..." Maria sat back against the seat with her arms crossed. Victor's ego would not allow him to admit it because Maria appeared to be arguing for the side of insanity, yet he and everyone at the table knew that she was for some reason right. He considered how the worms might react to them leaving in an organized panic. "Maybe it looks to them like we're trying to build a way in. Whatever it is, we have no choice. You can leave, Victor, but I will be in the lab."

Victor reached out and grabbed the hand of his wife. He squeezed it and nodded his head to her. "Okay... There's no way it's safe, but they probably know where we live anyway."

"Can I ask a question? If they decided all of a sudden that they were just going to kill dozens of people, then why are they wasting their time helping Enoch grow his corn?" asked Alice.

"Does it really matter? They decided not to kill that guy and great for him, but they certainly killed a lot of other people," said Mark. "We need to spend every day figuring out exactly how to stop this. No more wasting time arguing whether or not these things are trying to help us. They're not." Mark stood up and pulled out his wallet. He took out some money and threw it on the table. "If we're staying at the lab then that's where I'll be. We need to start working. We're less than forty days out."

"I'll come with you," said Victor.

"Listen, John. I know you're not one hundred percent in with us, but we need you to make up your mind. We need all the help we can get. Time's up on trying to weigh every single option. The decision's been made for us." Mark turned around and walked off.

Victor stood up. "What do you want to do, Maria?"

"Just go with Mark, and I'll drive us three back. We'll pay the bill and follow you back in a few minutes," said Maria.

"Okay, please drive safe," said Victor before giving Maria a kiss and walking away. John, Alice, and Maria sat alone. John was still recovering from the information and Maria was left stunned.

"Maria, what do you think about this?" asked Alice.

"I'm scared. I really thought that you might have been right, Alice."

"And now you don't? Your mind is made up?"

"Well, how could it not be? Did you not hear what he said?"

"Yes, I heard him, but it doesn't make sense. If they killed those people, then why not Enoch or us?"

"Maybe they don't care whether we live or die, or maybe they're using us and we don't know it. They're clearly much smarter than we are. But we can't ignore facts, Alice. It's a fact that people are dead. Everything else is just speculation."

"Well, if they're smarter than us, then I guess we don't have much of a chance to stop them anyway, so why even try?"

"Maria's right," said John. "I was on your side, Alice, and I'll admit that a lot of me wanted you to be right, but we cannot discount a tragedy, and it would take a lot to convince me that this was a coincidence. This is very bad. For all we know, seventeen is just the beginning."

"So, that's it? No more debate? Everything is decided?"

"It's not that simple, Alice. We have to consider all of the evidence, especially when that evidence involves a mass killing," said John.

"You don't know what made that building fall, John, and neither do you," said Alice to Maria.

"You're not being honest if you can't look at it from both sides," said Maria.

"Have you looked at it from both sides? Besides John, no one has considered anything that I've said."

"There are five of us. We're all entitled to an opinion, but don't judge us for closing our ears if you're going to do the same thing," said Maria as she got up from the table and walked away.

"You told me to keep thinking the way that I'm thinking," said Alice to John.

"I know I did."

"Why are you taking it back?"

"I'm not, but you can't ignore something so obvious. This isn't a cornfield or a lake full of fish. Everything just changed."

"Yes, and it's very convenient timing too, isn't it?" asked Alice. John nodded his head.

"I don't know what to say, Alice. We have to move forward, but we can't go in there like this. This is not the time to argue. Right now, you're only going to polarize them more, and it's hard to blame them."

Alice sat back in solidarity. "Then I guess it doesn't make much sense for me to go back. If my voice will only be antagonizing, then I'm not going to waste their time, your time, or mine. And if you're right, there's not much time left to waste."

"You're not wasting our time. I wish you would consider staying. You're very smart and very level-headed. I just think you need to step back and think about everything. I'm not saying that you're wrong."

"I think that you are. I'm going to go. We both know that you're the only one who pays me any mind anyway. I don't need to be ignored or silenced. If you have any thoughts, you can give me a call. Otherwise, I'll either see you at some point, or I won't."

"Where are you going?"

"Home. Another place where I'm not welcome."

★★★

John and Maria shared a silent car ride back to the lab. John sat still and disappointed while Maria quietly sobbed. John knew that the tragedy would slowly drive all of them apart. He had little experience with mass death, but he knew good and well what fear did to the human instinct.

They got back to the NASA/Thomas laboratory and remained silent on their walk to the east wing lab. Victor and Mark were already hard at work on their new set of pidimas. Mark had zero experience in the field of solar engineering, but he was great with tools and equally skilled in following meticulous directions. He filled in as Victor's assistant. "How can we help?" asked Maria. Victor looked up.

"Well... I may have to handle the small details myself, but you can start stripping down those solar panels if you're very careful. Just use the tools out of the box."

"Do we just take out all the parts?"

"Take it down to nothing," said Victor. "Where's the southerner?"

"Gone," said John. Victor and Mark stopped and looked at John.

"No way. She left?" asked Mark. John nodded his head. "Well... Her constant disagreements will be missed," said Mark.

"That's not true," said Maria. "She just had a different perspective."

"Honey, never once did she consider anyone else's opinion. Even after Mark told her that almost twenty people died, she still can't compromise. We're better off without her. I've been saying it for weeks." Victor continued putting together his machine. Maria sighed and walked over to a collection of solar panels. She pulled one out and began studying its design. John watched them work. He was slumped over, wearing his disappointment on his shoulders. Mark looked up at him.

"John, listen. Nobody here thinks that you're anything less than sensible... Brilliant even. Let's all be honest. You're brilliant. But you can't tell me that she wasn't steering us in the wrong direction. You said it yourself. You're an atheist, and she based all of her ideas on emotion and faith. She had no room for facts or reality."

"You know what, Mark? I can't even tell you that you're wrong, but she's the one person out of all of us who followed her gut. I'm a skeptical scientist, and so is Maria, and so is Victor, and we only believe in what we can see. Right now, we see death, so we're driven by fear. You and I are only trying to put a stop to this because we don't know what's on the other side, but that doesn't mean that we're any smarter. It only means that we're scared. She was scared of nothing."

"I'd rather be scared and alive than dead," said Mark.

"Well, that makes you exactly the same as everyone else then."

"If you want to risk your life, John, then you go ahead. Go spend the next month with Alice or that nut job on the farm. I'm going to stay here and make sure my son has a tomorrow to wake up to."

"Don't worry, Mark; I'll be here with you. I'll do what I can to help, but don't think that you're not risking anything. You're risking a lot. If we stop this thing from opening up, then your boy will have a future, but it may just be the same future that you and I have: pointless and brief. If that great machine that they're building holds any kind of opportunity, rest assured, you and I are responsible for its demise." John walked over to the table next to Maria and picked up a solar panel. He began dismantling it.

Chapter Thirty-Six
<u>A Most Curious Phone Call</u>

Maria watched her husband sleep beside her. For some reason, stress did not follow her home. She managed to leave all of her bad feelings in the lab for one night. Victor opened his eyes and saw Maria looking at him. He stared back at his wife who was lying naked next to him. He, in particular, was guilty about taking his stresses from the lab home, but at that moment, he only thought about how much he loved her.

"Did I wake you up?" she asked.

"No, I've been going in and out." He put his hand down and gently rubbed her belly. "Do you think it sleeps at night?"

"I don't know. It's quiet so far," she said. "I want a boy, but I know it's going to be a girl."

"How do you know that?"

"My dad told me. He said that he always knew that he would have a girl, and his girl would have a girl. Plus, I think I can just tell. It feels like a girl."

Victor smiled. "I wouldn't mind having a little Maria around here. Do you think she'll be as smart as you?"

"Absolutely. I won't even be close. That's something else my dad told me. He said that my little girl would change the world," said Maria. Victor laughed.

"I think you might have beat her to it, honey," he said. She paused.

"Do you think we're doing the right thing?" she asked. Victor looked at her for a moment.

"I do. I don't think we have a choice. We need to think about our kid. Everything will feel right when we have a family." They looked into each other's eyes and said nothing.

The phone rang.

Victor rolled over to check the clock. It read *one A.M.* "Who's calling us now?" he asked.

"Maybe it's Mark or John."

"We just left them an hour ago. I thought they were going to sleep." Victor picked up the phone. "Hello?"

"Hello…" said the voice from the other end. "Is this Mr. Delphi?"

"Yes. Who's calling please?"

"Hello, Mr. Delphi. This is Enoch Pricherwood from Sutton."

Victor looked at Maria. They were both surprised. "Yes, Enoch, how are you? Is everything okay?" There was an extended silence from the other end.

"Yes, Mr. Delphi. I apologize for calling so late, but I'm afraid that it couldn't wait."

"Umm… No, that's okay. What can I help you with?" asked Victor. Victor waited for an answer. On the phone, he heard calm, yet heavy breathing.

"I was visited again tonight, Mr. Delphi."

"You were visited? By who?" Maria hopped out of bed and ran over to the desk on the other side of the room.

"Something else came to the farm," said Enoch.

"What was it? Are you okay?"

"Yes, sir. I am. This was much different than the other creatures, though. In fact, It was no creature at all," said Enoch. Maria came back to bed with a voice recorder. She took the phone from Victor's hand and turned it on to speaker mode, then she started recording.

"I'm sorry, Enoch. I don't believe I'm quite following. What was it that you saw?" asked Victor.

"It was something higher."

"I see…" said Victor. He looked to Maria who was just as confused as he was. "What exactly happened when you saw It? Where were you?"

"It happened a few hours ago. I was finishing in the fields at right about sundown. Since Sunday, I have been so busy with the corn, I don't believe I've seen even half of the tunnels yet. I wanted to walk through one more before dark, and I noticed that one tunnel in particular didn't have any corn growing inside of it. I decided to walk down and see if I could find anything down in there.

"My flashlight had stopped working, but I just kept walking further and further. Before I knew it, I had walked several hundred feet into the dark." Victor and Maria sat silently and listened to Enoch. "Eventually, I made it to a place where four different tunnels intersected. It made sort of a small room. And then there I stopped.

"I couldn't tell you why, and I don't know why, but something in my body knew to wait right there. All around me was pitch-darkness. It was moist and cold, and it was completely quiet. I stood still and waited. Just as I started to feel that the darkness was beginning to get the better of me, I saw It."

"What was It?"

"Down the far end of a tunnel, a light slowly came towards me. From far, the light was just bright, but the closer It came, the more I could see the colors. They were beautiful. I saw colors that I have never seen before. Impossible colors. This Thing floated towards me, and the closer that It got, the more the stale air from the dirt suddenly turned warm and began to smell fresh like flowers." Enoch paused on the other end of the phone. Victor and Maria waited, but he did not continue to speak.

"Did It get close enough for you to see what It looked like?" asked Victor.

"Yes, It did, Mr. Delphi. It presented Itself before It spoke to me," said Enoch. Victor and Maria hung on impatiently. They heard Enoch take a breath.

"I stood in the very middle of the opening between the tunnels and looked down the one in which It was traveling. When It reached the end of the tunnel, It made Its way into the open space. It floated in front of me, maybe ten feet away, and It looked directly at me and into me. It was a giant Eye. It was only an Eye, but I will tell you, Mr. Delphi, that It was the greatest and most beautiful thing that I have ever seen.

"It glowed with gold and diamonds. They shined in circles and patterns, and they went on as far back as I could see. It was endless. And It would blink once in a while, and when It blinked, It revealed these incredible feathers. They draped It from top to bottom like the great headdress of an Indian chief. Right then, my legs gave in, and I fell to my knees." Maria and Victor clenched to each other's hands. Victor's face watered up with tears of shock.

"I watched as It made Its way around me, but It didn't move like regular things move. It appeared only in certain places at a time, but I knew that It was all around me at once, and I could only see what It wanted me to see. And as It shifted around me, the feathers disappeared and reappeared, and they twirled in and out of sight. I was seeing different colors every second. I could hear a sound of chimes echoing through the tunnels. It was soothing, and the Eye began to dance. It danced around me in circles and gave me the most incredible feeling that I've ever felt. Finally, I asked, 'Who are you?'

"The Being stopped and bowed to me. I could suddenly hear an orchestra of bells in my head. It sent shivers through me like somebody rang my heart. Somehow, It was talking to me, and I understood it. It said, 'Hello, Enoch. I am here for you.' Its voice was like nothing I've ever heard either. It did not sound like a man's or a woman's voice. It was pitchless and angelic. I asked It how It knew my name and It said, 'I have known you, Enoch, and you have known Me. We have been together before.'

"I found it very hard to speak right then. My chest was tight, but I asked It, 'When were we together?' It then floated up and over my head, real slow, and It looked down at me from the ceiling. It felt like a long while that It stared at me, then It floated back down in front of me. And then I heard It again. 'I want to show you who I am,' It said. I nodded my head to tell It *Yes.* It then told me to take the book out of my pocket. I couldn't believe it. I had been carrying my small Bible around with me all day in my inside pocket. I didn't even remember that I had it in there. I don't know how It knew, but I took it out. It then said, 'Turn to a page, and tear it out.'

"My finger flipped to the New Testament, and I pulled a page out. The Eye then told me to look at it and memorize what I could, and then turn it over and look at the other side. I did my best to read the front. I was very familiar with it already. It was Matthew, chapters three, four, and five. Then I did as It told me and turned it to the other side. It said, 'Hold the paper in front of your eyes'. So, I held it up. It then began reading both sides of the page at once. I heard It reciting exactly what I had read on the back, and at the same time, I heard Its voice also reading what I was seeing on the front. It finished both pages at the exact same time. Right then I could not hold back my tears." Enoch paused. His stuttered breathing told Victor and Maria that he was crying again.

"Enoch, are you okay? That sounds terrifying," said Victor.

"Yes, Mr. Delphi. I am. I did not feel terror. I felt awake for the first time. After I cried for a moment, It asked me to rise from my knees. As soon as I gathered myself up, I felt an immediate comfort. It looked deep in me and told me that I was safe, and I knew that It told the truth.

"It backed up to one of the walls of dirt and told me to watch. All of a sudden, the dirt began to separate. It opened up and I could see a blank space. It all just disappeared. I went over to look at it and I asked where the dirt went. It told me that it was all still very close, just in another space. Then I looked up and I saw the dirt above my head disappear, and then on the other wall, and near my feet. It said that there were endless places all around me that I could never see, but are always just right there. The dirt was just moving over.

"I looked up and told It that I want to know more. It circled around me again, staring at me the whole time. Then It said, 'I will show you something'. It opened up another spot in the dirt that kind of pointed up and away from where we were. 'Go this way,' It said. 'I will show you'. Then I walked through the opening. As soon as I took one step through, I couldn't see anything. It wasn't dark or blank like you would think a blind person sees, but it was almost like sight was no longer part of me. I didn't need it or feel it.

"I must have walked for one or two minutes and then something stopped me and turned me. I couldn't feel nothin' touching me, but I knew that my body was turning. And then all of a sudden, I could see my house. I was looking down on it from above, but I wasn't in the sky. My feet were on solid ground. Wherever it was that I was at, I could see my entire house. And then something moved me again just slightly, and now I could see inside of my house. It looked like somebody took the roof off and I could see everything inside. 'Look at your wife,' It said.

"I looked for her and I could see Delilah in our son's bedroom. She was crying. She sat on the bed with her face buried in a handkerchief. And then I was moved again, and suddenly I could see the inside and the outside of the house both at the same time. I could see Delilah and the top of the roof all at once. I can't explain it, but I can still see it.

"Then I was rolled over so I was looking up, and the only thing that I could see was the Eye. I was so overwhelmed. It said to me, 'This is where I exist, and where they exist, but your kind must not.' I asked, 'Why can't we,' and it said that we would not be safe. It said '*The Differents*' would get us. That's what it kept calling them: '*The Differents*'. It said that they were the ones that dug the holes. It knew that you and John called them '*the worms*'."

"Did It mention us by name?" asked Victor.

"Yes. It mentioned Maria too," said Enoch. Maria stood up from the bed. Enoch's words made her spine stiffen.

"How did It know our names, Enoch?"

"I don't know, but It knew many things. It knew much about all of us."

"What did It say about the worms? Did It say why they are here?"

"It did. It told me about Its world and Its relationship with the worms, but I found it very hard to understand what It was telling me. It was all so complicated."

"What did It say?"

"The best that I could make out was that It said, unlike our home where only humans are intelligent, Its world has many types of intelligent beings. One of those types is the Differents, and It finds them to be an evil race. It said that they cannot speak to each other in the way that we can, but they constantly build machines for communication. It said that right now, they are building a great machine that will span across many spaces, and that they will enter our world in order to use our space and our energy. It said that we are in great danger, but It has come here to help. It wants us to close the portal before it is open for good."

"Oh my God," said Victor. "Did It say why the worms dug the tunnels or killed your animals?"

"Some of it was very hard to understand, but I believe It said that the corn was given as a false hope, but eventually we would all end up just like the cows."

"Oh my God..." Victor sank into himself. He was unable to process his fear.

"Before It left, It told me that we would meet again in that same tunnel and It would give me more important information. It wants me to help It close the opening when the time comes. It promised me that we will all be safe, and just before It left, It said, 'I am very thankful to have spoken with you, Enoch.' I asked It if It had a name. It said, 'Yes, Enoch. My name is Diaphnerous. I will be with you again in a short time.' And then I said thank you and goodbye. And It left."

Chapter Thirty-Seven
<u>The Following Morning</u>

The tape stopped and Maria turned off the recorder. The four of them sat at a picnic table just outside of the lab. "Well, is he crazy or not, because that sounds exactly like John's story," said Mark.

"That's what we've been talking about all night. The way he describes this Thing, the Eye, is pretty much spot on to what John saw. Doctor?" asked Victor. John nodded, almost reluctantly.

"And It said that Its name is Daiphnerous. Just like the *D* from the picture It left John," said Maria. "It's been following us and watching us, and It knows what we've been doing and talking about."

"Then how do we get in touch with It? Let's ask more of the questions that this guy was too dumb to ask," said Mark. "John, feel free to chime in. You're the only other one who saw It."

John took a moment to answer. "I'm thinking that you should be careful what you wish for, Mark."

"Be careful about what? Maybe It can tell us how to close the tesseract. I hope It is listening." Mark looked up to the sky and began to yell. "Come tell us what to do! What the fuck are you waiting for?"

Maria reached over and touched Mark. "Mark, stop. Don't taunt It."

"Don't you find it strange that the worms have been showing up for over a year, and they do things that we don't understand, and then this Thing comes along in the end with the ability to speak our language, and suddenly we have all the answers?" asked John.

"Of course it's strange, but what's your point, John? Everything that It said falls in line with what we've seen," said Victor.

"My point is that these *'worms'* and their technology are far beyond our understanding, and they either can't communicate with us or choose not to. And this Eye for some reason comes to us individually and tells us that It wants to save us, and It needs our help. Why would It need our help? What could we possibly do that It could not do Itself, and why don't the worms just destroy us if we have the ability to stop them? Why are we even a factor?"

"We're acting according to the information that we have just like we've been doing all along. You want to just disregard this? It validates everything that we've learned up until now," said Victor.

"I'm not saying that, but these are questions that we should be asking," said John.

"If you had to pick a side right now, which would it be, John?" asked Maria. "We're running out of time."

"I have no idea. Just like every other time we've spoken about this, I still don't have the answers, but we shouldn't have spoken to Alice like that. There's absolutely no reason that anything this powerful should care what plans we have either way. This is all just too convenient. Nothing made sense for a year, now we have everything we've been looking for."

"Yesterday, you agreed to help us. You said yourself that Alice was being willfully ignorant. There are almost twenty dead bodies in Oklahoma. I find it incredible that you can't wrap your head around that," said Mark.

"Trust me, I can wrap my head around it fine, just like I can wrap my head around the fact that you weren't killed that day that you saw the worms. None of those dead bodies were any threat to the tesseract. You are. Why are you still here? These are intelligent beings and they have motives. That's the part that we keep ignoring," said John.

"Well, you do so much thinking for all of us that we don't really have to, Doctor." said Mark.

"Mark, stop. We can't keep fighting every time we get into this," said Maria.

"I'm sorry, but I got a kid to think about, and you do too. If you had more people in your life, John, then maybe you'd give a shit too," said Mark.

"Mark, stop," said Maria.

"Then there's your answer, Mark. You've figured out what the rest of us could not. Obviously, you don't need me. I'm the piece of shit who can't make up his mind, and you're the one with the plan. I don't want to slow you down anymore," said John as he stood up from the table. "You let me know how everything goes, and if we're alive in a month then I guess I'll owe you a drink."

"John, don't leave. We can't afford to lose any more time."

"I can't keep having the same argument over and over, Victor. We've been stuck on this for weeks now. I'm sorry that I said I would help you guys. Maybe I'm losing my mind, but the more I think about it, the less it makes any sense. If I stick around, I'll only get in your way. You can call me if anything new comes up." John walked away shaking his head.

"Jesus, Mark. Was that necessary?" asked Victor.

"What do you mean? He's just like Alice. How much do they need to hear before they change their minds? One day ago, the guy says that he's on our side, and now he can't understand what we're talking about. It's like he's arguing with himself." Victor pressed his face into his hands. Maria rubbed his back for comfort.

"We need help, Mark," said Maria.

"I agree, but not from those two. Anytime it's just the three of us, we seem to get a lot more done. Somehow, I think we'll be fine."

Victor stood up and began pacing. "Regardless of whether or not he's wrong, we still need bodies. We need to hit two different corners of the cube at once. That means that we have to split up into two different states to operate the pidimas at the same time."

"Well, then I guess we're lucky that there happens to be three of us. We have an extra body to spare," said Mark.

"Then I hope to God that there are still three of us around when the time comes. I'm the only one that knows how to work the machines. Maria's seen me use it, but she still needs help. Now do the two of us need to split up?"

"Absolutely not," said Mark. "We still have enough time for me to learn everything. There's no way you two are splitting up. God forbid this doesn't work and it turns out that... whatever. You two need to be together. I'll learn what I need to and I'll go by myself."

Victor shook his head. "We could have convinced him. Maybe he'll come back," said Victor.

"Forget it, man. He's irrational. He hasn't been the same since that week that he went missing. We have to accept that the three of us are on our own, and we need to do what we need to do."

They sat at the table for a moment and said nothing. The air was heavy. Maria sighed. "Wouldn't it be easier if we didn't know what was going on? I'm so jealous of everyone who just gets up and goes to work every day. Even if this kills us, I'd still rather live my last days happy and ignorant," said Maria. Victor rubbed her shoulder. She took his hand and held it. "So, what do you think this Thing is? *Diaphnerous,* our savior. Where does Diaphnerous fit into everything?"

Mark grinned as it came to him. "Deus ex machina."

Chapter Thirty-Eight
<u>A Drink With Himselves</u>

John sat at the bar and drank a tall red ale. It was not the one that he had been craving from the Davidson Hotel Bar, but it was powerfully crisp and doing its job. In fact, it was his fourth glass. Each sip felt cold and well-deserved, and the carbonation charmingly bit his chest on the way down. As he stared at the cypress wood bar, he wondered when the voice in his head would come back to greet him with a self-crushing observation. It had been over a month since their last conversation, which was the longest that his mind was ever so quiet.

On the rare occasion when John had the opportunity to think freely, an odd thing happened. He envisioned that his six-year-old self was sitting next to him on his right, and his eighty-five-year-old self was seated to his left. In John's day dreams, he did most of the talking. He would try to justify his position and accomplishments thus far in life to his younger self, and then he would turn and try to answer the questions from his elderly self before the old man had the chance to ask them. Six-year-old John already had great aspirations in the study of existence, and he had big expectations for the doctor which were not being met. And the lonely old man pressured John to explain why he allowed himself to give up on love. Neither of them was ever happy with his answers, and he spent most of the time feeling like he was sword fighting two people uphill, but it certainly beat sitting there with the voice insulting his eardrums all night. Nothing was worse or more annoying than the voice.

John took a big gulp and swallowed two-thirds of his beer at once. His past and future remained quiet for a few minutes and allowed John to drink, but he eventually looked over to young John and saw his eager eyes looking up at him. Without words, John could see that the child was wondering how he planned to move forward.

"I don't know," said John. He then looked towards his older self, hoping that he would be met with some advice, but the old man just shrugged his shoulders. He had been wondering the same thing himself. "I guess I'm running out of time, huh?" John shook his head and looked back down at the bar. He stalled as the pressure in his head built up, and then he slammed his fist on the bar. "Well, why the fuck is everyone relying on me? Why do I always have to have the answers? There are three other adults that are more than capable of using their heads. Go ask one of them." John stood up and pulled some money out of his pocket. He threw it on the bar and walked to the door. He opened it and looked back. The child and the old man stared at him with no expression, and their silence only added more weight to his back. He turned and walked out.

***

John made it back to his dorm with the relief that none of the others were there waiting for him. There was a phone call on his agenda that would ease his conscience, but his first order of business was a wheat style ale that he bought from a liquor store when he was in Nebraska. He intended to drink it for company.

He settled into his room and poured himself a tall glass. He drank it in large gulps and filled it up again. He regretted the conversation to come. With nothing but time to waste, John drank down another glass and then stared at the phone for five more minutes. Finally, his nerves had enough and he dialed Alice's number. She picked up before the end of the first ring. "Hello?"

"Hi, it's John."

"I know. What's going on?" Alice's straight-to-the-point tone was stinging.

"Listen… I'm sorry for how yesterday went. I never should have let you leave, and I shouldn't have spoken to you so arrogantly. It took me all of one hour to realize that I agree with you… I'm just not good at taking risks. I'm sorry, Alice." Alice took a long exhale on the other line.

"Thank you, John, but I wish you would have said this yesterday before I left."

"I know. I'm sorry. It hit me pretty hard when Mark told us about the people who died. And even now, it's difficult to reconcile it and separate that from everything else, but I don't think you're crazy to have questions about it."

"Thank you." Silence hung around in between their words.

"Where are you? Did you go home?" asked John.

"No actually. I came to Louisiana."

"Louisiana? Why?"

"I'm looking for answers. I don't have to be at work until next week and I found a cheap flight."

"Are you looking for the fig orchard?"

"I found it. I was there today."

"Really? What was it like? Did it look like the cornfield?"

"No, it didn't, but it was incredible. There weren't any tunnels, but they did something to the trees. The branches and the roots are all twisted up into each other. Whatever they did, the figs are huge. I'm afraid to eat any, but I bought a few."

"Does anyone there know about the worms? Did you speak to them about it?"

"No, I don't believe they know anything, John. I didn't come out and ask them exactly, but it's just one family that runs the farm, and they seemed like they were still amazed by the figs. I'm going back tonight too."

"Do they keep it open all night?"

"No, but I need more time to look around without being watched. The size of the area is about the same size as the corn tunnels. I'm planning on spending most of the night there." Alice paused. "The farm is supposedly directly under where I saw the orb in the sky: the orb that got me into this whole mess. I guess I'll be looking up to see if I can find that too..." Alice paused to take a breath. "So, how did the rest of last night go? Have you spoken to them at all today?"

"Yes. That's actually the other reason why I'm calling you. A lot has happened in twenty-four hours."

"What?"

"Enoch called Victor last night. Something else came to the farm. It spoke with him."

"Spoke with him? What was It?" asked Alice.

"From the way he described what It looked like and what It said to him, we think that It was the same Eye that I saw in the bathroom mirror that night in the dorms; and most likely the same Thing that drew me the picture and wrote the poem."

"Oh my God."

"I don't know that for sure, but I'm allowing myself to start making assumptions. It told him about why the worms are here and who they are."

"What did It say about them?"

"Unfortunately, Enoch ended each sentence with either *'I couldn't understand'* or *'it was very confusing,'* so he described very little, but the basic message was the same as we've been told all along. You know, they're here to destroy us and they're very evil. That sort of thing," said John.

"Shit. What a time for me to leave. I wish I could have asked him questions. Did you speak with him?"

"No, Victor and Maria recorded the phone call. They played it for us."

"Then, what are your plans now?"

"I'm not sure. I had a pretty good argument with Mark before I left, and I can't say that I would feel too comfortable going back right now. What are you doing after you leave Louisiana?" asked John.

"I was planning on heading to Florida. I have a few days before I have to travel. You're welcome to join me. Maybe we could figure a few things out with some time away from everything," said Alice.

"You know what? That sounds like a good idea. Since you're there for tonight, I'll start heading down south. It will take me a day or two."

"You're driving?" asked Alice.

"Of course. I have this little metal ball in my bag that I've been thinking a lot about. I'm not sure how airport security would feel about it and I can't let it out of my sight just yet."

"Then I guess I will see you soon, John. But listen… What if… What if we're wrong?"

"What do you mean?"

"About everything. What if we're wrong, and we've been arguing with them the whole time? Do we go back to try and help them close it? Can we go back at this point?"

"We have to. We're right to explore our options, but if we know at any point that we need to go back, then we need to go back. And they could always use our help. I promise you," said John.

Alice took a deep breath and let it out. "I guess it's time to make up our minds. The days aren't going any slower."

★★★

Maria stood outside of the NASA/Thomas building and looked into the night sky. She was beneath an ocean of stars that shined like lights. She looked at each one individually and imagined just how far away that it really was, and then she moved on to the next one.

"All of a sudden it all looks a lot different, huh?" Maria turned around and saw Mark lighting a cigarette.

"Yeah. I can't even wrap my head around it," she said.

"It's like everything that we can see is just one tiny page in a library of books. As significant as we feel to ourselves, we almost don't even exist."

Maria nodded. "We're so ignorant too. My father taught me science before I could even understand it, and I looked up to him as the greatest man that I have ever seen. He helped people get into space. My whole life, I thought that was man's greatest achievement. Now I think it's a joke. We've only been as far as the moon, and we can't even do that anymore. In the scheme of things, we're as small and simple as the flats."

"Well, when this is all over, I think you're going to be pretty famous," said Mark.

"What do you mean?"

"Come on. Even if we kill the tesseract, it's still going to make some sort of impact. People will want answers. You have all the answers," said Mark.

"I don't have any answers. Besides, when something like this happens, most people will assume a miracle or divine activity. It will be good business for the church," said Maria.

"Yeah? You have any more thoughts on that and where you stand?"

Maria took a deep breath and exhaled. "I don't know. Maybe God's around. Maybe He's even in one of those higher dimensions, but as far as this goes... no.

I don't think He's involved. As multifaceted as the creatures are, I still don't see anything that is beyond supernatural, and I don't feel any presence of God in this. I'm just scared. I feel fear." Mark put his arm around Maria's shoulder and squeezed her for comfort. They stood together for some time and looked up at the stars.

***

The sun rose over the field of corn. Its light covered the cold crops with warmth. It was only dawn, but Enoch was already in the field. He walked the tunnels all night in the hopes of running into his new Friend, but after hours of searching, he only found himself alone in the dirt. Enoch was filthy and sleepless, but his self-awareness was clouded by his mania to be visited again.

Delilah sat in the house over the long-past day, but she set herself up along the nearest window every time she settled into a new room. She watched Enoch as he climbed out of one hole just to walk down another countless times. She was the first to hear about his introduction to the great Eye. The righteousness and awe of her husband's story excited Delilah, but she also worried about him.

He spent the last two days under the sun, climbing around in the dirt until he was covered in it. He did not come into the house once since the previous morning. She periodically brought him glasses of water and forced him to drink them, but he refused to eat. He refused to stop for anything for more than thirty seconds before his patience ran thin, and then he would head straight for the next tunnel.

He stopped picking the corn and prohibited Delilah from even touching it. To Enoch, it was now seen as an overgrowth of deceit, intended to only poison their bodies and minds. His behavior was that to which Delilah had never seen in her husband. As much as she wanted to ask Enoch to stop and think reasonably about his actions, she knew that he had to wear himself down before he would be in any condition to hear a word that she had to say.

Chapter Thirty-Nine
<u>A Gift Under The Tree</u>

"I now understand how you can have a smoking addiction," said John. He sat across from Alice on her apartment balcony and drank a beer while she had a glass of whiskey and a cigarette. "I didn't look at the drawing at all on the drive here, but I wanted to. I wrapped it in a cloth and tied it with string just to make it harder to stop and look, but the longer I avoid it, the more I think about it."

"I can't stop thinking about it either. I don't understand how you can carry it around and not look," said Alice.

"It's not easy, but I know that if I look at it alone again, I'll probably die. I lost about five pounds over that week that I didn't have to lose."

"I can't imagine that. An entire week just gone," said Alice. She smiled and shook her head as she took a drag of her cigarette.

"So, now that I'm settled in here in the Florida heat, can we talk about last night?" asked John. "Did anything happen?"

"Oh yeah. A lot happened."

"Enlighten me," said John.

"I went back to the farm. I got there at about eight, but the last person didn't drive off until around ten, so I sat in my car for a few hours and watched the trees. And they were absolutely incredible."

"What did they look like? I know you said they were entwined with each other," said John.

"The roots were twisted into each other, and the branches looked like they reached out and held the branches on the other trees. And I swear the figs moved up and down a couple of feet from the time that I pulled up to the time I got out of the car," said Alice.

"You mean you could see them moving?"

"It's not that I watched them move exactly, but from eight o'clock to ten o'clock, each branch that held the figs migrated either up or down a couple of feet."

"What about when you got out of the car?"

"I walked up and down the rows of trees for a few hours. Each one was so unique; I could have spent the whole night just looking at them," said Alice. "After a while, I found this tree that had a trunk shaped like a seat, so I sat down. It felt like it was giving me a hug, and eventually I fell asleep. I was out for about an hour until I felt something on my face."

"What was it?" asked John.

"Static. My face was covered in static electricity. I felt it climbing down the tree and onto my face. I eased out of my sleep, and a tiny little light appeared about six feet away from me. It was maybe the size of a penny. I felt the static jump off of my face and onto the ball of light and it started growing.

"It looked just like you described, John. I couldn't tell exactly what kind of shape it was. At times it looked like a circle, then I was sure it was some sort of polygon, then I couldn't tell at all, but I do know one thing: It sure was beautiful. All of the colors inside of it were absolutely stunning. I crawled over to it and got a better look. You know what it was, right?" asked Alice.

"To me, it looked like a window. It seemed like I was looking through some sort of contorted lens into another world."

"Exactly. It's not just a window though. It's a doorway. It's a doorway that opens from outside of us. I could feel the breeze coming out of it. It was incredible… like a divine wind."

"What else happened?"

"I got close enough to feel it on my face, so I decided that I was just going to dive in, face first. I lunged, but before I could touch it, the orb shrank and I went straight to the ground. When I rolled over and looked up, it had grown back to its bigger size, and now there was an eye staring at me. It was looking from the other side."

"What did it look like? Was it the golden Eye?" asked John.

"No. It looked more like an eye of death. It was gray and pale and cracked. It looked at me very… intensely. It scared me at first, but I realized that the look in the eye was not angry or hateful. It looked like it was struggling. It was exhausting itself like it was trying to speak to me, but couldn't. I started talking to it, but nothing was getting through, so we just stared at each other."

"For how long?"

"I don't know exactly, but a long time. Eventually, the sphere just faded away. I don't understand why it didn't let me touch the orb because I wanted to go in."

"Maybe it's for the best. Maybe you wouldn't be able to handle it, mentally or physically," said John.

"I didn't care at the moment. I just wanted in," said Alice.

"Well, now at least you know what we're all talking about. You've finally seen a worm."

"But that wasn't the end of it. When it disappeared, it left something behind." Alice reached down into her bag and pulled out an object wrapped in a towel. She handed it to John.

"What is it?" he asked.

"I have no idea. Unwrap it." John carefully unrolled the towel and revealed a stonelike object. It was flat on the bottom, and turned cylinder shaped until it came to a point at the very top. It was about seven inches long, four inches wide, and very heavy. John judged it to be about ten pounds.

"This looks like a primitive tool or something. Something you would find in an ancient cave."

"Twist the top," said Alice.

"Twist it?" John gently twisted it and found that the top point came off, although it did not have any internal ridges like that of a jar's lid. It came off flat, giving no explanation of how it stayed together to begin with. John held both halves and examined them.

"Does it do anything?" he asked.

"Sort of. I mean, yes, but I'm not sure what. Take the flat end of the point and place it on that wall," said Alice.

"What do you mean?"

"Let me show you." Alice took the top end and turned it to where the flat end was facing the outside wall of her apartment. She then placed the object against the wall and it stuck on.

"How does it do that?" asked John.

"I have no idea. Probably uses the same magic that your metal ball uses. Now watch this." Alice then took the bottom half of the object and placed it flat against the wall. It also stuck. "Look it sticks now, but this half will only stick if the top half is on there first."

"How did you figure this out?"

"I've been playing with it all day," she said. John pulled out the metal ball from his bag. He held it down near the two objects that were stuck to the wall. As he held the ball closer, it began to resist.

"Look at this. I can't touch them together. It's like trying to force two north sides of a magnet together," said John. He tried his best to force the ball to the other objects, but his hand began to shake and struggle. He looked up at Alice. "Can we go inside and see what else this will stick to?" Alice smiled.

John and Alice proceeded to march through every room in her apartment and apply their unworldly instrument in an effort to understand its physics and makeup. It stuck itself to many things, and ignored many others. The surface material seemed to have no bearing on its decision. Metal, wood, brick, and glass all either worked or did not work depending on factors that remained unclear. They ran the apartment, and then doubled back, but still they learned nothing. The weighted pair of objects were proving to be even more baffling than the metal ball.

After a few hours of study, Alice flopped down into her armchair and placed the top of the object onto the side of her coffee table. John sat down on the couch directly across from her and placed the bottom half of the object on the other side of the table so that it was facing its counterpart. Both ends hung off of the table, defying gravity. John looked at his end and strained to understand it.

He finally took a break from the mental anguish and exhaled in exhaustion. He put his foot on the corner of the coffee table to give it a rest, and as soon as he released the weight of his foot onto the tabletop, it shot out from under him right into the chair where Alice sat. It smashed the chair's legs with great speed. Alice and John looked at each other with wide eyes. "Holy shit," said Alice.

"Don't move," said John. "Do you have a camera or camera phone?" he asked.

"Umm… yeah. There's a digital camera on my kitchen counter. Why?"

"I want to make sure we can recreate this exactly before we start messing around."

"Okay..." said Alice while trying her best to stay completely still. "Can I still not move?"

"No, you can move. Just don't touch the table."

"Okay," said Alice as she hopped to her feet and moved into the kitchen. She quickly came back with a camera in her hand and gave it to John. John moved over the coffee table and started examining it. He snapped a picture every few seconds.

"I can already tell you that the two halves are lined up perfectly across from each other. We must have just gotten lucky, but I think we're on to something here," said John. He touched the corner of the coffee table and nudged it towards the middle of the room. It slid across the floor as if he shoved it with all of his strength. He and Alice shared another look. Alice walked over and placed her palm flat on the table's surface. She began moving the table around in circles with little effort. "It's light," she said. She continued to move it. "The stones made it light."

As Alice continued to slide the table back and forth, John reached down and removed the triangular end from the side of the table. Immediately Alice could no longer move the table with ease, and the bottom end of the object ejected itself from the other side of the table. "Wow," said Alice. John put the pointed end back to where it was a moment ago.

"Can you move it," he asked. Alice extended her arm, but achieved no motion from the table.

"It's heavy again," she said. John picked up the cylinder end of the stone and placed it back on the table, lined up perfectly with the pointed half. As soon as he made contact, Alice's weight forced the table across the floor. She fell to the ground as it slipped out from under her. "It's light again."

"It sure is," said John.

Now with an assurance that they were dealing with yet another tool, John and Alice re-ran their experiments through Alice's catalog of appliances. The washing machine, the refrigerator, her bedframe, and the kitchen table all succumbed to the stones weight-draining powers. However, walls, counters, and other anchored structures experienced no difference from their ordinary nature. After only an hour and a half, they had rearranged Alice's entire apartment without even breaking a sweat. John then had one final test.

With the two halves of the stone sitting as a whole on the floor, John dropped the metal ball on the bedroom floor. The ball rolled its way over to Alice's large oak armoire, claiming it as the room's heaviest object. John then picked the stone up off the ground, unscrewed it, and placed each half on separate sides of the armoire. As soon as they were lined up, the metal ball retreated from the oak surface and made its way to the bed frame. "You know what this means, right? My little round friend, which always seeks the object in the room with the most mass, no longer considers your wooden dresser the king. Whatever this is that you have been given somehow removes the mass from objects, which is why they become easier to move."

"How do you think it does that? Is that possible in science?"

"Not as far as I know, but what do I know anyway? Maybe the stone somehow manipulates the Higgs field around the object and makes it pass under the radar."

"The Higgs what?"

"The Higgs field. Have you heard of the Higgs boson?" asked John. Alice returned an eyeroll.

"Please, John. Have I heard of any of these things that you talk about?"

"Fair point. The Higgs field is a field throughout the Universe that gives mass to particles. Massless objects move at the speed of light, but the more mass that something has, the more energy it requires to move. So, what I'm thinking is perhaps when we stick these two halves onto something, they minimize that something's contact with the Higgs field. It becomes lighter and requires less energy to move," John thought about it for a long minute and then shook it off. "I don't know. We have to look into this more, but one thing that I'm sure of is that this is the second gift that we have received from the worms that appears to be a tool of science, specifically mass related."

"Have you figured out the metal ball yet?"

"Not totally, but I'm not certain it's a coincidence that after my research on the gravity particle went missing, I received a ball that seems to act as a gravitational judge. It might even be silly to not suspect a correlation at this point," said John.

"So, why are they giving us tools? What are we supposed to do with these?"

"That's a good question. I don't know. My question is more specifically, why are these evil beings providing us with tools when they could much more easily let us join the poor souls from Oklahoma? And why is the golden Eye warning us against them?"

★★★

Maria watched from the far end of the laboratory wearing a pair of protective, dark-eye lenses. As the light poured in, her face was buried in brightness. Even through the dark lenses, she was forced to cover her eyes from the awesome light. "Okay, turn on number three!" shouted Victor over the loud machines. Victor stood dangerously close to the large pidima shell that he had been constructing. It was a six-by-six cubic metal frame with pidimas in each corner that all pointed at his original light pidima in the center. Mark stood on the other side of the shell and operated the machines opposite of Victor. As Mark turned on pidima number three, the room filled up with even more light energy as well as a deafening sound from the tandem machinery.

While Mark and Victor attempted to tame the great shell, they fought back the rising heat and force coming out of the center. Suddenly, pidima number one popped like a firecracker and began to smoke. "Turn it off! Turn it off!" shouted Victor. Mark ran around the cube and shut down the throwers of light. Victor tended to the smoking implement with thick, heat-resistant gloves and dismantled it. Maria made her way towards the action.

"Well, that's a definite problem," said Mark.

"No shit," replied Victor.

"Even if we can control the heat, how am I going to operate this thing on my own?"

"I don't know," said Victor in a frustrated tone. "I guess we need more distance, but we can't even get three of these to light at once. How are we going to get them all going? Are you sure we need to build two of these shells?"

"It doubles our chances at least. If one fails, we'll have an extra shot. If we learn how to use one, we can learn how to use two," said Mark.

Maria walked circles around the shell and looked for answers. Half of the metal emitted smoke from the loose dust that covered it. The other half remained cold and quiet. "I think it's your timing," she said.

"What do you mean?" asked Victor as he wiped the soot from his face.

"The first two pidimas were on too long," said Maria. "They were running for twenty seconds before you even started the third."

"Well, how do we avoid that? We need all of the energy they have."

"But we only need it for the moment that the orb opens, right?"

"How should I know?" asked Victor.

"Is there a way you can turn them on one by one, but only enough to warm them up?"

"And fire them all at once?" asked Mark.

"Exactly. Then you don't have to worry about overheating them until the second that you fire them up," said Maria.

"That's fine, but where are we going to get the energy to blast them all at once?" asked Victor. "We're in an aerospace lab and we can't figure it out. How are we going to get enough energy if the second location is outside?"

"Energy got us in this lab in the first place. Let's use it," said Maria.

★★★

John sat collapsed across from Alice on her couch. They both had a nightcap in front of them, although John was too exhausted to pick his up for a sip. Even after the successful day, they were both burdened with silence. John had been in his head for some time, when an old memory decided to find its way through.

"When I was very young, first grade, I made friends with a boy named Maxwell." Alice sat up and turned towards John to listen. "He told me that he was a hemophiliac, which I didn't understand at the time, but he explained that his body had trouble stopping him from bleeding if he got cut. He said that it was caused by a mutation, and he would joke around about being a mutant, which always made me laugh. I took an interest in him... I think he was the first boy I ever *liked,* you know, more than just a friend. I don't know if he felt the same way, but probably not. He was just a nice kid." John grinned thinking about it which made Alice smile.

"So, about a month or two into the school year, I went to his house for his birthday party. Not many other kids showed up because his family was poor, and his house was not the cleanest. I suppose some of the other children's parents decided not to let them go, but my parents were on the fringes of poverty as well, so we didn't care.

"At one point, we were all running down this stairwell that led to his backyard, and we must have been running too fast, and Maxwell tripped on the way down and ended up falling off of the stairs. When he fell, he was sort of sideways, and he ended up landing on the corner of a spade shovel, and its blade pierced through his rib. As bad as it was, I remember that he just stood up and held his ribs, but he didn't cry. Imagine a six-year-old who just got impaled by a shovel not crying. I mean, that's a tough kid. I remember seeing blood pouring out.

"Right away, his mom grabbed him and ran him over to the car. The other kids and I didn't really know what was going on, but our parents were all panicking. Half of them helped get Maxwell to the hospital, and the other half stayed with us and took us to one of their houses. My father went to the hospital, and my mother was one that stayed with us.

"Of course, all of the kids asked questions about Maxwell and what was going to happen to him. My mother kept telling us that the best thing we could do was pray for him. Then after a few hours, my father and the other parents got to the house, and I'll never forget, they all had the exact same look on their faces. It was the first time that I've ever seen that look on anyone, but now, unfortunately, I've seen it way too often.

"My father was probably the worst one. When my mother saw him, she immediately started fighting back tears, and that made me tear up, even though I didn't know why she was crying. So, I asked if Maxwell was coming back too. My father told me that we had to go home and we could talk about it later.

"After a silent car ride, they finally got me home and in bed. At that point, I had enough with all of the silence, so I asked them over and over what happened. Finally, they told me that Maxwell had died. They explained that his body could not stop his blood from coming out, and I would not be able to see him anymore. So, that day on this kid's birthday, he died."

"Oh my God," said Alice. "That had to be so hard to deal with at that age."

"Oh, it was, and that's actually the point of my long, drawn-out story. Respectfully to your beliefs, you know that I don't believe in the afterlife, and I'm pretty sure that I didn't believe in it even then. So, at a time much earlier than I probably should have, I began to think about mortality and the fragileness of life. If this nice boy could go from playing with his friends on his birthday to taking one slight misstep and falling to his death, then who's to say that anyone will make it to tomorrow? This haunted me for my entire life.

"People die every minute of every day, and a lot of them go young. I know for a fact that I haven't come close to achieving what I should have achieved, but I do know the value of existence. Every moment of time is a gift, but we're always just a nudge away from tragedy."

"Well, at least you're making the best of your time. That's more than I can say."

"What do you mean?"

"I mean, you're a doctor in physics, and you're really passionate about it, and you're smart. I haven't accomplished anything in my life. I'm on the '*back nine*' as my father would say and I'm living like a high school dropout."

"I think you're being way too hard on yourself. Look how well you're doing after being thrown out of your home. You picked yourself up in no time. Don't talk about yourself like that. I'm proud of you," said John. Alice grinned.

"That might be the first real compliment I've ever had. Thank you, John."

"Don't thank me. That's the truth." They sat quietly for another minute as they both reflected on their own state of being. "So, what's your plan for this week?"

"Unfortunately, I'll get kicked out of my second home here if I don't go back to work. I think I have a full week actually. How about you?"

"I need to go back to Amber Rock. I'm hoping that the hotel room is available again. I need to book it and get access to the closet."

"Do you think they've been back?"

"I don't know, but I need to contact them. I'll sit in there day and night if I have to. Do you mind if I take the stone with me? I want to show them that I know how to use it."

"Not as long as I can call you every chance I get. I can join you after next weekend."

Chapter Forty
<u>Behind The Eye Was A Soul</u>

John sat in front of the open closet door with his notebook on his lap. Both halves of the stone were attached to a chair in front of him. Three days had gone by with no activity from the closet, and John had half-a-mind to chalk it up as a waste of time. Besides the ever-ticking clock, his body was getting weak and numb.

Without quite noticing it, John began to mumble, "*The perfect genius is all that is made. It is made by the working machine. The perfect genius is all that is made. It is made by the working machine. The perfect genius is all that is made. All that is made is the theory of everything. The perfect genius is all that is made. It is made by the working machine.*" John realized that all of his chanting was beginning to sound like poetry, and John hated poetry. For that reason, he would never write any of it down. However, he did decide to record one thought into his note book for reflection's sake. *If the perfect genius is all that is made, is it composed of the theory of everything? If the theory of everything composes all that is made, will I be its death, or will my death be the working machine?*

With that, John decided that a few laps up and down the exit stairwell for exercise would be time well spent. He pocketed the metal ball and removed the stone from the chair. He twisted the stone together and laid it under the bed for safe keeping.

John left the room and checked the lock four times before he felt safe about walking away. He made his way to the stairwell and chose to walk down first. Each floor took its toll on John's legs, even on a decline. By the time he reached the bottom, his legs were shaking. He dreaded the trip back up, but it was evident that he needed the labor. He made it to the second floor, the third, and by the time he reached the fourth, his wobbling legs straightened, and the burden lifted from his muscles.

On the fifth floor, his chest relaxed, and every breath relieved stress. On the sixth, he sensed a peaceful aroma. Anything negative in his mind evaporated into a mist. When he turned the railing to climb to the seventh floor, there was nowhere to go. There were no steps in front of John. He looked into a deep darkness, not knowing if it went on for ten feet or ten miles. And then, out of the darkness, a fog of colors and lights appeared and flowed towards him. The cool fog welcomed John into a trance. He stared mindlessly until his instincts jogged his memory of his last trance. John had little doubt of who was responsible for the dramatics.

"Is that you?" John was met with silence. "Are you the one who came to me before?" He continued to fight the euphoria. One nerve of fear in his chest allowed him to stay cognizant. After another moment of silence, he took a hesitant step into the black, and then he heard Its voice.

"Come forward, John. I am here." John's throat filled with saliva, but he took another step. As he passed the threshold of the darkness, he lost his ability to see. He looked back expecting to see the light from the hallway, but nothing was there. His eyes were useless.

"Please. Continue this way," said the voice. John continued forward. After ten steps, he found himself under the brilliant, golden Eye, and he could see once again. He recognized the Eye from the bathroom mirror, but his memory served It no justice. It was far more astonishing than he remembered. Not only did It shimmer, but Its feathers stood flush in full bloom. They bled vibrant colors. John looked up at the Being as if he was face to face with God Himself.

The Eye looked more feminine than last time, like the eye of a beautiful woman. As John shivered in adoration, It circled around him. At certain times, It shrank out of sight and then reappeared back over his shoulder. As It moved about, It left behind the sounds of gentle ringing. After Its dance, the Eye stopped in front of John, just above his head.

"Who are you?" asked John.

"My name is Diaphnerous." The Being spoke eloquently, but Its voice was clearly non-human.

"Are you the one who gave me the poem and the drawing?" The Eye widened and Its pupil constricted as it focused on John.

"Yes."

"Are you the one who rang the bell?"

"Yes."

"Are you the one that visited Enoch?"

"Yes, John. You have known these answers before you have asked."

"I only heard Enoch's account second hand. He did not seem to understand much about you," said John. Diaphnerous swooped down so that It was only inches from John's face. He perspired.

"My connection with humans can be quite difficult."

"I can imagine," said John.

"I come from a place that is much more complicated than yours. Enoch sees your world through the eyes of faith, so I presented myself to him in a manner that suited his comprehension and his comfort." It began circling John, gliding up and down. John followed the strange dance with his eyes. "You have a greater reach in the method of abstract thinking. Out of all of your counterparts, you have the highest capacity for understanding. You, John, are the one that I need."

"How much do you know about me?"

"It is hard to say."

"Well… How do you know anything about me? Do you follow me?"

"Seldomly." John stared at the Eye, discomforted with Its reply. "I've only seen you enough to learn and recognize your nature. I am the one that influenced the worms to build an opening of their portal adjacent to your living space. Of course, this was done without their awareness."

"How did you do that? How did you influence them?"

"I studied the life and abilities of the shutterbur."

"I beg your pardon," said John. Diaphnerous stopped circling and turned Its gaze to John.

"I do not recognize this phrase," It said.

"Excuse me. It means that I do not understand what you are saying. What is a shutterbur?"

"Thank you for your clarification, John. The shutterbur is an organism in my living world. It is very instinctual and primitive. It does not carry a purpose outside of survival, similar to many of your world's insects or coldblooded reptiles. Its only function is to continue the existence of its species, but to achieve this, it goes through many labors and tasks. It relies on skills of camouflage, manipulation, and subtle influence. I used my knowledge of the shutterbur to apply its practices to my own objective. My resolve was to persuade a change in the worms' portal, and also to achieve access to it. You have found this portal and named it as the 'tesseract'. Your deduction traits are striking, but you have also used them in a custom that has alerted the worms," said Diaphnerous. It expanded Itself so that It doubled in size, and then It began circling John again.

"Why do you call them worms? Are they actually worms or is that your way of explaining them to us?" asked John. Diaphnerous paused. It closed Its eye and performed a bow to John.

"Very good, John. The decided label of their race is the 'Neolorgue.' In my tongue, this means *silent evil.*"

"I believe you referred to them as the 'Differents' to Enoch."

"Enoch is a man of good behaviors and intentions. However, his ability to comprehend is limited. I must practice simplification when speaking to him. You too have used this practice countless times when speaking to your people."

"I suppose I do practice that often. May I ask, what are they? What exactly are the Neolorgue?"

"They are a species of disturbance."

"Are they dangerous?"

"Yes."

"Do you know why they are here, or where they came from?"

"They build ceaselessly. They erect creations that present benefits only for themselves, and they destroy all else. Your worldly space, although small, holds a rich collection of life and energy. They have built a machine that spans across our skies. It is endless in size and even greater in power. They will use it to drain your world until it shrivels. This will create much pain and agony for your kind. This is a process that I have witnessed measureless times, but have never found the opportunity to intervene with. If they were to discover my entrance into your world, they would slay me before abolishing humanity. It is very difficult to cross to your side. I must wait for the rare moment and do so with caution."

"Why are you going out of your way to save us? I mean, why do you put yourself in danger?"

"Because I am alone, John. I have always been alone."

"Are there no others like you?"

"I am the sole existence of my species. There has always only been one."

"Do you mean that you are immortal? That does not exist in my world. Everything faces death eventually."

"As does everything in mine. I am not immortal, but I am a very special race. My memories span back to the beginning, although I am not the first to live."

"I apologize, Diaphnerous," said John. "I don't believe that I am understanding you. Are you not the offspring of two older organisms?"

"Do not apologize, John. It is not an area that you are familiar with. I am the offspring of myself. My existence goes back many generations."

"Oh. I see. In our dimension, we call that asexual reproduction. There are life forms in our world like that as well."

"But not your kind. From what I have gathered, humans practice heterosexuality, correct?"

"Most humans do. Some of us veer from that line."

"I have noticed. Unfortunately, I am confined only to self-replication. At the end of my time, my body will replicate itself and split into two separate beings, although we will have the same mind and memories. After the process is complete, I will be very weak and malnourished. The replicant will devour my body, slowly and precisely, in order to resorb the richness of my anatomy. And then, the replicant will carry on as the sole host of my race. That is how I came to be, and that will be my fate when my time is up."

John winced at the discomforting visual. "That sounds very painful, physically and emotionally. Does that scare you, knowing that you will have to endure that one day?"

"Fear is not an emotion that I am burdened with. My fate is my nature," said Diaphnerous.

"I respect your strength of mind. So, what specifically about humans has inspired your help?"

"I have been searching for all of time to find a companion that has the ability to communicate back. I have never experienced what you would label as friendship or meaningful relations. Your kind is much more simplistic than myself, or any other being in my world, physically speaking, but you are far more complex in the way of emotion and expression than any that I have come across.

"You have achieved art and ambition, and you have utilized the written word for the purpose of inspiration. I dwell in a vast realm of creative nothingness, void of anything abstract. Emotion does not exist outside of my mind. The creatures that surround me do nothing more than survive and continue without meaning. Even the Neolorgue lack the ability of expression. They have no spoken word. They communicate only through logic and symbols. Their creations are used merely to elongate their existence. My creations are made to inspire beauty, and they are wasted on the perceptions of the simple minded with whom I am punished to share an eternity."

"Well, if it means anything to you, Diaphnerous, I shared the picture that you drew for me with my acquaintances, and it is the most beautiful thing that we have ever seen."

"Thank you, John," said Diaphnerous. It took a long pause. "I have never felt recognition or compliment before. That alone has made my risks worthwhile. But I must tell you that the portrait that I have given you is only a simple example of my potential. Please forgive my pretension, but I was very limited in performing on a canvas that can only exist in your measurements. My absolute essence is to design works that change the onlooker for the better. To inspire."

"I can say truthfully that I was beyond inspired. And the bell... The bell blew my mind. The sounds that came out of that bell seemed impossible."

"And that is why I love bells," said Diaphnerous. "I learned long ago when I began crafting bells that they possess a special and unique quality. They can be so beautiful to look at, but one does not experience their full essence until they hear them ring. They have a duality... A duality of sound and light." Diaphnerous closed Its eye and revealed Its awesome coat of feathers. It opened Its eye and looked at John. "Will you enter with me into a compromise?"

"What do you have in mind?"

"If I pledge to save your kind, will you pledge to come share time with me in my land and speak with me? The place in which I live is safe from the Neolorgue. I have constructed a barrier in which they are incapable of breaching. I am building a creation that will undoubtedly be my life's best work. I would be privileged if you were to be the first to see it. Your opinion means everything."

"That sounds like a very fair trade, Diaphnerous." John did not know what to say. He assumed that any deal that he agreed upon would have to be honored in the future, but he also did not see much room for negotiation. "If you keep us safe, I will be happy to visit you."

Daiphnerous froze. It halted all movement and became silent. John remained as still as possible, fighting back his nerves from visibly shaking. A golden, red light then moved over Diaphnerous' eye like a wave. The light crawled across Its surface, then disappeared. Diaphnerous began to again move about normally. John's words became his regret. His body wanted the visit to be over, and it begged him to stop speaking, but once again, his curiosity won the fight.

"May I ask you one more question?"

"Of course, John."

"How did you learn to speak like us?"

"I have created thousands of languages throughout my existence. It is a skill in which I am proficient. Human language is uncomplicated, and after learning your natural ways through observation, I discovered your literature. I simply deduced the meaning of your symbols from the sounds and behaviors of your interactions. Since my first journey here, I have read many books about your world and its properties. I have learned a great deal of humanity's knowledge. It is informative, but vastly ignorant and incomplete. I choose now to focus time only on your literature that is written for the purposes of art. You refer to them as novels and poems."

"I understand. Thank you for the explanation."

"Thank you, John. I am regretful to say that I must leave you for now. If I stay longer, I will risk being discovered by them, which will bring harm to us both. I will return when a safe opportunity is presented, but if you would be so grateful, I do have one final plea to ask of you."

"Absolutely," said John.

"I understand that you have made plans with the female named Alice to stop the others from closing the machine."

"Yes. We've been working together for a long time trying to figure all of this out. The two of us have been leaning in that direction."

"Please, John. You must not take that action. Your hesitation is understandable, and this is why you are my most preferred of all the humans. Alice also operates exclusively with positive intentions, but her judgment is clouded by her faith. You must not let her influence your decisions. I have been cursed to watch the Neolorgue exterminate life on far too many occasions, but humanity is different. The human spirit is too valuable for me to allow them to succeed again. Even with my best efforts, we may not succeed because of the awesome power of their wicked machine. But I will extend my every resource to help you. My fate will be the same as yours."

John lowered his head. Every emotion hit him at once, and his eyes filled with tears. He did his best to hold his composure. "Okay… That's a deal that I can agree to," said John.

"And please, do not tell any of the others about this visit. Especially the female. I ask you to keep this among only us," said Diaphnerous. John swallowed his gut along with his hope. He knew that he would be held accountable for his words.

"Okay. This will stay between us."

"Thank you, John. We will meet again in time."

"Thank you, Diaphnerous. I look forward to seeing you again."

"Turn towards your right hand and walk forward," said Diaphnerous. And then It shrank into the darkness and disappeared. Before John had time to think, his body fell into an immediate terror from the absence of light, space, or any of his five senses. He turned to his right and walked. He paced ten uncertain steps, and on the eleventh, he arrived in his hotel room with the accompaniment of his full sight and hearing. He turned around to look back into the darkness, but it no longer existed.

Chapter Forty-One

<u>The Energy, The Debate, And Another Urgent Phone Call</u>

Maria stood over Harper Thomas' engine model and explained its design to Mark.

"This canister holds the liquid hydrogen, and this side holds the liquid oxygen, but it's the process in which they meet that's important. The hydrogen remains at a very cold temperature when it pours into the combustion chamber, but the oxygen is immediately heated which gives it its explosive reaction. Within the atmosphere, it works like any other rocket fuel, however, Mr. Thomas' engine is designed to create a unique pressure so that when the ship reaches zero gravity, the fuel expands and naturally rations itself into the chamber."

"How did your dad figure out the formula for this?" asked Mark.

"He came from a place where nobody had enough of anything to go around, so I think he idolized the idea of getting a lot out of a little."

"But how are we going to use this, hun? If somehow we can rig this to a generator, which is a huge if, where does the zero gravity come in? I don't think we have enough time to fly up to space and back," said Victor.

"Thank you for your input, *hun*, but at this point, every sarcastic comment crosses another day off of the calendar. At least we have something stronger than gas station premium," said Maria.

"I'm sorry. I'm just frustrated that every time we get one step closer, we unravel another ten problems. We're running out of supplies here."

"At this point, every idea that we have involves an extra fifty steps that we don't know about, so let's just prepare the best that we can," said Mark. "I know we're shooting to take down two corners at once, so the best we can do is over-prepare and hope that they both work. And what if we only really need to take down one corner? No building can support itself with only three corners. Maybe the tesseract is the same way."

"Can we set up one of the shells here in the lab?" asked Maria. "We have all of our equipment here."

"We can, but Mark has been looking at this for a long time. He says that, structurally, it makes the most sense to attack the inside cube. That's where we think the majority of the support is," said Victor.

"Okay, that leaves what? Oklahoma, New Mexico, Colorado, and Enoch's farm," said Maria.

"Well, you can forget about Oklahoma. That got blown to shit," said Mark. "And if the New Mexico spot is over a lake, then how will that work out? Do I have to build the shell out on a rowboat?"

"No. Here's what's most important: We need to be ready for the exact moment that the orbs open up. Where will they open up?" asked Victor. "Like you just said, Mark, Oklahoma is a pile of dust, and we've never seen the orb in New Mexico. But we know that Enoch saw it show up in his barn, and John's orb came from his closet. So, if we set up one of the shells here, it makes sense to build the other in Colorado or Nebraska. The hotel is indoors and so is the barn, although who knows what kind of electricity Enoch has out there?"

"At least in the barn, there's room. How can we fit a six-foot shell into a hotel closet?"

Victor took a big inhale and let it out. "I don't know."

"How about the generator? Can you rig that in less than a month?"

"No, but I might as well try. It's about time my degree paid off for something," said Victor.

★★★

John held the stone in one hand and the metal sphere in the other. His mind was split into its greatest debate yet. For a deliberation of this magnitude, splitting his brain into only two sides would not nearly cut it. For this, John brought out all twelve senators of his subconscious, which is something that he had not done since his decision to move into the mountains back in his earlier years.

The room was divided four different ways. One side argued to trust the evidence that pointed towards the worms being well-intentioned. The stone and the ball were presented as the prominent exhibits. They were tools; tools that were delivered specifically to John and Alice.

The second group of senators leaned in the direction of Diaphnerous. They did not view the ball and stone as tools. In fact, they labeled them as 'unworldly objects' that were to be treated as false vouchers for the one-eyed monsters. Additionally, they saw the worms' lack of speech or language as a sign of how far removed they were from humans. Diaphnerous, on the other hand, understood both human language and human emotion. It used that understanding to show John, with good reason, why he should fear the collective species, which the gorgeous, feathered Eye also feared. To that, the first group responded that eyewitness testimony may be regarded highly in the court of law, but remains less than considerable in the court of science, regardless of who the eye belongs to.

The third group simply suggested a plan along the way of fleeing and never looking back. The responsibility was never fit for one man, so why not leave it up to fate or the powers that be? That was undeniably tempting to John. It assured him no blame should the living world come crashing down. But then, the fourth group stepped forward and proposed the least popular opinion: Hold out. Hold out until the time comes where a decision must be made, for only then would the final verdict remain unforced. Although the first three groups immediately deemed this to be shapeless, lazy, and avoidant, John saw it as the only honest option.

On one hand, he was nowhere near choosing one way above another, and on the other, if time ran out before he could stamp his vote, then the decision would be made for him anyway. And to the surprise of the committee, John adjourned the court and suspended his verdict indefinitely.

***

Mark and Victor sat on a lab table and each drank a beer. They were covered in burnt dust from the experiment and its complicated cleanup. On the far end of the lab, the door swung open. Maria stormed in wearing the same sweatpants and shirt that she went to bed in.

"What are you doing, hun? Why aren't you asleep?"

"I tried calling you," said Maria.

"What happened? I guess my phone's off."

"Enoch called again. He said we need to get to the farm as soon as we can. The worms came back."

Chapter Forty-Two
<u>The Animals</u>

When they turned to drive down Enoch's long driveway, they saw right away that the cornfields were heavily overgrown. The elongated corn spread itself out abundantly, and the individual stalks appeared to be reaching close to ten feet in length. Looking at the unkempt field made Maria nauseous. The great Eye described the corn to Enoch as a 'false hope,' and as they drove deeper into the thick of it, Maria's skin turned cold. She did not want to walk through it, and she did not want to touch it. Even breathing in its mutual air gave her phantom pains in her lungs.

When they pulled up to the house, they saw Delilah sitting on the front porch in her rocking chair. Enoch's chair was empty. They parked and got out of the car. Delilah got up and walked down to greet them. Her face was pale and sickly, and her under-eyes were dark. She did, however, offer a kind smile, even if it was forced. "Hello there. I'm happy you made it here safely," she said.

"Absolutely. We're glad that Enoch called us," said Victor.

"Hi, Mrs. Pricherwood. How are you?" asked Maria.

"I'm okay, dear. You look very pretty."

"Oh wow. Thank you so much."

"Mrs. Pricherwood, this is Mark. He's the one that wasn't able to make it last time," said Victor.

"Hello, Mark," said Delilah as she gathered the strength to smile again.

"Hello, Mrs. Pricherwood. Thank you for having me," said Mark.

"Call me Delilah. I will go inside and fix you all something to drink, but please go out back. Enoch is waiting for you."

"Thank you, Delilah," said Victor. Delilah walked towards the house, while the other three headed towards the backyard. Maria glanced over and found that Delilah was looking right at her as she walked the other way. Their eyes were locked. With no expression, Delilah stared at her until she walked up the front steps and into the house.

Before Maria had the chance to think about it, they turned the corner into the backyard, and all three of them stopped. Enoch stood shirtless in the middle of the yard. He was still like a marble statue. On the ground before him were the bodies of ten dead animals, laid out in two perfect rows.

Victor, Mark, and Maria stood with their jaws dropped in front of the gruesome depiction. "Oh my God," said Mark. Maria and Victor could not even find the words to agree with him. One after another, they took slow steps towards Enoch and the animals. When they were close enough to see the fine details, they noticed that Enoch was covered in sweat, dirt, and blood, and he was shockingly thinner than the last time that they saw him. He was still yet to move. The animals were stale and lifeless, but their wounds were brutal.

The start of the first row was made up of three horses. All three had holes in their foreheads as if they were shot by a gun that was pressed against their skulls. That row was finished off by two headless goats. A dog was the first body of the second row, and it seemed to meet its demise by several blows to its right temple with a blunt object. The final four animals were cows, each with their throat slashed open.

"We've had these horses for ten years," said Enoch with his back still to them. "They were siblings."

"When did you find this, Enoch?" asked Victor.

"Yesterday morning. I came out here just after sunrise." Enoch turned around. His face was fried from the sun, and his mouth was covered in dried, dead skin. To Mark, Victor, and Maria, he looked no better than the animals.

In order to not stare, Victor focused back on the animals and studied their wounds. "Did you see or hear anything out here?"

"Nothing. There's no other sign of them being here either. The barn was locked at night and still locked in the morning."

"What do you think did this? The worms or the Eye?"

"The Differents. They killed them and laid them out just like before," said Enoch.

"This is strange though. Their brains are not removed like the others. This time it looks like they were just murdered," said Victor.

Enoch looked at Maria. "I'm sorry that you had to see this. Would you mind joining Delilah in the house?" Maria was thrown by Enoch's patronizing request, but she bit her tongue before responding. From behind Enoch, she saw Victor looking at her, who was also put off. She thought better about making waves, and gave in to Enoch's bizarre request.

"Yeah… sure," she said before slowly walking towards the house. Victor's comfort level vanished when Maria entered the house, and Mark was green since he came face to face with the deceased. He was not speaking because all of his energy was focused on holding his stomach down.

"Has the Eye returned?" Victor asked.

Enoch looked out to the cornfield and gazed for a moment. "No."

"Okay," said Victor with an uncertainty about everything. He was sick from looking at the animals, but he continued to walk around and pretend to examine them. From the color of Mark's face, Victor figured that he had less than five minutes before he had to check out and go sit in the car.

Enoch, on the contrary, was content with standing directly over the animals. "It will return," he said. Victor looked over at him, wondering if that was a very late response or the start of a new conversation.

"I'm sorry?"

"It will return. It's very difficult for It to travel. But It will again. I've been waiting for It."

"Oh… I see."

***

"Are you sure you're okay? There's a lot going on. It's okay if you are feeling worried or stressed," said Maria from her seat at the kitchen table.

Delilah set up glasses on the counter and filled them with ice. "Oh, I'm okay dear. It's a lot to deal with, but we feel that we were chosen for a reason," said Delilah.

"Okay, because it's been a long time since we have experienced anything ourselves, but the stress has never gone away. You're actually experiencing contact. That must be frightening."

Delilah kept her back to Maria as she prepared a pitcher of tea. "The surprise of seeing something like the animals can be a bit shocking, but like I said, we feel lucky that God chose us," she said. Maria watched Delilah as she stirred the tea. Her stiff posture looked forced and put on.

"So, you're still feeling strongly that God is behind all of this?" asked Maria.

"Of course."

"What about the Creature that spoke to Enoch? How do you feel about that?" Maria recognized that Delilah was over stirring the tea as a stalling tactic.

"What do you mean, dear?"

"Well, when he told Victor and I the story of what happened, it didn't seem like the Eye spoke much about God," said Maria. Delilah hindered.

"Yes, well… I think It was just speaking as if we already know about Its connection to God. It only spoke about new things and… we're waiting for It to come back and then Enoch can ask It more questions. It's very… intelligent." Delilah stopped stirring and dropped the spoon into the pitcher. Maria got up from her seat. Delilah was frozen. Decades of pressing her sadness and emotions deep down below her chest had left her heart solidified. Her nerves were all but dead. Maria took small steps towards her, moving slowly so as to not alarm Delilah. She gently reached out and touched the arm of the tired woman. Her limbs were stiff and cold. Maria felt Delilah's living rigor mortis.

Maria teared up, and when she got close enough to see Delilah's face, she found out that she was not alone. Delilah broke down. Maria rubbed her back as the farmer's wife cried with another person for the first time in years. "It's okay, Delilah. It's okay. Take your time." Delilah sobbed to the point of almost screaming.

"It's Enoch," she said through her tears. "I'm worried about Enoch."

"What's wrong with him? Is he okay?"

Delilah took a deep breath and found some of her voice back. "He's been acting so different ever since the Eye came."

"What's he been doing? What has changed about him?"

Delilah stood up straight and stopped to catch her breath. She got herself together and pulled back her tears. "He's completely obsessed over it. After the tunnels came and the corn grew, we both agreed that it was an act of God, but since he spoke with the Eye, he stopped calling it a miracle. He won't let us eat the corn, and he thinks that this is all for a different purpose. It's not like him. Every day, he walks through the tunnels waiting for It to come back. He refuses to eat or sleep until his body collapses."

"Have you ever seen It? Did you see It the day that Enoch spoke with It?" asked Maria. Delilah hesitated. She looked out the window into the back yard.

"We shouldn't be talking about this. Enoch would be very upset if he found out that I was saying this." Maria grabbed Delilah's hand and held it.

"He won't find out, Delilah. This is between you and me. You need to be able to express your thoughts and feelings." Delilah looked Maria in the eye.

"I never saw It. But I do know for sure that he's telling us how it happened."

"How?"

"Because he told me that the Eye took him into a place where he was outside of the house, but he could see me inside and he could see everything that I was doing. He was right. I was in our son's room crying. It told Enoch that It preferred to speak to him alone. It chose Enoch to reveal Itself because he is a special man. But I'm scared of how he is behaving now. He cut off all communication with everyone and stopped answering the calls from the people that we used to do business with. He won't even let me near the tunnels. But he is willing to show you and your husband what he has found because the Eye told him to trust you. It wants you to see what Enoch sees," said Delilah. She paused and thought about something. "Many nights I wake up and find that he is not in bed, so I look around for him. I see him standing in the middle of the yard just looking out into the cornfield, waiting for It to come back. He cannot go on like this much longer," Delilah looked out the window into the backyard again. "Please don't tell him I told you any of this. He cannot afford to get upset."

***

"Something was very wrong with that. All of that," said Victor as he drove the car down the driveway. "He was in some sort of trance, and Delilah looked like she just awoke from a coma." Victor looked over at Mark in the passenger seat. He was sitting purposely still, trying to recover. "Are you okay, Mark? I thought we were going to lose you back there."

"Yeah, I'm okay. I've just never seen anything like that before."

Victor laughed. "Yeah, who the hell has?" He glanced at Maria in the back seat. "How about you, hun? What did you two talk about?"

"Nothing good. I've never met a person with so much imprisoned emotion."

"What do you mean?"

"She clearly has no avenue for sharing her feelings. She can't say anything to or in front of Enoch, and she's scared to death."

"About what?"

"About the way he's acting. She said that he's so completely obsessed with the Creature coming back that he's running himself into the ground. He's not eating or sleeping, and he spends all day out in the dirt. I mean, look at him. He's clearly losing it."

"Well, what does that mean? Should we not trust him? Frankly, I don't really want to come back here after today," said Victor.

"I don't know. According to her, he hasn't lied about anything so far, but apparently, he no longer feels that God is responsible for everything. All he can talk about is Diaphnerous."

"Okay well, let's keep our distance from them while we figure this out and decide how to deal with them."

"Agreed. Absolutely a good idea," said Mark as he took deep breaths.

"If they call us again, we can answer and hear what they have to say, but there's nothing about what just happened that I feel right about," said Victor. While Maria looked out the window and watched the cornfield shrink into the distance, she couldn't help but think that Delilah had a lot more to say if she ever found the time to say it.

★★★

John dialed Alice's number and held the phone to his ear. As it started ringing, he still did not know what he was going to say. The conversation he had with the unexplainable Diaphnerous left him in a bit of a jam. He now had to figure out how to tell Alice about their talk without breaking his promise with his new feathered friend. He was now dealing with the feeling of being watched at all times, and as pleasant as the articulate Eye had treated him so far, John had no intentions of disappointing It. After the third ring of the phone, Alice picked up.

"Hey, how's it going?" John hesitated, fully regretting reaching out to Alice without a plan. He was hoping that the solution would come to him at the very last moment. It had not. "Hello? John?"

"Hi. Can you hear me?" he asked.

"Yeah, I can hear you fine. What's going on? How's everything over there?"

"It's umm… Everything's good. Just been kind of quiet."

"Oh yeah? I'm guessing you still haven't seen anything."

"Not that I know of… Nothing yet." John rubbed his hand over his eyes. "What umm… What's going on with you? How's work?"

"It's actually not too bad, although I can't really concentrate. It's hard to work when you think the world might end in a few weeks. I wish I could afford to take off, but if it turns out the world doesn't end, I'd rather not be homeless." Alice intended for her joke to be taken lightly, but John returned only silence. Of course, he was too distracted to even hear her. "You okay, John?"

"Yeah, I'm okay. Just trying to think about everything and uh… you know, just trying to figure everything out." Something clicked in his head. "Hey, remember those things that you took from your husband before you left the house?"

"Umm… Oh. Yes. You mean the—" John cut her off.

"You showed us those at dinner and told us about them. And then something happened to them later that night."

"Yeah, right. John, what are you—"

"And then you had that other thing with you that you were reading when you were trying to make yourself feel better? But then you didn't have it later on," said John. Alice was not exactly caught up to what John was doing, but she was pretty sure that he did not want her to say too much.

"Yes. I do remember that," she said.

"Well, now I think I understand how you felt." John let a quick moment go by so that Alice had time to think about what he was trying to say. "But anyway, I'm getting restless here. Not much has happened in a week and I was thinking that maybe you can head this way on your next break from work."

"That sounds good. I have a few more days, but maybe I'll just leave straight after my last flight. I can get on another plane to Denver."

"Yeah. I'll pick you up. Just call me when you know exactly when you can get here. Hopefully by then, I'll have something to tell you about."

Chapter Forty-Three
<u>The Confession</u>

Maria and Victor sat at the dinner table with plates of chicken parmesan in front of them. There was a third plate in front of where Mark was sitting before he left the room to answer his phone. When he saw that it was his ex-wife's home number, he excused himself thinking that it may have been Jake calling. Maria and Victor enjoyed the few minutes of silence and just sat together.

Mark walked back in from the other room and sat down at the table. He was quiet. He cut his chicken and began to eat. Maria and Victor looked at him concerningly. "Is everything okay, Mark?" asked Maria.

"No, not really," said Mark without looking up.

"Well, if you feel like you want to talk about it, we're happy to listen. Otherwise, we will totally leave you alone," said Victor.

"Um, okay. My son will most likely never speak to me again, and my ex-wife more or less told me that he would be much better off if I was dead. So, instead of speaking with my son like I hoped, I was reminded once again that I'm a piece of shit failure."

"Why would she say those things? No one has a right to speak to you like that, Mark. You don't deserve that," said Maria.

"Oh, trust me, I deserve it. She opened the conversation by telling me that Jake was accepted into Vanderbilt, which was his dream school for the past four years, but because of my financial fuck-ups, we'll never be able to afford it. So… I'd say I deserve it, Maria." Mark continued to saw his chicken and eat it, but he never did pick his head up. Maria and Victor both shook their heads. They felt empathy for Mark regardless if his punishment may have been deserved.

The house phone rang. Feeling a mixture of wanting to give Mark his space and wanting to silence the ringing, Maria walked over and picked it up. "Hello?"

she said. Right away, she heard a woman crying on the other end. "Hello? Are you okay?"

"Maria, I don't have much time. This is Delilah."

"Delilah, hi. Is everything okay?"

"Maria, I'm sorry. I have not been honest with you. I don't have much time, but I have to tell you something."

"What is it? What do you need to tell me?"

"It's Enoch. It's much worse than I told you about," said Delilah. Maria got the attention of Victor and Mark and waved them over to join her. She then put the phone on speaker mode.

"What's going on with him?"

"He's changing. He's becoming violent. When you came out to see the animals, it was not the creatures that killed them. It was Enoch. He shot the horses in their heads with his rifle, and he used an ax to behead the goats. The cows and our dog too. He killed all of them."

"Oh my God, Delilah. Why would he do that?"

"I'm sorry for telling you this. Please don't let him know that I told you."

"I won't say anything to him; I promise. But why did he do that?"

"He believes that if he kills them, then the Eye will come back again. He wants the Eye to think that the other creatures are responsible like they were for the cows. But they're not. Enoch is responsible."

"Alright listen, Delilah. Do you feel like you are safe? Is there anywhere you can go or do you have somebody that you can stay with?"

"No. I need to be here. I need to help him. He's changed so much in the last few weeks. I can't leave him now."

"Delilah, you need to stay safe. It doesn't sound like he is in a good place right now."

"Yesterday, he told me that he was going to one day live with the Eye. He wants to follow the Eye into the upper world and live with It. That's what he called it. The 'upper world'. It's all he talks about. He doesn't even pray anymore."

"Is there anything I can say that would convince you to leave? This does not sound like he is in his right mind. I'm happy to help you find a place to go."

"I can't leave. I'm sorry…" Delilah stopped talking. Maria and the guys heard rustling coming from Delilah's end of the phone. "I see him walking back to the house from the field. I have to go, Maria."

"Okay, but call me back when it's safe again," said Maria. Nothing was said back to her. "Hello? Delilah, are you there?" Maria hung up the phone. "Oh my God."

"He's the one who killed them? This motherfucker is crazy," exclaimed Mark. "What a goddamn lunatic."

"I told you that something was off," said Victor. Maria held her hand over her mouth in shock.

"We have to do something. We have to go down there and get her," she said.

"Are you crazy? We're not going down there. We'll end up like one of those horses," said Victor.

"Well, what about Delilah? Should we just leave her?" asked Maria.

"Listen, Maria, I hate to take sides here, but I think I have to agree with your husband. I don't want us to end up as the third row in his little pet cemetery out there. Maybe we can find a way to help her, but we can't go over there again," said Mark. Maria looked at him and looked at Victor. She knew they were right, but she also knew what that meant for Delilah.

Chapter Forty-Four
<u>Who Is Not Being Honest?</u>

John sat in the same chair that he had been sitting in all week. It had become his thinking chair, and at the moment, John was thinking about how and when he would explain everything to Alice. He did not know how often he was being watched by Diaphnerous, nor did he know the limits in which the Eye could travel. John considered bringing Alice to the loudest bar that he could find and try whispering in her ear. He also thought about getting her into his car and driving as fast as he could down the highway, thinking that maybe the Creature would not be able to keep up. But there was a major risk involved with both.

John had watched Diaphnerous expand Itself twofold, and he had watched It shrink down into the size of a fist. His assumption was that the size and shape of Diaphnerous was based on how much or how little It immersed Itself into the third dimension. Unfortunately for John, if his hypothesis was true, then his privacy ceased to exist. Diaphnerous could enter the smallest cross-section of the third dimension, and be able to watch and listen from an unseeable speck. He concluded that to be safe, he should live as though he was an actor on a stage: always watched and always heard. Spatial control was lost, so John had to find the upper hand in the art of communication. But even the human language of English was dominated by Diaphnerous.

It taught Itself the language of a race that It did not even share a dimension with. John could not compete in speech on any level; however, he did give himself a chance in the game of numbers. If he found a way to disguise a hidden message within a page full of numbers, then perhaps he could get something across to Alice without the watchful Eye knowing. He pulled out his journal and opened it up on his lap. The front section of it was cluttered with equations, proofs, and the sloppy, disorganized notes from his failed experiment.

John's plan was to somehow mark different numbers with disguised symbols in a way that could be later examined by Alice to uncover his message. If he could circle the number *one* to represent the letter *A*, *two* to represent *B*, and so on, then he could probably write out most of his story in only a few hours, but the higher Being was too smart for that. It was decodable and obvious. John decided that he would start on a certain page and write out equations. He would then solve these equations using the solution numbers as the encoded letters. It would take much longer and be very difficult for Alice to decipher, but it at least sounded safe. Even if Diaphnerous was watching him throughout the entire process, it would just seem as if John was practicing his profession.

He started with a differential equation that he remembered from graduate school. He became friends with his professor because John showed a great interest in numbers, and often found time outside of class to meet with his teacher to introduce him to new equations. John's insomnia allowed him a lot of extra time to scour through books on math from the library, looking for problems that presented new challenges.

The most interesting book that he ever came across was called *The Pangea Solution*. It was a non-fiction account of a man named Arthur Caine who traveled across all six populated continents seeking to discover the different practices of math from dissimilar and hidden societies. Mr. Caine centered his book on the fascinating, yet predictable fact that all problems that were based in numbers concluded in the exact same solutions, even if the means to finding those solutions were practiced in unique, uninfluenced ways. *"Numbers remain constant across all borders,"* wrote the author, and he littered the book full of the most obscure numerical riddles that he came across. John and his professor found remarkable joy in solving those riddles.

While carving the numbers into his book, to John's surprise, he found little trouble in scripting his secret message. He quickly hit a rhythm and got lost in the unconventional art. To him, putting a mathematical equation onto a blank piece of paper was like mapping the coordinates of the Universe one number at a time. He was a painter depicting the measurements of all existence.

The solutions that concluded his number sentences all remained true, but also gave Alice a small bit of needed information about John's predicament. And when he finished with his first piece of the puzzle, a smile grew across John's face. He was proud, and he rediscovered the thing that he was so good at. But then he picked his head up and looked across the room, and his smile shriveled.

Stretched across the far bedroom wall was the glaring eye of Diaphnerous. It glowed with a color that John was yet to see out of the Traveler. It was somewhere just above a gushing green emerald. Its glow advised John's spine to quiver. He shut the book on his lap and placed the pencil on the table beside him. He stared at the Eye and the Eye stared back. He could do nothing to hide his guilt. He gulped down his nerves, and he fought back the urge to weep.

"Hello, John," said the Eye. John took a deep breath.

"Hello, Diaphnerous." Diaphnerous separated Itself from the wall and hovered in the direction of John. For some reason, John thought that it would be polite to stand for his Guest, but he quickly realized that his numbed legs would not be joining him, so he sat up straight the best that he could. Diaphnerous reached a point just in front of John's chair, and then rose above him, never breaking eye contact.

"You look ill," said the Eye. It then shrank to the same size as John's head and descended down to his level. The Being hung only inches from John's face and looked directly into his eyes. John stared back, but only because he feared the consequences of folding. Diaphnerous extended Its examination for twenty, bitterly long seconds. John scraped together enough willpower to speak.

"I'm actually okay today. Just a little tired from traveling so often."

"It is interesting," said the floating Voice. "You left the female from the south, and then you came here to be alone." It hovered behind John and stopped when It was between him and the wall. It looked down on his back. Too timid to turn around, John remained facing forward, but he could see his half-reflection from the mirror in the next room. He saw Diaphnerous looking down on his back, and as he looked into the reflection of the Eye, he could see that It was also looking at him through the mirror. Its gaze was held to no limit and It could watch in any direction that It pleased. Feeling rather vulnerable, John cleared his throat.

"Yes, I just thought that I would reserve the room and keep it occupied. I didn't want someone else to rent it and get involved somehow." John knew that his lie made little sense at best.

"It would be best for you to head north to be with the others," said the Eye. "Being here alone is not safe, John. And your time is precious. Much more precious than theirs."

"Yes, I had thought about that. I planned on calling them later today actually. It's been some time since I have spoken with them... But how about you? How have you been, Diaphnerous?" Even just the stare from the Eye put a weight on John's back, and he came close to giving out, until the Light Bearer finally moved out from behind his chair and into the center of the room.

"I am very well inspired," It said.

"Really? That's good. What about?"

"My most recent trip has demonstrated just how rich and beneficial this world is. The space here is undoubtedly round and limited, but its worth exceeds its weight," said Diaphnerous as it hovered up and down in a pattern. "I spent my hours consuming your greatest works of literature. Shakespeare is admired by your species, so it is there that I began. Are you familiar with this collection?"

"I like classics, but I don't know too much about Shakespeare honestly. 'To be, or not to be?' is pretty popular. I know that it's from *Hamlet*, but that's about the extent of my knowledge," said John. "Did you come across that?"

"Yes, quite fortunately. The solution to his dilemma was blatant, even to a human of youth, however, his soliloquy posing 'To be, or not to be?' was the most profound query ever asked by man." Diaphnerous rose to the ceiling and looked down on John. "To a human, the answer is simple: to be. Be amongst others to gather and to share. For myself, the question is so deeply conflicting." Diaphnerous expanded as It spoke. "To be alone, or to be not at all. All of my ancestors have suffered this curse, and to exist is to continue suffering, continue creating to please the eyes of no one, continue watching the mutilation of the innocent." Diaphnerous grew many sizes throughout Its emotional plea. It caught Itself when the size of the Eye reached nearly half of the ceiling. It slowly reduced Itself back to normal, and blinked a number of times, revealing Its magnificent feathers. They dazzled John as intensely as they did the first time, however he watched the transformation with a stone face, trying his best to hide any emotion. "What others did you read?" he asked. Diaphnerous shrank down and out of sight. John held still, waiting for Its return. The Eye reappeared over his shoulder.

"I took an interest in the struggles of Iago. Are you familiar with this character?"

"I'm not. Like I said, I've heard about a few of the plays, but I don't know many of the characters or stories," said John with a stiff posture.

"Iago appeared in the work entitled *Othello*," said the Eye. "Othello, the Moor of Venice, was the focus of the story, however the man of most intrigue and intelligence was Othello's true enemy, Iago."

"It sounds like Iago was the antagonist. Many times, they are the most interesting characters," said John.

"Why would you label him so negatively?"

"Well, the antagonist essentially means that he is trying to do harm to the main character, I'm assuming Othello is the main character," said John. Diaphnerous stopped and stretched Itself wide.

"I do not agree with that assessment, John. If this is the consensus on him as a man, then he is simply misunderstood. He was the victim of a great betrayal in both vocation and in love by his friend Othello."

"Shakespeare is known for writing a lot about betrayal," said John.

"This held no exception. Othello is weak. Iago performs a simple act of manipulation with the use of a well-placed cloth, and he tricks Othello into killing his own wife just before himself," said Diaphnerous.

"But why does that make Iago the better person?" asked John. "In general, humans consider killing to be the worst act possible. And in stories, trickery and deception is usually a tool used by the 'bad person'. Honesty is the trait given to the 'good person'."

"Nothing of worth should ever be simplified into the limits of 'good' and 'bad,' John. It is always more complex than that. Iago was led to believe that Othello engaged in a sexual betrayal with his wife. In return, he simply tricked Othello into believing that he had returned the sin by the placement of her personal cloth of hygiene: her handkerchief. The handkerchief was used to represent infidelity. But it was Othello that committed the horrid acts of violence. Of the two, Iago was the superior of intellect.

"Othello, in contrast, was simple-minded and brutish. His actions mirror that of the Neolorgue. When I ingested the words of Iago, I felt a shared vibration with him. He was alone, as am I. Alone in thought and in communication. I have been deprived of connection for all of my time, but there still remains a craving to speak and to be heard, as well as to listen and to hear. Just our discourse alone has brought me indescribable bliss. Thank you, John."

"Of course. Thank you, Diaphnerous."

Diaphnerous swung down to John's level. "May I ask you, John, do you have a preferred character of literature?"

"I do, actually. Huckleberry Finn. Have you come across any of Mark Twain's books?" asked John.

"Yes, all of them. I spent the fourteenth hour of my visit covering nineteenth-century American and European fiction. Structurally, they differed from the stories coming out of the East during that time period, but even with the title 'The great American novel', one could trace its inspirations back to the comedies and dramas of Ancient Greeks, if not even further. The narrative of the human comes from the mind of the human, and is therefore simple, but that is not to say that it is not inspired," said the Eye. "What is it about Huckleberry Finn that you find intriguing?"

John could not help but stop and breath as he realized that Diaphnerous may have read everything that was ever written. He felt that any point that he made would be sub-elementary to the Great Mind above him, but staying silent would not do him much good either. He accepted it and pushed through. "Huckleberry is only a young boy, but he is wise beyond his years. He makes decisions based on what he thinks is right."

"So, you appreciate his insight and bravery," said Diaphnerous. "Do you feel the impact that he has made on your own self?" asked the Eye. It floated in slow circles around John, and Its color shifted from a sharp green to a soft gold. John suddenly felt emotions that were tied to the character of Huckleberry, whom he had not thought about in a while, but he realized that the boy's convictions influenced his own on a daily basis.

"He was driven by the want to be good. His principles were formed from his empathy."

"And how did he practice those principles?" asked Diaphnerous. John's fear subsided. He found himself deeply focused on Huckleberry's soul.

"His desire was to help his friend, Jim, escape from slavery, but he had to battle with his conscience."

"By what means?"

"His conscience told him that slaves were the property of people, and helping them escape was wrong. It told him that he was stealing."

"What was the enlightening moment for the boy?" asked Diaphnerous, still circling around John.

John began to slide into a state of comfort and understanding. A warmth embraced his skin. "He was presented with a dilemma. Save Jim from being captured, or write a letter to Jim's owner, and tell her where her slave could be found. So, he wrote the letter up and told himself that if he sent it, then his soul would be forgiven, and he would not be thrown into hell for his sins. He could save himself."

"How did he handle his inner struggle?"

"He thought about what Jim had meant to him as a friend and the experiences that they shared, and he tore the letter up. He accepted an eternity of burning in flames in order to do what he believed was right. He was unaffected by fear." John and Diaphnerous shared a quiet moment.

"It seems that the boy's courage has inspired you to also be courageous, John." John nodded his head. "Yes."

"But what would the boy think about your numbers?" asked the Eye.

"What do you mean?" he asked back.

"The numbers that you have written in your book; the ones that you plan to show to the female."

All of John's comfort and calm feelings fled his body. *This is impossible,* he thought. John took a deep breath, hoping to dig up some strength, but when he exhaled, he was left with only defeat. He said nothing.

"Your number message is oddly similar to the letter written by the boy that you idolize, but unlike him, sending the letter will deliver you into damnation. Not by me, John. By the Neolorgue." John closed his eyes and took another deep breath. His muffled sobs made his emotions known to both of them.

"Do not feel shame. Do not cry. It is the instinct of the human to combat that which it fears by way of deception, but I came here to help, John. You are the one that I have chosen to rely on. You revere this boy because you see in him what you want to see in yourself. You desire to have courage, but you are hesitant to bear its weight. Open up to me, and I will show you how to harness your courage. You have something that very few have, John. You are a man of true worth."

John hung his head, too hopeless to cry. He could feel the Eye watching him, waiting for some recognition. John weakly nodded his head.

"You are by a great distance the most important human in this. I need you to help me. Enoch is important as well, but he does not understand what you understand. None of the others do. You must keep them all in line with our goal. You had differences with them when you were in the north, but those differences must be mended. They will listen to you. You were put here to lead them. I think you should share with them the new tool that the Neolorgue have left behind."

John somehow managed to look up at Diaphnerous. He sniffed his running nose. "The stone?"

"Yes, John. You must show them the stone."

"But why did they give it to me? Why are they giving me tools if they are going to harm me?"

"Why does the fisherman give the fish a worm?" asked Diaphnerous. "Next comes the hook." John did not respond. "And perhaps it would be best if you cease any further relationship with the female. You can close your ties with her when she arrives to see you." John looked up at Diaphnerous in the way that he would look at a judge who just ordered him to a life sentence. He tried to plea with the Eye, but nothing came out.

"She will put all of you in danger if she finds a way to interfere. Sending her away will expire the issue. If she then returns a final time, then she will have to be removed." John understood quite well what Diaphnerous meant by that. He nodded his head, unable to hide his discontent.

"Do not despair, John. This will all be over soon, and we will be able to enjoy our future. I will be happy to show you the art structure that I have been building. I am nearly satisfied with it. It is powerful to observe, but it still lacks a crucial piece before it is complete. Favorably, my trip to your world is providing me with exactly the inspiration that I desire to finish it," said the Artist. "You will be the first to see it in its completion."

John nodded, but he could only move his head up once. His energy was depleted.

Diaphnerous slowly retreated towards the closet, but hovered backwards so that It was still facing John. John could not even look up. The Eye drifted into the wall and sank through it until It could be seen no more, and John was alone again.

Chapter Forty-Five
It's Not Alive

"Turn it to two!" shouted Victor over to Mark who cranked up the gas-powered generator from afar. They watched on edge as all of the pidimas in the cubic turret warmed up equally. They were taking it slowly this go around. They attached the generator to a custom-built power source. Within that power source was a precisely crafted tank that held a small amount of Juan Carlos' rocket brew.

"Turn it to three!" yelled Victor. After hitting the third out of five levels of output, the pidimas glowed. Victor stood way too close to the machine. The light from each of the eight corners reflected off of his darkened laboratory goggles, and the heat pounded his face.

He planned to let the pidimas heat up just enough to hold energy, then when Mark turned the generator up to the fifth level, Victor would fire all of the pidimas at once and crash the center. On this particular dry run, nothing was in the center, but on the night that the tesseract opened, a bright orb would be there waiting.

"Four!" Mark's hand shook as he raised the setting from three to four. Victor dug his heels in the ground and held fast against the might of the pidima shell, awaiting the exact instance to fire it off.

As the glowing lights turned bright white, Victor yelled, "Five!", and he pressed the red button as Mark fired the generator up to full power. And it turned off. The generator lost steam and hissed as its residual heat melted off. The eight light pidimas in the corners of the metal cube lost their fire and dimmed to a dark, faded grey. The only sound that remained was the crisping dust from the hot metal. Victor stood quiet and still, looking at his most elaborate invention, and he hated it. He hated things in the past that were created by others, but he never felt such disdain before for something that was his own. Mark watched

Victor, awaiting the inevitable conclusion, and sure enough with little suspense, Victor slammed the button pad to the ground and smashed it to pieces.

"It's too weak. The fucking generator is too weak. Even with the rocket fuel. I told Maria this wouldn't work. The fuel is useless like this. It just acts like regular gas." Mark tried to open his mouth and interject, but before he could get a word out, the pacing Victor jumped in. "I thought that if the canisters were suctioned out then maybe it would create some sort of vacuum, but it didn't work." Victor took off his goggles and gloves, and threw them across the room. He stomped over to a cooler, opened it, and grabbed a beer. Mark took his protective gear off more humanely, and set them down on the desk. He walked over and grabbed his own beer, and cracked it open. He took a long sip. He patted Victor on the shoulder and hopped up on the desk. Victor shook his head and caved to his disappointment.

***

After twenty or so minutes, Victor found himself sitting next to Mark on the desk. They were both two beers in, and Victor had exhausted all of his anger. He now sat relaxed, and puffed on a cigarette that Mark had given him.

"How many days left?" asked Mark.

"Twenty-six."

"Twenty-six?!" I thought it was twenty-seven or twenty-eight."

"Well, if it happens right around midnight like we think, then it's more like twenty-five," said Victor. "There may be only three more weekends ever."

"Jesus Christ. What happened to the past three days?"

"Try to enjoy the next three," said Victor. They traded moods with each other from one extreme to another, which was something that happened at least twice a day for the three of them.

"How long do we have until students start coming back to class here?"

"I talked to the school the other day and told them that I found several gas leaks around the building. They're sending someone to come look throughout this week, so I figured I would open up the valves for a few minutes before they get here. I think I can buy us another week or two of keeping it closed," said Victor.

"This is not good, man. I thought we were okay, but you were right. This isn't working. We're running out of time. Even if we get our little machine here to work once, what are the odds of it working the night of?"

"Please repeat everything you're saying now to my wife," said Victor as he casually took a drag of his cigarette

"We have to do something. We need more help," said Mark.

"You are the help. We don't have anyone left."

Chapter Forty-Six
<u>Missing Communication</u>

John stood on top of the hotel's roof and looked out onto the great city of Amber Rock. Most of the summer's warmth stuck around, and on that particular evening, nature took its time when it painted the night's sky. A long time had passed since John wiped the slate and just appreciated something beautiful. He paid his dues.

Somewhere out in that gorgeous black space was Alice, traveling at half the speed of sound, drinking small amounts of liquor in an airplane bathroom. John was yet to find a fundamental belief that he and Alice could agree on, but he saw the principles on which her mind operated, and he cherished her for it. He looked up to her as the most open minded out of them all, and it was this level of admiration for Alice that sickened John for what had to come next.

***

Maria looked at the ceiling, and the ceiling looked at Maria. Both of the bedside lamps were on, and her covers were all over the place. Even though she was physically comfortable, she was not able to sleep. Her husband was putting another night in at the lab, and she was starting to obsess over the calendar as she watched it cross off days by the hour. On nights when the anticipation got the better of her, Maria's imagination would strap her down and read to her a well-worded horror. She was learning that the best antidote was not to drown out the thoughts, but to avoid them altogether. So, she tossed and turned constantly in order to gaze onto something new and keep her mind fresh. From the ceiling, she looked down across her body.

Her belly showed no signs of its current responsibilities yet, but she checked it often. Maria was excited about the new clothes that she was going to need considering her disinterest in fashion or shopping. But she figured that a pregnant woman could get away with a lot more than a professional scientist. Maria envisioned a closet full of clashing colored dresses that were sewn for comfort over style, and on the days where she really felt cheeky, she could pull out something that left her belly uncovered altogether. Right about the time that she decided to turn onto her left side, the phone rang. She looked over at the clock and saw that it read *two-thirty-one.*

She rifled through all of the bad scenarios that Victor could be calling about. Because of how dangerous their new operations were, Victor limited her time in the lab. He recently banned her from being on the premises at any point that the pidima shell was being operated on.

The phone rang again. She rolled over and picked it up. "Hello? Victor?" There was a hesitation on the other end. "Hello?" she said again. She waited a few seconds because she knew that somebody was there. Finally, she heard a sigh.

"Maria. Hi… It's John."

***

Delilah kept her eyes shut as Enoch crawled out of bed. For the fifth night in a row, he came to bed at two A.M. covered in filth. He stiffly settled on top of the covers. Normally, he would remain still for three hours before returning to the cornfields, but tonight, Enoch was up in only an hour.

His continuous weight loss made him lighter on his feet and quieter at night, but Delilah always knew when Enoch got up. She was sleeping less than he was. He leaned up and set his feet on the floor. He took eight steps and then stopped. To the best of her ability, Delilah guessed that he was looking out of the bedroom window. Behavior like this was no longer abnormal for her husband, but she worried that his lack of sleep was building a solid case against his heart.

Enoch stood still for a long time, which told Delilah that he saw something outside, or more likely, he believed that he saw something outside. If Enoch spotted any sort of movement in his fields, he seized all possible measures to investigate it, and Delilah would not see him for six to ten hours.

The floor creaked as the farmer turned around and walked out of the room. Delilah opened her eyes to see that he was naked. She stayed in bed until he walked down the stairs and out of the house. When the door closed shut, she hopped out of bed and hurried to the window. She watched Enoch walk across the yard. He stopped as he reached the threshold of the corn. For some time, he simply stared at the wall of corn stalks in front of him like he was waiting for something. Delilah searched the dark field with her eyes, trying to determine what that something was. It was quiet and still. She looked out in the direction that Enoch was facing, and she saw that he was directly in line with the tunnels. About two-hundred yards of corn separated them. And then Delilah understood that something would soon be joining Enoch.

From then on, the tired woman focused only on the tunnels. She had wondered what It would look like if she ever saw It. Enoch described It to her many times, but with each retelling, the appearance of the Entity changed. The first time that he spoke of the encounter, Enoch called It *an indefinable collection of beautiful awareness*, which was a mouthful of words above and beyond his vocabulary. Later on, however, he began to define It in more physical terms, almost to where Delilah could imagine It.

A light breeze passed over Enoch's shoulders and brushed through the tassels and leaves of the corn. From above, Delilah watched the wind travel from every direction and end up somewhere over the tunnels. The pageant of nature had her pressed against the glass. Then, from the most central tunnel came a Light. Whether there was a source of light, or just a buildup of light, Delilah could not tell, but soft colors filled the air in a fog. The glow of the Light surfaced from underground and cut through the field.

It progressed to the wall of corn on the far, opposite end of Enoch. As it approached the first line of vegetation that guarded the field, the stalks bent forward and to the ground, clearing a path for the Light to travel. Delilah trembled. As It proceeded onward, the corn not only lowered itself to the ground in waves, but it leaned towards the Migrator as if all of the stalks were bowing to It.

When It arrived to where Enoch was waiting, the final row came down. And now that It was close enough for Delilah to see clearly, she once and for all understood why her husband was now a different man. The Eye greeted Enoch with a warm, affectionate gaze and a display of Its feathers. Enoch fell to his knees, and sobbed for several minutes.

The Eye slowly circled him until he rose to his feet. Enoch made a strong effort to stand up tall and straight. Then, side by side, they made their way into the field and through the already flattened path. Enoch walked next to his Guide all the way until they reached the tunnel from which It came out. Delilah watched Enoch walk to the start of the incline, and down into the hole. The feathered Eye followed behind him, but just as It began Its way down into the ground, It spun around and looked directly at Delilah. From two-hundred yards away, she saw It staring right back into her eyes. And It slowly descended, watching her the entire time.

***

John, Maria, Mark, and Victor all went to bed that night with the eighteenth of October on their minds, and not one of them slept. The looming date on their calendars was closing in faster than the speed of time. As the days slipped by, they could not figure out how to sit down for a moment and appreciate it. And so, with the morning light imminent, the days remaining were now somewhere in the teens. Before they knew it, they would each open their eyes to the number ten, and then five, and then three. And then after that, they wondered if there would be an after that.

Chapter Forty-Seven
The Broken Promise And The Next Step

"I don't understand. Why would you tell them that you were going? I just flew all the way here to meet you," said Alice. She and John shared a small table at the airport food court.

"I know. I'm sorry. It's not something that I can explain right at this moment; it's just very important that I head straight to the lab. I have to leave right from here."

"John, what are you talking about? I just flew across the country to meet you because that's what we talked about. What do you mean you can't explain it? Just explain it," she said. John tried to find the words that would tell Alice something without telling her anything.

"Listen… Something happened, and it made me realize certain things."

"Okay… What things?" asked an angry Alice.

"One night at the hotel… It just started to make sense. And I don't think you should change your mind. I wouldn't if I were you," said John. He had rehearsed the conversation all morning, but now that he was in the limelight, he was choking. He looked Alice in the eye. She looked back at him, baffled. John began to lower his shield and share with her a sign of trust. He softened his gaze on her and used his eyes to speak to her without words, but just then over her shoulder, he saw a small blip. Something flickered. He wasn't completely sure if what he saw had actually happened or if he imagined it, but regardless, he felt like he was being watched from the inside out. From then forward, he let the fear do the talking.

"I've felt things and have seen things lately that I can't quite describe out loud, but the way that I'm seeing them in my head… they're making me aware of what I need to do. I need to be in the lab. It's the best place I can be right now.

And you should head home. It's not safe to be so close," said John, doing his best to not fold over in shame.

Alice leaned in. As much as John tried to look away from her, she found him anyway. "What's going on, John? Why are you saying this? Do you really believe that we are wrong, and they are right? Forget about the worms that came to you and came to me and gave us something. Even though we both know that they picked us and only us because we are doing the right thing… Tell me you believe we're wrong, John." The pain in Alice's chest was usually only brought on when her husband, Tom, confronted her with his latest affair. She thought for sure that with the collapse of their affection, she would be free from betrayal, but here she was again. John became someone to look up to for Alice. Besides her father, John was the only person in her life who was purely an apostle of truth. She trusted him, and that's why her heart was breaking.

"Tell me we're wrong, and I will let you go. Just like the last time that you agreed with them, I will leave and I won't bother any of you," said Alice. John's eyes were damp but not wet. He believed that if he broke character and cried, then the watchful Eye would be quick to protest, and Alice would meet her ruin. He had to choose right then and there to either lose her physically or lose her emotionally, and for that, his heart broke too.

"I believe that we are wrong, Alice. I'm sorry. I have to go to Wisconsin." John shook as he kept eye contact with Alice. His eyes hurt from holding back the tears. Alice was feeling more disgust than anything. Suddenly, she found herself not thinking so much about their plan that they created together, but instead about her inability to build and hold a fellowship with anyone. John was hardly different. A true connection was rarer than gold to both of them, and Alice felt every bit of it as it was pulled out of her. She stood up silently and walked away. John watched her and wondered if ripping her heart out to save her life was worth it.

★★★

Mark poured himself a tall glass of vodka. He was covered in dried sweat, and only showering at a third of his normal rate. He was forgiven though. Maria and Victor were maybe washing every other day. They were all sitting around in Victor's office.

"There's no other way. We'll have plenty of access to electricity here in the lab. We'll have to pray that we figure out the generator for the farm, but what else can we do?" asked Victor.

"Maybe John can help," said Maria.

"In what way?"

"Well, he's worked with all sorts of equipment and machinery, I'm sure."

"We could use his brain power, but do you really believe that he's coming to help? He's changed his mind three or four times now," said Victor.

"I'm not just saying this because he and I had our thing, our argument, but I don't think we should tell him a whole lot," said Mark. "He's on his way to 'help' us I guess, but we've spent a lot of time figuring this out together. We're on the same page, but who knows where his head's at? For now, I think we should lie to him, and assume that he's doing the same."

"But what if he isn't? How will we know?" asked Maria.

"We're three semi–intelligent people. We'll be able to tell."

"How about for the time being, we explain the plan, but give him the wrong details? Maybe he can help us with the generator, but let's only show him one pidima shell, and give him a false location where we're going to be working," said Victor.

"Dealing with John is only half of it. The real question is, how are we going to get that nut job farmer to stay out of his barn for the night?" asked Mark.

Maria sat down on Victor's desk and dangled her legs back and forth. "I'm going to call Delilah and ask her to help."

"What are you going to say?"

"I don't know yet, but we need him distracted for most of the day. Maybe we can somehow convince him that the tesseract will open a week later than it actually will."

"Keep me updated on all that," said Mark as he took a long sip of his vodka. "I'd like as much distance between him and myself as possible."

"What are you talking about?" asked Victor.

"You're out of your mind if you think either of you are going near that farm again. He's too crazy."

"Well, what about you? You'll be safe there?" asked Victor.

"I also don't have a kid on the way."

"You have a kid who's already here."

"Yeah, well… I'm not sure he would agree with you. I already blew it. At least this might help him."

"Maybe we could figure out a better place to do this—" Maria was interrupted mid-sentence by Mark.

"Listen, we all agree that using two shells is better than one. There are two spots that make the most sense. That's where we're going to hit it, and you two are staying here. That's the end of it." Maria stepped off of the desk, walked around, and hugged Mark. He hugged her back with one hand while the other secured his glass of vodka. "Alright now, alright. I'm sure there'll be plenty of hugs to go around afterwards. We'll all be alright." Maria kissed him on the cheek and walked back to her spot on the desk.

"I've been thinking a lot about how we're going to build these shells while on location," said Victor. "I think it's better if I use aluminum and make it in six parts. We'll each have two squares along with four connecting posts to make the cube. I'll have the pidimas already attached to the corners of the two squares. That way when you assemble it, you can place down the bottom square, attach the four posts, and then put the top on. I'll try to keep the wiring as simple as possible."

"Let's do plenty of practice runs. I don't want to try and figure it out when I'm looking over my shoulder for this guy and his machete. If he laid me out in that pile of goats and horses, I don't think you could tell me from them," said Mark. Victor chuckled, but stopped when there was a loud knock on the front door of the building. Even from Victor's office with the door closed, they could hear it.

"Who's knocking?" asked Mark.

"Maybe it's the people coming to check the gas leak again," said Maria.

"They were just here this morning. They said they wouldn't be back until tomorrow," said Victor. The harsh knocking repeated again. It was rhythmically slow, but it came from a heavy hand. Victor stood up and walked out of the office. He made his way down the hall and into the stairwell.

Again on the stairs, he heard the echo of the visitor's knock. When he came in sight of the glass front door, he saw the outline of a tall man with broad shoulders standing inches from the door itself. The man pounded again, even though Victor was clearly walking over to greet him. When Victor was close enough, he saw the man who was responsible for the noise, and he became nervous. Enoch looked at him from the other side. He did not smile or wave. He simply waited for Victor to open the door.

***

Riding along in their engineering machines, they traveled along the surface of the much larger machine. Their vehicles were not so much for transportation, but more to repair the constant complications of the vast structure. They operated in perfect order. Most of the colony mentally and physically contributed to the machine, however a smaller portion of them worked on the tesseract itself.

The completion of the hypercube was on schedule down to the second. Interference from the Watcher was the only collective worry that was shared across the species of the worms. They had no means of stopping It. The Stranger was intelligent in ways that they were not, and It buried Itself outside of their reach. But they decided to devote resources to tracking and capturing It, so long as the execution of the tesseract was not delayed. For then, the round humans would slip from their grasp.

***

Alice sat on her balcony next to a pack of cigarettes and a pint of whiskey. She had the intention of smoking the entire pack and drinking the whole pint. It didn't take but a minute before she thought about John looking her in the eyes and betraying her. The whiskey started flowing as she replayed their conversation in her head, over and over. Alice never knew what disbelief felt like until then, but she didn't blame herself. Her mind was always spoken, and her opinion was always shared, therefore Alice regretted nothing. But she did harbor resentment and disgust due to the massive waste of innovation by John and the others. John brought with him to Wisconsin the poem, the stone, and the metal ball, and Alice was sad that he had accepted the words of the Poet over the instruments of the engineers.

Chapter Forty-Eight
The Collision Of Heavy Things

John stood on the top of the hill and looked down onto campus. Groups of students walked around everywhere, which made John forget about his predicament for a moment and feel at home. Then he turned around and stared up at the NASA/Thomas Laboratory. There were no students in sight, and the heavy-rock building was looking more like a house of straw and sticks just waiting to be tipped over.

Irrational is not irrational, he thought. *Rational is not real.* As far as he could guess, he was still safe to think freely without Something listening, but the thoughts themselves were starting to turn an odd color. John had little confidence in determining reality from fiction, and even less of an idea on who or what was deciding it.

His car was parked in the far end of the lot, and he backed into the spot so that he could see the front door. He had been standing outside of his car for an hour, and although his bladder was sending him alerts, he was not yet ready to face them. He had nothing prepared to say, even after the long drive up, and the thought of lying to more people was eating at his stomach like an ulcer. With his mind jumbled, John heard the front door open from across the asphalt lot, and then he saw a little pregnant lady walk out.

Despite their differences, and all of his anxieties, John grinned at the site of Maria. She made her way over to John's car. She was also smiling, although hers seemed more cordial than natural. "Hey, how are you? You look really healthy," said John.

"Thank you. I'm surprised. I haven't been sleeping much. How are you?"

"About the same. Not sleeping," said John. Maria's smile disappeared, and she stepped closer to John.

"Listen... I need to tell you. Enoch showed up. He's inside."

"Did you ask him to come?"

"No. We had no idea. He's gotten a lot worse since you saw him."

"What do you mean?"

"He's lost his mind. He called us out to the farm again and claimed that the worms came back and killed his animals. They all had either their throats cut or their heads removed, but his wife told me that Enoch killed them all himself."

"Wait a second... He killed all of his animals? Why?"

"Delilah thinks that he was hoping for the Eye to return. He killed the animals trying to make it look like the worms did it."

"Jesus. Well, why is he here now?"

"He came to tell us that It came back. I called Delilah a few hours ago and she saw It. We mentioned that you were on your way and he wanted to wait for you to get here before he told us about everything," said Maria. John grew nervous as he wondered whether or not Diaphnerous told Enoch about his own conversations with the Eye.

"Okay then... I guess let's hear what he has to say," said John.

"There's something you need to prepare for."

"What's that?"

"He has a gun."

"Why does he have a gun?"

"We don't know. He says that he travels with it now for protection against the worms. We told him that we don't allow them on campus, but he basically ignored us. We don't know how to handle it. Just know that it's there."

"Are we safe?" asked John. Maria took a deep breath.

★★★

They walked down the hallway surrounded by the echo of their own footsteps. When they turned the corner into the lab, John saw Mark and Victor sitting at two seats in the front row, and Enoch standing behind the granite island. Next to the pidima, there was a wooden box on top of a cloth. When John began down the aisle, Enoch watched him with a grin. Attached to his right hip was a revolver. "Hello, Doctor," said Enoch. His presence and stature were nothing like John remembered from their first meeting. There was a noticeable confidence and even arrogance about him. John looked at Victor and Mark who looked back at him. Their wide eyes spelled discomfort. John nodded to them, and took a seat across the aisle.

Enoch stood behind the desk and looked at each one of them. His eyes were sleep deprived and blood shot, yet popping with excitement. "Today, I am a messenger. I am a messenger from the One who was sent here to save us. It has a plan for all of us, and It has shown me mine. It has shown me the other side." Enoch stopped and took a breath. He fought back a sudden emotion. "One day soon, I will live with It on the other side. It has chosen me." Enoch took a deep breath, and then another one. On his third, he choked on the air and began to cry. He sobbed for half a minute and then began laughing. The laughter lasted as long as the crying did. As he settled down, he looked at the wooden box on top of the cloth and froze. A smile sprouted from his lower cheeks and grew across his face. The others looked at each other. Enoch's slideshow of emotions was only upstaged by his loose-hanging revolver.

Maria leaned up in her chair. "Enoch… Are you saying that It took you into the higher dimension?"

"It is not yet safe to travel, but the wonderful Artist has shown me Its paintings. I've seen what Its world looks like."

"Well, what did it look like?" asked Mark abruptly. John recognized anger below Mark's impatience.

"It was unspeakable. There were impossible directions everywhere, and it was open. So much more open than here. It was hard to recognize much, but I did see the Differents. Diaphnerous had many paintings of them. They looked nothing like they did on my farm. They were not worms; there was much more to them. And they are evil. Diaphnerous showed me them working all day on a big machine. It expanded as far as the eye could see."

"Was it the tesseract?" asked Victor.

"I don't know what you mean," said Enoch.

"Did it look like a big cube or big square opening?"

"No. Diaphnerous showed me that too. It said the cube is what they use to get in and out of here, but the machine is different. It's a weapon. They are building it so that when they open up our world, they can drain the life from us. They want to remove our souls… But Diaphnerous will not let that happen. And It needs my help. It has chosen me."

John looked across the way at Maria. She side-eyed him back.

"I have come to ask for your help too. Once I am on the other side, we will need your support. We're going to shut down their machine."

"And how did Diaphnerous propose that we accomplish this, Enoch?" asked Victor.

"Once I am on the other side, everything will make sense, I am told. You must all continue to do what you are doing. It has plans for each of us, and we will be instructed very soon. Diaphnerous knows each one of you. It has even spoken of your child that is on the way." The air in the room stopped.

"What did you say?" asked Victor.

"The child that you are expecting. The Eye has spoken much about it. It is excited for the birth."

Maria stiffened. "Enoch, what did It say? Why were you talking about our baby?"

"Do not worry, ma'am. It wants the best for all of us, including the child. We will all be taken care of. You must trust me to be the first with the great Eye. I will join It up there, and then when the time is right, you will be given instructions," said Enoch. Maria squirmed in her seat. Victor took and held her hand.

Mark stared at Enoch with hatred. "Have you ever taken medication in your life?" he asked. Enoch looked at him either confused or insulted.

"What do you mean?"

"I mean you came here assuming that you could just tell us all how everything is going to happen, and I guess you expected us to buy into your bullshit. But you're crazy."

"Mark, stop. Let's just let him talk," murmured Maria.

"I am not crazy."

"You are. You're a crazy person."

"You have no right to talk to me like that. I'm the one who was chosen to help, and I am helping you."

"How are you helping? Why would you bring a gun? You can't have a gun on a campus, you moron. Normal people don't need to be told that."

"Mark, just let him finish. We can talk about this later," said Victor.

"Fuck him," said Mark. "He's crazy. Why are we giving him our time? This probably didn't even happen."

"LIAR!" shrieked Enoch. He slammed his fist down on the podium. "Don't ever say that again! I am the one It chose, and you are who It warned me about. It mentioned you by name. You are an obstacle, but nothing more," said Enoch.

"No, It didn't. It didn't tell you anything because you're not important. Nobody believes or cares what you are saying. You went from thinking that God sent angels to your farm to dig you holes to believing in some new god that you just made up. You're unintelligent, and you're crazy. You're a fucking liar."

Maria turned quickly to Mark. "Stop it. Just let him finish and we can talk about it later. Stop calling him crazy." Enoch heard enough and slammed his hands on the podium. Soundwaves traveled across the lab.

"You will be sorry. The Eye will remove you. We are here to help It save the world, and we will start with you." Enoch walked out from behind the podium. His silver revolver shined under the ceiling lights. He stared a hole through Mark, and Mark stared back at him. He stood his ground, although his conscience began to worry that perhaps he pushed the crazy man with the gun a bit too far.

"Enoch…" said Maria, carefully. "Would you feel better if Mark left? We're all a little on edge right now, but maybe it's best if Mark goes and cools off." Enoch said nothing, but his heavy breath got heavier. "I think your story with Diaphnerous is just a lot for us to understand right now, and maybe we're saying and thinking things that aren't true… Mark, why don't you go on a walk and cool off?"

Mark's face tightened. His ego refused to bend over to the will of the madman. The only thought that turned him over was the possibility that his defiance could lead to the death of a pregnant woman and two undeserving men. Mark blinked and broke eye contact with Enoch. He reluctantly walked to the aisle, and began his way towards the laboratory door.

"Stop," said Enoch. "You have no right to walk away." Mark halted. He remained with his back facing the farmer.

"Enoch, maybe let's just let him go for now—" Maria was interrupted by Enoch's determination.

"No, ma'am. He has said things that must be dealt with." Enoch spoke directly to Mark. "You have defiled and blasphemed the One that has come to save us. You will apologize and ask for forgiveness." Mark was yet to turn around and face Enoch. He did not want to meet his demise by the hand of someone that he had such little respect for, but he could never apologize to him either. It was not in Mark's makeup to kowtow to authority. He was fired off of multiple jobs because he refused to bite his tongue in the face of upper management. So, he decided that if it was his time to go, then he would go out with some dramatics. He turned around and faced his accuser.

"What about God, Enoch?"

"What?"

"What about God? You talk about this Thing like It's God. Did you replace God with a false idol? That's a broken Commandment."

"This isn't about God!" shouted Enoch. "Diaphnerous is different than anything we have known. It is here to help us. You need to correct what you have done."

"Well, when we're all dead soon, you will have to face God and explain to Him why you started worshiping a false deity."

"Mark, stop it," said Victor.

"Stop what? He's going to be burning in Hell with the rest of us if he continues with this sacrilege. I'm trying to help him see the light."

"Shut up, Mark," demanded Maria.

"You and your soul will pay for this, and you will be sorry," said Enoch.

"Nah, I won't be sorry. I've fucked up too much in my life to care about this. You're the one who's full of shit; you should be sorry. You lived your entire life claiming to believe in something, and then one golden Eye came around and made you betray it. You're a weak, goddamn hypocrite."

Enoch lifted the revolver and pointed it between Mark's eyes. He cocked back the hammer.

"Thou shall not kill, Enoch. Does your new God believe in that?" asked Mark.

"This was not my decision," said Enoch. "You brought your words upon us, and I will set us free. Anything in the way of our plan must be removed." Mark closed his eyes. Enoch closed his eyes.

"It showed me a picture too," said John, desperately. "The Eye. It drew me a picture and left it for me to find," said John. Enoch opened his eyes. He was yet to pull the trigger. "I found that the more I looked at it, the more it came to life. It was like looking into an entire world on a page… Is that what the paintings were like?" Enoch kept his aim on Mark, but his eyes briefly shifted to John.

"I spent two weeks straight looking at it, and it didn't even have color. I can imagine how incredible the paintings must have been," said John. He reached into his jacket and pulled out his journal. Cautiously, he stepped closer to the aisle with the book outstretched in his hand. Without much feedback from Enoch, John passed by Mark in the aisle and tiptoed up to Enoch's podium. John placed the open journal in front of Enoch, being very careful not to catch a glimpse of the masterpiece himself. Enoch's eyes rolled down to the page.

★★★

The book was pulled away from his gaze, and Enoch was humbled and calm. At some point in his stretch of tranquility, Mark safely left the room, and Enoch's gun had been put back into its holster with the bullets removed, although Enoch was much too distracted to notice. He took in a long breath and let it out.

"Is that anything like what it looked like in the paintings?" asked Maria. Enoch nodded.

"Yes, much of the land was beautiful, but the Differents contaminated it with their machine and their hive. The other creatures were there too," said Enoch.

"What other creatures?"

"John knows. He called them centipedes. They came out of his closet."

"How do you know that happened?" asked John.

"Diaphnerous told me. It watched the whole thing," said Enoch. "They didn't look like centipedes though."

"What are they?" asked John.

"They were very hard to look at. Very disturbing. They were ring-shaped and they had millions of squirming limbs around them, like hideous insects. Diaphnerous told me that their relationship to the Differents was like the relationship between a horse and a human. They spend all of their lives working for them.

The Differents are big and unable to work in small spaces. The ring creatures are forced to do the work that they cannot. They do only as they are told."

"When are you supposed to go to the other side?" asked Victor.

"It has not told me yet, but it will be very soon. Diaphnerous is happy that we will be together soon. After we do our work, we will be able to invite you over as well. It wants us to be with It as soon as possible."

"But if we close the tesseract, how will we or the Eye get in and out? And where will the worms go? I'm sure they won't just leave."

"It's all part of the plan. Once the opening is completely closed, the Differents will have no reason to stay. They were only there to build the opening. When they're far enough away, me and Diaphnerous will reopen the portal. We will surely need your help."

"Okay, but won't they want to kill you two if you're responsible for destroying their plans?" asked Victor.

"They will never get to us. Diaphnerous has created a fortress that can never be entered by the beasts or their slaves. Diaphnerous alone can get us in and out… It is the smartest being in all of their world, and It has chosen me to be the most important human." Enoch looked to the mysterious wooden box that had been sitting on the granite island. They all looked to see what Enoch was motioning to.

"What's in the box, Enoch?" asked Victor.

"A gift from the Artist. I've been excited to show you." Enoch walked over to the box. His hands began to shake, and his knees trembled. He took out a key from his pocket and unlocked the box. When he lifted the lid, there came a blast of light. It was hallowed and full of color. Enoch froze in the sight of the box's contents. Maria peaked out from over his shoulder to get a glimpse of the beautiful artifact, and she too froze.

Enoch began to cry. When he was able to catch his breath, he wiped his hands of the sweat and tears, and he gently reached into the box. Carefully, he lifted out of it a shining, royal crown, and he cradled it under its swaddling cloth. It was a stunning mix of gold and silver, and it was sprinkled with jewels of the most unique colors. It was nearly as beautiful as The Feathered Eye. Enoch softly turned the crown to reveal every last of its details. They all adored it. They were surrounded by its glowing warmth. They loved it.

"Diaphnerous crafted it from the rarest metals of Its world. It spent Its entire life collecting each individual jewel." Enoch admired the crown. He smiled through his tears. "It gave it to me as a *thank you.*"

They stood around Enoch and stared at the crown. After an hour had gone by, no one had noticed that John's jacket, which was down on his chair, was slightly elevated. Its shoulders were hooked on the back of the seat, but the pocket was stretched out in the direction of where they were standing. As it stretched further and further, the pocket ran short of fabric, and from within its clutch appeared the metal ball. Its natural desire to seek mass encouraged it to fight its way to the edge of the pocket's grip. And when it made its final slip to freedom, the metal ball fired from the jacket and sailed straight into Enoch's crown. The two metal objects slammed together and sent thunder throughout the laboratory. Everyone fell to the ground out of either force or fear, and the crown shot through the air. When it came crashing down, the metal ball clung to its side.

"No!" shouted Enoch. He rose to his knees and shrieked. He dove back down for the crown. He held it up and sobbed as if he was holding the lifeless body of a loved one. The crown was squeezed tight to his chest, and when he noticed that the ball was attached, he jammed his fingers in and tried to pry it off.

He grunted and pulled until his face turned blue. Seeing that death would come to Enoch before he would be able to separate the two rare objects, John ran over to his seat. From his bag, he pulled out a cloth and quickly unwrapped it. Out came the stone. John brought it to where Enoch was on his knees. Three of Enoch's fingernails were ripped off in the struggle, and blood was filling his hands. John untwisted the stone into two pieces and carefully applied each piece to opposite ends of the crown. As soon as he felt them lock into place, the crown went light, and the ball fell off. It began its way toward the granite island where John snatched it up. It was covered in the farmer's blood.

Enoch tried wiping the crown clean in search of the damage that had been done. There was a noticeable indentation from the collision, and the absence of one of its most beautiful jewels. Enoch whipped his head around, looking for it. He spotted the glow from the gem, which was close to the color of the dark-blue ocean. He picked it up and held it to his heart. It was clear that glue or any man-made adhesive would not be suitable for repair. Enoch let out another deafening shriek before falling to the ground in a flood of tears. They stood above him. Between all of their years, not one of them had ever seen someone in such emotional agony.

"I'm sorry! I'm sorry!" cried Enoch. "It's ruined." He rolled around in unbearable pain. John leaned down and put his hand on Enoch's shoulder to try and calm him. Victor kept Maria back to a safe distance.

"Enoch, it's okay. Maybe we can fix it," said John.

"It can't be fixed!" yelled Enoch. "It was perfect." John looked at Maria and Victor. No one had a thought.

"Enoch, I'm sorry. I didn't realize that the ball was left in my pocket," said John. Enoch suddenly caught his breath.

"What do you mean?"

"I don't know how it got out like that. That's never happened."

"You mean this was your fault?" Enoch rose to his knees. "This happened because of you? You ruined it!" Enoch lunged towards John who sprawled back and fell over. He sat up and crawled backwards on his hands and feet. Victor jumped in and grabbed Enoch's arms from behind. Even after weeks of malnourishment, the farmer was strong enough to throw Victor off of his back and rise to his feet. He walked towards John who scooted backwards until he hit the wall. With nowhere else to go, Enoch stepped to him and lifted him up by his shirt. John was little more than bones and skin. He looked to grab for Enoch's gun before he remembered that they had removed its bullets.

Enoch held John against the wall and pressed his forehead into John's. They were truly eye to eye. A great deal of debate polluted the farmer's head, and John recognized it immediately. He realized that perhaps the tormented man suffered from the same mental unrest that he himself did. It was no longer a battle of good and evil for Enoch. His mind had been taken into a harshly profound place, and it was changed for the stranger.

When Enoch slowed down his breathing, John assumed that a decision was made, and once again, he awaited his sentencing. Enoch relaxed his grip of John's shirt and took a slow step back. He nodded his head as if some internal agreement had been made between he and himself. "We do not need your help," he said. "We will do it on our own, and only we will share the kingdom." John hardly heard what Enoch said, but he was happy to have his torso back.

Enoch walked over past Maria and Victor and picked up the crown. He placed it into the wooden box, closed the lid, and locked it. Without another word or even a look, Enoch gathered his possessions and left the laboratory.

John walked over to the podium and watched the door, hoping that it would stay closed. "Maybe we should pack up and get out of here," he said.

"Good idea, doctor," said Victor. They kept an eye on the door. "So, what's the deal with that thing you put on his crown? What was that all about?"

John looked at Victor. "Do you have any booze at your house?"

Victor looked at John. "Plenty."

"Let's go to your place. Pour me a tall drink, and I'll tell you all about it."

***

"Thanks for trying to help earlier. That definitely could have gone the other way," said John to Victor as they made their way to the front door. John carried the stone in its cloth.

"Sorry I couldn't do more. After he threw me, I tried to get up, but the left side of my body stopped working," said Victor.

"I guess science hasn't really kept us tough. I tried to wrestle in high school, but my first match was against a guy his size, and I got thrown around... Actually, it looked pretty much identical to what just happened," said John.

"Are you sure you're okay? We can go get you checked out at the medical center," said Maria. "And maybe we should call the cops on him. Besides assaulting both of you, he's driving around with a gun. What if he kills someone?"

"I don't know, hun. Maybe you're right, but how do we even know where he is?"

"We know where he's going."

"What if he kills the cop that pulls him over?" asked Victor.

"We took the bullets from his gun," said Maria.

"He probably has more in his truck. I couldn't even get the door open..." As Victor and Maria argued, John thought about what side to take. Maria was making complete sense, but he was far less worried about Enoch and the police than he was about Diaphnerous and Its feelings on getting Enoch taken away and locked up. As many problems as taking Enoch out of the picture would solve, John made a *'promise'* to the Eye that he would help in Its plan. He had the feeling of being watched since before he crossed state lines into Wisconsin, and he could almost smell the fresh scent that always preceded the great Eye's arrival. He was nowhere near ready to betray his promise yet.

"What about the school?" asked John. Maria and Victor stopped arguing and looked at him. "If the police want to investigate what happened, they'll want to speak with the school, and they'll probably investigate the lab."

"That's right," said Victor. "We're not supposed to be in the lab right now." They reached their stoop and stopped at the bottom of the stairs.

"We can say it happened somewhere else. We'll tell them it happened here," said Maria.

"He's so crazy that, if he doesn't kill them, he would probably tell them the entire story, and insist that we were in the lab. All of our equipment belongs to the school technically. If they walk in there right now, what are we going to tell them we're doing? We're too close to worry about getting him arrested."

"I can't imagine Mr. Pricherwood going quietly," said John. "It would end badly for him and the police. Probably his wife too."

"Oh my God… Delilah. He's going home to Delilah right now. She needs to get out," said Maria.

"She's crazy too," said Victor. "With everything she told us, why is she still there anyway?"

"She doesn't know what to do, Victor. She's scared. That's her husband."

"If anything, she needs to help us. Only she knows what's really going on over there, and she can help us get rid of him. Otherwise, Mark might have to… um…when.." Victor caught himself talking in front of an audience. "When he decides to show up again. She can warn us." Victor and Maria got uncomfortably quiet. John pretended to not hear any of it, and Victor pretended that he didn't say it, but they all knew that he did.

"Is the door open?" asked Maria, changing the subject. They looked up at the front door. It was a few inches ajar. She walked up, and Victor and John followed. They walked through the front of the house and back into the den. The sound on the television was blasting as *The Flintstones* played. Mark was passed out drunk on the floor.

"What the hell happened here?" asked Victor.

John set down the stone and picked up a beer mug from the coffee table. He smelled the dark brown liquid inside. "He filled it with whiskey. That's a tall drink," said John, impressed.

Victor looked at the mug. "I'll get some glasses. The ice still looks fresh." Victor walked over to the kitchen and grabbed two tall glasses. "Can I get you anything, hun?"

"Water please," said Maria. Victor returned with a glass of water for his wife, and two empty glasses for himself and John. John poured the remainder of Mark's mug evenly into both cups. They both took a large sip.

"Alright, let me show you what this thing does." John set down his glass and picked up the stone. He walked over to their large recliner and attached the stone to both sides of it. "Hand me that pillow." Victor handed John a pillow from the couch. John threw the light cushion into the recliner, and it slid six feet back into the wall. He then walked over and picked it up with one hand and brought it back.

"Oh my God," said Maria. "How did you do that?"

"What's in that chest?" asked John as he pointed to a thick wooden chest in the corner of the room.

"Books," said Maria. "It probably weighs four-hundred pounds."

"Is there anywhere else you want it?"

"Yes, I've wanted to move it for years. I hate it there. Can you move it next to the shelf over there?"

"No problem. Let's roll Mark out of the way, and I'll slide it over," said John. Victor bent down and pushed on Mark's belly in an attempt to roll him over. He dug his feet into the ground, but only managed to push himself backwards.

"He might be heavier than the chest," said Victor. Victor looked down at Mark, then at the stone in John's hands, and then up at John. He gave John a shoulder shrug.

John looked at the stone and weighed the possibility. Mark was in fact a large person. He shook off the idea though. "We better not. I don't want to pull his molecules out of alignment." He and Victor instead both grabbed a leg and drug Mark across the floor the old-fashioned way. John then went over to the chest and applied the two halves of the stone, pulled it from the wall, and slid it swiftly across the room, next to the shelves. It moved like a cardboard box across ice.

Maria was thrilled. She had John rearrange the entire room which was something that she had been putting off since she and Victor moved in. They stood in the center of the new decor and admired their work. Maria was ecstatic.

"Does Mark have any cigarettes?" asked John as he took another sip of whiskey.

"I didn't know you smoked," said Victor.

"I've had one about every twenty-five years. Seems like a good time to have my third."

"Right on. I'll grab his pack and join you for one."

★★★

Outside, John and Victor stood on the sidewalk as Maria sat on the stoop.

"But how does it remove the mass?" asked Maria.

"I'm wrestling with the idea that it somehow manipulates the Higgs Field. Perhaps it makes the object no longer interact or interact less with the field," said John.

"So, basically it hides the mass?" asked Maria.

"Yes, but that's just a guess," said John.

"It could also have something to do with the difference between weight in dimensions," said Maria.

"What do you mean?"

"What if it somehow connects the object's weight with the higher dimension, or maybe even shifts its weight?" asked Maria.

"That's possible as well. Like it's just nudging it slightly into the fourth dimension and ridding its weight," said John.

"Why are they giving you things like this? Between Enoch and his crown, and your weight tools, it's like both sides are trying to win us over with gifts," said Victor. "Which one is the Trojan Horse?"

John took a drag of his cigarette. He wanted nothing more than to tell Victor and Maria what he really thought, but again, at that exact moment, the sweet smell came back, and he could almost hear the faint ringing of chimes. He took a deep breath.

"I'd like to think that these are here to help us... but it's just too convenient. I think you guys had it right." John's face was covered in shame despite his best efforts to hide it. Maria and Victor shared a look of mistrust.

"So, you think we're on the right track, huh?" asked Victor. John stared at his feet for a long minute.

"I do. Nothing is clear cut, I suppose... but I think you're doing the right thing."

***

John stayed in a hotel just off of campus. He had nothing more than the clothes in which he wore, the ball in his jacket, and stone wrapped in its cloth. John rested on the bed and stared at the ceiling. He wondered what he was doing there, where he had been, and if this would ever end. As the days passed, John lost his sense of what was happening and what was not. He could only guess whether or not the forty-second night would actually come. Perhaps the meeting of dimensions broke a link in the time-space continuum, and he was doomed to float freely in a time that took place in-between days. Or perhaps he was just waiting to die.

Chapter Forty-Nine
<u>One Final Goodbye</u>

John opened his eyes to a dark room full of waving colors. The walls were covered in a flowing movement, like moonlight reflecting off of water. Clouds of mist hovered above him and created a soft glow of dark purple and blue. There was an ambience of meditative music that coincided with the flow of the colors. He felt himself lift off of the bed and float in the mist, free from any negative feeling. As he drifted in the air between the floor and ceiling, the moisture thickened, and John found himself in a beautiful nowhere. A cool breeze blessed his face, and somewhere out in the distance, he saw the impression of a Light.

John knew who It was, but he was not scared. He was comforted. The Light grew in size as It got closer, and the universe of colors deepened. Ecstasy swallowed him. He looked forward with reverence as the Eye presented Itself. It first arrived closed, showing Its full dress of feathers. They were radiant in tone but soft in texture. John could feel their embrace just by looking at them. Then the feathers spread as Diaphnerous opened Its eye, and It looked deeply saddened. All of the diamonds within the golden spiral were emotionally broken. The borders of Its eye were covered in a delicate nectar. It had a sweet aroma and appeared to be glittered with sugar, but John knew that it was the tears of Diaphnerous. Just like himself, the great Eye was fighting the urge to cry. John's heart broke.

"What's wrong?" he asked.

"They have caught me," said the Eye.

"Who?"

"The Neolorgue. They have caught me trespassing. They have destroyed my home and all of my work."

"Your art?" asked John, breaking into tears.

"Yes. It is gone, and soon I will be gone," said Diaphnerous. "I will not be able to see you again."

He became overwhelmed with sadness and wept.

"Soon, I will be exiled to a place of total isolation. I will be alone for the rest of time."

"I'm sorry, Diaphnerous. I'm very sorry."

"Do not be sorry. It is no matter. I have always been alone," said Diaphnerous. The Eye straightened up and gathered Its pride. "My memory goes back for uncountable days, but the brief interactions that I have shared with humans means more than any other part of my existence. Most important was my time with you, John."

John was unable to speak, but he never looked away. Tears poured down his face.

"I am sorrowful for the way in which I have acted and spoke to you. I know that it has been mysterious," said Diaphnerous. "I apologize for the behavior which confuses you and scares you. It is difficult to communicate with you in a method that is suitable to your understanding. I have tried my best.

"You are the only singularity in this Universe who I have ever truly connected with. Thank you, John. You have given all of my days value. You are my friend."

"You are my friend too, Diaphnerous. Please… How can I help you?"

"Thank you, John, but you cannot. It is beyond your power, and much is already in motion. I had only one last opportunity to see you."

"What will happen to you?" asked John hopelessly.

"I will face my solitude. My Being will continue in a place of void. My words and thoughts will be heard by only me. I will feel nothing. I will create no more… But I will do so in peace. I will know that my actions have assured the permanence of a species. And you will prosper. You will prosper in language, and love, and art. My eternity of nothing will pass parallel with your eternity of everything. The eternity of man. And that, John, has given Me worth."

"Diaphnerous, I am sorry." John was broken.

"Just do your best. You can save everything, John. Close the opening. They do not know your plan yet. From here on, Mankind will be the only creator of art. Existence deserves art, and that is your responsibility."

John's head remained hung. "I will try my best," he said.

"So long, my dear friend. I will remember you for countless lives to come."

"Goodbye, Diaphnerous."

***

"She said that he's been sleeping since he got home. He hasn't moved," said Maria.

"That's good I guess," said Victor.

"She has an idea."

"What is it?" He and his wife held hands in bed and stared at the pitch-black ceiling.

"She wants to get him out in the fields somehow. She thinks that she can convince him to stay down in the tunnels for the night, that way he's nowhere near the barn."

"Can't she just get him off of the property for the night?"

"There's no way. Coming here was the first time that he's left in months," said Maria.

"Okay, so the plan is to get him into the tunnels, and keep him down there all night? What if he tries to leave, what is she going to do?"

"She's going to write him a fake note from the Eye that will instruct him to wait down there. And then she'll go down there with him and make sure he stays."

"That's great until he realizes that It's never coming," said Victor. Maria let it sit for a moment.

"Yeah… I guess it will have to be timed perfectly," she said. They held still in the dark.

"Everything will have to be timed perfectly." Victor took a deep breath and let it out. He turned over and held onto his wife. "Maybe tomorrow we'll wake up and forget about everything. I want to be one of the people who don't know it's coming."

***

Alice walked along the trees and ran her hand across the incredible twists. She prayed to God to either intervene or give her the ability to do so herself. She knew when the end was due, and she could see it coming. Like a wall of water rushing towards the beach, Alice could see the moment in time when the two realities would meet and become one. She had exactly that duration to stop the others from stopping the merge. For now, she prayed for help from her Lord while waiting for the worms to find her.

All of the larger figs in the trees were picked and gone, but they were followed immediately by a bloom of smaller fruit. The covered branches hung heavy and full. The leaves blended into the entirety of the green spectrum, and the figs bunched together, purple and blue. It was nature in a way that Alice had never seen, and for that, it came with a cost.

Alice could only imagine that this was a subfraction of what could be done if the complex worms were given more time. To her, the beasts from above were sharing their secrets to success, and everyone was ignoring them. It was no different than the field of corn that was turning to waste under the watch of the mad farmer. But ironically, Enoch was the only other person involved that Alice could find empathy for.

He was a man of extreme misfortune and grief, and he was led down a path of false promise. In her opinion, the Eye of deceit found a man who was broken and vulnerable, and It mutilated his soul. Alice looked at herself honestly and knew that she could have done little more if she were in the farmer's shoes. Enoch's faith was taken by something more cunning than himself, but when it came to the others, Alice succumbed to the primal human emotion of anti-sympathy. She could do nothing but blame them. In the face of the highest opportunity, they only defeated themselves.

★★★

John woke up with moist, puffy eyes like he had been crying all night, but he could not remember a thing. When he sat up, his brain squeezed itself into a pounding headache. It took him rather long to get his feet down onto the floor, and when he stood up, his knees wobbled. He swore that he did not drink all that much, but his body disagreed. He was dizzy and displaced.

The room was stale, and the more that John stumbled about, the more that he felt the need to vomit. Either he began to tilt or the room began to tilt, but John quickly lost the ability to stand. He collapsed onto the filth-covered carpet. His eyes slid up while his eyelids slid down, and everything went quiet.

***

Juice covered Alice's chin and spilled down her shirt. She sat in the shade with a full bushel of figs and ate one after the other. She figured that she may as well indulge in the fruits of the worms' labors if their time of contact was reaching its limit. Alice often filled a basket before going to her waiting spot, and then she ate figs and waited. They were sweeter than sugar, and they always left her feeling healthier. She could only ponder how a room full of professional truth seekers could ignore so much proof of good intent.

Sometimes, she even got mad at the worms. Alice could not understand why they were watching the other humans openly devise their plans against them. *What is the plan?* she often wondered. *How could a being with so much higher power and ability have such little control over its subjects?* Then, she wondered how much control the worms had over anything.

She thought that maybe on their plane, they were as clueless as her fellow humans. Maybe her fellow humans were as clueless as the flat creatures. And maybe there were others higher up, and maybe they were all clueless too.

***

John came to cognizance. He was on the floor of his hotel room with his notebook beside him. It took him a few seconds to remember that he was still in Wisconsin, but as soon as he did, he struggled to his feet again and rubbed his face until he fully came-to. He picked up his notebook off of the floor and placed it on the night table beside his bed. Looking down at it, he realized that it had been through just as much as he has, even more in fact. The book had been to the other side and back, and somehow, it was still with him. With that thought, his head began pounding again.

He cleared the bed to make room for his body to collapse again. He pushed back the blanket and moved the pillows. From under the pillow, he was greeted with a surprise. John kept the stone rolled up inside of a towel, which was then rolled up inside of a bed sheet. He knew for a fact that he did not leave it under the pillows on the bed because he never removed it from his bag of belongings. With some befuddlement, John picked it up and gave it a good look.

He unspun it from the bedsheet, loosened the towel, and released the stone along with a small piece of paper. The piece of paper caught his eye first, so he picked it up. Written in accomplished cursive was the note, *Art mimics life.* After the sleepless night of who knows what, John's cognitive assembly was nowhere to be found. Instead of trying to interpret the message's meaning, he filed it away in the overflowing folder of *"Things to Figure Out"* in his great mental library, and then he shifted his focus back to the stone.

Right away, something seemed off. When John felt it in his hands, he noticed an unfamiliar texture on its surface. And upon a closer look, he realized that he was holding something that he had never seen before.

It appeared to also be a stone or a rock of some sort, but the color was different and it was covered in ridges. The ridges themselves were individually carved out peaks and valleys. Hundreds of them wrapped around the rock, each one with its own unique design running through it. He focused in on one and studied it from the bottom up. This particular canal used imagery to tell the life story of an organism. It was like no other creature that John had seen before.

Its birth from its mother, whom was only partially depicted, introduced the being into a serene living environment. John's mind could best describe it as a warm, aquatic atmosphere. It lived comfortably and safe. Its only inherent labor was to find a mate for the purposes of companionship, and to reproduce something that would also be blessed enough to enjoy such a life. As John followed the sketched ridge to its conclusion, he witnessed the creature and its mate give birth to an offspring of their own before dying peacefully together. Their bodies then floated on continuously for the rest of time.

John welled up. He felt the tranquility that this creature experienced through its time, and he was able to share its emotions. He rolled the stone over just slightly and was greeted with a new carving. This canal was not so much a story as it was the evolution of a landscape over time. It started desolate and dry until it was introduced to a shock of energy. Slowly but surely, this world was transformed into the home of an incredible ecosystem of life, minerals, and complex terrain. Every state of matter blended perfectly into the next. John got halfway through its transformation before he started to visualize himself surrounded by the luscious, fertile nature.

Chapter Fifty
The Missing Variable

Maria ate her breakfast bagel sandwich out of its wrapper. She was parked outside of the laboratory. Her seatbelt pressed against her as she perched forward to see into the building. Before she spilled a pepper onto her shirt and looked down, she could have sworn that the hallway light turned on. When she looked back up, it was on, but then she began to convince herself that it was on the entire time. She took another bite from her sandwich and watched closely.

★★★

"Mark, get up," said Victor as he shook Mark's shoulder.

Mark sat up with his eyes half closed. "What time is it?"

"It's nine. We should get over to the lab."

"Okay. Where's Maria?"

"She's meeting us there. She wanted to pick us up breakfast first."

"Shit... sorry... I didn't mean to send your pregnant wife to go get us breakfast," said Mark.

"It's alright. I told her that I would get you up and we'd be a little bit behind her."

"She shouldn't be there alone."

"She'll be okay. She won't go inside. I think she wanted some time alone to think."

★★★

Maria was pasted to the windshield as she looked inside the building. A Shadow moved across the hallway wall before the lights shut off again. Maria unbuckled, opened up her door, and stepped out. Even with the light shut off, there remained a glow of Color.

***

Mark leaned over and tied his shoes. Victor stood in front of the television while he waited. "Turn that up," said Mark. Victor turned up the volume as news footage hovered over the scene of a small, collapsed bridge with a mess of crushed cars and rubble. "Did they just say sixteen people? What town is that?" asked Mark. Victor ran over to his book shelf and pulled out a book of maps.

***

Maria faced the long, open hallway. She regretted pursuing this on her own, but like John in the past, she was too curious to turn back. The only noise throughout the hallway was that of her creeping feet. When she came within ten feet of the laboratory door, she stopped. She was alone with whatever waited on the other side. The laboratory door slowly opened and a soft Glow welcomed her from inside.

***

"Where is it?" asked Mark impatiently. "And why do you have a map book of the northwest?"

"Shit…" said Victor.

"What? Why shit?"

"It's like fifty miles from the storm."

"Is that good or bad?"

"It's a lot farther than the other places, but I don't know. Fifty miles… It's not that far."

"Well, is it too far or not?"

"How the hell should I know?" yelled Victor. "It's Idaho. Everything seems to be spread out. Fifty miles there is like one here."

"Okay, listen, let's get to the lab, and look at the map. We'll find out exactly how far it is."

★★★

Maria stood in the doorway, hesitating to walk in. The entire room was pitch black except for one light that shined straight down onto the granite island desk. On top of the desk, and well illuminated, was the original pidima. Just in front of that was a smaller object that Maria could not make out. She walked down the aisle, and a warm Breeze kissed the back of her neck as she got closer. When she reached the front of the room, she recognized the object. Reflecting brightly from the lights above was John's missing stone.

★★★

Victor jogged circles around the laboratory floor. Mark stood face-to-face with the stone and pondered, afraid to actually touch it. Victor continued around when Maria hung up her phone and walked over to join Mark. "No answer?" asked Victor from across the room.

"No answer," said Maria.

"Well, he didn't just leave. That doesn't sound very John-like. Even after our arguments, he's been vocal about everything," said Mark. Victor trotted over and pulled it in.

"You didn't see his car when you were sitting out there?" asked Victor to his wife.

"I didn't see anything. The only reason why I knew he was here was because the light turned on and off, and the stone was here."

"Well, he didn't just leave," said Mark as he tried to connect the dots.

★★★

John marched back and forth across an old wooden floor. He could not take his eyes off of the window because he was nervous for what was going to happen outside. The roaring fireplace behind him provided the only light in the room, and through the window, he could see only darkness.

Without making any noise, something long and black slithered out from above the fire behind John, and then made its way into the room. John was too nervous to notice the movement behind him, nor could he hear anything, but the countless legs of the elongated creature propelled it across the air. In graceful swirls, the visitor spun itself through the room and arrived just over John's head. As he addressed it, he kept his eyes on his pacing feet.

"If you can read my numbers, then why can't you help me?" The many-legged creature did not reply. "I know that you know what I'm doing because you made me the ball. Or the worms made me the ball… Either way, you all left me on my own."

John turned around and looked up at the being. "Do you think that we're trying to help you or something? We're not. In case you can't figure it out, they're trying to close you out. I wanted to stop them, but I guess I can't do a whole lot about it now, can I?" A light grew across the room. John looked out the window. The sun rose above an endless green field. By the time he could walk up to the window, the sun had already set. Then it happened again, and again. The sun was rising and setting, and days and nights were flying by. John pointed to it and began snapping his fingers at the creature to take notice. "You see? Look! It's happening. This has been happening since you took my book. There was never enough time."

John looked up at what still appeared to him to be a large centipede hovering just above his head. "You really have no idea what we're doing down here, do you?"

★★★

Delilah came into David's room seeking aid from God or her son, but before she could finish even one prayer, the tears started. The voices from above never came, and she was left by herself to figure out how to handle her husband on the upcoming night.

*S*he dried her face with David's handkerchief and looked across the room at the dark window. Her husband was somewhere off in the corn, but she needed him in one place and one place only when the final hour came, and the clock was ever-ticking.

She took three deep breaths and put a stop to her tears by force. Delilah inhaled deep, held it, and let it out. Again, she inhaled deep, coughed on some moisture, and let it out. By the third and final deep breath, Delilah caught her balance, and her face cleared.

The room was suddenly quiet, and she could feel the full wetness of her tears on her neck and chest. She wiped herself with the handkerchief until she was dry and the cloth was wet. Looking down on it, she was amazed at how fresh and new the silk appeared. She never took the time to admire it because it reminded her too much of David, but it was undoubtedly gorgeous. Its surface shined with a smooth pinkish-white, and the golden *D* that she stitched in for her son had not lost one thread, nor did the multi-colored trimming that surrounded the *D*. She could finally appreciate it as her best work.

As she rubbed her hand across the embroidery, she felt a faint rush inside of her. It was a subtle feeling of life, and it was not horrible. She only felt either horrible or numb for decades, so this mysterious sensation was more than welcome, whatever it was.

With the new feeling came a rhythm, and that rhythm caused a spark. She was struck by a revelation. She held in her hands her lost son's only possession, but instead of seeing grief in its stitching, she saw a canvas. The smooth pinkish-white surface of the handkerchief was an empty page, and the golden *D* was a well-crafted signature.

Delilah ran into her room, grabbed her sewing materials, and retreated back into David's room, locking the door behind her. She threaded her needle with her darkest black. As the needle inched towards the handkerchief, her fingers began to shake. The action that was necessary to save her husband also involved the mutilation of the only object that still represented her son, and Delilah found it hard to swallow. It felt to her like she was burying him again. As the horrific memory passed through her, the tears started again. Delilah fell into the deep hole of dread once again. But then her mind stepped in and offered her a thought: *David is dead. Enoch is not.* Those intriguing words replaced the image of her son's still body, and then she came up with a thought of her own: *Have I cried enough?* Delilah sat up straight, stuck the needle through the silk, and pulled.

★★★

The dark shades protecting Victor's eyes reflected the light of the glowing pidima shell. He waited behind the switchboard as the energy machine warmed up. This time, he demanded that Mark and Maria watch the spectacle from the observance room above the lab floor. It took an hour of arguing, but he finally convinced them to stay far enough away in case the presence of the stone caused the generator to backfire. He told them that if he went down, then the two of them could possibly still get the job done on the night of.

As soon as the engine purred, Victor turned the lever up to two. The shell brightened and the generator shook. He waited thirty seconds and then turned it up to three. The entire lab floor rumbled. Victor hopped off of the switchboard and placed one half of the stone onto the far end of the generator. He returned to the lever and pushed it up to four. The engine roared, and the lights blasted whiteness into the center.

Victor turned and looked up to see Mark and Maria, but everything behind him was voided from the blinding light surging from the pidima. He counted to three in his head. He grabbed the other end of the stone and applied it to his side of the generator. With the generator now weightless, he smashed the lever up to its fifth and highest level.

The zero-gravity fuel expanded itself into its optimal form, and combusted into energy. The pidima shell maximized its concentration of light, and it poured all of its activity into the very center.

The visibility in the room returned, and what remained was a concentrated ball of light and heat. Victor looked up to his wife and friend. Their awed faces glowed from the powerful weapon.

Chapter Fifty-One
Both Cannot Be Right

The news played at a low volume on the television. Mark kept his eyes half open as he ate a bowl of melted ice cream. Maria and Victor had gone to bed hours ago, leaving Mark in his semi-drunken state. Before he could nod off with the ice cream bowl on his fat belly, his phone buzzed. He felt around for it and checked the caller ID. With a smirk of curiosity, he opened his flip phone and held it to his ear. "I didn't think I'd hear from you."

"Hello, Mark," said Alice from the other end.

"What can I help you with, Ms. Day?"

"Are you still going through with it?"

"Has anything changed?"

"No, but that's the point. You're looking at it wrong."

Mark sat up in his chair. "Listen… From day one, I saw a lot of similarities between you and me, so I figured that we might get along, but we just think differently. We don't have the same beliefs. And that's all fine and well, but you gotta stop telling us we're wrong. It's arrogant," said Mark.

"How many times have you told me I was wrong? You've made it clear that you don't believe in God, and that's okay, but you also never took me seriously."

"Okay, Alice, what are your thoughts? Keeping in mind that I don't believe in God, what is happening?"

"What's happening is that the worms are here to help. You still have never answered my question?"

"And what question would that be?"

"Why didn't they kill you? I've asked you a hundred times."

"I don't know. Like the last time you asked me, I still don't know. And who gives a shit? They killed other people. A lot of people."

"I read about the building, Mark. I read all of the articles and saw all the pictures."

"Yeah? Nothing like seeing a mass grave to put your mind at ease, huh?"

"The building was wrong from the start. They think that it had structural problems from the way it was built. It was the architecture."

"Oh okay. So, did any of these articles mention bus sized worms roaming the halls or ramming into the scaffolding?"

"What if they were there to warn you? Have you thought about that, Mark?"

"I've thought about the people who are dead, one of whom that I knew. Look up what happened in Idaho. Did you happen to catch that? Sixteen more people, Alice. That makes it thirty-three if I'm counting correctly. Although I'm not a math genius like John, so I could be wrong."

"What happened in Idaho was nowhere near where Victor mapped the sight. I looked it up. Accidents happen all the time and coincidences happen."

"Yeah, well somehow you're the only one that thinks that, and that's why we stopped listening to you."

"John agrees with me. We've talked about it--"

"He's gone, Alice! John's gone! He left. John doesn't agree with you. We haven't seen him in over a week. Have you seen him?" Mark was met with silence. "He hasn't called you back either, huh? Sounds like you two are really on the same page."

"Something's wrong. He would never leave without telling us. He was not acting like himself."

"He seemed like himself to me. He came here for one night, and he took off in the morning. Haven't heard from him since. Maria called the hotel in Colorado, and they haven't seen him in weeks. He got out while he could, and he left us here to deal with it." Mark paused and waited for a response. None came. "Alice, they're trying to kill us, and you're trying to help them."

"I'm trying to stay out of the way. This is not our decision to make. If it is supposed to be stopped, then it will be stopped."

"Then say a prayer to God. Maybe He'll come down and stop us."

"You might regret saying that."

"Yeah, well... maybe I will. We'll find out soon. You, me, John, the lovely Delphi family, my son, the crazy goddamn farmer... We'll probably end up in the same place anyway. After our spines are gone, maybe they'll throw us in the same pile."

"Or it could be worse. You may have to spend the rest of your life with yourself, knowing what you've done. Believe me; that will be far worse." Alice hung up the phone. Mark hung up, looked up at the ceiling, and sighed.

★★★

Victor kneeled down and put together two pieces of the aluminum pidima shell. Mark watched closely. "Each corner has a slip. Slide in the flat end until the holes meet, then close the clip. No screws, no tools," said Victor. He tugged on it to show Mark its stability.

"You would be good with scaffolding," said Mark.

"Thanks. I recommend we leave the top and bottom squares together because the pidimas are already in place and calibrated to the center. Put the bottom one down with the pidimas facing up, obviously, then do one arm at a time. All of the arms are identical and the top and bottom square are interchangeable. Just be careful that you don't break the pidimas. We need all of them... I think."

Mark took a slow walk around the shell with a beer in his hand. "Pretty solid here, Mr. Delphi. How about the generator? Is it easy to hook up?"

"All you'll have to do is plug the heavy chord into both sides. Plug it into the shell first, and then the generator. You've seen how I turn it on, right? It's like a stick shift. You can't shift the gear until the lights have a chance to heat up." Victor held the lever on the control box. "When you see that they're ready, push the lever on the box, and then wait again. It's a balancing act though, so you have to be careful. If you shift too early, you'll blow out the pidimas. If you wait too long, they'll pull too much energy, and the generator will short. If you're lucky, you'll have another shot at it, but maybe not. You've seen how this thing gets."

Mark scratched his head. He never had to handle pressure like this. "So, after the fifth gear, I have to put on the stone?" asked Mark.

"After you shift to four, put the first half on. When you're ready to go to five, throw on the other half, and shift. That's how I did it. Put the stone on first, but don't wait. There's a lot of power in there.""Yeah, no shit," said Mark. He took out a cigarette and sparked it.

Victor did not look up as he continued to put the shell together. "What did she say about John?"

"She said he's on her side and he agrees with her, but she didn't even know he was gone."

"I guess he didn't tell anyone he was leaving."

"Any of this make sense to you?" asked Mark. "The guy shows up for a day with this thing, teaches us how to use it, and then leaves. Not to mention that we didn't even show him how to use the shell. How would he know that we needed this? And why just disappear? I mean… Should we be worried about him?"

Victor continued to build the shell. "I suppose it's possible. I hope he's okay, but even if not, what can we do? We can't get a hold of him, and we can't stop what we're doing. Considering how many times he's changed his mind, I think he wants us to close it, but doesn't want to be here for it. Convenient for us."

★★★

John stood behind a camera tripod in a single-colored room. It was too big and unicolored to see where the floor or ceiling separated from the walls. John wore a black suit and a black tie, but the tie was covered in a pale-gray crust. John held the tie and used his fingernails to scratch off the crust, but every bit that he scraped away revealed an even thicker layer below it. When he looked down, he realized that his pants and shoes were covered in the pale-gray soot. John turned around to look for some water to clean his hands.

Behind him and across the room, Alice was sitting on a couch. She could not lift her head up to look at John. She was paralyzed with sadness. John wanted to help her, but no matter what he did to get Alice's attention, she would not look at him. No matter what he tried, he could not get closer to Alice or convince her to look up.

He turned back around to the camera. Standing in one line in front of him were Maria, Victor, Mark, Enoch, and Delilah, all dressed in black. They were smiling and patiently waiting for John to take their picture. John made eye contact with all of them, but he could not smile back. Their lack of compassion for Alice sickened him, and he blamed them almost as much as he blamed himself. The only one whom he truly cared about would not even look at him. John bent down to look through the viewfinder, and only then could he see how scared everyone was. Through the viewfinder, nobody smiled.

John stood up again to see them all happy, and he pressed the shutter-release. Out came a flash, and simultaneously, Maria, Victor, Mark, Enoch, and Delilah each had their brains and spines pulled out from the top of their heads. Their lifeless bodies fell to the floor, and their central nervous systems slowly lifted into thin air. John was not convinced though. He leaned back down and looked through the viewfinder. Everyone was normal with their insides still inside them, and just over Enoch's shoulder, was the watchful eye of Diaphnerous.

"I didn't believe you, you know. I only cried because you made me," said John. Diaphnerous just stared at him. "I know we're weak… but at least we're trying to get better." The Eye and everyone just stared at John. He said nothing more, and accepted his share of the blame.

John pulled away from the viewfinder. He knew what Alice was thinking, and could not work up the nerve to look back at her. He knew that she was right.

Chapter Fifty-Two
<u>Staging The Scene</u>

Maria, Mark, and Victor sat on tall stools around the granite island in the east wing laboratory. Mark had a pad of paper and a pen, as did Maria. "You should park on the road outside of their property, but be able to see the front door. She's going to turn the porch light on when they leave the house. After that, you're good to go," said Maria.

"Where are they going?" asked Mark.

"To the tunnels. She's going to bring him down there for the night."

"How does she plan to do that? For sure, he's going to have a gun. So, how do we know that he's not going to wander out of the hole?"

"She's telling him a good story," said Maria.

***

Enoch pushed the front door wide open and walked into his house. He was covered in dirt from head to toe. He walked into the kitchen and poured himself a glass of water. The farmer was thin to his bones. Except for the few meals a week that Delilah forced on him, he did not eat. His joints were giving out and he was nearing exhaustion. Enoch had not seen Delilah for over a day, and the house appeared to be empty. He shuffled over to the stairs, leaving behind a trail of filth.

The doors upstairs were all shut except for his bedroom. Enoch approached it. The closer that he got to the open door, the more he could feel the breeze on his face. He placed his palm on the door and pressed it forward. The sunlit window was open, and the air was moving.

On the center of the bed was Enoch's wooden box, which at first nicked him. He did not leave it there, therefore it was touched by somebody else. But once Enoch noticed how neatly the key was placed beside the box, he rushed to it.

Drunk with excitement, he lifted the top open and gazed down at his priceless belonging. He could not open the box without paying his dues to the crown's beauty. He was careful to not look at the dent that it had suffered in the laboratory as it caused Enoch to break down in screaming tears, but even with that caution, he could not deny his love for the crown. He laid out the cloth that Diaphnerous had given him, and he placed the crown softly onto it. When he looked back into the box, Enoch saw another cloth. This one was unfamiliar to him. He pulled out the folded square of silk and opened it. In carefully sewn-in cursive lettering was a note:

After sunset on the Eighteenth of October,
take your wife into the darkness where we first met, and wait.
From there, I will lead you to the other side.

Enoch could hold his tears no longer. They poured out of his eyes while he cried and laughed at the same time. He squeezed the silk cloth to his chest and embraced it. When he looked at it again, he saw the signature of its author. Below the message was the golden *D* surrounded by beautiful colors, just like the Eye that he loved. Enoch fell back onto the bed and rolled around in total joy.

★★★

Mark looked down at the notes that he had taken so far. "So, I park on the north side of the barn?"

"Yes, with your lights off, obviously. The north side is essentially the back of the barn, so you will be hidden from the house and the tunnels. Look at the outline I drew you. Delilah basically described it over the phone to me," said Maria.

"She knows he needs to pull the truck in, right?" asked Victor. "There's no way in hell he's lifting the generator out of the truck by himself."

"Yes, hun. I told you. There's a huge door that he can slide open and back the truck into. She's leaving a key too."

***

Delilah walked out of the barn. She was filthy herself from clearing out an opening big enough for Mark to work. She closed the large door behind her, then she slid it open and back closed again, testing it. She locked it with a padlock, and then she placed the key directly under the window to the left of the door. Delilah pulled a smooth grey stone out of her pocket and placed it on the key.

She made her way out from behind the barn and walked towards the house. When she reached the middle of her yard, she heard Enoch screaming from the house. She stopped and looked up at her open bedroom window. From the top of his lungs, Enoch hollered in ecstasy.

***

"When you get in there, build the shell as fast as you can. Wherever that orb shows up, you've got to get the shell around it quick, and blast it. We're going to try to do the same here. Just in case we lose power, we'll have a generator too, but there's only one stone," said Victor.

Mark lit a cigarette and looked over his notes. "I guess the best you can do around here is use the power while you got it and at least slow this thing down."

***

Alice prayed as the sun set. She was curled up under her tree and asked God for a last-minute connection. She knew that time was up, and she contemplated whether to spend the next twenty-four hours driving far away or just staying in the orchard until the tesseract appeared. But somewhere in the hunt for a decision, Alice dozed off in the tree that had become her second home. The roots curled into the perfect shape for her. Somehow even the bugs left her alone. She felt this spot to be as good as any to spend what could be her final day.

***

Mark sat at the dining room table, smiling as Victor and Maria unwrapped their gift. Maria unfolded a tiny shirt that read *Little Scientist* across its belly. "Aww", moaned Maria as she looked at the shirt.

Victor picked up the hat that came with it. It was dark blue and had each planet from the solar system stitched onto it. "A little hat too."

"Yeah, I figured since he or she is probably going to be a genius anyway, might as well start them early," said Mark. Maria stood up and walked over to Mark. She gave him a hug and kiss on the cheek. Victor wrapped around his wife and Mark, and turned it into a group hug. "Okay, okay… There will be plenty of hugs to go around after. Don't wear yourselves out now," said Mark.

Victor let go. "Hold on. I got you something too." He ran into the kitchen ."Oh wow. Now I feel important," said Mark with a grin. Victor returned with a small wrapped gift. "What do we have here?" Mark unraveled it revealing a pack of cigarettes and a flask. "Oh nice. What are these?"

"They're from India. It's supposed to be very good tobacco. The professor of statistics here gets them shipped in. They're all he smokes," said Victor.

"And the flask is for tomorrow night. For you, it's not enough to get you drunk, but maybe you'll need a sip at some point to take the edge off," said Maria.

"Thank you…" said Mark with his lip quivering. "Well, now it feels like Christmas morning. God bless us, everyone, huh?"

***

A light shone onto Alice, and she opened her eyes to a glowing orb. It was the largest that she had seen, and in its center was the eye of an onlooker. She rose to her knees and crawled towards it. The eye was expressionless, and Alice was not scared. The orb grew and revealed the worm of whom the eye belonged to. Alice could see that there was much more to the worm than any of them had seen prior. Its shape continued in many directions, as did its eye. When the orb grew large enough, Alice could see that it was not alone. There were many others like it, all just as oddly shaped. She felt connected to them, and safe now that they were so close.

From behind the group of creatures, an even stranger black figure made its way towards the orb. It was formed by many black circles connected together, and had countless extremities sticking out from its frame. It came to the threshold of the orb and then pressed through. From the edge of the orb, the being spiraled out towards Alice in a twisting motion. As soon as it crossed over to her side, it was no longer a collection of rings or circles, but one long, thin body. She too observed it to be an elongated centipede, but even then, she was not scared.

It made its way to Alice's face where it traveled around her. As she watched the unexplainable openings in its body pass her by, she saw that it possessed something that was coming her way. It was a book, one that she recognized. When it came closer, the being stopped moving and opened its clutches. The book fell into Alice's hands. It was John's journal. The centipede made its way back into the orb where it grew in complexity. She saw the eyes of all the worms looking back at her, and she knew now why they found her. "Thank you." Without warning, the orb closed up and shrank into nothing. She stood in the silent dark and looked at the journal from her friend.

★★★

Mark rested his hand on his glass of whiskey while Maria and Victor sat arm-in-arm across from him. "Don't even start to think that you didn't do everything you could have. You've both devoted the last two years of your lives towards this."

"It's not that. We just wish we could have figured it out sooner," said Maria.

"That's bullshit. What could you have done better? You traveled to every goddamn corner of this thing until you found out what you were looking for. Even if John is the one who finally labeled it, you two did all the leg work. No matter what happens, you're both tremendously good people. And after tomorrow night, when us three are sitting at this table, we'll have a real celebration together. Pizza and alcohol. I'm buying."

"If we're still here tomorrow, we're going to be explaining a lot of things to a lot of people. You should consider moving in here. Even though you pass out on the couch more often than you make it to the guest room, we'll make the room for you," said Victor. "Something tells me that we're about to get a lot more funding from NASA after this is over. We'll need an assistant, and we'd love to float you a salary."

"Since I'm already squatting in your house, you might as well start paying me too." Mark smiled and held up his glass. Victor tapped his glass to Mark's and they drank.

***

Alice sat in her car across the street from the fig orchard. With the reading light on, she leafed through John's journal. Every page brought her more empathy for John. Most of the entries either began or ended with an insult about his own mentality, which showed her a side of John whom she was not familiar with, and it got worse as she read on. As the self-berating intensified, so did his handwriting. Some entries were almost torn up by the pressure of John's scrawling.

After the last daily log, Alice turned to the one part that she remembered seeing herself, except it was now altered. The poem that Diaphnerous had written for John was smudged out to the point of incomprehension, and the sketch of the landscape was scratched over with some kind of heavy ink. Even as she focused on the few details that were left, the drawing had no effect on her.

She turned the page again and was presented with equations laid out like a list. Alice's incompetence in math went back to birth, or even further, but she found an interest in stepping into the mind of John. In her head, she gave the first one a crack, and to her disappointment, it was simple to figure out. The answer was one. She mentally placed it on the solution line and moved on to another one. It was longer than the first, but no more difficult. She remembered the number seven. She tried one more and got yet another easy answer. Determining that it offered little insight into the mind of the doctor, she moved along.

On the next page, there was a paragraph:

It came at a time that is long forgotten. It spent its days making a nest. It called itself me. It always started with a lie, which meant nothing to anyone else. It never had a chance to know you. Do was its intention always. Not ever did it change, no matter what it would believe. Because no matter what, it was always me.

Alice cringed with the utmost confusion. Never would she peg John as the poetry type, and reading that only reinforced her opinion. She read it over again hoping to find a lost message, but it was just not there. She began to wonder why she was delivered the book in the first place. Alice cranked her car and headed towards her hotel for further dissection.

***

After two hours of a close examination, Alice's eyes burned, so she closed the journal and fell back onto her bed. She always wondered how she would spend her last day on Earth. Even with the belief that life would continue well on after her tomorrow, she felt a bit pathetic spending the night alone in a hotel room in Louisiana. On top of the self-pity, her thoughts could not stop racing. There was still no clear decision on where she would be spending her next twenty-four hours. Most likely, she would curl back up under the fig tree and wait for what was coming, but that would leave her right on the edge of the opening. She contemplated driving further north and putting herself in the center of it all. Either way, she knew she would be alone just like John.

Alice had not heard from John in weeks, and she had no interest in letting him back into her trust. The empathy that she felt for him after reading his journal was a just reaction in her eyes, but that was as far as it went. He was a good friend and a good person, but something happened, and she was let down. Out of principle, she could not let him back in, and the more that she thought about it, the angrier she became.

After heating up, Alice turned her light on and grabbed the journal. If nothing else, she thought that she may be able to find something in his entries about why or how he could turn on somebody that he cared about. She flipped through the pages looking for any kind of revealing language that would give her some light. She read through the inception of the search for the graviton, the excitement he felt when he mistakenly thought that he was on his way, and finally his great downfall. But her search came up empty. There was no mention of interpersonal relationships or responsibility to anyone else. In fact, the entire journal was void of mentioning anyone outside of John. That infuriated her. She came upon the final entry with much less empathy this time around:

June 22, 2015

Sulking in my regrets about all the time that I have wasted is in itself a waste of time, and therefore an act of hypocrisy. I would like to drop this journal into the lake under my feet and move on with my life, but that would be unearned. I have a debt that can only be paid in my time and effort. If string theory is in fact the theory of everything, then devoting myself to finding it will give me true worth. If this theory turns out to be the manual for the Universe, then I will be there to see it through. If it turns out to be a fallacy, then I will do my part in dismantling it. Either way, this is my act of contrition, and I will see it through until death or completion.

The perfect genius is all that is made. It is made by the working machine. I am NOT its mortality.

John

She dropped the book onto the bed. *This is not right*, she thought to herself. John was not one to make a promise to himself and abandon it. Even with his actions being clear evidence of his dishonesty, she did not believe it. Just like the deaths of so many people in Oklahoma being the evidence that everyone needed to close the tesseract, Alice looked deeper. She opened back up to the list of equations and began filling in the solutions with her pencil. She wrote down the line, *one, seven, fourteen…* She filled in every answer until the page was complete. Then she flipped it over and looked at the paragraph.

She reread it one last time to catch anything that she may have missed. Alice knew that John knew her well, including her lack of intuition with numbers and puzzles, so she took it at face value and counted the words. She wrote down each word to its corresponding number:

It, is, making, me, lie. Alice immediately regretted leaving him in the airport. She regretted not trusting him. *to, you, do, not, believe, me.* She gasped. She understood what John was not able to tell her in person. *It is making me lie to you. Do not believe me:* simple and straight to the point. Alice reached over and grabbed her phone. She shook as she dialed John's number. Without even a ring, it went straight to voicemail. "Fuck." Alice got up and paced the room. She tried his number again, and again it did not ring. She dropped the phone and paced. "He tried to fucking tell me." Alice stopped to think. After ten seconds of silence, she picked up her suitcase and threw it on the bed. She opened it up and began packing.

***

John was in darkness. He heard nothing. As he stared forward awaiting his accuser, he started to think about all the days that passed since he sat on the end of the dock over the lake in Colorado. He made a promise to himself and his mind, but now after so much tribulation, he wondered if he had learned anything at all. Failure led him to that dock, and after walking away a free man, failure found him again. He was bested by fear.

While existing somewhere in the pitch dark, John began to feel like his hands were cuffed, and he fell to his knees in a prisoner's pose. He saw this coming for weeks, but he neglected preparation. He chose to run until the inevitable happened. And here it was.

Footsteps came out from the darkness. Three figures made their way towards him. When they were close enough, he could see the disappointment on their faces. From left to right stood John's old man, his six-year-old self, and his mind.

The fact that nothing was said yet told John that they decided to start their assault with silent guilt. If he saw it once, he saw it a thousand times. John knew how to handle the silence temporarily, but after only a short amount of time, it became worse than Chinese water torture. He had to hold out for a few moments before speaking; otherwise, his weakness would be evident.

From his knees, John looked each one of them in the eye. He started with the old man, then moved on to the kid, and then to his mind. It was clear that they chose to stick together regardless of anything that John did or said. He was frustrated that he always felt alone in these meetings and never once did they argue with each other.

His stare of intimidation was not working, and the silence on their end was suffocating. For a second, they may have even looked sad for John. Perhaps they were offering to share some of the burden, but John was not buying it. He saw it as their second method of attack, so he reacted.

"What do you want me to say? You want me to say sorry?... I'm not," said John. "Isn't it easy to be you and not me? I'm the one that has to do everything. You get to just criticize me."

John looked directly at his mind. It stared back at him as if he was looking in the mirror, and for the first time ever, it was not disappointed. It understood John's position. But once again, he rejected the offer of peace.

"Remember what you asked me that time? 'Is life more important than truth?' I've thought about that a lot," said John to his mind. "I ask myself if anything is more important than truth. Is my life more important than truth? You want to know my answer? No. It isn't, but guess what. I'm too fucking scared to do anything about it. I'm scared of what's happening and what's going to happen to myself and everyone else, so I lie. I lie to Alice, I lie to Maria, I lie to the Eye, and I lie to me.

"I don't like it, okay? I hate it, but I'm scared, so I do nothing... Do you have a solution?" John asked his mind. He looked to his other selves. "How about you? What should I do? Tell me. Should I get us all killed?" Thinking that he just made an indisputable point, John went quiet, but his strongest defense fell flat, and they all three shared the same look.

"I know I'm wasting time... But why wake up? I can't do anything anyway. I'm as useless as you've always told me. Nothing but unreachable expectations from all of you. It's easy to judge when you never have to risk anything. Try being me for one day. You'll put a bullet in your head. You live comfortably in here. I'm out in the world eating shit every goddamn day so that we can all survive... You think you could do what I do?" John was desperate for one of them to break, but they held strong. Even he had trouble believing in his words. He was forcing it, and they all knew it. John put his head down, took a heavy breath, and trembled. Tears came down his face.

"Am I too late?" he asked. "I've wasted so much time. Am I too late?" Expecting only the worst, John once again looked up to his other selves. They were crying too. Each one felt the pain and helplessness that he felt. For the first time in his life, he was given their compassion. At that moment, John realized that it was not him versus them. They came to be together, and the only one left for him to appease was himself. To do that, he needed to finish what he started.

John got to his feet and stood up tall. He set his eyes on the old man, and the old man softened. He turned to the young boy. The boy straightened up and looked at John proudly. John turned to his mind, and they shared a moment alone. When the moment ended, John and his mind were of total equality. From over his shoulder, there came a light. John turned around. An orb glowed ten paces away. He looked back one more time to other selves and found no one there.

He turned and faced the orb as a complete man. He took one more deep breath and walked forward. John knew that on the other side of that orb was the most meaningful day of his life. There was no more time to waste, and if he could finish what he set out to do, then his life would have true worth. He placed his foot in front of the orb, and he walked through.

Chapter Fifty-Three
<u>The Night Of The Tesseract</u>

John sat up on his bed and gasped for air. Like a near-victim of drowning, he panted and coughed. He rolled over and fell to the floor. As he leaned onto his elbow and looked around the room, John saw the evidence of days gone by, maybe even weeks. Like the first time that he fell under the spell of the Artist's work, his living space was littered with half-eaten food, towels thrown about, and lights left on. And yet again, he remembered none of it. He concentrated on slowing down his breath. John had no recollection of his actions in the real world, but his dreams were as clear as day. He knew the promise that he made to himself, and without the need to look at a calendar, he knew what day it was.

***

Alice flew up the highway with very little thought of what she would do when she got there. Now that she was deep into middle America, the clouds were forming as far as she could see, and they were getting darker.

***

Enoch bathed for the first time in forty-two days. The bath water ran black with filth as he scrubbed his withered skin. After washing, he walked into his room where his nicest pants and shirt were folded on his bed.

As Enoch dressed into his now oversized clothes, his hands shook. The excitement for his new life was electric. He buttoned up his shirt and stood tall in front of the mirror, paying no mind to his thin, malnourished body. Tears seeped from his eyes and ran down his face. With the crown's wooden box under his arm, Enoch looked at his reflection and smiled at the man that would soon meet his savior.

***

With the unassembled pidima shell and gas-powered generator strapped down and covered in the bed of his truck, Mark headed southwest towards farm country. The only thing that rode with him in the cabin was the stone which was strapped down on the passenger seat.

He drove all the way through the early morning, but it was about the time that he crossed the Iowa border that the rain came on heavy, and coincidentally, his doubts came on heavy too. The lack of accomplishments and achievements across the entirety of his life played as a slideshow in his mind. In between all of the long voids of productivity were the broken relationships that resulted from his behaviors. Mark Schmidt looked back on his time in shame, and then he looked at the road ahead and wondered if it could possibly be different.

***

Victor assembled the pidima shell on top of the granite island desk. Using the original pidima as a mark for the orb that would soon show up, he took his time to align the aluminum frame in exactly the right spot. Maria ran wiring in ten different directions across the lab for backups to the shell. She also gassed up their backup generator in case that the power blew out altogether.

Once the laboratory was equipped with all of the power that they needed, Maria pinned the doors locked from the inside. "I hope you're ready to unlock them back shortly here," said Victor without turning around.

"They're staying locked."

Victor stopped what he was doing and looked over his shoulder at Maria. "Are we really going to do this now?"

"I sure hope not. I would hate to argue if this is our last day together."

"Maria… Honestly, just stop it. I don't have the energy to fight about this. You're out of here in ten minutes."

Maria walked up to Victor and hugged his waist as he knelt on top of the granite desk. "What would I do if something happens?"

"If something happens and you're here, then you won't be doing much of anything. Seriously, I packed the car with everything you'll need. You're heading north."

"I unpacked it," said Maria. Victor released himself from her hug and slid around to face her.

"Why would you do that? We have a plan, Maria. We went over this."

"I lied. I'm not raising our kid without you."

"What the fuck, Maria? Why are you doing this?"

"I'm going to start testing the connections."

***

John got to his knees and used the bed to pull himself up. When he looked on top of the sheet, he immediately dropped back down to the floor for cover. The fraudulent stone remained next to his imprint on the mattress.

John closed his eyes and stood up. He took hold of the bed sheets and thrusted them into the air. Along with some stray pillows, John heard the object crash into the wall on the other side of the room and fall to the ground. He kept his eyes closed and felt his way to the other end of the bed. He avoided laying his sights on the stone in fear of its spell. He shuffled over and made contact with his foot, and then he slid it under the bed. When he opened his eyes again, he became aware of his physical and mental state. His body was weak and tired, his vision was cloudy, and he was unprepared for decision making.

He wandered the room looking for something to jump out at him, and the first thing to catch his eye was his cell phone. He picked it up, opened it, and turned it on. The phone showed no response. He dug around through his towels and clothes on the ground until he felt his phone charger. John stumbled over to the wall and plugged it in. He slid down against the wall and waited for it to charge.

***

Mark trekked down a paved road with cornfields to both horizons. Rain pounded his windshield, and the sky was dark grey. His dashboard GPS lost signal, so he was traveling by map, waiting for his dirt-road turnoff. After that, he would be traveling by memory.

***

Enoch opened the front door for his wife and led her out onto the porch. The farm was a mud field, slowly turning into a lake. At Enoch's request, Delilah had on her wedding gown and he wore the suit jacket from their wedding day. He held the wooden box in one hand, and with his other, he took his wife's hand. They made their way across the muddy lawn with an ocean of water falling from the sky.

Over the past day, Enoch chopped down a path through the corn that led directly to the tunnel in which they would meet Diaphnerous. He looked at Delilah with a grin. "Are you ready?" Delilah looked back at him. Even with her best efforts, she could not smile.

"I'm ready," she said. And they walked into the path.

***

Alice prayed with her hands folded as she drove. She was just starting to panic that her decision to drive north was made too late. The road flooded more by the hour, and lightning flashed across the sky.

Her phone buzzed on the seat next to her. She grabbed it and opened it. "Hello?"

"…lice…Al…." she heard from the other end. She looked at her phone to read the caller ID, but the screen was blank.

"Hello?" she said again. The other end popped with static, and the call ended. Alice hung up, and pressed the *End* button rapidly. "Come on." The phone then rang again. She answered immediately. "Hello?"

"Alice! Can you hear me?"

"Hello? Yes. I can."

"Alice, it's John."

"John! Where are you? Are you okay?"

"Yes........." Her phone spat out more static.

"Shit!" Alice pounded the *End* button again. She redialed John's number.

★★★

"You're sitting in the back row the entire time," said Victor as he adjusted a corner of the pidima shell.

"That's fine."

"Even if this works, there's going to be radiation. Forget about the pidimas. The whole room could turn into an oven."

"These are all very worst-case scenarios, hun."

"Don't start with me. Hand me that screw driver, please," said Victor. Maria complied.

"Do you think NASA will come to us when it's over?"

"Well, we laid out the evidence to them a year ago. If they don't come to us, I'll be more than happy to rub their faces in it." Victor hopped down from the granite desk and walked over to his control box. He held the lever and practiced his movements. "Which wire are we starting with?"

"The yellow."

"Okay, plug it in, please." Maria reached down and plugged the yellow cord into the control box. "So, I'm thinking… we should have the generator running, and I'll switch over to it the second we lose power. Maybe even if we can't light all of the pidimas, we might be able to keep a few warm enough to slow this thing down. Give Mark an extra minute on his end."

"I wonder how he's doing," said Maria.

★★★

Mark sat in his truck on a dirt road. He looked down at his phone and noticed the first reception bar since he hit the Nebraska border. He thought that he would have figured out what to say by now, but he didn't. Although he did not want to lose the opportunity. He dialed his son's number. It rang only twice and then went to voicemail. As he listened to the recording of Jake's voice, he tried to make it last forever. The voicemail came to a *beep*. He took a deep breath.

"Hey buddy… it's your dad. Listen…" Mark struggled as he made the call that he never dreamed of making. "I want you to know that I'm sorry for how everything turned out. It's my fault. I know I blamed your mom a lot, but it's me. I know you know that, but it's important that I tell you. Everything that happened was because of me, and I'm sorry.

"I think after tonight, things are going to be a lot different. If you hear this tomorrow, or later on, or whatever, you'll know what I mean. I know you're mad at me, and you'll always be mad, but I'm hoping that tonight I can do one last good thing for you. I'm doing it for you, and I hope I make you proud. I love you, Jake." Mark hung up his phone and began sobbing. For a moment, he cried intensely, but he pulled himself together.

He pulled out a cigarette, lit it, and then slapped himself in the cheek. Mark shook off his heavy thoughts and wiggled his neck and shoulders to loosen up. He put the truck in gear, and pulled back onto the road.

***

Alice answered her phone as she flew down the highway. "Alice," said John on the other end.

"Yes! I can hear you."

"Okay, listen I don't think we have much time. All of my electronics are shutting off."

"Same here. My car is running, but my phone and my headlights are starting to go in and out."

"Alice, listen. I'm sorry. I wish I had more time to explain, but I didn't mean anything that I said in the air—"

Alice interjected quickly. "I know, John. I know. You don't have to apologize. I have your notebook. I read your message. I figured it out."

"My notebook? How do you have my notebook?"

"They gave it to me, John. The worms gave it to me." There was silence on the other end.

"How… How did they find you?"

"John, let's catch up later, I'll tell you all about it. We're going to lose the call soon."

"You're right. Okay, where are you?"

"I'm north of Missouri right on the border of Nebraska and Iowa. There were closed roads in Missouri, so I had to detour. But I'm on my way to Wisconsin to the lab."

"How long will it take you to get here?"

"I don't know. I could still be four or five hours out."

"Okay, I don't think you have time to make it here. I'm going to the lab, but if you keep coming this way, you're going to be too late."

"What should I do? You can't do this by yourself."

"I may not have a choice, but listen. When I first came here after we spoke in the airport, I heard Victor say something about Delilah helping them with Enoch on the farm when the time comes. I think there's a chance that they are going to the farm."

"Why would they do that? Wouldn't it be easier in the lab?"

"I don't know exactly; they might have figured something else out. How do you feel about splitting up and going to the farm? If that's where they're actually going, then being here won't do us any good. They're in Sutton. Do you remember what the farm looks like?"

"Umm… Yeah, I guess so. What do I do when I get there?"

"Number one, it's very important that you be careful. Enoch might have a gun. He almost shot Mark in the lab."

"Oh my God. Why?"

"He's really lost his mind. So, be very careful if you see him. Park far away from the house, and the only thing you need to do is stop Mark. I've seen what they're building. They look like metal-framed cubes with pidimas attached. Try to break the pidimas."

"I have a crowbar in my trunk. I'll take it with me."

"Now you're thinking. But remember, don't go near Enoch, and be careful."

"I will. You be careful too, John." They shared a quiet moment.

"Did you think that this is what it would come down to?" asked John. Alice laughed,

"Not exactly. But I don't know what I thought."

"Me either… I'm sorry, Alice. I've been a real shitty friend. You don't get the credit you deserve. You're a pretty fucking smart lady. You were right all along. I'm sorry that no one else could see that." Alice laughed again.

"Well thank you, Doctor Robins. You're no dummy either. And if you really feel bad about it, I'll let you buy me a whiskey the next time we see each other."

"If we make it through this, I'll buy you whiskey for a year," said John.

"You better have some savings stashed away then," said Alice, and then with a loud *pop*, the phone call ended. Alice looked down at her phone to see it completely dead.

John's phone still had life. He tried to call her back, but the call went straight to her voicemail. He walked over and looked out of the blinds. Rain poured harder than any storm that he could remember, even back to his days growing up on the Wyoming farm. He looked back at his phone and noticed a number of missed calls from days earlier. There were seven missed calls from Jack. John grinned and dialed Jack's number. Without even a full ring…

"Dr. Johnny! Where are you?" yelled Jack over the roar of pounding rain.

"Wisconsin, Jack. I'm in Wisconsin."

"I thought you were dead!"

"I think I was, Jack," said John, calmly.

"I'm heading back to Amber Rock, but I got caught in this crazy storm. It's fucking pouring water out here, Johnny! You coming back?"

John grinned as he heard Jack's voice for the first time in a long time. "Not today, Jack. I got something I gotta do… but listen. There's something you need to see."

"What's that Johnny?"

"As soon as you get to Amber Rock, go to my hotel room. I mean the minute you get there. Ask for a key, bust in the door, get in there anyway you can."

"Not a problem, John. Us hotel people help each other out. I'll get in there."

"Good. Go to my closet, open the doors and wait. You're going to see something you've never seen before."

"Is this it? Is this what changed you?" asked Jack with enthusiasm.

"This is it, Jack. Something's going to appear. It's easier if you see it than if I explain it. But as soon as that thing appears, you go into it. Head first, Jack."

"You say it, I do it, Johnny… I appreciate that, pal…"

John took a breath and welled up. Whether it was from hearing his friend's voice or from fear that he may not see him again, John did not know, but he savored the moment. "How's your brother?"

"He's okay, John. Eric's going to be okay."

John nodded his head. "… good. Glad to hear that, Jack… Hey listen--" The phone popped once again and went silent. John looked down to see it go dead. He let a few more tears out and nodded his head. He stood up, threw the phone in his bag, and marched towards the door.

★★★

Enoch and Delilah sat on the dirt floor of the tunnel. The corn had grown through most of the opening and began to pierce into the floor. With the light of only a flame lantern, Delilah took notice of the water coming in through the tunnels opening on the far end and creeping ever so slightly towards them. Her dress was ruined with mud, as were all of Enoch's clothes. With a grin on his face and the pistol in his hand, Enoch stared ahead, dreaming of his life to come.

"Why did you bring the gun?" asked Delilah. Enoch looked at her, wide-eyed and smiling.

"I'm going to help It fight the Differents. I bet they've never seen a gun before. Just wait. When we get there, you'll see how important the Eye is to Its world. And you should feel so special that It asked you to come too. Do you know how special we are?" asked Enoch. Delilah remained quiet. "Do you know how special we are? Have you thought about that? It chose us. It could have chosen anyone, but it chose us. And we are grateful. Are you grateful?" The smile on Enoch's face turned into desperate seriousness. Delilah looked him back in the eye.

"Yes. I'm grateful," she said. Enoch smiled again.

"You just wait. I haven't seen Its home yet, but It showed me paintings. It's going to be so beautiful…" As Enoch continued to ramble on, Delilah looked at the pistol in his hand and his finger that wrapped around the trigger.

***

Mark turned off of the main street onto a small dirt road that was cut out between two vast fields of corn. As soon as his tires hit the dirt, he felt the slop of the mud. Enoch's property greeted Mark. The atmosphere was polluted with unbalanced energy, and Mark felt it immediately.

Rain continued to pound his windshield as he made his way down the curved dirt path. He looked out into the field where he could see the outlet to one of the tunnels. A large cow crawled out into the rain, and it took off into the cornfield. Right behind it came another. It followed the other into the wall of corn and falling water. When Mark returned his eyes to the road in front of him, he shrieked and slammed on the breaks. His car slid sideways into the mud. Crossing the road before him was a herd of cows. Five adults walked from the cornfield to his left and headed into the cornfield to his right. He watched them in wonder of where they came from until the last of them cleared the road.

When he turned the bend and came within sight of Enoch's house, Mark saw dozens of more cows grazing his front lawn.

***

John cranked his car and pressed the gas pedal to give it some life. While it warmed itself up, John looked in the mirror. He thought about this moment many times throughout his life. Everything that he learned and everything that he believed in would be put to the test. He looked back at himself with tired eyes. His face was long and pale. He realized that whatever the outcome of his actions that day would be, they might be his last. "Don't blow it, old man," John said to himself. He pulled the car out of his parking spot and drove onto the road.

***

Victor lit up the pidima shell to a minimum glow. He turned the dials on the control box up and down to test them. A cigarette hung out of his mouth. "Where did you get that?" asked Maria.

"Mark gave me a handful before he left," said Victor without looking up.

"Since when are you suddenly a smoker?"

"I know… I really got addicted, I think. Or maybe I just like it a lot. I'll quit in a few days when this is all over." Thunder rumbled outside and the lights within the lab flickered on and off. Victor looked up at the lights, and then to Maria. "Time to start the generator, hun."

***

Mark's truck came to a sliding stop through the mud. He hopped out and ran to the window beside the large barn door. The ground was quickly becoming a lake. As he trotted through the water, Mark came to grips with the toll that he had put his body through over the years. His excessive drinking, smoking, and lack of exercise had never been so obvious. He threw himself to the ground, submerging his hands and knees in the water. He searched through the slush of dirt and grass until he felt the rock that Delilah had left for him. Underneath was the key.

Mark came to his feet and unlocked the barn door. Anxiety was never one of his inconveniences, but he could not shake the feeling that he was about to get brained by a machete, so he kept his head on a swivel. He slid open the large barn door. He ran to his truck, backed it into the barn, got out, and slammed the barn door shut.

***

Alice leaned forward to better see out of her windshield as she sped down the road. The rain was torrential, as was the lightning that accompanied it. Looking up at the storm, she experienced flashbacks to her dreaded night in the sky. She did not know whether to feel cursed by the sight of that first orb or to feel grateful, but regardless, it brought her to where she was: flying down a dirt road in Nebraska, trying to stop someone from stopping a merge with the higher dimension.

★★★

The parking lot hosted six inches of water. The tires of John's car pushed waves across the asphalt in both directions. The NASA/Thomas Laboratory stood dark and menacing under the flashes of lightning. John pulled his car to a halt and jumped out into the water. Through the pouring rain, he ran to the front door of the building to find that it was locked and barred shut. A large stone in a flower bed caught his eye.

John lifted the heavy stone, and tossed it into the glass front door, shattering it into a mess of shards. He ducked his head and stepped through the opening. His wet feet slapped the floor as he ran down the hallway. When John reached the doors to the east wing laboratory, he grabbed the door grips with all of his might and heaved. They moved not one inch. John tried shaking them loose, but he made more progress dislocating his shoulders than he did the doors. He slapped and banged on them with his fists. "Maria! Victor! Open the door!" he yelled.

Victor looked over his shoulder at the door. "He can't get in," said Maria. Victor turned back to the shell and gradually raised the lever on the control box. In small intensities, the pidimas grew brighter. The banging on the door stopped.

John ran down the hallway and into the lobby. He grabbed a wooden chair, and then ran full speed back to the door and slammed the chair onto it. He fell backwards to the ground. John stood up, and again slammed the chair on the door.

Victor kept his eyes on the pidima shell but his attention on the violent slamming behind him. "You sure he's not getting through?" he asked. Maria looked up to see the door unaffected. The banging stopped again.

★★★

Delilah watched Enoch out of the corner of her eye. He stared at the wooden box in his lap. With a smile, Enoch pulled a small key out of his pocket, and unlocked the box. A glow brightened his face.

Enoch lifted the crown and turned it so that it shined in the lantern's light. Delilah could not deny its beauty. It was so well crafted and priceless in value, but its presence made her uncomfortable. Her husband never adored an object or even a person the way that he adored the crown.

Enoch placed it gently on his leg, and pulled out the handkerchief. He held the silk to his cheek and pressed it. Delilah avoided looking at it in the hopes that he would just put it away. He buried his nose into the cloth and inhaled. When he lowered it again, there were tears in his eyes. In an effort to keep the silk clean, Enoch used his shirt collar to wipe the tears away. Delilah watched him travel through his emotional spectrum.

When he was good and ready, Enoch spread the handkerchief out to read the words of his Guardian. He read aloud. "After sunset on the eighteenth of October, take your wife into the darkness where we first met, and wait. From there, I will lead you to the other side…" Enoch squinted, focusing on what was written next. He could not believe his eyes. "David?" he said. Enoch looked at Delilah. "What is this?"

Delilah's heart raced. Whatever it was, she knew it was not good. "What do you mean?" she asked.

"Why does it say David? Is this a joke? Did you write this?" Enoch's face turned blood red.

"Did I write what?" asked Delilah. Enoch held up the handkerchief. After the golden *D* at the bottom of the note, there was a stitching of the letters *avid* written in cursive. Delilah turned white. "Enoch… I… I don't know how that—"

Enoch stood up and threw the handkerchief at Delilah. "What did you do?" he screamed. "Why did you write that?"

"Enoch… I…" Delilah choked on her words. She opened up the cloth and saw the name *David* written out. She was awestruck. And then her eye caught the bottom of the cloth. Under the signature, three words were written: *Life mimics art.*

"David is not coming. Diaphnerous is coming," said Enoch. He stood above Delilah. His hands trembled. Delilah looked up at him; her eyes wide with guilt. Driven by judgement, Enoch became aware of what he was holding in his right hand, and Delilah did too. He gripped the pistol tight with his finger on the trigger. He looked at the barrel of the gun, and then he looked at his wife.

***

Mark pieced together the last section of the pidima shell, and cranked the generator to warm it up. He walked over and opened the passenger side door of the truck. The stone was still strapped in with the seatbelt. He released it and walked back to the generator. Slowly and carefully, Mark unspun the stone from its cloth, and then he placed it next to the generator.

As he connected the wiring of the shell to the control box, a strike of lightning shook the barn, and for a split second, the room went dark. Mark saw a marble-sized orb light up six feet in front of him. "Thank you," he said, and then he hopped to his feet and slid the aluminum shell across the ground until it was centered over the area where the orb appeared.

He jumped back onto the control box and turned the first dial. The pidimas progressed to a low light. Mark leaned over and turned up the generator's power. Its engine roared, and the pidimas turned another shade brighter. The room began to dim.

In the dead center of the pidima shell, a bright dot appeared. As it expanded, Mark could not tell whether it was a sphere or a cube, or both. Even looking at the object, Mark could not justify how it was possible. But before he got lost in the interesting, gaining object, he pushed the lever up to two, and he turned up the heat.

***

Maria stood behind her husband as he increased energy. With a crack of thunder, the power failed and the room went dark. In the center of the pidima shell, a coin-sized orb freely floated. As the room darkened, the orb grew. "Hook it to the generator" said Victor. Maria plugged it in, and Victor dialed it up.

He turned it to two. The gas-powered machine resisted the energy drain of the orb and continued to feed the pidimas. He pushed it up to three. Maria stood next to Victor as he manned the controls. After he felt the heat on his face from the white-hot shell, he pushed it up to four. With an explosive pop, the pidimas shut off, and the lab turned dark. The generator burned out, and everything went quiet. "Shit… It shorted. The fucking generator shorted," said Victor.

The emergency exit doors in the corner of the room crashed open and flew off their hinges. John's car, now smoking and totaled, slid into the lab from the pouring rain.

"Jesus Christ!" yelled Maria as she moved five steps back. The car's headlights dimmed in the face of the orb across the room. The driver's door opened, and John fell out onto the floor. "John, what the fuck?" said Victor. "What are you doing?" John got to his knees and pushed himself up.

"You can't do this," John said as he stumbled over and leaned on the hood of his car. "Turn off the machine."

"You could have killed us, John," said Victor. John found his balance and made his way towards the shell.

"You don't know what you're doing. Turn this off," John grabbed the nearest connection of wires and pulled them apart. Victor ran to John and grabbed him.

"Stop it, John," said Victor as he struggled to take the wires from John's hands.

***

The generator roared in full. The orb had grown to a diameter of about three feet, and its battle against the pidima shell was dead-even. Mark waited for just the right time before lifting the lever to four. After watching Victor several times, he memorized the perfect degree of brightness that the pidimas needed to be. He placed his hand on the lever. Once he pushed it forward, he was prepared to apply the first half of the stone onto the fuel tank.

The large barn door to his right flew open. Standing under the falling rain was Enoch. Mark first saw the eyes of the farmer, staring at him with hatred. Then, he saw the smoking gun in his right hand, and the crown's wooden box in his left.

"We have to stop it. We're doing the right thing," said Mark. Enoch walked into the barn. "You've lost it. Whatever that Thing convinced you of, It's lying." Enoch walked between Mark and the pidima shell. He looked at the orb that was stifled by the shell. "Enoch… You cannot do this. I'm doing the right thing."

Mark looked down at the lever of the control box. Enoch saw it and made the assumption of its purpose, then their eyes met.

Enoch raised the pistol and pointed it at Mark. The two men stared into each other's eyes. Just as Mark showed fear, Enoch lowered the gun. Mark remained still, and he began counting in his head, hoping that by the time he got to ten, the mad farmer would turn around and leave, but Enoch did not break eye contact. Mark breathed heavily. His vision darkened and tunneled until he could only see Enoch's face. Enoch looked at the orb, back at Mark, and then he lifted the gun and fired.

Mark fell to the ground and grabbed his stomach. Enoch turned around and ran straight to the orb. When he made contact with its edge, Mark watched him get absorbed by the sphere until he vanished completely. Alone on the dirt floor, Mark cupped his hands and pressed, trying to hold the blood inside of his gut.

★★★

John and Victor fell backwards in their struggle, and spilled down a step onto the floor. Victor grabbed his knee and winced. John stood up and ran towards the pidima shell. "Don't do it, John," said Maria. "What if you're wrong?"

"If I'm wrong, then I'm sorry." John grabbed hold of the shell. He found the connection on the top corner. "But if you're wrong, I can't let you destroy it." John unlatched the corner clip and pulled the shell apart. He slammed the disconnected section to the ground, and then pushed the rest of it off of the granite desk. He looked into the glowing orb. There was an entire world inside. Maria cried as she watched him.

"Don't do it, John."

"I'm sorry, Maria. They need my help." John touched his hand to the orb. Maria watched his body become shapeless, and get pulled into the sphere of light. She screamed in tears. Victor limped over to her and held his wife. An explosion of light shot out of the orb and forced them to cover their eyes. Victor protected Maria as a force of energy blew over them.

When the pressure stopped, the Delphis took a step back. They looked up at a giant structure. With the orb as its corner, they stood beneath two walls of the tesseract. The walls were formed by light and energy, and through a blurred filter, they could see the colors and makeup of the higher world. Unable to look away, but too scared to move forward, they stood completely still and watched from the outside.

★★★

Alice crossed the town line of Sutton, and then, at the speed of light, she found herself driving through a place beyond her comprehension. She slammed the breaks, and came to a stop. She peered through the window, and she saw an existence that she did not recognize. She lost touch with her senses. Intertwined with the unrecognizable colors were angles that her eyes were not familiar with, and they struggled to interact with them. Alice panicked as she tried to fathom her surroundings.

★★★

The door of John's hotel room blew open. Jack, who was soaked and wet from the rain, barged into the room. He glanced from his right to his left, and he saw the closet. Jack ran over and swung the doors open. Before he had a chance to look inside, his attention was completely stolen by the inside surface of the doors. The wood was masterfully carved from top to bottom, side to side, inch by inch. Jack gazed upon what was even more intricate of a creation than the stone or the drawing that trapped John for so long. Jack reached out and rubbed his fingers through the grooves of the brilliant creation.

★★★

John stood alone inside of the tesseract. The orb was still visible, and it seemed to create the bottom corner of the structure. The edges of the tesseract formed visual barriers that led all the way up into the sky where there appeared to be a ceiling, even though he could see far beyond it. John could not decide if the boundary was made up of a solid wall or a spaceless wall, but he kept his distance from it in fear of falling out. He carefully approached the orb and looked into it. He could see a distorted image of the laboratory where Victor and Maria looked back at him from the other side. Knowing that they were not going to join him, John turned around and walked deeper into the hyper-space.

As he moved into the intricate environment, all of his senses were hammered by a phenomenon. From a point of standing still, John saw a three-dimensional space that spanned in all directions. However, when he moved, it was as if he was entering an entirely new three-dimensional space that also expanded infinitely. The nature that surrounded him was astonishing, and with every next step, he saw it from a new angle that revealed all new details. He felt like a flat creature that had just been tossed into a pool of endless depth, and even then, he knew that his understanding was so very limited.

John stopped moving so that he could experience the visual presentation honestly and unbroken. And, in fact, it was a masterpiece. The sky was soaked in colors that he would describe as sacred. They were bright and stellar. Behind them was a black outer space with planets infinitely rounder than the ones from his own night sky. Miles above his head, flying instruments blazed about, carving streaks of color into the black. He returned his gaze to the ground and moved forward to a new line of sight.

When he looked into the distance, he saw a large group of worms. There were thousands of them. He now understood that in the third dimension, they appeared to be worms, but in this higher space, they were so much more complex. With every next step that John took, a new angle was opened that revealed another portion of their mighty physique. Their bodies stretched and extended in many directions. They formed into the shape of domes. One continuous eye went through the center of their heads and bulged out. It could be seen at every curve. As John watched the creatures from his limited vantage point, he knew that he would never experience their complete forms at one time.

And from behind the worms, John saw a great machine. It looked like a long, metal cylinder, hundreds or thousands of feet in the air, and it stretched as far as his eyes could see. As he continued forward, the exterior of the structure exposed new turns and additions. It protruded in every direction. Symbols flashed across its surface which John assumed to be measurements of information.

He hypothesized that he was looking at some kind of super computer. Worms covered its surface.

Some of them took on what seemed to be the role of mechanics. They rode along the sides of the computer with vehicles that acted as robotic tools, stamping and correcting physical issues as they went. Others gathered at ground level where the legs of the machine met the land. The bottoms of the legs were covered in holes. The holes projected indiscernible symbols in the form of light. The worms read the symbols through their single eye, and then they split up into smaller groups.

The first group made their way into large metal rooms that sped back and forth at implausible speeds. When one of the large rooms came to a stop to let the worms in and out, John spotted stones lined up across the top of the vehicles. They were identical to the stone that was given to Alice.

The other group of worms formed circles around smaller machines that created new projections. The light that formed these symbols floated in the air, and traveled over into the holes on the legs of the super computer. John debated over whether he was seeing a form of written language or a written number system. He quickly favored the latter. He knew scientists and mathematicians when he saw them, regardless of dimension. As overloaded with sight as he was, John managed to continue forward.

★★★

Alice got out of the car and found her footing. After she gained some composure, she began to make sense of the landscape and environment. Without frying her brain, the best she could determine was that every surface was three-dimensional, the way that her world was covered in flat, two-dimensional surfaces like floors and walls. However, she found out rather quickly that trying to understand its true make-up was a labor that her mind was not built for.

When she took her first step, her vantage point changed completely, and she got nauseous. For as much trouble as she was having, there was something inside of Alice that craved the visual feast. She took a moment of concentration and opened herself up.

Alice panned her head and took in the incredible realm. The colors of the sky bled onto the terrain. The ingredients of the nature may have been above her grasp, but Alice recognized clear signs of organic life. The rounded land was covered in soft growths that extended in every direction, each with its own shape and hue. Above her, very distant in the sky was the machine that stretched to both horizons. The machine was covered in moving specs. When Alice squinted, she could see just enough detail of the specs to realize that they were the worms that had visited her in the orchard. A countless group of them traveled along the face of the machine.

Alice recognized the fortune of being invited into the cross-section of her world and the doorway to the great beyond. She climbed onto the hood of her car, and looked out at the most abundance that she had ever seen. She turned her gaze ever so slightly, and witnessed a new eternity in every direction. It was the open of openness.

★★★

Jack had been looking at the doors for a few moments, but even with the Artist's calculated patterns carved into the wood, he was not stuck. Unlike the others, Jack did not get lured in by Diaphnerous' fine work. In fact, he found it synthetic and unappealing. He saw through the true intentions. After he finished scanning over the doors, Jack turned his gaze to the orb. His eyes reflected the warm light from the glowing sphere. Whatever colors he was seeing were spectacular. A smile grew across his face.

He spent the appropriate amount of time admiring the orb, and then he took a step forward. Remembering John's advice, he braced himself to enter the new world. "Head first," he said to himself. Everything unworldly and supernatural that he had been looking for waited for him beyond that open portal, and his smile grew bigger. With not one second more to waste, Jack leaned over and jumped in.

★★★

John got lost in all of the extensions of the super computer, trying to imagine what each component was responsible for. The second path of the machine's extension actually grew in size and led straight up. The machine expanded countless miles into the sky, all the way to the orb in the higher corner of the tesseract. Surrounding that orb there was a much larger opening. Beyond that, John saw the beginning of a dimension even higher than the fourth.

In what John believed to be the fifth spatial dimension, there was an existence too extreme for the worms to comprehend, let alone himself. Beings that were indescribable looked down onto the simpler worms, as they themselves worked on the extension of the machine that crossed into their reach. Symbols were passed down by the fifth-dimensional creatures into the tesseract where they were immediately translated into codes for the worms to decipher. From his best viewpoint, John could see that the machine kept stretching into yet higher and higher dimensions until he could no longer fathom what he was seeing. The only thing that he knew for sure was that the machine continued on. Needing to see more, he moved forward. John walked to the top of a hill that overlooked a dark valley. And then he heard laughter, but it was not a welcoming laughter; it was sinister.

John looked to where the sound came from and he saw Diaphnerous. It was spinning in circles and dancing as It mocked the worms. John immediately recognized the Creature's true place in their world. It was wicked, and spiteful, and deceitful. All of Its beauty turned insidious. Its golden, feathered eye was only Its partial appearance. John could now see that the single eye was attached to a prolonged, leathery neck. On its neck, there was a beak that stuck out pointed and rotten looking. Beneath the beak and neck was a body resembling that of a bulbous insect. It had a dozen legs that gnarled out of Its buttocks in every direction. The legs were sharp and daunting, connecting at long, arachnid–like joints. It towered in the air taller than even the worms. John beheld Diaphnerous' stature and recognized It, as he had seen many images of Its micro-counterparts. The Creature was a gargantuan single celled organism. It appeared to be the product of a bacteriophage that infected a stentor. Over countless generations, It evolved from a simple instinct driven speck into a brilliant rhetorician. It was demented by virus, but awesomely perceptive.

The colossal Thinker had one front hand that was slender and prickly, and in that hand, It held Enoch. It swung him around like a rope as It continued to dance and laugh. Enoch screamed and yelled as he was thrown in directions that he had never experienced before. Diaphnerous raised Its front legs into the air, and revealed a belly that was covered in long, needle-like hairs. It rubbed Enoch across the hairs, poking him in countless places and covering him in his own blood. He screamed louder and louder, spewing the sounds of absolute, pure dread.

Diaphnerous dwelled in a lair that was surrounded by an intricate, wired barrier that twisted up and around itself. The material of the barrier resembled a hardened, transparent plaster, which John assumed to be a biological discharge produced by the Creature. The appearance of Its home looked as disturbing as Diaphnerous Itself. It was not just a home but a palace, fortified securely at its base, and extending high into the air.

At its tallest point, it formed the arches of a bell tower. A gigantic bell tolled every few seconds sending a horrifying sound across the land that made John shiver with sickness. He covered his ears and tried to focus again on the base of the palace. It had elaborate openings that would only allow such an oddly-built creature in and out of. The worms had no means of entrance, however, through the openings and transparent walls, everything inside could be seen.

There were works of art all over the walls, floors, and ceilings, like a museum created by and for a mad genius. The highest ceiling of the palace was designed in a thrilling scene of exploding colors and images, all telling the story of time. In the center of the ceiling was a life-sized painting of Diaphnerous asexually reproducing Itself into Its next generation. The two separate cells were almost fully formed except for one feather of each eye still barely touching. John was so astonished by the detail of the Artist's own binary fission that he actually felt ashamed about having no memory of his own birth. Other paintings showed the patterns of nature, and the timeline of light. Within the high walls was the single most important collection of art to ever exist. John looked upon it with the utmost inferiority. And in the very center of the deranged kingdom, there stood a magnificent sculpture, twice the size of Diaphnerous. And the sculpture mimicked Diaphnerous.

At one end, It was beautiful beyond understanding, filled with colors that bred with one another, which gave birth to new colors. It flowed outwardly into sprouts of brilliance. Each curve along its surface told the story of a goddess being born from the almighty. As John rested his sight upon the great wonder, he became tranquilized. All of his anxieties quieted down until he could hear only his own heartbeat, which sounded like waves of the ocean. Its design made all of John's and humanity's questions about the meaning of life obsolete. It was greater than existence. *No heaven or paradise could understand this beauty,* John thought. An eternity of staring at it would be too short.

And then John heard Enoch's scream, followed by a vile laugh.

John awoke from his peace and turned his vision to the opposite end of the sculpture where it turned ghastly. It was dark, stricken with intolerable twists and spines. It resembled an abandoned creature that was born mutilated and tortured. It writhed in pain, and it tormented John. It was agony itself. John felt the legs of countless insects crawling under his skin and behind his eyes. The more that he saw of the creation, the more that he suffered and burned. He was living the subject's reality first hand, and the paradise that he experienced seconds ago, quickly turned into hell. But then, he heard another laugh and broke free of the spell. His attention turned to the focal point of the piece.

On top of the hind legs of the sculpted beast, sat a throne covered in tiny needles and prongs. As John struggled to look at the throne, the music of an organ surrounded him. He was doused in a deep, gothic melody. Its vibrations pulled John's darkest emotions from his gut, and he began to quiver and vomit. Diaphnerous played an elaborately chaotic sound machine that was constructed into the walls of Its home. It used Its legs to pound on different keys and pedals. Long pipes blasted sound into the air, and bells rang all over the kingdom. The palace was alive.

As the song evolved, Diaphnerous turned a crank. Enoch, who was strapped onto a flat plank, was slowly lifted into the air. The crane-like device placed him onto the needled throne, and squeezed him in tight. As Enoch screamed, Diaphnerous strapped down his wrists and ankles. With pure joy, It then crawled down into a hole in the ground. John watched, as he knew that he was powerless, and Enoch was without hope. When Diaphnerous arose, one wretched leg at a time, It carried the crown. In its fourth-dimensional state, the crown was far more beautiful than John or Enoch could imagine. The place where it had been damaged was heavily embellished by Diaphnerous. It drew John's attention right away, and because the Artist was skilled at telling story through visuals, John knew immediately that the garnished dent represented Man's carelessness and ignorance.

Diaphnerous bowed down to Enoch and then twisted the crown down onto his head. Diaphnerous broke out into laughter and began dancing around Its creation. It was truly happy. Its greatest piece of art was complete. "Thank you, John! You have kept your promise. You came to see my creation. It would not be possible without you." John trembled with disgust. His knees buckled. "What do you think, John? What do you think?" It continued to laugh louder and louder.

John covered his sight of the Beast with his hands and forced himself away to where he could no longer see It. He pulled himself up to his knees and wept. He blamed himself for Enoch's pain and thought about all of the opportunities that he had to intervene in the past. He told himself that he allowed this to happen. John's mind turned to a darker place than it had ever been. He struggled to accept breath into his lungs after such guilt, but then he heard one more laugh, and he knew that if he did not continue forward, then he might too share the farmer's fate. He vowed to reach the worms and aid them in any way possible.

He ran towards the herd of creatures, but by the time that he had taken only a handful of steps, he was able to see a group of worms already coming his way. They rushed towards him in their large transportation room. It was the size of a small building, yet it moved from place to place faster than the sound wave that followed it.

They traveled alongside an extension of the great machine that was built in his direction. This particular length of the computer forked off into a path that was very thin compared to the others. It was only about one foot in diameter, and it was aligned directly at him. It was noticeably incomplete, but when John looked behind him, he determined its destination: It was being built to run straight into the orb. He came to the obvious presumption that it was sized to accommodate a human's use once it breached the portal into the NASA/Thomas Laboratory. Right then, John began to understand.

He watched the equations come down from the fifth dimension and into the fourth. They were translated upon arrival, and then studied by the worms. John saw the direct results of the information that came down the line. The worms used it to transform their world. They also relayed their own information up to the higher beings.

John envisioned all of the ways that the worms and the higher creatures could help mankind when their equations traveled through to the third dimension. They would create safe methods of high-speed traveling. Cities and societies would be recreated in order to accommodate everyone within them. They could now understand the mysteries that occurred at each incident around the country over the past two years, and use the practices to their advantage. Vegetation would multiply overnight, and world hunger would be eliminated. Then, John went deeper and thought about the responsibility that would fall upon humanity; it was a responsibility that he would be proud to take on.

After fully understanding the power of the higher equations, he and his people would take on the obligation of sending their own equations into the lower flat dimension to teach them. With the knowledge gained from the spaces above, he could help connect their piece of the machine to the flat dimension below. After that, the flats would then pass it on to those below them. Then finally, all of the dimensions would be connected together by the working machine. And as the overall picture became crystal clear, John recognized himself as the missing link in the great chain of all existence. To the worms, he would soon be the mouthpiece of humanity, and to humanity, he would be the transcriber of the worms. He was the ambassador between his world and all of the worlds above him. From that moment on, John was a man of true worth.

The large traveling room arrived and opened its gates. A group of worms came out. They spread around to different computer stations located around the area. Three worms approached John and surrounded him. Even with their incredible stature, looking down at him from such heights, John felt safe. There was a mutual trust. Along with the worms, two of the centipedes slithered up, carrying equipment for the worms. They too were much different looking than they were in his hotel room. Although they still had all of the features that were so unpleasant to look at in the third dimension, their elongated shape completed around itself like a ring. Their countless legs and extremities also formed smaller rings along their bodies. John bowed his head to all of the creatures, having no idea what would be an appropriate greeting. Looking at each of the entities before him, John felt the gratitude of sharing a moment with such great minds. And then, with a deafening pop, they disappeared, as did the tesseract, and John stood alone outside of the laboratory.

***

Alice walked along the road. Her destination was the closest corner of the tesseract. She could clearly see where the walls of the hypercube met, and she was curious what she would find at its limits. Suddenly, the tesseract vanished and Alice found herself traveling through a cornfield. Her heart dropped. She looked around, hoping to God that it was not gone for good. When she lined up the place that she was traveling to, she saw Enoch's barn, standing tall above the corn. And then once again, the sky changed and Alice was back under the celestial colors. The tesseract was back, and Alice ran towards its corner.

***

John watched as the worms panicked. The tesseract flickered in and out of existence, and John found himself standing outside of the laboratory, and then back in the hypercube a second later. Another large moving room pulled up, and worms poured out of it on smaller vehicles. They charged the edge of the tesseract and began shocking its boundary walls with bolts of electricity. Others came in on machines that resembled tanks, and blasted the walls with rippling waves of light. As they scrambled to keep the tesseract open, John turned around to see that the corner orb was deteriorating.

He sprinted over to it. When he looked through the orb, he saw Maria and Victor still watching. "Turn it off!" he yelled, but when he realized that Maria and Victor had not moved since he left, John knew that they were not the threat.

***

Mark was flat on his back. His belly continued to purge blood, but he paid it no mind. His only focus was on the sight of the pidima shell, which had every corner pidima blasting light into the center of the orb. He smiled at its beauty. His eyelids became heavy as the fueled engine purred. The stone on the generator brought it to its optimal state, and streams of light from the pidima shell collectively intensified. The orb attempted to resist the assault of energy by absorbing the light and expelling it outwardly, but the tremendous force of heat eventually became too great, and the orb began to collapse inward.

***

As the group of worms continued to blast the border of the tesseract with energy, John saw as a small flock of them rush over to a nearby computer station. As John took a few steps towards them, he saw that he was within an entire field of computer stations. At the top of the computer occupied by the closest worm was a sphere made of a transparent material. Symbols began to flash through the sphere. The symbols were similar to the ones that were written across the great machine in the sky. After a number of complicated codes appeared through the sphere, numbers began to show up: human numbers that John recognized. *One* appeared, then *two*, then *three* all the way through *nine*, and finally the all-important *zero*. They scrolled around the circular display, then symbols showed up again… and then numbers.

The sphere then presented a number and a symbol at the same time. The number *one* appeared, and right next to it was an unrecognizable figure. Then, the number *two* flashed up along with another emblem of complexity. This continued again with *three* all the way through *zero*.

The spherical display lit up and omitted a loud sound. A worm that was operating the computer then forced its weight into a switch and changed its location. From an opening on the computer came out a small object. One of the ring-shaped centipedes that John once thought of as a monster, extracted the object and then rolled its way over to John. It held out its extremity and offered him the object. It was a hand sized cube of glass. John's nerves made it hard for him to clutch the cube, so the ringed creature gently removed it from John's hand and placed it in his coat pocket.

With tears in his eyes, John looked up at the ring. "Thank you." Before he could say another word, the environment turned a shade darker and started to fade. "No!" screamed John. He tried to grab the ring, but it quickly retreated away. With the beauty of the world slipping away, John was approached by a worm. When he looked into its eye, John recognized it as the worm that first looked at him in his hotel in Colorado. It stared at him again with the same look, but instead of giving into the fear of ignorance, John stared back at it. They were two creatures separated by dimension, but they shared the same curiosity and desire to connect. John apologized to the giant with his eyes. He reached out his hand, and the tesseract faded away. The last thing that John heard was Diaphnerous' wicked laugh. He would hear it for the rest of his life.

John stood in the lab looking up to where the worm just was. He could not bring himself to turn around.

"John…" said Maria. He did not budge. "John, what did they want? Did they give you something?"

***

Alice ran out of the cornfield and across the grass. She opened the door to the barn and felt a wave of heat rush over her. It was dark inside, and a layer of smoke filled the air. The only light was that of the pidima shell, however, it was dimming by the second. The generator puttered as it burned the last bit of its fuel. Alice turned it off. Upon feeling its light weight, she recognized the use of her stone. She twisted both halves off and put the stone together.

Alice approached the hot pidima shell. Smoke seeped off of its surface, but the orb was gone. With nothing left for her, Alice turned around to leave, but she was caught by the sight of Mark's body. It was still and surrounded by a pool of blood. She began to cry. Alice walked over and sat next to Mark. She took his hand in hers, and she prayed.

***

"There was too much going on, John," said Victor. John paced back and forth trying to gather his head. "We're better off with it closed."

"You think we're better off?" asked John, halfway between extreme sadness and fury. "They were here to help. You didn't see them. I did. You have no idea what you just fucked up." Maria sat on the ground with her face in her hands. "They were reaching out for us," said John.

"What about the Eye? It told Enoch that they were coming to kill us. How do you know who was right?" asked Victor.

"The Eye lied! It was a cockatrice. It only said what we wanted to hear. It was out for Itself. It lied about everything. The worms were here to help."

"How about all of the people who are dead, John? They collapsed that building."

"No, they didn't. It didn't make sense from the start. If they killed those people so easily, then why did they stop there? Why wouldn't they kill any of us? We were the ones who stopped them."

"What about the animals that they mutilated? Or the river in Mexico? What good did that do anyone?"

"The river came back! It came back. Whatever they did to it, they had a reason. They multiplied the fish along with every crop that they came into contact with. Enoch wasted that corn because he was lied to. They never touched a human. You call yourself a scientist? Use your goddamn head. How about you, Maria? Do you have any thoughts?"

"Do not yell at her," said Victor. Maria picked her head up, but was not ready to speak. John took his jacket off. He removed the glass cube and placed it on the desk. Tiny symbols were imprinted into every side of its surface.

John squinted to see better, and he noticed that the top was covered in the symbols from the worms, and the other sides of the glass were covered in what seemed to be human numbers. They may have been equations, but they were set up like no other equation that John had ever seen. They were not written out in linear number sentences, but rather structures that were shaped by numbers built on top of one another.

When he lifted the glass off of the desk to see the other side, a shadow of the numbers spread flat across the desktop. He looked up to see lights across the ceiling. As he moved the cube up and down and twisted it, the numbers on the desk became more and less organized. He walked over to the dry-erase board and grabbed a marker.

John looked at the original light pidima that was still bolted to the granite desk. He turned to Victor. "I need this turned on." Victor looked at John and thought about questioning him, but chose to keep his words to himself, and he obliged. Victor connected one of the power cables to the pidima. "Turn out the lights on the ceiling," said John. Maria walked over the wall and switched off the lights. Victor turned on the pidima which naturally projected a vivid light straight towards the ceiling.

John picked up the glass cube from the desk and placed it onto the lens of the pidima. The ceiling was covered in a shadow of numbers surrounded by a striking light. However, the numbers were unorganized and indecipherable. He flipped the cube so that the side facing down was the only side without any writing on it which corrected the disorder. Then, John spun the cube clockwise until all of the numbers faced their proper direction, and the ceiling was filled to the edge with a mathematical challenge.

John approached the dry-erase board with the marker in his hand. He looked up and studied the presentation of numbers above him. Their arrangement was not self-explanatory, so he began sifting through them in smaller sections, searching for a method of solution. At the forefront, there were the symbols used by the worms, which were followed by the human numbers. John assumed this to be the translation key. Below that was the puzzle.

He eventually recognized separations in the larger pattern, and identified them as individual equations. He wrote them all out separately. In total, there were forty-two. Each of the forty-two equations were structured in quartets. Each quartet was made up of four equations laid out in a square. He needed to complete each of the four equations in order to build its solution, and then he could move on to the next quartet. He dove in and scratched away on the whiteboard. Victor and Maria watched from behind him.

"How do you know which to start on?" asked Victor. John ignored him. He filed down the first piece of the puzzle. Maria was amazed at John's ability to simplify four lines of numbers and variables simultaneously. He started off slow, but as he gained the confidence to anticipate his next step, he developed a rhythm. When he believed that his answer reached its most basic form, he moved on to the next group. He spent almost five minutes figuring them out, but as he finished and moved on to the next, his pace sped up. When John was fully in stroke, he knocked them out in less than sixty seconds each. When he marked in the final number, he looked up at forty-two solutions.

Victor and Maria remained over John's shoulder trying to figure out what the numbers meant along with John. "I don't believe they understand language. This is how they communicate," said John.

Maria noticed a few patterns in the first set of numbers, and then again in the last set of numbers. She grabbed a marker and began jotting down her thoughts. "Look," she said. "This is here three times, then it happens again at the end." Victor looked at the board, trying to figure out what they were seeing.

"What about this?" asked John. Maria looked over and wrote something down. "They're letters?" Maria nodded her head as she continued to write. John caught up with her and began decoding. They split up the first and second half of the numbers. Maria ran through the first half and caught up to John. Realizing that she was much better than him, he stopped and allowed her to proceed.

Much like John with the equations, Maria gained speed as she turned numbers into letters. When she completed all forty-two, she looked at the letters and placed lines in between where she believed the words broke. She filled in the last one and read the message to herself.

"What does it say?" asked Victor.

"I don't understand what this means. *'the working machine teaches theory of everything.'* What does that mean?" she asked. John's heart jumped. As he re-read the words written across the board, his soul left his body. He picked up his jacket and walked to the edge of the lab's stage.

"John, what does that mean?" asked Victor. John said nothing. He was lost in his head. "What is the working machine? This doesn't mean anything," said Victor.

John turned towards the exit door. He could not look back at the couple. "I only blame myself. I was afraid, and I let fear make my decisions."

"You blame yourself for what?" asked Maria.

"We all knew that the flat creatures made the wrong decision, and we went right ahead and followed them. We're no better. No smarter." John put on his jacket. "We needed their help, and they tried to give it to us."

"Who? The worms? How were they going to help us?" asked Victor.

"They tried to give us the ultimate solution, and we ripped it in half. We spit in their face."

"Wait a minute… What did they do?" John ignored Victor and walked away. Victor looked at the board and then at Maria.

John slipped by his crashed car and left the building. When he made his way to the front parking lot, he heard students in hysterics from every direction. The campus was in a full panic. John's body moved across the sidewalk on autopilot while his mind tore itself apart. It pulled out every file that it had on *Self-Value* and lit them on fire. He passed by a young couple who argued about whether it was best to stay or leave while cars drove recklessly through the parking lot and out to the street, but John did not pay them any mind.

He made his way to the sidewalk on the campus' main street, and he slipped into a sea of frightened people. With his hands in his pockets, John walked. He did not know where he was going or what he would do; he was not thinking about that. His mind was torching itself to the ground, getting rid of any evidence of beneficial thought that John may have once had. As he watched it all burn, he wondered if anything of true worth would be left. He wondered if he would ever see numbers in the same way again, or if they would forever haunt him for the perfection that he had left behind. The only thing that John knew for sure was that he would forever see the eye of the worm that reached out to help him, and he would never forgive himself.

<u>After Chapter</u>

Rod Serling was the creator and head writer of "The Twilight Zone" as well as one of my favorite American writers. He was insanely creative with the limited medium that television was at the time, in contrast to today where many writers rely far too heavily on spectacle and technology over story. Anyway, Serling once said, "If you need drugs to be a good writer, you're not a good writer." I was sober for maybe 2% of the writing of TesseracT, so I wonder what Mr. Serling would think of me. Perhaps I am just not a good writer. Oh well, what can I say? I'm a pothead and I like to drink.

I would now like to thank some personal friends and family who took the time to read my book before it was published. For the record, most of them did not like it, but I appreciate their honesty. I wanted to list them in the order that they read it, but I don't quite remember, so I'll just list them alphabetically by first name.

★★★

Andrea Wright (first person to tell me my book sucks), Frank Schuenemann (future literature expert), Grant Hutchinson (Emmy winning TV editor), John Calogero (my dad, who pulled me out of some tough spots and truly supported me at all times in my life), John Calogero (my brother, who I will be writing my next book with, also the man who produces all of the music for our company), Katie McHugh (my very attractive and sexy future wife, who saved me from a very difficult time in my life), Kerry Moles (my sister-in-law, also the editor of TesseracT. very sharp lady), Kyle Wright (who claims he is incapable of reading), Laura Knight (my mom, who I am sure is responsible for any creativity that I may have), Peter Carmody-Burns (Pete C.B. my "pal"), Samantha Bianchi (spectacular Jeopardy player), Sam Croce (who reads more than anyone I've ever met), Scott Knight (my uncle, who has not read this, but taught me how to format my art for the book cover. he is a very talented artist himself), Spencer Brown (another amazing artist and creative mind).

***

I do not actually have a whole lot in common with John Robins, that is to say that he is certainly not a self-inserted character. He is braver than me, smarter than me, and is probably better looking. However, I do strongly agree with his philosophy on life and death. Specifically, I do think that wasted time is the biggest sin of all. I envy those who believe in the afterlife, and in a way, I hope they are correct. But if not, then this is all we have. I will never understand those who go through life never striving for something greater: "True worth" as John would call it. People act like life isn't short. That is not a judgment, nor is it ego. I, at this moment, am nowhere near my goals in career or overall accomplishment, but the great clock is ticking and time is running out.

I've had heavy anxiety my entire life, but it was not until I started writing TesseracT that it skyrocketed. I think it's because I started deeply obsessing over all of the greater questions about existence on a daily basis. Also during this period, I lost my good friend, Eric. Shortly after that, I got into a car accident that I was very lucky to recover from with only a minor head injury. (I think my brain recovered fully, but who knows?) Between those two events, mortality blended itself into my brain and changed the chemistry forever. I fear death, and I think about it constantly.

I found medication extremely helpful in dulling my anxiety, unfortunately it also dulled my creativity and energy altogether. So, I had to stop taking it. I am stuck with the anxiety. I fear death. At every passing moment, I am afraid that the phone will ring and the caller on the other end will tell me that someone I love is dead. Every time I leave the house, I hug and kiss Katie as if it will be the last time because someone on the road is going to ram into me and turn my lights off for good. Every time I look up to the sky, I imagine the mile-long, unstoppable asteroid that is going to smoke the planet and kill us all. I fear death. However, what I have learned about myself while I was taking way too long to finish this book is that I fear death, but I absolutely do not fear life. Life is beautiful. I love life, I appreciate life, and that is what drives me to achieve something greater. I have no plans to remain stagnant and let life pass by. Too many places to see, too many experiences to conquer. I'm beyond tired of wasting my life working regular jobs. Fuck jobs.

When starting my writing "career", I never planned to write a book. (I wrote career in "quotes" because it is not a career until it generates enough money to live off of. But if you are a stranger who is reading this, then maybe at this point I have forged a career.) I moved to Los Angeles from New Jersey to pursue television writing. That did not work out after three years of hard work, and quite frankly, I did not see the path to success, so I shifted. And that is a decision that I will never regret. I truly believe that I was on a straight path to a lifetime of Hollywood production work, which is an abyss of misery and anguish that swallows 99% of people who move out there to be writers, directors, actors, etc. In doing this, I fell in love with the world of literary fiction and I will continue to write novels for the rest of my life. I also rediscovered art, which I have not attempted since high school. But after taking the time to draw and paint this book cover, I will continue to do that for the rest of my life as well.

TesseracT has taken a long time to create, but it was well worth it. Having said that, I dearly hope that my next book goes a bit smoother in its production, which I am excited for. To end this rant, I want to thank you dearly for reading my book. I understand that it is not for everyone. Tragedy is not a crowd pleaser, but it is important. Not every story can end happily; that is not realistic or interesting. The Ancient Greeks taught us that, and we are better for it. But even if it is not your style or taste in story, in the interest of practicing what I preach, I hope I did not waste your time. Your time is very important to me. I hope you got something out of it. Feel free to reach out to me with your thoughts: Chris@strangetheatreproductions.com. Also, please visit my website if you are into that sort of thing: Strangetheatreproductions.com. I hope you continue reading. There is little on Earth that is better. Have a beautiful rest of your week.

With all sincerity and gratitude, Thank you,
Chris Calogero